Something
I Keep
Upstairs

Something I Keep Upstairs

Philip Crawford

PROVENÇAL
PRESS

This is a work of fiction. Names, characters, organizations, places, events, and incidents are either products of the author's imagination or are used fictitiously.

Published by Provençal Press, Paris
www.philipcrawfordauthor.com

Edited and designed by Girl Friday Productions
www.girlfridayproductions.com

Cover design: Paul Barrett
Project management: Sara Addicott

Image credits: Cover © Shutterstock/Dana Mauer
ISBN (paperback): 978-2-9571108-0-3
ISBN (ebook): 978-2-9571108-1-0

Printed in the United States of America

For my family

1.

I'd just finished eating dinner in the hospital dining room, lobster tails if you can believe that, and headed back to my room in the Northwest wing to get what I needed: a single-edged razor blade I'd hidden five months before. My roommate, Mr. Schloss, was lying on his bed reading when I came in, which was pretty much the only thing I'd seen him do since he'd been admitted about a month after I was. But I ignored him as usual, shuffled myself into the bathroom, closed the door, and reached into the side pocket of my shaving kit. The blade was still there, wrapped tightly in wax paper. Mr. Schloss didn't look up when I grabbed my jacket and left. Then again, he never did.

It was a Sunday, and quite some time ago by now, at least ten years. Back in the seventies. And Sunday was the day a lot of patients liked to gather in doorways after the evening meal and talk about weekend outings with their families, meaning I'd have to run the gauntlet to get where I wanted to go. Take my word, it was no piece of cake trying to look relaxed and nonchalant as I made my way down the corridor. I'm a pretty nervous guy on the best of days, never mind on this particular one. Just so you know.

I'd started walking at a fairly brisk pace, fast as I dared without attracting attention, but couldn't help overhearing a few snippets of conversation. As pretty much always, people were talking about a drink or a drug that'd been put in front of them at a party or a restaurant on Saturday night, and how seeing it had been like coming across a fountain of ice water in the middle of a desert or something. There was laughter and hugging, assuming whoever was telling the story had resisted the temptation, and I remember thinking how much I envied the togetherness the detox folks seemed to have. At least they all shared the same problem, more or less. It wasn't like that with the head cases. People like me, that is.

Only one of the nurses looked up when I walked past the station. It was Stacy, the pretty one, and I felt compelled to glance back. She gave me one of her great smiles, the soft dark hair falling down in front of her face like it always did. But my exit through the side door didn't set off any alarms for her because, clever me, I'd made a point of stepping out every night after dinner for the past couple of weeks to get a breath of fresh air. I'd thought that was pretty smart—laying the ground-work and all—but I still couldn't help feeling a little guilty. I knew the doctors would rake Stacy over the coals, maybe Mr. Schloss too, when my death was investigated. They'd want to know every detail of what'd happened before the nurses real-ized I wasn't there for the evening head count.

Don't get me wrong, it's not like I couldn't understand that. I mean, in a joint like this, one guy offing himself could give other patients ideas. Never mind that the publicity wouldn't be too terrific either. The Plains Clinic was a private hospital that had to compete for patients with other mental health facilities in the state. The brochures made the place look like a country club, which maybe it kind of was, what with the outdoor pool, the lobster tails once a month, the gym, and everything else. But Plains' reputation wasn't my problem. Pretty soon I wouldn't have *any* problems.

The late-September air hit my face as soon as I made it outside, just the kind of chill I'd loved as a child because it meant basketball season was coming, and I headed for a thick row of bushes between the main building and the old gray house where the doctors' offices were located. I burrowed in, sat down, and pulled the blade from my pocket. It had rained that morning, so the ground was wet underneath my jeans.

Game time.

I might as well just tell you from the beginning that slashing your wrists isn't the easiest thing in the world to pull off. I mean, cutting *one* is a breeze as long as you're in the right mood. But try cutting the second, or even gripping the blade, with a hand whose nerves and veins were mangled a few seconds before. Typical me, that was a wrinkle I hadn't counted on. You don't have to take my word for it either, because when you look at the scars today, the ones on the left wrist look like nice, straight lines. The ones on the right wrist look like a little kid tried to draw a road map. And in case you're wondering, it hurt like hell when I dug the blade in. I just didn't care.

When all the slicing was done—I'll spare you the play-by-play—I lay back, closed my eyes, and waited. I thought about all the loony bins I'd been in over the past five years, since I was about eighteen. A full series of shock treatments, all the Thorazine, Stelazine, Haldol, and Prolixin you could eat. A parade of shrinks, each one weirder than the one before. At another hospital a few years earlier, go figure, one of my doctors had even been carted off *himself* when the nurses realized he was more bonkers than his patients. I remember how he used to get right up in my face and stare into my eyes from about an inch away. Then when I told the nurses he was crazy, they all acted like the complaint was a symptom of *my illness*.

"Of course you don't like Dr. Smith, but that's because he's helping you. Deep down you don't want to be helped, you want to stay sick. But in time you'll see his wisdom."

Standard loony-bin crap. Saying stuff like that is why half the patients leave the bins a lot more screwed up than the day they walked in. Don't get me started.

Anyway, leave it to me, as I was lying there in the bushes waiting to croak, I remembered something: I'd had an argument on the phone with my mother the day before. It suddenly hit me that when they found my body, she'd think it was her fault. She'd be sure it was something she said that finally did me in, when the truth was that anything good in me came straight from her. None of it came from my stepfather, Terry, one of the biggest creeps who ever lived, by the way. He was the guy Mom married after my real father died when I was young.

And here's something you can take to the hoop: there aren't a whole lot of things more annoying in life than trying to kill yourself, and be doing a slam-dunk job of it, only to realize you've got to call time-out and fix something before you can kick back, relax, and die. Kind of like being in a warm, comfy bed late at night, just drifting off, and remembering you left your front door wide open. Something like that, anyway.

Well, any idiot, meaning me, could see that trying to sneak back inside the hospital to call Mom wouldn't be too brilliant. That'd be rich, standing at the pay phone outside the TV room, blood dripping all over the carpet, chatting away. That said, if some jerk started bugging me for being on the phone too long, I could just smile and stick my wrists in his face. That'd be the end of that one.

The doctors' building? Probably locked on a Sunday night. But if I could get inside, maybe I could find a phone that worked. Never mind that my head was getting pretty woozy, kind of like the feeling from the anesthesia they give you just before the shock treatments. And typical me, another wrinkle

I hadn't counted on was having to get up off the ground. So here's one more thing you can take to the hoop: never slash your wrists and then put all your weight on one hand as you try to stand from a sitting position. I shouted from the pain, but no one was around.

I'll tell you this: if they were casting a spooky-looking house to be part of a loony bin, the doctors' building at Plains Clinic would've gotten the role from day one. All dark and gothic. And once I made it over there, just as I'd thought, the side door was locked. There was a row of windows I could reach, though, about shoulder-high on the ground level, and the first one I tried slid open pretty easily. The pain from pushing upward on the wooden frame wasn't even too bad, which unfortunately wasn't the case when I had to grip the windowsill and hoist myself up and in. I screamed from the pain again. How stupid can one person be, really?

Now I was inside a doctor's office, didn't know whose, and it was pitch black in there, but the lights outside in the parking lot gave me just enough light to find my way around. There was a rotary telephone on a big wooden desk, so I stumbled over and picked up the receiver. Things were getting pretty messy by now, blood dripping all over the place, but I wasn't too worried. It's not like I'd be around later to get yelled at.

I got a funny dial tone, but called my home number anyway. A voice came on the other end.

"Dr. Peroni?"

Christ, the hospital switchboard. I slammed the receiver back down. But there were three buttons on the base of the phone, so I tried pushing one of those. I got the same funny tone. Then I tried dialing 9, and the normal tone kicked in. I called home again, the line rang several times, then a click.

"Hello?"

My mother's voice.

"Hi, Mom, it's me."

"Hi, honey. How are you today?"

"Look, I just wanted to say sorry about yesterday. It was my fault. Don't worry about anything."

A long silence. I hate those.

"Thanks, Coleman," she finally said. "I've been pretty upset."

"I know, I know, and it's my fault. Everything's my fault."

"I don't think that's true, dear, but at least you're in a place where you're getting the help you need."

"Right, Mom, that's the way to look at it. Thanks for everything. Hey, listen, I better go. There's a few people lined up to use the phone, OK?"

"Well, talk to you soon, dear. Thanks a lot for calling."

"Right, Mom. Bye."

There. Now I could kick the bucket with a clear conscience. But not in some idiot shrink's office; that'd give them too much satisfaction. They'd probably think I was trying to reach one of the genius doctors for help, maybe this Peroni guy I'd never heard of. Had to make it back to the bushes. But had to get out the window first, never mind fast, because the lady at the switchboard would've already called security.

I leaned on my right forearm for leverage to climb onto the windowsill—a lot less painful that way—and got to a sitting position. I was starting to feel light-headed again, and it dawned on me that the impact of landing on the ground would pack a wallop on my wrists.

Well, Geronimo.

I was right about the wallop, but at least I didn't fall over. So I hustled back to the bushes, crawled in, and lay down—my face, my hands, my white T-shirt, my jacket all covered with sweat and blood. Right, *finally*. Any other errands to run, eggs to buy, cleaning to pick up?

Just think of the blue sky, I told myself. Or maybe the ferry ride to Martha's Vineyard. That always calmed me down. Or swimming on the club team in the summertime, going to the picnic area after practice, eating the butter-and-honey sandwiches Mom had made for me in the morning. For dessert, two crackers with peanut butter in between. "Gourmet special," we called them. Mom even wrote "gourmet special" on a piece of paper one time in her loopy script and left it in my lunch box for me to find. How nice is that?

I waited for maybe ten minutes, lying there like an idiot, my mind churning away as always. The only problem was that nothing seemed to be happening. I mean, I wasn't dying—at least as far as I could tell. So I finally leaned up and looked at my wrists. After all that, go figure, the blood was starting to dry and cake. Which got me to thinking: more slicing maybe? The blade, filthy with dirt but still razor sharp, lay next to me on the sodden ground.

Sorry, I wimped out. Nothing like committing suicide to help you find your limits. Still, enough blood *had* to have flowed out of my body to do the trick. Had to think positively, that was the main thing. *That's right, lie back again. Close your eyes, go to sleep.* After another few minutes, I thought I was starting to feel it. The life draining out of me. Getting very faint now, very faint. All . . . slowly . . . going . . . darker. *At last.*

"Coleman!" A voice shouting from the hospital door. "Coleman! Where are you?"

Another voice: "I'll take that side, you take this side."

A third voice saying something I couldn't make out. Heavy footsteps everywhere. Cries of "Colemannnn! Colemannnn!"

One set of footsteps came close to where I was lying, now all curled up in a fetal position. What a perfect autumn night it was. Cool, crisp, clear. Basketball season right around the corner.

Just lie still.

More people coming out the door. Another set of footsteps near the bushes. Heavy breathing. I could see the vapor just a few feet away. A hand reaching in, swishing around. A touch on my leg. Now *grabbing* my leg.

"I've got him! He's over here!"

It was George, one of the nursing assistants. Not that much older than I, not a bad guy. I'd played some one-on-one hoops with him in the hospital gym. His voice turned softer.

"Coleman, that *is* you, isn't it?"

Game over.

I just wish you could've seen the look on his face when he got a load of my wrists.

2.

Stacy, the pretty nurse, sat beside me in the ambulance, siren blaring. To be honest, after hearing and seeing ambulances go by on streets all my life, being inside one and being the reason it was screaming down the road in the first place was pretty weird. And just so you know how crazy I am, I started to pretend I was in a movie, one of those film-noir things from the 1940s or 1950s. I imagined I'd cut my wrists because I was in prison for armed robbery and in love with the prison nurse, who wouldn't give me the time of day because I was a convict. But I, the thief, knew she'd *have* to pay attention if I were badly injured, because that was her job. Then we'd be in the ambulance together, like Stacy and I were now, she'd fall in love with me, my conviction would be reversed, and we'd get married and have a few kids. I've been imagining myself in movies like that ever since I started watching them with Mom when I was little.

Then the real Stacy sneezed and snapped me out of it. She put a gentle hand on my chest, not saying anything, just looking down at me one second and off into space the next. Finally, I broke the ice.

"Stacy?"

"Yes?"

"I feel a lot better now. Like a weight's been lifted off my shoulders."

"That's because you've done this terrible thing, Coleman. I think somewhere inside you don't like yourself very much, so doing something like this makes you feel better in a way."

We got to the emergency room and they wheeled me inside on a gurney, parking me in a treatment station where I had to cool my heels on my back for a good ten minutes. Then a pudgy little guy wearing a white lab coat came in, stethoscope around his neck, the whole doctor getup. A badge on his pocket said "Peter Thornhill, MD." He sighed as he looked down at me, but I couldn't tell if it was a tired sigh or a fed-up one that meant *Christ, now I have to deal with something like this.* He unwrapped my wrists and stared hard at them. The bleeding had stopped completely, but the cuts were all moist and puffy. In the clear light, I could see for the first time what a mess I'd made. He looked into my face, and his businesslike expression turned softer.

"What happened?" he said. "Red Sox drop a doubleheader?"

I give him a lot of credit for that.

"Will there be permanent damage?" I asked.

"Not if you're lucky," he replied, loading up a syringe. He gave me a shot of anesthetic in each wrist, which hurt like hell.

Know what we talked about next? Football, if you can believe that. He was a big fan, had played in college—Princeton, no less—even though he looked about as much like a football player as I did. He sewed me up using two steel tongs, weaving the sutures around and tying them in tightly. Pretty impressive, actually. Then a nurse, an older lady, came in and the two of them put my wrists in hard casts reaching halfway up my forearms. Dr. Thornhill said there was no point in keeping me at the medical center, so they'd be sending me back to Plains right away. He wished me luck, and the next thing I knew, I was back in the ambulance with Stacy.

It started to hit me when we pulled into the Plains parking lot and two orderlies I didn't recognize came out to get me. "I'll come see you, Coleman," Stacy said, turning to walk toward her car. It was after ten, she was going home, and I realized I was not going back to the Northwest wing.

***

Since you've probably never been in a locked ward in a mental hospital, I can tell you from experience that you don't want to be. And the one at Plains, known as Southeast, was pretty tame as these places go. Some patients you could talk to, others you couldn't. Some stood in corners clapping their hands and muttering all day. Not the type of place that gave your self-esteem a lift, if you know what I mean. Never mind that I was the only person in the whole ward with casts on his wrists, putting me at the bottom of the pecking order.

They'd designed the place to prevent hiding places. There was an open space known as the Big Room where a television blared away, and a small dining room off to the side. The main hallway, with patients' rooms on either side, ran the length of the unit, and the nurses' station was halfway down. There were no doors on the rooms or the bathrooms, which had shower curtains for privacy. It was all fair enough, I guess, the only problem being that we could hardly breathe because everyone, including me, smoked cigarettes all day. That was allowed, and there wasn't anything else to do. It added up to the unhealthiest atmosphere you could imagine: a bunch of drugged-up dullards sitting around in a cloud watching sitcom reruns from morning to night. On the positive side, we got our three meals, and the food wasn't half bad. There was also a beat-up piano in a corner of the Big Room.

I happened to be sitting at that piano, two weeks after I entered Southeast, trying to plunk out the melody to "American Pie"—not so easy with the casts, but I could use the index finger on my right hand—when I met my new doctor. One of the nurses told me he'd just been hired. Since no psychiatrist—four in all—had been able to do anything with me in the five months I'd been at Plains, they probably figured they'd stick the new guy with a hopeless case.

It was about six o'clock, just after dinner, when he strolled into the Big Room, sidled over to the piano, and gave me a smile. He was pretty nondescript—aren't they all—maybe in his midthirties, stocky build, full head of dark hair graying at the temples. Not a bad-looking guy, I guess.

"Hello, Coleman. I'm Dr. Christie."

I raised my right arm to attempt a handshake, cast and all.

"Don't bother," he said. "I'll be seeing you tomorrow in my office. We can talk then. Would that be OK?"

"Sure."

"Just one question. What exactly are your symptoms?"

My symptoms. *Take a look at my wrists, pal. Is the message somehow unclear?* That's what I *wanted* to say. I remember starting to cough, my nervous cough, and staring down at the piano keys.

"I mean what's bugging you?" he said calmly. "Are you mad about something, sad about something?"

"Well, I'm—"

"Because most people I've met who've done something like that"—he nodded at my casts—"are *really* angry about something. They just can't put their finger on what it is or express it in the way they need to. So they turn the anger on themselves."

"Just a lot of anxiety. I don't know, really."

"It's OK not to know," he said. "To be at a loss sometimes."
He smiled again and glanced at his watch. "See you tomorrow
at five. One of the orderlies will bring you over."
He gave me a pat on the shoulder and left.

***

Dr. Christie's office turned out to be small, as befit (or so I figured) a new physician at the hospital. He'd put his diplomas up,
though: Amherst College, University of Pennsylvania School
of Medicine, Fellow of the American College of Physicians,
and a few others. Books were already on the shelves, and the
purple curtains looked right out of the store. He smiled tightly
when the orderly, another new face who looked barely out of
high school, ushered me in.

"Half an hour?" he asked the doctor.

"Just fifteen minutes."

I helped myself to a chair. It was a move I'd made so many
times in front of so many shrinks over the years that I'd developed a certain style: the mental patient swerve and plunk.
Then I'd offer up my patented sulky gaze and wait for it all to
begin again.

On this particular day I was in a playful mood—call it
mental patient giddiness—seen it all, talked about it all, heard
it all, ingested it all, now slashed it all. Dr. Christie stared at me
like the rest always had and surely always would.

"So," I said, trying and failing to achieve a wry expression.
"When did these feelings start?"

He laughed, I'll give him that. Better than the last shrink
I'd had at Plains, Dr. Johnson. In my first session with him, I'd
talked for ten straight minutes without coming up for air, the
same old story. When I stopped and asked if he had any reac-
tions, he just stared at me, folded his hands in his lap, and said,

"No." How these guys get licenses to be shrinks is what I'd like to know.

Dr. Christie sat back in his chair and took me in for a moment.

"Coleman, tell me something," he said. "What do *you* think is wrong with you? What made you want to harm yourself?"

My mood changed in an instant. It can do that sometimes. "I'm always *anxious!*" I blurted out angrily. "I'm *sick* of it! The more I try to get better, the worse it gets!"

"By 'get better,' do you mean feel less anxious?"

"What do *you* think?" I fumed.

He picked up a thick folder from his desk, held it up in the air for a second, and let it fall back down. It didn't take a genius to know what was in it.

"I've looked through all the charts on you," he said. "There are no chemical imbalances or anything physically wrong that I or anyone else can see. So whatever your problem is, it's an emotional issue. Would you agree with that?"

I shrugged.

"It seems a few years ago you had a psychotic episode. The doctors you were seeing gave you shock therapy and high doses of some pretty potent drugs."

"That was at Redwoods," I said, calming down a shade. The Redwoods Clinic was my first loony bin, the place where the crazy doctor used to get right up in my face.

Dr. Christie shifted in his chair and stared me right in the eye, but not in the aggressive way a lot of shrinks did.

"This may surprise you, Coleman," he said. "But I don't think there's anything wrong with you at all."

I think I gave him a look like the one my dog Frosty used to give me when I was a kid. I'd be saying something, and all of a sudden he'd tilt his head to one side as if to say, *What the hell are you talking about?* I'm sure it wasn't nearly as cute when I did it.

"Let me put it another way," Dr. Christie said. "I think what's wrong with you is you *think* there's something wrong with you. For the past few years you've been trying very hard to figure out what it is. My guess is it's all that introspection that pushed you into psychosis."

It was my turn to shift in my chair.

"See, if you keep *trying* to get better"—he made quote marks in the air around "get better"—"it just reinforces in your own mind the idea that you're sick. For years doctors have been giving you medicine, because that's what docs do, and that reinforces in their own heads the idea that they're docs. Not to say patients don't need medication sometimes, sure they do, but less often than you'd think. All your anxiety started somewhere, probably with your father's death and your relationships with your mother and stepfather, and we can talk about that. I think over time you just got a 'sick' label"—more quote marks in the air—"and it stuck. All the docs and meds just made it stick tighter until it became your identity."

He took off his wire-rimmed glasses, set them on his desk, and rubbed his eyes. He suddenly looked very tired.

"Now, you *could* have some physical problem that hasn't been identified, but I don't think that's the case. So I'm taking you off all the medication you're on. You might be a bit uncomfortable for a few days, maybe more anxious than usual, but you'll be OK."

He put his glasses back on.

"And by the way, stop trying so hard. I'm convinced that *trying*, in the sense we're talking about, is completely futile. All this self-analysis. You're just spinning your wheels. Let your thoughts and feelings flow naturally, as they will. Just let yourself be." He smiled. "Like the Beatles used to say."

He glanced at the clock on the wall behind me.

"They're taking your casts off tomorrow. You might take a shower, clean your hair. You've got a little BO."

There was a loud knock at the door. Back to Southeast. But I was suddenly starting to like Dr. Christie. You've got to be pretty cool to tell someone right to their face that they've got BO.

3.

Four days later, Dr. Christie was on my shit list. Ever since he'd taken me off the meds I'd been on for years, I'd slept a total of five hours. When I did sleep, my stepfather visited me in my dreams and punched me around. Dr. Christie'd also had the nerve to go away for a medical conference without telling me, leaving orders not to give in to any pleas I might make for pills. I'd made the pleas, and they'd been duly refused by Heidi, the charge nurse on Southeast.

But on the fifth night after I'd gone cold turkey, a miracle happened: I slept for eight solid hours, a record since I'd arrived at Plains. The next morning I showered and put on clean clothes, something I hadn't done for a week. I even shaved with an electric razor they had, combed my hair, and—*gadzooks*, as my mom's father, Grandpa Coleman, used to say—slapped on some cologne I'd found in a plastic bottle in my bathroom cabinet. When I came out for breakfast, Heidi told me I was leaving the locked ward and going back to Northwest. She said I'd have what they called "Ps," for privileges, meaning I was free to go to the snack bar, wander outside in the picnic area, and eat in the main dining room like a real person again.

"Dr. Christie left orders: if you got through the week without driving us crazy, we could let you out of jail," Heidi said. She even winked at me. And in that instant, Dr. Christie was crossed off my shit list.

The thing was, once the meds had started to wear off, I'd gone kind of crazy again. Not ranting, raving crazy—I'd never been like that—but mind-racing, sweating, nervous crazy. If I sat in a chair, my right leg bounced up and down and I couldn't stop it. If I got up, I'd pace from one end of the main Southeast corridor to the other. The nurses tried to joke about it—*whoops, there he goes again* type of thing—but the best thing they could do was leave me alone, and they did. I kept thinking about what Dr. Christie had said, so I found a mantra to keep myself company: "Let it be, let it be, let it be, let it be" over and over and over again. I still say that to myself today when I get anxious. The phrase just pops into my head like a safety valve that opens when a pipe is about to burst.

Anyway, part of my renewed status as a human being was the right to walk over to Dr. Christie's office alone the following week when he got back from his conference. His door was open when I got there, but I knocked anyway. He got up from his desk to shake my hand. My casts were off, so I could do that again.

"Coleman, how are you?"

"OK, I guess."

We got settled, and he looked across his desk. He knew he'd been right about the meds.

"You look good," he said. "All spruced up. Sorry for taking off on you like that. It was a last-minute thing." Then his expression turned more serious. "I'm afraid I have a bit of news that may upset you," he said. "I got a call from Dr. Berbick."

William D. Berbick was the Plains Clinic's president, referred to by the patient population as The Man.

"Apparently you'll have been a patient here for six months at the end of next week. That's the maximum stay permitted by the hospital. I'm afraid you have to leave, and I'm not happy about it. I would have liked to work with you a bit longer."

How many shrinks over how many years, how many loony bins, how many cocktails of meds, how much of the endless mental patient song and dance before I finally find a doctor who knows what the hell he's talking about, who doesn't have his own agenda, who isn't pushing his own sick problems onto me, who doesn't say that if I stop the meds I'll go insane? And now, a couple of weeks after I meet him, I have to leave?

"Can I see you as an outpatient?" I said meekly.

"I'm afraid not, and I'm sorry about that too. The patient load is so heavy here that the clinic doesn't let us see private patients. It's a rule I don't agree with but unfortunately can't change."

When I was admitted to Plains, I'd been tending bar at a steak house and living with four of the waiters, frat-house style. I didn't think either place wanted me back. Going to live with Mom again was out of the question. I sat back in my chair.

"Coleman, I think you're on the right track and are going to be just fine," Dr. Christie said. "There are options we're looking into. I'm not sure that moving on is the worst thing. But you might benefit from a supportive environment."

I nodded, lamely.

"The problem is finding a facility that your mother's insurance will cover, but we *have* found such a place. It's an accredited hospital, and that's why the insurance company said OK. It has an open structure, no locked doors. You can even look for a local job. You'd see a therapist four times a week, and there's a nursing staff and a patient support staff. It's one of the few places of its kind in the country."

The thought of starting over yet again, easily the tenth time, with another shrink who'd peer across his desk in the breed's bizarre way, was too much. My eyes started to mist, and I couldn't remember the last time that'd happened.

"I'd stick with that," Dr. Christie said gently, as I let the tears flow.

He sat silently for a couple of minutes, aside from pushing a box of tissues across his desk in my direction.

"Coleman," he finally said. "You may not see it this way, but the fact that you can *feel* instead of just *analyze* is a step forward. We've arranged an appointment for you at this hospital and transportation to get you up there this weekend. If you like it and they think you're a good fit, you can stay. If it doesn't work out either way, they'll send you back and we'll find another solution. But I think it would be good for you. It's where I went last week for a conference, and it's quite a nice setting."

"What's it called?" I asked.

"The Buchanan Institute."

"Where is it?"

"Up north, in Maine. In a town called Pierrevert."

He reached into one of his desk drawers and pulled out a large manila envelope. "I brought you a copy of the local newspaper. Give it a look, if you'd like. Might give you the flavor of the place."

"Thanks," I said, taking the package.

He stood up, and I took that as my cue to do the same. His desk was between us, but I felt a powerful urge to embrace him, to give him the kind of hug a young boy might give his father. He just gave me a warm smile and extended a hand across the desk, which I shook.

"The folks up there will let me know how your interview goes and what you decide to do," he said. "Good luck, Coleman."

***

I went straight over to the hospital snack bar to get a soda and opened up the envelope. The newspaper was some sort of regional thing called *The Northeast Telegram*, published in a town called Hargrove, Maine, which I figured must be close to Pierrevert. The front page was all about a local election and something called the Board of Selectmen, whatever that was. Pretty snoozy stuff. It was when I turned to the second page that I saw a headline you couldn't miss, and I read the whole article. I remember wondering if this was what Dr. Christie had meant when he said maybe the paper would give me the flavor of the place. But he couldn't have meant that.

Murder of Prominent Attorney Stuns Pierrevert

By Hayley Blossom
Telegram Staff Writer

PIERREVERT—A Pierrevert lawyer was found dead in his home on Thursday morning, the victim of an apparent homicide.

The body of Ronald L. Sanders, 60, was discovered by a housekeeper after she reported for work at the victim's home on Daffodil Lane at approximately ten o'clock, police said. The attorney had suffered multiple stab wounds.

Sanders, who was self-employed, had represented numerous local businesses for more than two decades.

Chester Cody, Pierrevert's chief of police, said there was no sign of forced entry to the victim's house. He added that, according to the housekeeper, Sanders frequently left his doors unlocked even at night. The name of the housekeeper was not released.

"This crime appears to have been directed at a specific individual," Cody said in an exclusive interview with the *Telegram*. "Although we're all upset by something so awful happening in our peaceful town, residents should not be overly alarmed or think similar crimes will follow."

Cody said Sanders' home was being closely guarded and that a full investigation would begin immediately. Asked if any suspects had been identified or if he had any information regarding a motive for the incident, Cody declined further comment.

Outside Town Hall, local residents expressed a sense of shock.

"This sort of thing doesn't happen in Pierrevert," said Marvin Glickman, the newly reelected chairman of the town's Board of Selectmen. "Ron was a fixture on Main Street. Everyone liked him."

Asked whether he had confidence that the police would solve the crime, Glickman said, "Sure I do, but right now they got nothing. Bupkis."

According to *Telegram* archives, the presumed homicide would be the first in Pierrevert since 1949.

4.

Excerpted from the book *The Maine Murders: What Really Happened in Pierrevert*

By Hayley Blossom
Originally published in the United Kingdom.

The town of Pierrevert, Maine, has one main street, a white colonial church, a café, a post office, a hardware store, and a big hotel—the New England country-inn variety, with a restaurant that most locals can't afford.

At the time of the first Maine murder, the King Richard Inn had already been around for a good hundred years in one form or another, and seen its share of dodgy times. But unlike the king after whom it was named, Richard III, it was a survivor, limping through each winter and spring to get to the high season when tourists from New York, Boston, Providence, and farther-flung cities flocked in. They came for the classical music festival, the storytelling festival, the lobster festival, the maple syrup festival, and every other money magnet the local chamber of commerce could dream up. Then autumn brought the leaf peepers, busload after busload of people who came to admire the glorious fall foliage in the daytime and dine at the King Richard at night.

The surrounding towns of Douglas, Edmond, and Hargrove had good restaurants too, and plenty of small inns and bed-and-breakfasts. But no other village had quite the cachet of Pierrevert, where real estate prices had risen steadily since the end of World War II. The rise steepened after the East Coast Philharmonic—a summer-only, sixty-piece symphony composed of musicians whose home orchestras throughout the country did not perform in July and August—made Pierrevert its home in the early 1960s, providing an alternative to the Tanglewood Music Festival down in Massachusetts. The town's population, barely 20,000 in the winter and spring, soared to 60,000 in the summer and stayed above 40,000 until the leaves began falling in earnest in late October.

Yet even at the height of summer, Pierrevert felt like a small town. It was, as the locals liked to say, an incestuous place. Everyone knew everyone. No one had ever been a selectman, a town clerk, a police officer, or any other type of official who had not been born and raised there. The only off-note in what seemed like a New England picture postcard was an earthy pub on the outskirts of town with a pool table and a blaring jukebox. That's where the locals went to drink, dance, and hook up.

The selectmen had been trying to close Erin Go Bragh's for years, but they never succeeded because Erin—there really was an Erin—always managed to stay within a hair of the law when it came to excess noise and keeping underage drinkers off the premises. In her midsixties, a native of County Cork in southern Ireland, she was known for both her down-to-earth directness and a fondness for the whiskey that came from her homeland.

Ronald Sanders had been a regular at the pub—also known as Bra's, the notion of female lingerie fitting right in with the place's pick-up-joint reputation—for many years. A decidedly middle-aged man frequenting a bar that was primarily a haunt for much younger people, Sanders was also the kind of drinker who became a fighter, not a lover, when his alcohol level reached a certain point. Erin's son, Seamus, in his early forties, both bartender and bouncer, had been called upon more times than he could remember to grab Sanders by the collar and drag him out into the parking lot, often needing assistance because the attorney was a large man, not to mention physically powerful when fueled by single-malt whiskey and adrenaline. Yet the following day in a court of law, Sanders could usually argue a case cogently, appearing every bit as sober as, well, the judge. Many of the townspeople, according to interviews conducted long after the fact, were sure that Sanders had finally insulted the girlfriend or spit in the face of the wrong person at the wrong time in order to earn his fatal comeuppance.

5.

The ride up to Maine, slowed by the weekend traffic, took seven long hours. Plains had a driver, a white-haired guy named Ray, who ran a local taxi service and did contract work for them, take me up there. It was late October, and the trek through Massachusetts and New Hampshire was kind of pretty, at least as pretty as the view from an interstate highway can get.

The farther north we drove, the colder it got, and by the time we wandered into Pierrevert it'd started to snow at a good clip. There was a small business district, maybe a few blocks long and a few blocks wide, and the deal was for me to spend the night at a hotel called the King Richard Inn. My admission interview would be at eleven the next morning, and if it didn't work out, Ray would take me back to the Plains Clinic. Then Dr. Christie would look for plan B.

We parked in front of the inn, which turned out to be a big federal-looking structure in the center of town with six tall pillars and a small lawn surrounding it. The building was painted a lightish shade of blue, which struck me as kind of warm and welcoming. So I told Ray I'd let him know, grabbed the suitcase

I'd brought, ambled up a short walkway, and pulled open the heavy front door of the King Richard Inn for the first time.

Boy, talk about New Englandy: all rocking chairs and sofas, plus a blazing fireplace. People were sitting around chatting and drinking, and there was even music in the background. I thought it was a record until I peered into a little side parlor just off the main room and saw an older guy sitting behind a grand piano, looking absorbed in whatever he was playing. There was a reception desk to the right of the front door, and what looked like a fancy dining room on the left. The whole place was carpeted in light blue, matching the paint job on the outside.

The desk clerk suggested the bar in the basement of the hotel as a good dinner spot after I registered, and when I went down there later on it turned out to be another cozy, blue space—but with a big fish tank that separated one side of the room from the other. The bar was across the back wall, so I sat on a stool, ordered a sandwich and a beer, and watched as people slowly drifted in. At about nine, a fortyish guy carrying a guitar showed up on a small stage in one corner of the room, introduced himself as Charlie Biggs, and started singing country-sounding stuff that the audience pretty much ignored. I struck up a conversation with the bartender, a girl about my age who told me the place had live entertainment on some nights and that most of the acts were decent, except maybe for Charlie Biggs.

Dr. Christie had given me a brochure for the Buchanan Institute that had a map of Pierrevert, so the next morning I took a right out of the hotel and walked for a good half mile, eventually finding myself in front of a group of red brick buildings that reminded me of a trendy New England boarding school, complete with a big cupola. There was a sign out front. Dr. Christie'd said the back door to the largest building would be open but that, it being Saturday, the reception area would be deserted. I was supposed to take a seat and wait. Always one to follow orders, that's what I did. And after twenty minutes of reading a six-month-old copy of *Sports Illustrated*, someone finally came down the hallway. She was a tall, thin brunette who seemed about my mom's age, that'd be fifty, but cut from a different cloth: severe face, black turtleneck, army fatigues.

"Mr. Cooper? I'm Dr. Nelson. Come with me."

She didn't offer to shake hands, so neither did I. Once we were in her office, she got right down to business.

"I'm not crazy about being here on a Saturday," she said. "Not your fault, I realize, but I hope we can get this over with quickly. So, why do you want to be a patient at the Buchanan Institute?"

Great bedside manner from the get-go.

"I'm not sure I do," I said. "It wasn't my idea."

"Whose was it, then?"

"My doctor at Plains Clinic."

"Exactly what are you looking to accomplish?"

"I've been really anxious for a few years and don't want to feel that way anymore."

"I understand you recently tried to kill yourself."

That crazy doctor who used to stare into my face from an inch away was looking pretty good just then.

"I'm glad I failed, I guess."

"You guess?"

"No, I'm sure."

"Why are you sure?"

"I met someone who helped me see things differently."

"Who was that?"

"My doctor at Plains. My last doctor."

"What makes you think you can find someone here who can help you?"

"I don't know if I can or not."

She settled back in her chair and crossed her arms. "I can tell you we don't go for that suicide crap here," she said. "You try it, assuming you mess it up again, you're out the same day. It's only happened once at Buchanan, and we didn't appreciate it, I'll tell you that right now. Young girl named Pearleen Porter. Couple of years ago."

What was I supposed to say to that?

Then she went into what I took for a standard spiel. If I stayed, I'd be assigned a therapist to meet with four times a week. I'd be given a room in the patients' residence, called the Manor, which was in a wooded area behind the doctors' office building we were sitting in. For the first few weeks, I'd have a "buddy," a patient who'd take me around, introduce me to people, and accompany me to meetings called coffee clubs, which were run by one of the doctors and gave everybody a chance to talk about stuff and air gripes. We got three meals a day, served in the patients' dining room. I could try to find a job in town so long as it didn't interfere with my therapy schedule. Some local businesses were OK with hiring Buchanan patients, others weren't. If I wanted to spend a night away from the institute, I had to let the staff know. Did I understand everything?

I was about to say yes when a knock came at the door. A female face popped in.

"Hi there!" she said, looking right at me.

"Coleman, this is April," Dr. Nelson said, her scowl lightening a bit. "She's part of the patient support staff. She'll give you a tour of the grounds."

A couple of minutes later, April and I were walking down a long, winding path behind the doctors' building toward the Manor. She looked about thirty, an athletic five foot eight, with light brown hair tied back in a ponytail. She wore jeans and running shoes.

"Don't let Nelson bother you," she said. "Not the most welcoming person in the world, I know. A lot of people think she shouldn't be admissions director."

"She couldn't be my therapist, could she?"

"It's the medical director, Dr. Bellino, who makes all the patient assignments. I think there's only one doctor with any space right now—Dr. Haynes. He's a little confrontational sometimes, but I really like him."

The Manor was far enough behind the doctors' building that you couldn't see it from Main Street. And we hadn't been in the door fifteen seconds when a very tall guy with shoulder-length black hair came up to us. He looked even younger than I was, and was skinny like me but still had kind of a belly that stuck through his unbuttoned shirt. He offered his hand, which I shook. "It's not such a bad place," he said, taking a swig from a bottle of diet soda and walking back in the other direction.

"That's Lenny," April said. "He drinks twenty bottles of that stuff every day. When he got here, it was thirty. The goal is fifteen by springtime."

I got the deluxe tour, all four floors. On the ground level was a main hallway, the walls painted a faint shade of pink, with a big sofa on each side. A few people who seemed about my age were sitting there, all of them smoking, a habit I'd quit the day I got out of Southeast at the Plains Clinic. They all had a certain air about them, the same one I saw in the mirror every day: the look of the career mental patient. To the right was an oval-shaped living room with more sofas, some easy chairs, and a big wooden table in the center with a collection of books and magazines on it. On the far side of the living room, through a doorway, was a dining room with six round tables. Upstairs was all hallways and bedrooms, except for the top floor, which was kind of a recreation room with a pool table, a chess table, and some chairs clustered around a large TV. The basement, our last stop, had a little exercise room with some free weights, a closet-like space with an upright piano, a laundry room, and a smaller TV lounge. We sat down in front of the TV, which was already on, and took in a few minutes of a dance show that featured Black people only.

"I've always wanted to be able to dance like that," I said.

"Me too," April said. "I'm such a klutz."

Just so you know, I'm a terrible dancer. But I was such a nerdy outcast in high school that I tried to attract attention by whirling around like a madman at the dances we had in the cafeteria on Friday nights. The only thing that kept me from being ostracized by everybody was that I could play a little basketball—couldn't dribble but could shoot passably—and a little piano because Mom had forced lessons on me in grammar school. I was glad she did, because once I got into it I really liked the piano. Not that I had any talent, but it helped me forget about my stepfather. Then I got so screwed up that I couldn't concentrate enough to practice and ended up letting it all slide. The only other thing I had going for me was that I was the best chemistry student in my grade. I even won a prize my senior year, not that it was the type of thing that made people like you. More the other way around, unless I let the football players copy my homework, which I did because I was afraid of getting beat up.

April looked at her watch. "It's almost noon," she said. "Wanna go upstairs and have some lunch? The patient dining room should be open."

"Sure."

Lunch turned out to be a buffet, and April and I were the first ones there. We each took a hamburger and some potato chips and sat down, and within a few minutes the room was pretty full, maybe twenty-five people in all. As a group, they looked less strange than the patients I'd seen in the front hallway earlier, and compared to the population of Southeast, they looked like an Olympic team. They didn't seem like the friendliest bunch, though. No one came over to sit with April and me, even though there were four free chairs at our table.

"Don't worry," April said, picking up on my gazes around the room. "Most people here are shy with new folks for a couple of days."

Just then, a small, very pretty girl with shoulder-length brown hair came over to our table, tray in hand.

"How ya doin', Marie?" said April enthusiastically.

Marie looked confused by the question. She laughed and sat down. "I'm not sure, really," she said.

"Marie, this is Coleman. He's having an interview today and decided to join us for lunch."

Marie stared down at her plate, piled high with nothing but chips, and said, "Hello," just above a whisper. Then her head jerked up, and she looked at me with daggerlike eyes. "Did you come here to kill us?" She broke into a fractured smile that as much as said, *Don't forget you're in a loony bin, mister, and I'm just as nutty as the rest of them.*

"That's not funny, Marie," April said. "Coleman didn't come here to hurt anyone." Then, to me: "Someone was killed in town last week. It's been in the papers. The police are investigating. Nothing to worry about."

"I saw an article."

At that moment, a short, freckled, lady who looked about thirty-five arrived at the buffet table. She picked up a plate, put a hamburger on it, and thrust the plate high above her head, like a waitress carrying a cocktail tray. Then she just let the plate drop to the floor. The loud bang made everyone look up.

"BRITNEY, DON'T YOU DARE!" April screamed.

Before she got it all out, the lady upended the whole buffet table with one big jerk of her arms. The crash was awful, the plates and serving dishes shattering, the food making a huge mess on the floor. A stream of tomato soup flowed halfway down the room.

"GODDAMN IT, BRITNEY!" April shouted, taking off after her as she ran away. I looked across the table at Marie. "That's not the first time she's done that," Marie said amiably, crunching into one of her chips.

***

April came back five minutes later and asked me to take a stroll outside. It'd started to snow, and we walked back by the doctors' building, out to Main Street, and in the direction of the King Richard Inn. I remember shivering as the air got colder, my excuse for a winter jacket not at all up to Maine standards. April apologized for everything and said the kitchen staff would clean up the dining room. The freckled offender, Britney, was on her way out, this being the third time within a month she'd pulled that particular stunt.

"Only you can decide whether you want to stay, Coleman," April said. "But I'd hate for you to base your decision on Dr. Nelson and what just happened. I've seen a lot of people really be helped here, and I think you'd do well. I have to let Nelson know before two o'clock, so what would you like to do?"

I'd already made a decision. I hated the place. I couldn't imagine living in that house with those people. My shrink would probably be as crazy as all the others in my past, except for Dr. Christie. The Buchanan Institute would be the worst thing in the world for me.

So I looked at April and said the only thing I could think of: "I've got no place else to go."

6.

Excerpted from the book *The Maine Murders: What Really Happened in Pierrevert*

By Hayley Blossom
Originally published in the United Kingdom.

One week after the murder of Ronald Sanders, police chief Chester Cody and his deputy, Kevin Kincaid, sat down to lunch at the Cauldron Café, a small eatery just opposite the King Richard Inn on Main Street. The officers had no leads on the murder, and the selectmen were anxious to have something to tell the townspeople. After a young waitress took their order—lobster bisque, the house specialty, for both—Kincaid started in with the case he'd been making since the body was discovered.

"The housekeeper had something to do with it," Kincaid said. "Don't know how you can think anything else."

"There's no motive," Cody replied. "Two young kids? Happy to be in the USA?"

"Try telling that to the state cops."

"Anyone's capable of anything," Cody said, testily for him. "But she'd have to be one heck of an actress to pull that off. She was trembling when we got there."

"I'd be trembling too if I'd just murdered someone in cold blood," Kincaid retorted.

Ronald Sanders had been killed in his den, just off the sitting room of his three-bedroom Colonial on Daffodil Lane. At least that's where the corpse, or what was left of it, had been lying, sprawled amid a clutter of legal documents. There was no sign the body had been dragged or carried. But few people, least of all the petite Asian housekeeper whom Kincaid couldn't stop carping about, could have moved such a hulking figure. Sanders stood six foot three and weighed 250 pounds.

"Did what we saw strike you as cold-blooded in any sense of the term?" Cody inquired.

"Damn straight."

"Kevin, cold-blooded is killing someone with no feeling," Cody declared, in a tone an English professor might use with a class of freshmen. "That's not what we saw. Most of the stab wounds were made after Sanders was dead. Whoever killed him hated him. He was *butchered*."

Cody sat back and sighed before adding, "At least we managed to keep that little detail out of the paper."

"Looked like a hunting knife to me," Kincaid said. "The kind I use to skin deer."

Cody, at age forty-five, was still a relatively young police chief, but well established. He'd joined the force when he was twenty-two, a freshly minted state university graduate with a degree in American history, and had been appointed to the top job by the selectmen at thirty-five. Trim, nearly six foot seven, with a full head of thick blond hair, he commanded respect as much for his calm, even disposition as for his physical stature. He'd lost his wife,

Darlene, the Two Rivers Regional High School cheerleader he'd married three weeks after graduation, to ovarian cancer when they were both forty. They'd had no children, and he had not remarried. Shy by nature, Cody avoided places like Erin Go Bragh's unless he was called to sort out a disorderly conduct incident or to tell Erin, for the umpteenth time, to turn down the jukebox after eleven p.m. so people who lived nearby could sleep.

Kincaid, by contrast, was every inch the townie toughie he looked. Although his overall appearance was pleasant enough at age thirty-three—thick, bushy dark brown hair, decent features, a muscular build from regular gym going, and a swarthy complexion—he sported a thick moustache that turned downward at the corners. The facial hair gave him a distinct *don't-mess-with-me* aura, exactly the effect he wanted, as by all accounts Kincaid had carried a chip on his shoulder since childhood, always the kid looking for a fight. Some of the townspeople put the blame on Kincaid's father, a retired Marine Corps colonel who— before his death at age fifty-eight when one of the guns he was cleaning in his garage misfired—had regularly subjected his son to the type of merciless criticism typically reserved for boot-camp recruits. There was also the fact that Kincaid's mother had left both him and his physically abusive father when Kevin was ten, never to be heard from again. It didn't help that Kincaid was barely five foot seven, giving him one more reason to have something to prove.

Cody had hired his deputy five years before, shortly after the senior Kincaid's demise, because he thought the younger Kincaid had promise. The son also had an associate's degree in sociology from Hargrove Community College and knew Pierrevert from back to front. But he wasn't the brightest bulb on the chandelier, Cody well knew, and he could still be a bully.

"You're wrong on this one, Kevin," Cody said as the waitress delivered their piping-hot bowls of soup. "Let's just keep digging."

Never one for proper table manners, Kincaid dropped a glob of bisque onto his blue patrolman's shirt as he raised a spoon to his mouth.

"Damn," he said. "Should've ordered a sandwich." He couldn't resist adding, "I could've called that housekeeper to cut it for me. Looks like she knows how to use knives."

***

Although the name had not been released in the press, many locals well knew the identity of Ronald Sanders' housekeeper. Sunisa Singhaboon was thirty-one years old, had been in Sanders' employ for only a few months, and was so youthful-looking that she could just about pass for a teenager. But her freshness of appearance belied a background that was unknown in Pierrevert and beyond the imaginations of most Mainers.

Originally from Chiang Mai in northern Thailand, she'd been sold to a prostitution ring by her father at age fourteen and worked in the filthiest of brothels for several years before migrating to the locus of the Thai sex industry, Patpong Road in Bangkok. With soft jet-black hair cascading to the small of her back, light-caramel skin, a Barbie-doll figure, and an ability to move to pounding disco music on a bar stage in a way that drove men wild—typically clad in nothing but a G-string and stiletto heels—"Sunny" had been a top earner at Wonderwomen, a preeminent Patpong establishment. Swept off for weekends and even long holidays by well-to-do sex tourists, she'd made more money some years than half the physicians and lawyers in Bangkok. She'd banked these funds with the single-minded objective of getting out of "the business" and moving to America, where a better life presumably awaited. Her two daughters were not her own but those of her best friend at Wonderwomen, Mai, who'd been beaten to death on a yacht in Monte Carlo after refusing to service three high-paying but particularly sadistic customers at the same time.

Sunny was a practical woman. She'd used her earnings to buy a small flat near Patpong, a reliable used car, and English lessons three times a week at a language school near Lumpini Park. As quick a study in English grammar as in the Kama Sutra, she'd become reasonably fluent by the time she was twenty-one, a skill that vastly enhanced her earning power. When an American tourist who bought her out of Wonderwomen one night when she was twenty-eight turned out to be a high-ranking US diplomat, she saw the opportunity in the blink of one of her turquoise-shaded eyelids. He was sixty, long divorced, and had saved enough money and holiday time to come to Bangkok every few months and stay in the finest hotels. One morning after a particularly torrid sex session and a room-service breakfast of exotic fruits and freshly baked croissants, he'd asked Sunny if there were something extra, anything at all, that he could do for her. Three months later she had a five-year visa to live and work in the United States. Three months after that, she and her daughters landed at General Edward Lawrence Logan Airport in Boston carrying the name and phone number of a Cambodian woman, the mother of another Patpong girl, who ran an Asian restaurant in Hargrove, Maine.

It wasn't long before Sunny realized she did not want to live in Hargrove, nor waitress in the lady's restaurant. So she'd gone to nearby Pierrevert, which she found a lovely little town. She bought a small house for herself and the girls, Lamai and Lawon (then eleven and nine years old), and started a housecleaning business.

Sunny was an industrious worker, impeccably polite, and knew how to dress down to make herself look plain— or at least as drab as a woman with her natural gifts could appear. After one customer, an elderly woman, fell ill and asked Sunny to prepare dinner for her, word got around that the little Thai housekeeper was also a chef and a half, a wizard with spices such as lemongrass, coriander, and turmeric. When Sunny would occasionally be asked to cater a party, her *gai ping* appetizer and *kaeng hang le* entree were big hits. The catering provided extra income that she needed, even if it came with a dose of unwanted attention from whiskey-breathed husbands who hovered as she and the girls circulated with platters of hors d'oeuvres, and a few snide remarks quietly exchanged among their wives.

It was at one such gathering, about six months before the murder of Ronald Sanders, that Sunny first crossed paths with Chester Cody. The chief had been particularly fond of another of her appetizers, the spring rolls with hot sauce, and had sensed an extremely self-possessed woman. He'd also taken note of her understated elegance. But he'd done nothing to flirt or chat with her, even though, nearly five years after Darlene's death, he'd finally begun to feel a rekindled interest in women. It was just as well. Sunny's interest in men—having experienced literally thousands in her relatively young life, most of them smelly and drunk— was nil. Her life was her daughters.

As for Chief Cody, who since the murder had harboured a nagging feeling that another killing was coming to Pierrevert, his life had narrowed to coming up with a single clue as to who had done a very thorough job of eviscerating the torso of Ronald Sanders.

7.

It took several days of initiation before I got to meet my new shrink at the Buchanan Institute. On the first day, the one after my interview, I was assigned a small room on the second floor of the Manor. I went to my first coffee club, run by a skinny, goateed guy called Dr. Zinn, and met a few patient support staffers besides April. I even read through a little booklet that described the hospital's rules and regulations. My soda-swilling friend Lenny seemed to have been right, at least so far: the BI, which is what all the patients called the place, wasn't so terrible.

On the second day, I had a meeting with the nursing supervisor, a silver-haired Black lady in her seventies named Ruby Calhoun. It turned out she'd been at the BI for over forty years, having left the Deep South to study nursing in New York when she was young, and had even known Hamish Buchanan, a Scottish doctor who'd founded the hospital. She was tall and heavyset, with a warm smile, and April said she ruled the Manor with an iron fist and a kind heart. Ruby gave out the night meds at ten o'clock from a locker on the top, recreation-room floor, but I was off the pills, at least for now.

I also met Freddy Cruz, the head patient support guy, who'd gotten out of Cuba and come to America in the 1950s, or so he said. He introduced me to my buddy, the patient they'd assigned to take me around and introduce me to people. She was a girl who couldn't have been any older than twenty, called Amy, and the first thing you noticed was her long, straight red hair. Then it hit you how skinny she was. I'd known two girls like that at Plains, but Amy looked so skeletal that it unnerved me. When I told Freddy that I'd rather have a different buddy, maybe someone a bit more upbeat, he asked if it'd occurred to me that upbeat people wouldn't be at Buchanan in the first place, and that maybe Amy didn't think I was such a great catch either. I give him a lot of credit for that.

It was on the morning of the third day that Ruby told me I'd have therapy at four thirty in the afternoon, so I went over to the doctors' building at the appointed time. There was a receptionist, Mrs. La Motte, who said to take a seat and wait. So I picked up the same copy of *Sports Illustrated* I'd read before and started an article about illegal drug use by pro basketball players. I was pretty caught up in it when a deep male voice broke my concentration.

"I can find you a more recent issue of that magazine."

I looked up and saw a trim, athletic-looking Black man with an Afro hairdo. He looked about my height, that'd be six foot three, maybe in his late forties, and wore one of those African shirts with a loud design that hangs loose below the belt. He held out his hand.

"Coleman? I'm Dr. Haynes."

Except for Dr. Christie, pretty much every shrink I'd ever had *looked* like a shrink: geeky and soft, the high school nerd whose real goal was to take revenge on the jocks who'd kicked him around the gym and the girls who'd looked past him in the cafeteria. Dr. Haynes seemed to be a break in the mold. That said, once we got settled in his office on the second floor, he started giving me the hairy eyeball so typical of the breed. It was the stare that said, *Even though I just met you, I know you better than you know yourself. If you ever want to feel better, you'll do what I say. And by the way, I make no promises, and everything is up to you.*

They must teach that look in shrink school.

"How are you finding life over at the Manor?" Dr. Haynes asked, clearing his throat.

"OK, I guess."

"Room OK?"

"Fine."

"Food?"

"Better than the last hospital I was at."

"That was Plains Clinic, right?"

"Right."

"I've spoken to Dr. Christie on the phone."

That one threw me a bit. "Really?"

"We didn't talk for very long, but he told me about the problems you've been having. I'm not sure I'll take the same approach, but we should be able to work together. Is it safe to say you have a nervous disorder, one you've had for a few years?"

"I don't really like that word, 'disorder,'" I said. "But if you want to say I'm anxious all the time, then sure. I guess you have to call a spade a spade."

The look on his face changed in an instant.

"Are you calling me a spade?" he said.

"What?"

"I said, are you calling me a spade? It's a slur for a Black man. Is that what you're suggesting?"

"It's just an *expression.* I mean . . . like . . . I don't know, but—"

"You don't know *what*?"

He looked like he was about to take me apart.

"I didn't *mean* that!" I said, tensed on the edge of my chair.
We sat for maybe ten seconds, and it flashed through my
mind to jump up and bolt the hell out of there. Then he broke
into a toothy smile.

"I know you didn't," he said calmly. "I was just testing you."
Like I said, how these guys get licenses to be shrinks is
something I'll never understand.

"Maybe this is one of the ways I'm different from Dr.
Christie," he said. "I believe in pushing people's buttons to see
how they react in uncomfortable situations. I think you can
learn a lot about folks that way. Behind all the words are the
emotions, and that's where the action is. Why don't you just tell
me your story, Coleman, in your own words?"

Who else's words would I use? That's what I *wanted* to say.
But as usual I went into the tired old tale again: from Dad dying
when I was seven, to Mom marrying Terry when I was eight, to
Terry abusing me in pretty much every way except sexually—
thank God at least for that—to Mom's hopelessness in getting
us out of it, to me hating her for that, to me hating myself for
hating her, to my anxiety going through the roof, to the parade
of shrinks, to Mom finally breaking free, to living with her in a
small apartment, to getting a bartending job, to my first loony
bin, and to the long line of bins ever since.

When I was finished, he sat back and said, "That's quite a
story." Then we were out of time.

"We have to stop here," he said. "By the way, I noticed
down at reception you were reading an article about basketball. You're kind of tall. Are you a ballplayer?"

Like I told you, I'd played a little basketball growing up. But
I was never any good, just gawky and uncoordinated. The thing
was, I'd reached my full height by the time I was fifteen and
made my high school team because of that. Plus the coach, Mr.
Glover, needed a couple of white guys at the end of the bench.
The town I grew up in had a pretty big Black population, and

those guys dominated the team. One of them, Harold Cherry, got a scholarship to a Division I school and made a splash in the NCAA tournament one year. He was always getting on my case in practice, rolling his eyes at stuff I did. Off the court he could be pretty nice, though.

"I used to play," I said. "I haven't for a while."

"Well!" he said. "Some of the locals play over at the town gymnasium a couple of nights a week. Maybe you ought to give it a try. Might be fun. I play myself."

The idea of playing basketball with my shrink was about as appealing as another round of shock treatments. But I had to give Dr. Haynes credit for one thing: the guy was original.

8.

Over the next few months and through the winter, I fell into a daily routine at the Buchanan Institute. Therapy with Dr. Haynes was Monday through Thursday at four thirty. The coffee clubs were every Monday, Wednesday, and Friday morning at eleven in the top-floor recreation room of the Manor. Breakfast was from eight to nine, lunch from noon to one, and dinner every evening at six thirty. I usually got up around eight thirty, came down to breakfast, then went for a walk. Pierrevert was a nice little town with lots of hilly, wooded areas full of dirt paths. The only people I ended up hanging out with were Lenny, who was still downing about twenty bottles of diet soda every day, and Amy. I'd gotten over my discomfort at how she looked and felt sorry for her because she had Dr. Nelson for a shrink.

I remember the first time she invited me up to her room, after I'd been at Buchanan for a few weeks. I'd just sat down on her floor when she said, "Coleman, let me show you some old photos of my friends back in California." She took an album off a shelf and put herself next to me.

"This was my best friend at Stanford freshman year," she said, pointing to several pictures of a girl in a short skirt sitting on a park bench. "What do you think of her?"

To be honest, I didn't want to offend Amy by saying how pretty her friend was. I figured she wasn't too pleased with the way she looked now, and probably the last thing she'd want to hear was me going on about the other girl. Then again, I figured it'd be stupid to lie and say the other girl was just "OK" or "not bad" or even go full tilt and say she was homely when it was obvious to anyone with a pair of eyes that she was a real beauty.

I cleared my throat a few times. There's my nervous throat clear, my nervous cough, my nervous head jerk, and my nervous laugh—take your pick. Throw in a few other random tics and you've got me pegged.

"Well, she's obviously very attractive," I ventured.

"Guess what her name is," Amy replied.

This time it was my nervous laugh.

"Well, I've never seen her before. Is she here in Pierrevert or something?"

"Her name is Amy Blair."

It took a few seconds before it dawned on me. The girl was Amy herself, maybe forty pounds heavier and with a different hair color. I know that makes it sound like she was fat in the photo, but she wasn't; she was perfect. The thing was, Amy in the here and now couldn't have weighed more than ninety pounds, and she was a good five foot seven.

The next time she invited me up was in the spring after some crazy stuff happened down in the snack bar. That was a small room off the front hall where they had a fridge packed with stuff we could help ourselves to, hot coffee, and little packages of cookies. I'd gone in to grab a yogurt, and just as I was closing the fridge, a new patient named Mark Williams walked in. He was a few years older than I, a skinny guy with blond hair halfway down his back and thick sideburns.

"Oh, hi," I said, peeling the lid off the yogurt. He edged past me on his way to the fridge and opened it up as I headed out to the hallway.

The punch came from behind, on the right side of my face just underneath the temple. My legs buckled, and I hit the linoleum floor, my head taking a hard bounce. I might've been out for a few seconds, I don't know to this day. When I looked up, Mark was standing there grinning. "Just a joke, man!" he said. Then he took off running.

I'd been hit in high school, not sucker punched like that but beaten up plenty of times. I usually just walked away, ashamed. I can't tell you exactly what'd changed, but this time I went after Mark Williams. I chased him down the main hallway, out the front door of the Manor, and onto the small patch of lawn. I'd just caught up and landed a punch on his back when Freddy Cruz, who'd been sitting in the hallway, grabbed me from behind.

"All right, *COOL IT!*" Freddy shouted at both of us.

April came running up too and stood between Mark and me. Then another man I'd never seen before came trotting out of the Manor toward us. He was an older guy, maybe pushing sixty, rake thin, full head of gray hair. He had a lit cigarette in his hand, and when he got closer, I could see that his teeth and fingernails were badly stained—the chain-smoker look I'd seen plenty of times in loony bins. I was almost one myself when I was admitted to Plains.

"What's the trouble here?" he asked in a pretty aggressive voice.

"We've got it under control, Dr. Frazier," said Freddy. "Nothing to worry about."

"Well, what happened?"

"He punched me for no reason!" I yelled, sounding like a sixth grader.

Typical me, I was worried no one would believe me. I spend half my life feeling like a little kid who's trying to convince an adult he didn't open up a box of cookies or something.

"Mark?" Freddy said challengingly.

Mark just kept grinning, not saying anything, until Freddy took him by the arm. The two of them went off, probably up to Mark's room to talk it through.

"We'll take care of it, Dr. Frazier," Freddy said over his shoulder.

"Are you OK, Coleman?" April asked.

"Sure."

"I haven't met this fellow before," the older guy said, meaning me, and changing his tone. That's when I caught a whiff of whiskey on his breath.

"Dr. Frazier, this is Coleman Cooper," said April. "He was admitted last fall. He's working with Dr. Haynes."

Dr. Frazier stood and pondered for a few moments.

"Ah yes, of course," he finally said. "Now I remember the name. Sure you're all right, Coleman?"

"Fine."

Suddenly friendly, he extended his hand and smiled at me. I shook the hand and did my best to return the favor.

"Well, I'll let you all deal with whatever this was," he said, puffing on his cigarette and turning away in the direction of the doctors' building.

"I better go see what's going on with Mark," said April. "But don't worry, Coleman, I believe you. See you later." She headed back toward the Manor.

I was still rubbing the side of my head when Amy, who'd just come outside, sidled up and invited me to her room again. Once we were up there, she started telling me how she was eating better, how she'd had two apples that morning and kept them down. I didn't believe her because the only thing I'd ever seen her eat was an ice cube. Then she started saying how bored she was at the BI and how Pierrevert was just a little hick town with nothing to do.

"Why don't you go over to the King Richard?" I asked. "To the bar downstairs."

I hadn't been back to that bar since my first night in Pierrevert, the one when Charlie Biggs had brought the house down with his twangy guitar.

"The entertainment's lousy," she said. Then her face brightened up. "Have you been to Bra's yet?"

"Where?"

"Erin Go Bragh's. It's a bar a few miles out of town. I'd go more often, but guys are always trying to pick me up."

To be honest, I didn't think too many guys were vying to pick up Amy in bars, but even someone as awkward as I could see she needed to think that. So I nodded and said what a pain in the neck it must be.

"Let's go together sometime," she said. "I have a car."

I'd already seen Amy tear out of the BI parking lot in a little foreign job that probably cost three times what my mother made every year as a legal secretary.

"OK," I said. "When?"

"I'll let you know."

***

Dr. Haynes had a way of smirking when you came into his office. He was always sitting behind that big desk giving you a look that seemed to say, *You think you're getting to know yourself, don't you? Well, think again. You've got a long way to go.* It didn't feel mean or anything, and I admit he was what you might call a cool, confident guy. He reminded me of Harold Cherry in the way he walked, which was kind of a strut. He was also trim and a snappy dresser. I was trim too, but in a soft, dorky way.

Anyway, he was giving me the smirk when I went to therapy the day after the fight with Mark Williams. There was no coffee club that morning, but the fight would've been topic number one, front and center, so I lucked out. I really didn't want to talk about it. The problem was that Dr. Haynes, having been filled in by the staff, wanted to talk about nothing *but* that. He was always saying people got screwed up because of emotional traffic jams, and that I should think of a huge intersection with cars going every which way and none of them able to get through—the whole idea of therapy being to unclog the congestion. He said there were only a few basic human emotions and that it was easy to recognize them once you learned how.

"So, other than the physical pain, how'd you feel after Mark slugged you?" he asked.

"I don't know. I don't know why he did it."

"Well, once you realized what'd happened, what'd you say to him? Anything?"

"What could I say?"

Another thing that Dr. Haynes liked to do, and this is pretty strange, was make up sentences and tell you to repeat them.

"Let me give you a sentence," he said. "'Mark, you fucking asshole!' Now you try."

"Mark, you fucking asshole," I said, rolling my eyes.

"Come on, Coleman, put a little mustard on it. Pretend it's the moment just after he hit you. Try again."

"MARK, YOU FUCKING ASSHOLE!"

"That's better. Then you went after him, right?"

"He started running and I chased him."

"And you caught up and socked him in the back."

"Right."

"How did that feel?"

"Good, I guess. I've been punched all my life without punching back."

"By your stepfather."

"And by kids at school."

"Why'd you hit back this time?"

"I don't know."

"Try."

I stared at the floor for a while.

"Why didn't you fight back in the past?" he said.

"Because I was scared."

"Scared of what?"

"OF GETTING BEAT UP!"

He was really starting to get on my nerves, I can tell you that.

"Let's recapitulate," he said calmly. "Which basic emotions have we just talked about?"

My mind went blank, like it used to at school when I got called on. I'm not too good when people put me on the spot.

"Being afraid," I said.

"And what else? How'd you feel after Mark punched you?"

"I was mad."

"And the times you didn't fight back?"

"I don't know . . . *humiliated*, maybe. But that came later, once I started thinking about it."

"Those are three biggies, man," he said. "Fear, anger, humiliation. You get a handle on what you're really afraid of, who you're mad at and why, what makes you feel ashamed and how to avoid that . . ." His voice trailed off for a second, then picked up again. ". . . you can probably unclog that traffic jam and get folks on their way home."

His eyes wandered behind me to the clock that sat on one of his bookcases. "We have to stop for today," he said. Then his voice changed tones. "Hey, you used to be a bartender, right? Dr. Christie told me."

"I wasn't very good at it."

"I saw an ad in the *Telegram* yesterday. Summer's coming, King Richard's looking for help."

"I don't—"

"You've got experience, right? Might be good for you, put some money in your pocket. Make some new friends. You've been here a while now."

"I don't know."

"Think about it, OK?"

I got up and headed for the door, looking back just before stepping into the corridor. He was giving me the smirk again.

9.

Excerpted from the book *The Maine Murders: What Really Happened in Pierrevert*

By Hayley Blossom
Originally published in the United Kingdom.

As the owner of the King Richard Inn, Patricia Sorensen was the acknowledged grande dame of Pierrevert. Nearly six feet tall, fine-featured, stylish—she wore her (dyed) dark brown hair in a short bob—and in her midsixties, she was an astute businesswoman, having long ago perfected the formula of employing only a handful of managers to whom she had to pay proper salaries, the rest of the workers being young people to whom she could pay a relative pittance. Other than the rooms manager and the chief accountant, the highest-paid person on the staff was the head chef, Leroy Little, a large Black man who had started at the King Richard as a dishwasher in the early 1940s. Patricia's father, the late Charles Turner—a former history professor and Shakespeare buff who bought the inn in

1920 (with funds inherited from his mother) and changed its name from the Hotel Pierrevert—had hired Leroy as a favour to the boy's father, Lamont Little, the house handyman. Lamont, a widower, had left town one night when Leroy was around thirty, leaving nothing behind but a note to his son saying he had other "fish to fry" in his life.

If Patricia (known behind her back among the staff as Queen Trish) was the brains of the hotel, Leroy was its soul. He knew the recipe for every New England favourite by heart and could put any of them together just as fast as executive chefs from the most fashionable restaurants in Augusta, Portland, or even Boston. Now in his fifties, after a lifetime of long hours behind the stove, he liked to leave work early. On nights when only a few stragglers remained eating after nine thirty, Leroy would urge the waitresses to hurry their customers so he could clear up and go home. "Just crisp 'em and let's get outta here," he'd say, which meant for the girls to push the apple crisp for dessert, get it served, and get the bill paid straightaway. Variations included "Just cream 'em and let's go home" when Boston cream pie was on the menu, or "Roll 'em and let's get a drink" when profiteroles were on offer. "Cream 'em" was the girls' favourite, and they'd shout it out to each other as the dining room's ten p.m. closing time drew near. "Let's just cream 'em and leave!" they'd cry over the stacks of plates, pots, and saucepans.

The girls adored Leroy's baritone voice and the twinkle in his eye when it came to females. When chickens, ducks, or turkeys were roasting, filling the kitchen with wonderful aromas, he'd open the cooker door, peer in at the bubbling birds, and say with great satisfaction, "Ahh, look at that. They gonna come out golden brown, just like Lena Horne." He even had a framed photo of the famous singer, taken in the 1940s, hung in his cramped office behind the kitchen.

Gentle at heart as he was, Leroy ruled his domain with a steel spoon. He was the only person on the hotel staff who could talk back to Queen Trish and live to tell the tale. When he got fed up with her presence in the kitchen— she'd occasionally linger too long over his stove, eyeing the simmering pots, or even touch a plate waiting to be served to make sure the food was hot—he'd tell her to "go back to your castle where you belong." That meant the sprawling modern house several miles out of town that she owned but where she spent very little time, preferring to live in a flat she kept on the hotel's top floor. In a business where just about everyone is replaceable within a day, she needed her chef and they both knew it. There was also the fact that she had known Leroy for most of his life, had even, as a teenager, played with him on the front lawn of the King Richard when he was a toddler.

Leroy made sure the King Richard was known for its food, but the hotel was also large enough to host three bars. One was a tavern—Bosworth's, so dubbed for the battle that claimed Richard III's life in 1485—which served as a holding tank for people waiting for tables in the main dining room. The tavern had a few booths of its own, decked out with blue tablecloths that bore the White Rose emblem, acknowledging Richard's status as the last king of the House of York. Queen Trish loved English history as much as her father had done—she even chaired the local historical society—but as a high school student reading Shakespeare she'd questioned Charles' infatuation with Richard III, not the most popular of English kings after all. She'd eventually accepted it as one of her father's many quirks and decided, when she inherited the hotel in 1950, at the age of thirty-seven, to bring whatever tidbits of culture she could to the state of Maine that did not involve lobsters or maple syrup. She'd also pledged to be the type of hands-on owner that her father was not.

The other bar inside the hotel was in the basement. Its name, aptly enough, was the Tower, a nod to the London landmark where Richard was suspected of having imprisoned and murdered two young princes, the sons of Edward IV, to ensure his succession to the throne. You could enter the Tower by descending a winding ramp outside the hotel on Main Street, or by a rickety, wooden staircase that led downstairs from the reception area. The design was such that anyone entering the Tower by the inside staircase got to make an entrance of sorts, since all the tables and chairs faced in that direction in order to view the small stage where local musicians held forth several nights per week. Customers watching the players first saw pairs of legs coming down the staircase through a large window in the wall behind the stage, limbs that would turn into real people at the bottom when they turned left to enter the bar.

The Tower was a more genteel spot than Erin Go Bragh's. Still a pickup joint, perhaps, but you needed more effort in the way of conversation to make things happen because there was no dance floor. The Tower also had the distinction, on weekends, of being the primary gay hangout in the county. The gays tended to stay on one side of the large fish tank that set one section of tables and chairs off from the rest of the room, and crossing that piece of real estate, which you were obliged to do if you entered from the street, was like navigating a London Underground crush at rush hour. The gays generally carried on with great glee, much to the stony disapproval of Queen Trish, who sputtered in disbelief at the sight of men kissing men and women kissing women.

Such scenes didn't bother Leroy, no homophobe. He usually tried to calm Queen Trish when she went into one of her antigay huffs.

"Any of 'em ever do anything to you 'sides pad your bank account?" he'd say.

"Well, not exactly, but—"

"Then let 'em have a good time. They good people. Their money just as good as Rockefeller's."

"But the way they behave!"

"You just jealous," Leroy would say, and he may have had a point. Queen Trish had been a widow for more than thirty years. She and her husband, Major Rupert Sorensen, a chemist by trade who had been killed in World War II, had been childless. She had never remarried nor, to anyone's knowledge, consorted with another man after her husband's death.

The hotel's third bar, called the King's Court, was outside in the courtyard, which served as another dining area during the warmer months. Queen Trish had fashioned the bar from the old woodshed where Lamont Little had kept his tools decades before. On fair summer nights in high season before the East Coast Philharmonic concert—which always began at nine o'clock sharp at a huge amphitheater built on the site of an old military airfield about a mile out of town on Route 27—the courtyard was full of holiday conviviality. There was an intoxicating mélange of scents, the highlights being fresh flowers on every table, lobsters boiling and steaks sizzling in the main kitchen (whose windows were left open for ventilation), and enough heady French perfume to make a Chanel wholesaler swoon. It was the good life in real life, the combination of lovely food, fine wine, and women in summer dresses as potent as ever. The pop of wine corks, clink of glasses, and

constant laughter rounded out the feast for the senses—
and the evening's music hadn't even begun.

One night in early June, nearly eight months after the
murder of Ronald Sanders—for which no arrests had been
made—three local blokes sat on barstools at the Tower discussing the crime, still by a mile the hottest watering-hole
topic in town. More specifically, they were discussing the
relationship between the victim and Sunny Singhaboon,
his Thai housekeeper.

"He was screwing her," said one. "Had to be. Ever get a
look at her?"

"No way she's gonna get naked with that fat pig," said
another.

"Alls she does is clean houses," said a third. "Got two
kids. It was a payin' arrangement. One day he wants it for
free, don't wanna pay her no more, gravy train's over, and
she freaks. Grabs the kitchen knife when he's not lookin',
and thank you very much."

The three theorized until long past midnight. By the
time a final round of beers had been ordered, the topic
had shifted to the Boston Red Sox—every evening's coda—
whose early-season pitching woes were enough to depress
them all.

***

Sunny Singhaboon had a few idiosyncrasies, one of which
was taking very hot showers. She wasn't happy unless
the steam billowed and her skin took on a slightly pink-
ish tint, quite a trick given her natural caramel coloring.
Immersing herself in scalding water was a habit she'd
developed in her Patpong days when she was having sex
with as many as five customers a night. Once she returned

home, she couldn't feel cleansed until she'd boiled herself sterile.

A bit earlier on the same June night that found the three Red Sox fans in lively discussion at the Tower about her alleged role in Ronald Sanders' murder, and having lived through a winter of discontent during which the suspicions of more than a few townspeople about the killing had gotten back to her, Sunny found herself thinking about the old days. She'd put the girls to bed and taken a shower that might have cooked a couple of two-and-a-half-pound Maine lobsters to perfection. Toweling herself off in front of the large mirror in her sky-blue-tiled bathroom, she stood still for a moment and stared at her naked reflection. Still a force to be reckoned with, if she did say so herself: tiny waist; full, natural breasts; skin soft as the finest Thai silk. Turning sideways, she could see that her small, high-perched bottom showed no discernible sign of sag. No question, in a pair of spike heels she'd still be a money machine at Wonderwomen.

Sunny could even admit to herself, although she found her former life abhorrent and would never dream of going back to it, that there had been something empowering about grown men being reduced to little boys simply because they wanted *her*. The look in their eyes when they stared at her on the stage, the way she could wrap them around her little finger with a swaying dance move or a smoldering wink—how strange men were!

She also knew that part of her popularity had been her personality, the way she made men feel with her mind as well as her body. There were plenty of beauties in the Patpong bars, confections of every conceivable ethnic mix, many of whom Sunny perceived as far prettier than she. But Sunny had a special sense that permitted her to trawl the depths of the male psyche. She knew how to make the ugliest of men feel like movie stars, the flabbiest like bodybuilders, the most painfully insecure like catnip for women. Demand for her services rose steadily throughout her career, as did her rates, enabling her to stash away sizable sums.

When Sunny arrived in Maine, she used a chunk of those funds to remodel her little house in Pierrevert, particularly the bathroom. This was her inner sanctum, the place where, amid the clouds of steam, she could commune with her deepest thoughts beneath a round showerhead that was more than a foot in diameter, giving the effect of a small waterfall. She'd first seen one of these at Claridge's hotel in London, where she'd stayed with Alistair Stevens, Lord Stevens actually, who'd fallen under her spell in Thailand and brought her to England for several weeks when she was twenty-five. He'd sent her back to Bangkok after the two of them, walking through Burlington Arcade one evening, had come within seconds of running bang into a well-known investigative journalist who was on the warpath against naughty behaviour by peers of the realm. The close call had put the fear of God into the old aristocrat, and Sunny was on a flight the next morning, economy class, a bit deflated but wiser when it came to political scandal and luxury bathroom fixtures.

Having admired her reflection for more than a few moments, Sunny lifted her silk bathrobe off its hook. It was far too big for her, always had been, but that's the way she preferred it. As she pulled the sash around her waist to tighten the robe, she heard a knock at the back door. She glanced at her watch, which lay faceup next to the sink. It was ten thirty, long past the time anyone had ever come calling in Pierrevert. She ran a comb through her hair and, descending the stairs, heard a second round of knocking, louder and more insistent than the first. Unnerved, she turned into the kitchen and flicked the switch for the dim light over the sink. Through the small windowpanes in the back door she saw a man in uniform. He had a swarthy complexion and a thick, dark moustache that turned down at the corners. Almost immediately she recognized him as Officer Kevin Kincaid, one of Pierrevert's finest.

10.

It was a Friday night in July, all hot and muggy. Amy had suggested at lunch that we go to the bar everyone called Bra's that night, and I'd said sure. But after dinner she wasn't up for it.

"Go anyway, Coleman," she said. "Take my car. You know how to drive a stick, right?"

The idea of getting behind the wheel of an expensive sports car scared me to death, not that I'd ever had a bad accident, just a few fender benders, but they'd all been my fault. In the end, I took Amy's keys anyway and said I'd be extra careful. She gave me directions.

The bar was two or three miles from the BI, through town and down a couple of country roads, and I figured I was getting close when I heard loud music through my open window. As it turned out, the place was a barn-like structure set back from the road. There was a big guy standing in front waving a flashlight, and it took a second before I realized he was trying to steer me toward a parking space. Amy's car purred as I eased it in. A group of girls was standing just outside the front door smoking cigarettes, all dressed in cutoff jeans and halter tops, and as I approached they looked at me in the time-honored way that pretty females reserve for nonentities.

Inside, Bra's looked like a gin mill straight out of film noir. Cheap card tables, each surrounded by three or four folding chairs, lined the walls. A jukebox blared in one corner. The bar stretched across the far wall, and through a passageway I could see another room with a pool table. The air was so thick with cigarette smoke that it was hard to breathe, but that didn't seem to bother anyone. The place was packed.

It took a few minutes of inching through the crowd to reach the bar, and I was lamely trying to get the bartender's attention when the guy sitting on the stool in front of me stood up, slapped down a ten-dollar bill, and walked off—angrily, it seemed. He was good-looking, the mountain-man type with a square jaw and closely trimmed beard. I watched him ease his way across the room, then turned around to grab the seat he'd left. What stopped me was a glance at the next barstool over, just to the right. It was occupied by the type of girl you almost never see in real life. The kind who, if you're a loser like me, makes all your self-loathing rise to the surface in about half a second. I froze solid, like in a cartoon.

She had thick blonde hair, shoulder length, and the kind of face that made me think of old songs by the Beach Boys. Her outfit matched the concept: a backless denim dress with a strap around the neck, clearly designed to show off a meadow of soft skin. She wore pink platform sandals that matched her lipstick and fingernails, and golden earrings with the symbols for Mars and Venus dangling down, one on each side. I remember the bar seeming to fade into a strange blur, kind of like the rush you get after a hefty shot of Thorazine, until a loud slapping sound got my attention. I looked down. She was rapping on the stool next to her.

"Hel-LO up there!" she said in singsong, her voice giving Lauren Bacall a good run for her money. "You're blocking my view! Why don'tcha have a seat?"

Always afraid of authority, I obeyed.

"Are you all right?" she asked. "You don't look so good."

She took a sip of her drink in the girly fashion I'd seen a million times in my bartending days—pinky in the air, squeezing the top of the straw between her thumb and forefinger. I started to say something, and my lips began to move, but there was no voice behind them. The bartender, a big burly guy, came over and said, "Whaddya havin'?" I could feel that old sense of panic creeping in, the kind I used to get when I heard my stepfather come home and slam the front door. The bartender looked down at the girl knowingly. She shrugged as if to say, *Don't look at me, I just met him.*

Then something remarkable happened: I calmed down. My mouth opened and some words came out. "Just a beer," I said.

"Draft or bottle?"

"Bottle."

And off he went.

"Are you *sure* you're all right?" said the girl, eyeing me curiously.

"Um . . . fine. I thought you might be saving that seat for someone."

"No, nobody," she said, taking another sip of her drink. If my instincts were right, it was a whiskey sour. Some kind of sour, anyway, judging from the color, the froth on top, and the orange slice and cherry at the bottom of the glass. Not that Erin Go Bragh's struck me as the type of place where the barkeeps cared about drink recipes and getting the fruit right.

The burly guy returned and slapped a bottle down in front of me, which I grabbed and tilted high for a couple of gulps. My nervous system sighed with relief.

"I've never seen you before," the girl said. "New in town?"

"I'm one of the local loonies."

She knew exactly what I meant. "Oh, don't worry," she said. "I've had lots of friends who went to Buchanan. Sometimes I think I oughta be there myself."

A long silence followed, at least too long for me. "Is that a whiskey sour you're drinking?" I finally asked, searching for witty conversation.

"It's dark rum and OJ, with a splash of grenadine."

"I used to be a bartender. I just applied for a job at the King Richard Inn."

No reaction to my claim of professional knowledge or potential employment. Instead, she said, "I always ask Seamus to add a little sour mix to give it a head at the top."

Her gaze turned toward the center of the room where a group of people was lurching around to the music. She downed the rest of her drink in one swill and gave me a smile straight off the cover of *Playboy* magazine. What she said next was the biggest surprise of my life, at least up till then.

"Wanna dance?"

I couldn't help myself. I pointed at my face and said, "Me?"

"Well, I'm looking in your direction, and the person behind you is a girl. I don't dance with girls, and we've been chatting. So I guess I mean you. I'm tired of sitting here, and I like this song. Drink up, your beer won't be here when we come back."

I followed orders, and next thing I knew she'd slung her purse over her shoulder, taken my hand, and dragged me through the crowd to the center of the room. When we reached a spot where some oxygen seemed accessible, she stopped, turned toward me, and began swaying her hips. Then she did a little pirouette in perfect time with the beat. I still remember the words to the song, which sounded like:

> Ba dee ya,
> Say do you remember,

Ba dee ya,
Dancin' in September

She was really getting into it, *getting down*, as people said back then, spinning all around despite the cramped quarters, and within about ten seconds every guy in the place and more than a few of the girls were staring. Her lush back, bronzed to perfection and on full display, was starting to glisten with little beads of perspiration. As she twirled away, tossing her hair this way and that and sending little gusts of perfume in my direction, I noticed the mountain man leaning against the jukebox, eyeing me like he wanted to break every one of my bones. But my main concern was trying to look less like the dork I was and more like one of the guys on that Saturday morning dance show. That meant moving no more than one inch in any direction with jerky little gestures and clamping a scowl on my face worthy of the meanest power forward in the National Basketball Association.

It didn't take much peripheral vision—something my high school basketball coach, Mr. Glover, once told me I had even though I was a benchwarmer—to see that people were laughing at me. Some were trying not to show it, but others were openly sniggering. Welcome back to my real life. I kept going gamely until the song wound down, and that's when the girl grabbed my hand and pulled me across the floor again, this time toward a side door. There was a delicious wave of fresh air when we made it outside. She leaned up against the house, fished around in her purse for a cigarette, lit it up, and exhaled loudly.

"They're *jerks* in there," she said, eyes blazing. "Don't pay attention to them."

"I know they were making fun of me," I said. "I'm used to it."

"They're idiots. I've known most of them since kindergarten." She took a deep drag of her cigarette and offered it to me.

"No thanks," I said.

"Don't smoke?"

"I quit just before I came to Buchanan."

"Good for you. I'd do the same, but I know I'd gain weight." She looked up at the moon, which was nearly full. "You don't have a car by any chance, do you? Mine's in the shop."

"Actually, yes."

"Could you give me a ride home? It's not far."

"Sure!" It came out with way too much enthusiasm, but who was kidding who? She burst out laughing, and I instinctively braced for her next line, which would certainly be: *You really thought I'd get in a car with* you? *Oh my* God! Then she'd dash back into the bar, unplug the jukebox, wave her arms above her head, and shout, *Hey everybody! He* believed *me!* And the whole place would erupt with mirth.

"What's so funny?" I asked, staring at the ground.

"Just that I don't know your name!"

"Coleman," I said.

She held out her hand for me to shake. "Well, I'm Cheryl."

⁂

We listened to an oldies station on the way to her house, and she kept bobbing her head and snapping her fingers in perfect time as we drove along a dark country road, her window halfway open, hair blowing in the wind as she gave me directions. I'd never felt more out of my league in my life: Coleman Cooper, class scapegoat, butt of jokes, loser deluxe, career mental patient, driving a sports car on a sultry summer night, beautiful blonde at his side. Cheryl had commented on the car, and it crossed my mind to say it was mine, but I knew she'd sense the lie. In any case, the bubble would burst as soon as I dropped her off.

"Turn right, here," she said after a short while, pointing me onto a small, flat street lined with old houses. "Over there," she said, nodding. "On the right."

I pulled up in front of a yellow two-story house that had no driveway and was badly in need of a paint job. That much I could see from the headlights. The rest of the street was pitch black, but there were a couple of dim lights on inside the house. I put the car into neutral and pressed down on the emergency brake pedal, leaving the motor running.

"Well," Cheryl said. "If you want to come in for a nightcap, you better lock the car. We've had some vandalism around here."

She opened her door and stepped outside. There was a flagstone path leading to the house, and she started up the walkway, stopping once to look over her left shoulder. When she reached the front door, about twenty yards from the car, she did an about-face.

"Hey, Coleman, you coming or not?" she said. "It's getting chilly out here."

For the second time that night, I couldn't move or speak. She stared at me for a few seconds, shrugged, entered the house, and closed the door behind her.

It was at least ten minutes before I managed to turn off the car. That's how scared I was of not measuring up—to what, I didn't exactly know—if I went inside. But after another five minutes it hit me that sitting there was outright cowardly. I'd always been OK with that, too timid to be anything except a coward all my life, but I suddenly found myself getting out of the car and walking up the path toward the front door. There was a brass knocker, which I hit softly three times. I heard footsteps coming down a staircase. Then the door opened.

Cheryl was combing out her hair and seemed just out of the shower. She was dressed in a satiny pink robe that ended at least a foot above her knees, tied at the waist with a little belt, and the same platform sandals she'd worn at the bar. She leaned against the doorframe and sized me up.

"Well, look who's here. Clearly a man who likes to think before he acts."

"Sorry, I just—"

"Are you *sure* you want to come in? I don't bite, all appearances aside."

"Yes."

"Come on up, then. I've got a nice bottle of wine."

She grabbed my hand for the third time that night and led me up a wide, wooden double staircase that seemed too grand for such a modest house. Her room turned out to be huge, confirming my imaginings of what a beautiful girl's boudoir must look like. There was a king-size bed with night tables on each side, and a small sofa with a coffee table in front. A large chest of drawers was positioned against one wall. She had posters: the Eiffel Tower lit up at night, Stevie Wonder grinning in front of a bunch of electronic keyboards, a Maxfield Parrish art exhibition in Boston. A few candles had been lit, providing the only light in the room, and there was soft jazz coming from a cassette player.

"Have a seat," she said. "I hope you like Fleurie. It's my favorite wine. I have to go all the way to Hargrove to get it."

She'd obviously figured I'd come to my senses because a full bottle had just been opened, two glasses by its side. She filled them up, sat down next to me, and crossed her bare, tanned legs.

"We have to keep the music soft," she said. "My roommates are sleeping."

"Um, how many do you have?"

"There's Kim, she's in nursing school, and Julie, she teaches third grade."

"Do you work?" I asked.

"Not now. I've got a year and a half to go for a bachelor's in psych at the university. I dropped out last year when my father died."

"Oh, I'm sorry."

"Don't be, he was a real prick, pardon my French. When he died I got some money, so I don't have to work. At least not for a while."

She downed her wine in three gulps and poured herself another glass.

"And you?" she said. "How'd you end up at Buchanan?"

"Oh, it's a long story."

"Aren't they all?"

I took a sip of wine and coughed. My nervous cough. "I just realized I didn't pay for my beer at the bar," I said.

"Don't worry, Seamus'll put it on my tab."

"That's the bartender?"

"Yeah, his mother owns the place. No changing the subject, now. How'd you get to Buchanan?"

"I was in another hospital and had to leave. I'd been there too long."

She was polite enough not to push it. "And your parents?"

"My father died a long time ago. I was brought up by my mother and stepfather." Boldly, at least for me, I ventured, "He's a prick too."

"So," she said, smiling. "We've got something in common."

Cheryl leaned back on the sofa and gave an exaggerated yawn, holding the back of her right hand up to her mouth to cover it. At the same time, she extended the tip of her left foot so the sandal dangled off her toes. I noticed for the first time that her toenails were also painted pink. Then she got up, walked across the room, leaned backward against the dresser, folded her arms just underneath her breasts, crossed her legs at the ankles, and struck a pose.

"So, Coleman," she said. "Watcha feel like doing?"

"Um . . . anything you'd like. I don't know, really. I mean . . . I guess." Move over, James Bond.

She slowly untied her robe and let it fall to the floor.

I'll always be grateful for that image, despite everything that happened later. It was a gift, really, a generous one, never mind other motives she might have had. She was wearing very tight, lacy bikini underwear, the precise shade of pink as everything else. Her breasts poured out of the brassiere. The panties were sheer enough between the designs to reveal a narrow strip of pubic hair, and she was clearly a natural blonde. Not that I knew anything about such things.

She let me take her in for a moment, gave me a sly look, and let out a lilting sigh, tipping her head and peering down at me with a smile that actually felt quite tender even if it made me feel like a little boy.

"Tell me the truth, Coleman. Have you ever been with a woman before?"

"Of course."

She looked at me the way a first-grade teacher looks at a fibbing child. "Are you *sure*? Because it really doesn't matter."

"Sure I'm sure. Why would I lie?"

"I can think of about a hundred reasons."

"Well, I'm not lying."

The truth was that my only experience in this particular realm had been in one of the loony bins I'd frequented. A fifty-five-year-old schizophrenic woman came into my room in the middle of the night, I think I was nineteen at the time, and pretty much raped me in one of my Thorazine/Stelazine hazes. My body had responded despite all the meds, and afterward I thought I'd had a strangely exciting dream. It wasn't until I started talking about it in therapy that my shrink told me what'd happened. Somehow I didn't think that episode would count for Cheryl, who was obviously aware of her weapons-grade allure and the power it provided over men—the real kind, the self-confident kind, never mind one who knows he's not worth the paper he's printed on.

As the candles flickered, casting dancing shadows across the walls, I concentrated on the poster of Stevie Wonder to buy time. The only question was how long it would take before she sighed in exasperation, put her robe back on, and asked me to leave.

"Coleman, let me tell you something," she said. "When we were at the bar, I could've picked any guy in the whole place to come home with me. They all would've jumped at the chance. I'm twenty-two and it's been that way since I was fourteen. Why do you think I chose you?"

"You felt sorry for me?"

Here came the exasperation. She looked skyward, rolled her eyes, and shook her head from side to side as if to say, *Well, I tried. But this one really is hopeless.*

What flashed through my mind was this: When I was a senior in high school, I was the last man on the basketball team. If we were winning by a lot, Mr. Glover would put me in with about a minute left in the game. I could never tell whether he was being mean or kind, trying to embarrass me or give me enough quarters to earn a varsity letter. But one time, when we were way ahead, he put me in with twenty seconds left. There were a lot of people in the gym, the game being against our big rival, Malvern, and I could see people laughing as I trotted onto the court.

One of the Malvern guys missed a shot, and the rebound came straight at me near the foul line. I grabbed it, and as the crowd started to count down, "Ten . . . nine . . . eight . . . ," I heaved the ball underhand toward the other end of the court. Everyone in the gym couldn't help but watch its flight, and a few seconds later, just as the buzzer sounded, the ball swished through the basket about eighty feet away.

The place went nuts. It was my only moment of glory, ever, and the team mobbed me. I don't think I'd ever smiled so broadly in my life, and I'm sure I haven't since. Mr. Glover came running over with a huge grin on his face, slapped me on the back, and cried, "Attaboy, Coley, attaboy! What've I always told you guys? When the pressure's on, don't think, just react!" Then he walked away with his arm around Harold Cherry, who'd had his usual thirty-point game.

In fact, there hadn't been any pressure on the team at all. We'd have won if I'd just stood there when I got the rebound. But there *was* pressure on me because I never got to touch the ball, let alone take a shot. That's what he'd meant. And in practice he'd always preached that we should study the plays, engrain them in our minds so we could run them in our sleep, but once the game started to just trust our instincts and have some fun out there. Not bad for a seriously overweight, alcoholic high school basketball coach in the early 1970s. Mr. Glover died of a heart attack about a year later, and I went to the funeral. Harold Cherry was a no-show.

Anyway, as Cheryl stood there staring down at me, I imagined a ten . . . nine . . . eight . . . countdown going through her own beautiful head. In a few seconds the buzzer would sound, the game would be over, and I'd be driving back to the BI alone, ready to explode in shame and frustration. And in that moment, I decided to take Mr. Glover's advice one more time: don't think, just react. I got myself up off the small sofa and walked over to her. She smiled radiantly, relieved not for herself but for me. The candles flared, and the soft jazz soothed.

Maybe Mr. Glover had been trying to be kind to me after all, way back when. Because in the back of my mind, as Cheryl took my hand yet again, I was sure I could hear his raspy voice whispering, *Attaboy, Coley, attaboy.*

11.

I woke up to the smell of frying bacon and the sound of hushed female voices downstairs in the kitchen, Cheryl nowhere in sight. Having never been privy to private conversation among women, I slipped silently out of the covers, pulled on my boxer shorts and jeans, and tiptoed over to the bedroom doorway at the top of the stairs. Now I could hear more clearly, although it was obvious they were trying to be quiet.

"He's got the message," said one of the voices. "Why don't you tone it down a bit?"

"Why should I?" said another voice, which I recognized as Cheryl's.

"I'd say *definitely* tone it down," said a third.

"Easy for you to say, Jules," Cheryl replied. "How long's it been?"

"That's not nice."

"I don't mean it *that* way."

Jules must be Julie, the elementary school teacher; the other voice, Kim, the nursing student.

"I'm not jealous, I just don't know how you do it," Julie said.

"I'm having fun," Cheryl replied. "Hey, the bacon's gonna burn."

A chair scraped against what sounded like a wooden floor, then some footsteps.

"Nice and crispy," Julie said.

I heard a toaster pop up and plates and silverware being plunked down on a table.

"Shhh!" Cheryl hissed.

"OK," Kim said with a giggle, "let's cut to the chase. How was this one?"

"Nothing to write home about."

"Like the guy last weekend? What was *his* name? Or did he bother to tell you?"

"Ha ha ha. This one was just awkward. It was his first time."

"Oh my *gawd*."

"He could do a lot worse on his maiden voyage," said Julie. "Miss blonde bombshell."

"They're all big boys," Cheryl said. "And if Jason sees me doing it, all the better."

"Was Jason there last night?" Kim asked.

"He's there every night of his life, and he wants to get back together. I told him no way, and he got pissed off. That's why I picked up what's-his-name in the first place."

"What *is* his name, pray tell?" asked Julie.

"Coleman."

"That's his first name?"

"That's what he said."

"No worse than Jason Mason," said Julie.

"He's a patient at Buchanan," added Cheryl.

"A *virgin* living in a *mental institution*!" Kim sputtered. "Wouldn't the Salvation Army be easier? I mean if charity's your new thing."

"Shhh!"

The girls fell silent, and a few minutes later I heard dishes being cleared and rinsed.

"Let's go sit in the sun," Julie said. "Bring your coffee. I've got half an hour."

I heard the three of them clamber out of the kitchen and head down what sounded like a back staircase. So I eased my way across the upstairs hallway and into the bathroom, which had a small window with a backyard view. They emerged onto a wooden deck that had a picnic table and a few wicker chairs. All three were barefoot, dressed in cutoff denim shorts and tank tops, and smoking cigarettes. They sat down on the deck and turned their faces toward the sun, which was shining brightly. I guessed it was about ten o'clock. A perfect summer Saturday.

"Hey, Kimmy," said Cheryl. "Ya got an ashtray?"

The girl sitting to her right reached over to the picnic table and grabbed a glass dish, placing it between herself and Cheryl. At least now I knew who was who. Kim was about Cheryl's size, with short dark brown hair. Julie was taller, very slim, and dirty blonde. Neither were in Cheryl's league, but both were pretty enough to laugh at someone like me.

"Whatcha gonna do when he wakes up?" Julie asked, glancing over at Cheryl.

"Same thing I do with all my mistakes. Get rid of him. Fast."

"Maybe you should go check on him."

"Not sure I can bear to look. He's kind of zitty. Skinny and zitty."

"The anti-Jason!" cried Kim.

"Shhh!" Cheryl hissed again. "All right, all right. A girl's gotta do what she's gotta do."

Cheryl pulled herself up and started back into the house, stopping to pick up everyone's coffee cups.

That was my cue.

I dashed back into her room, grabbed my T-shirt and sneakers, and tore down the stairs, flinging open the front door and hauling ass down the flagstone path. Typical me, I tripped over my own feet about halfway out to the street, which sent me crashing down on the walkway with a loud *slap* just in front of Amy's car. The fall knocked the wind out of me, but I made it back to my feet and yanked open the car door—which, thank the powers that be, I'd forgotten to lock the night before. Tossing my sneakers and T-shirt in ahead of me, I dove in headfirst, a brief silence taking me over save for the pounding of my heart. Wriggling around to close the passenger's side door, I noticed that my jeans were ripped and my knee was bleeding badly, doing a great job of ruining the white upholstery in Amy's car.

Where were the damn keys? I reached into the left front pocket of my jeans, but it was empty. I tried the right front pocket, then both rear pockets. Nothing, except for the panic creeping in. I was trying to stay low but couldn't stop myself from lifting my eyes just above the ridge of the car door to see if I'd been noticed. There was Cheryl, looking blithely out the kitchen window as she dried a plate with a dishcloth. Then she turned away, vanished into a passageway, and reappeared at the front door with a perplexed look on her face. Who the hell had opened the door and *left* it open? But she didn't put two and two together because the car was still there and she couldn't see me.

I shifted position and stared down at my smelly pair of Converse All Stars. Then I raised my head once more, just in time to see Cheryl's perfect round backside scurry up the stairs toward her bedroom. Nothing to do now except prepare to face more humiliation than even *I* was used to.

But looking down again, I caught sight of a stringy piece of brown leather inside my left sneaker. I reached in gently. What I touched at the end of the string was hard and metal.

It was also the second gift from above I'd been given in the past twelve hours. In the haze of Cheryl's bedroom, I'd forgotten that Amy's keys were attached to a thin leather strap, that they'd fallen out of my pocket as I'd struggled—no doubt comically so—to get my jeans off, and that I'd stuffed them into the sneaker.

I sprang to a sitting position, got behind the wheel, shoved the keys into the ignition, and revved the powerful engine. Just as I cranked the car into gear, I heard Cheryl's shouting voice.

"Coleman, wait!"

She was framed inside the front door, looking straight at me. Our eyes met for an instant. Then I was gone.

12.

Excerpted from the book *The Maine Murders: What Really Happened in Pierrevert*

By Hayley Blossom
Originally published in the United Kingdom.

Second Brutal Killing Rocks Pierrevert

By Hayley Blossom
Telegram Staff Writer

PIERREVERT—A prominent local physician was found dead of multiple stab wounds early Friday morning, police said.

The body of Dr. Gregory Frazier, 55, assistant medical director at the Buchanan Institute, was found in his car at seven a.m. by a group of joggers in a rear parking lot of the King Richard Inn on Main Street. Police said Frazier had been a patron at the Tower, a bar located in the basement of the inn, on Thursday night and had been among the last customers to leave.

The apparent homicide comes roughly nine months after a local attorney, Ronald L. Sanders, was found dead last October, also of multiple stab wounds, in his home on Daffodil Lane. Police are still investigating that incident.

Pierrevert police chief Chester Cody said Friday afternoon that there were no suspects in either killing but that investigations would intensify and state police would be called in to assist.

"I wish I could tell you differently, but as of now we have no viable leads," Cody told reporters gathered in his office.

Frazier, a longtime therapist at the Buchanan Institute, had moved into an administrative role several years ago alongside the hospital's medical director, Dr. Angelo Bellino. In a telephone interview, Bellino said he was "stunned and saddened" by the news of Frazier's death.

"No one in this part of the country has done more to advance the development of modern psychotherapy than Gregory Frazier," Bellino said. "This is a devastating loss for the Buchanan Institute, for Greg's family and friends, and for the greater psychiatric care community in New England."

Patricia Sorensen, owner of the King Richard Inn, said she was in a "state of shock" over the alleged murder and the discovery of Frazier's body in a car parked behind her hotel. She said the inn would remain open for business as usual and that extra security personnel would be hired for the remainder of the summer season, traditionally the busiest time of year.

According to several sources contacted by the *Telegram* who insisted on anonymity, Frazier was heavily intoxicated when he left the bar just before one o'clock Friday morning. Asked about the possibility that Frazier had departed the hotel in a state of inebriation, Sorensen defended her staff.

"Whatever happened is obviously a terrible thing," she said. "But I want to be clear that our bartenders and waitresses have been trained never to serve a patron who appears to have consumed too much alcohol."

Frazier was a widower with three grown children, all of whom reside on the West Coast. Funeral arrangements are not yet known.

13.

I got lost on my way back to the BI, so it was nearly noon when I pulled Amy's car into the parking lot. Soon as I did, it hit me that I'd missed the bed check the staff did around midnight. You were supposed to tell them if you'd be out for the night, and I hadn't. Maybe Freddy Cruz, usually the night supervisor, had called the police and reported me a missing person—make that a missing mental patient, one notch below escaped convict.

The thing was, when I slunk in the back door of the Manor, the front hall was deserted. I went up to my room, and the upstairs hallways were empty too. A lot of people went out on Saturday mornings, but I'd never seen it like this. Maybe they'd mobilized everyone to canvass the town for the AWOL and presumed dead Coleman Cooper. Then I went up to the recreation room, and both doors were closed. That usually happened only for coffee clubs, but those were during the week. I tiptoed up and cupped an ear. A man was talking, but it wasn't a voice I recognized. I thought I heard "obviously a travesty," or maybe it was "tragedy." Then the voice behind the door turned murky, and I thought of Mr. Glover again: don't think, just react. I took a deep breath, turned the knob, and eased the door open. There was a horrible creak.

A sea of eyes turned toward me, and it looked like every Buchanan patient and staff member was crammed into the room. Ruby and Freddy were stone-faced. April looked like she'd been crying. Amy was sitting in one of the larger chairs with a bowl of ice cubes in her lap. When she saw me, she looked toward the ceiling as if to say, *There he is, the biggest moron who ever lived.* She picked up an ice cube and started crunching on it.

But just as fast as everyone turned to look at me, they turned back in the other direction, like at a tennis match. At the other end of the room were two uniformed policemen. One was very tall, had kind of a friendly face, maybe in his mid-forties. The other was younger, short, with a mustache, and looked like a hard-guy type. I closed the door softly and leaned my back against it.

"Does anyone have any questions?" the older officer asked.

Dead silence.

"All right, then. Thank you for listening. I want to stress again that there is nothing to be afraid of. No one should hesitate to contact me or Officer Kincaid. That's what we're here for." He looked to his right and said, "Dr. Bellino?"

Dr. Bellino was the honcho of the BI, the medical director. He was short and pale with a full head of salt-and-pepper hair. You could tell he was a big shot from the way he carried himself and the way people seemed nervous around him. I'd heard there were articles written about him and that his picture had been on the cover of some magazine that shrinks read. To me he was just another example of the breed, if slicker-looking than most. That morning, turned out in one of those sporty shirts with an alligator on the chest and loafers that shined like new, he looked ready for lunch at the Hargrove County Country Club. Maybe he and Dr. Haynes, who was standing off to one side in a fashion-plate sport coat and slacks, were competing for best-dressed shrink at the BI.

"Thanks, Chief," Dr. Bellino said, moving into the spot where the policeman had been standing. "Just so you all know, the arrangements for the service aren't complete. Dr. Frazier's children should arrive tomorrow or Monday, and they'll decide. We'll keep you posted. Everyone hang in there."

As people started to get up and leave, Amy shot me a laser look and mouthed the words, "My room. Now."

***

Five minutes later, Amy and I were sitting on the floor in her room, the bowl of ice cubes back in her lap. She told me about what'd happened with Dr. Frazier.

All I can say is that it felt pretty weird. I mean, I didn't really know Dr. Frazier, but I'd met him and shaken his hand. He'd smiled at me, bad teeth and all. Other than my dad and my old basketball coach, Mr. Glover, he was the only person I'd ever met who'd died. It's different now, because after living in Pierrevert for a long time I've known quite a few people who ended up that way. I've never gotten used to it, especially after what I did to end up at Buchanan in the first place.

Then Amy remembered how many things she had to be mad at me about, so I had to make up a story. I wasn't about to tell her what'd really happened the night before, not that she'd have believed me, so I just said I'd gotten too drunk to drive back to the BI, and that since I'd had no way to get in touch I'd slept in her car in Bra's parking lot. I told her I was so smashed that I'd fallen down a few times, which explained my ripped jeans and bloody knee, and that I'd clean the stains on her car seats. She bought the whole thing.

Then she said Freddy had asked just after midnight if she'd seen me, and that she'd covered and said I'd gone to bed early.

She knew Freddy was pretty lazy about bed checks and might not look in my room, which I guess he didn't because he never said a word to me. In the end, nobody on the whole staff knew I'd been out all night. Go figure. Anyway, Amy and I made kind of a pact to come looking for each other if either of us started feeling spooked out about the whole Dr. Frazier thing, and to do more hanging out together in general.

I never followed up.

14.

On Monday morning, I got a call from the King Richard Inn. Mrs. Ryan, the lady who ran the switchboard in a little office on the second floor of the Manor, came running out to tell me when I passed by on my way to breakfast. The switchboard was only for the hospital operator to use, or maybe the doctors and staff in case of an emergency. For the patients, there was a phone booth in the snack bar that everybody fought over, especially at night after dinner. Mrs. Ryan said the call was about the bartending job I'd applied for.

I admit I didn't jump for joy at hearing from the hotel. Even though I was running low on the money I'd saved from my last bartending job, I'd gotten kind of used to hanging around doing nothing, just whatever I felt like. I'd read a couple of books and was even practicing a little piano on the junky upright they had in the basement of the Manor, just trying to figure out stuff I heard on the radio. I'd play chords with my left hand and melodies with my right, which I'd learned how to do when I took lessons as a kid.

The thing was, I knew if I didn't call the hotel back, Dr. Haynes would find out. Then he'd be *disappointed* in me. You'd think I'd be used to disappointing people at this stage of the game, but it still bothered me. On the positive side, maybe it wouldn't be so bad to get out of the BI a little more, what with everybody moping around after Dr. Frazier got killed.

Anyway, after Mrs. Ryan filled me in, I went ahead and called the hotel back. The guy I was supposed to ask for, Mr. Simons, answered and told me to come by at four that afternoon. He said to wear dark pants and a white shirt. Even I, fashion-challenged as they came, could manage that.

***

I had to wait in the hotel reception area for about fifteen minutes before Mr. Simons showed up. He was one of those guys who looks like he's never been outside: pasty complexion, belly hanging over the belt, little beads of sweat around his eyes like he'd just come out from under a rock or something. Maybe forty years old. His handshake was limp and clammy when he introduced himself as the hotel's food and beverage manager.

"I don't care if you're a patient at Buchanan," he said, "so long as you can stand the pressure here. We run three bars—Bosworth's Tavern, the Tower, and the King's Court. They get very busy this time of year. Between your bar customers and the orders you fill for the waitresses, you can be pouring a few hundred drinks a night. Think you can handle it?"

"The steak house where I used to work got pretty busy too," I said lamely.

"Yes, I've seen your application, and if I weren't desperate I wouldn't take a chance on you. Tell me, what's in a Brandy Alexander?"

I hadn't mixed a drink in over a year and drew a blank. It didn't even occur to me there just might be some brandy in it.

"Sorry, that's one I forget," I said, my nervous throat clear starting up.

"How about a Tequila Sunrise?" he countered.

I'd made a few thousand of those but couldn't remember anything but the tequila. There had to be some juice in it, though.

"Tequila and orange juice?"

"Where does the sunrise color come from?"

I drew another blank and here came my nervous head jerk.

"The answer is grenadine," he snapped.

"Ah, that's right."

"Think you can manage a scotch on the rocks?"

I remember standing there thinking maybe I should just sprint out of the hotel and forget about the whole thing. Believe me, I've wondered plenty of times how my life might've turned out if I'd done just that.

"I think it'll all come back once I . . . well . . . get *started*," I said. "Behind the bar, I mean."

"I certainly hope so," he said. "You're the only option I've got tonight for King's Court. Come on then."

He took me down a back corridor to a small laundry room and gave me an official light-blue King Richard Inn vest and tie, each decorated with a small white rose. Then he led me out to the bar in the hotel courtyard. It was a wooden shed, painted the same shade of blue, with five barstools in front and a small counter off to the left where you put the drinks for the waitresses. There was a tiny door on one side, and I had to duck to get through it. Inside were four rows of liquor bottles against the back wall, each higher than the other so the customers could see the labels, and coolers for beer, wine, and sodas. Mr. Simons showed me where everything was and how to use the cash register.

"Normally each new bartender starts with an experienced hand beside him," he said, "but I've got nobody. Anything comes up you can't handle, ask one of the waitresses to come get me. There's a book of recipes behind the register if you need it." With that, he turned and waddled his way back through the courtyard toward the main building.

It was still early, not even five o'clock, and the courtyard was pretty empty. I have to admit that wearing the blue vest and tie did something for me, kind of like my basketball uniform used to do when I was in high school. I'd been the dregs of the team then, and I was sure I'd be the dregs of the hotel staff now, assuming I didn't get fired on my first night, but at least I wasn't *just* one of the local loonies for that particular day.

By seven o'clock the tables in the courtyard were half full, and the waitresses seemed nice enough, introducing themselves, dropping off order slips, then coming back to fetch their drinks. At one point it started to hit me that I wasn't making a fool of myself. The rhythm and the drink recipes were coming back. I had to look up a few cocktails, like a Singapore Sling and a Sidecar, but mostly I was making sours, highballs, and martinis. Any idiot can do that. It was just starting to get dark outside when a tall, well-dressed, older lady with short dark brown hair wandered into the courtyard. She stood with her arms folded like she was surveying everything, and the waitresses all nodded or smiled nervously when they passed by. After a few minutes she strolled over to the bar where I had three customers talking about the Boston Red Sox. She came around to the side counter.

"Hello," she said, holding out her hand, which had some pretty big rings on it. "I'm Patricia Sorensen."

"Hi."

She had a firmer grip than Mr. Simons.

"I don't recognize you, so you must be new," she said. "What's your name?"

"Uh . . . Coleman. Coleman Cooper."

"Very nice to meet you, Coleman."

And that was that. She turned and walked away, heading for a small spiral staircase that led up to the kitchen. A couple of minutes later, one of the waitresses told me she owned the place, and I was glad I hadn't known when I shook her hand. I probably would've knocked tomato juice or something all over her nice dress. I have a knack for that sort of thing.

As it happened, I had to take that same staircase into the kitchen about half an hour later because I ran out of ice. There was a big plastic tub for it, and Mr. Simons had said the ice machine was in a storage room behind the kitchen. To get there you had to walk straight past the cooking line where the chefs prepared the food and the waitresses picked up their orders. As I headed back by the line after filling up the tub, I heard a big voice say, "YO!" Nobody knew me, so I kept going. When I reached the door to the courtyard, the big voice came back: "I said YO!"

I turned around to see a large Black man in chef's clothes staring at me from behind the line. Maybe nobodies like me were supposed to take a different route to the ice machine.

"Who are YOU?" said the chef, jabbing a carving knife in my direction.

"I'm Coleman," I said in a voice that probably sounded like a third grader's. "I'm new."

"I KNOW you new," he boomed. "Know how I know? 'Cause I never seen you before, and I know EVERYBODY who works here!"

"I just started . . . today, I mean." My nervous throat clear was starting up again.

"Yeah, I saw Simons talkin' to you earlier. Don't pay Fauntleroy no mind. See, I got only half his name, but the ladies like me ten times as much. I'm Leroy."

At that moment, another chef who'd been facing the stove turned around. She was a small woman with a young Asian face.

"This here's Sunny," said Leroy. "She new too, but she a lot prettier than you."

Sunny giggled, as did a few waitresses who were standing around.

"Get movin' with them ice cubes 'fore they melts and Simons send you to the dungeon," he said. "Queen Trish don't like no loiterin' neither."

"Who?"

"The boss lady."

He gave me a big smile and turned back to the stove.

"Come on, girls!" he shouted as I exited. "Let's cream these folks and get outta here! There's a movie I wanna watch on cable." I took his exhortation as some sort of kitchen code I hoped to stick around long enough to learn.

"Let's CREAM 'em!" several of the girls yelled, all together.

The baseball fans were gone by the time I made it back to the courtyard bar, but I had a new customer: a lady with light brown hair, maybe about thirty. She was all by herself, sitting on the middle stool, scribbling something into a small notebook. I clambered through the side door and eased the ice tub onto the low counter next to the sink.

"Hi," I said. "What can I get you?"

"A gin and tonic would be lovely. Beefeater's. Thank you very much indeed."

You could tell from the first words out of her mouth that she wasn't from Maine or anywhere I'd ever been. I mixed her drink, taking a particularly fresh piece of lime from the fruit tray to squeeze into it, and put the glass in front of her with some extra flourish.

"I don't suppose you have any of those lovely crisps the chef makes, do you?" she said.

"Sorry . . . what?"

"Sometimes you have little bowls of crisps here on the bar. I'm *besotted* with them."

"Bowls of *what*?"

"You Yanks call them potato chips. Where I come from they're crisps."

"This is my first day."

"I thought you looked new," she said, which came out like, *You clearly have no idea what you're doing.*

She took a long sip of her gin and tonic.

"Mmm, spot on," she said. "Well done."

She reached into the glass to squeeze the lime a little more and took another gulp.

"I turn up here often," she said, "so we may as well meet. My office is just round the corner, and I *do* fancy a tipple after work. I write for the *Telegram*." She held out her hand. "I'm Hayley."

"Coleman," I said, shaking the hand and worrying that mine would be too cold and wet from handling all that ice.

Remembering that feeling, I could never have imagined how something as simple as running out of ice could affect a person's life.

I'd find out soon enough.

15.

Mr. Simons put me on the schedule four nights a week, starting at five and working until eleven thirty. The King's Court closed at eleven, but it took about half an hour to clean up and get the bar ready for whoever did the lunch shift the next day. He said if I ever worked in the other bars, I'd have to stay later because they closed later. He also made a point of telling me a second time that he was desperate, the message being that I hadn't distinguished myself on my first night. I felt like reminding him I hadn't made any big mistakes either, like making a bad drink or falling way behind, but I wimped out as usual. I think I already told you I almost never say what I *want* to say or what I *should* say.

Anyway, being told I was a last resort was nothing new because I'd always been the player nobody wanted in pickup basketball games. And I don't even remember what the hotel paid me, except I'm sure it was minimum wage for restaurant workers in Maine, plus tips. I had to ask Dr. Haynes to change my therapy time, and since the bartending thing had been *his* idea, he couldn't really say no. So we went from four thirty in the afternoon to eleven thirty in the morning.

All in all, the first week didn't go too badly. There was only one waitress, an older, crusty one named Gladys, who was unpleasant. It was over a drink recipe.

"There's no orange juice in a Golden Dream," she snapped one night, watching me mix it up.

"I think there is," I said, confidently as I could, which came out sounding scared, which I was. You didn't want to mess with Gladys, though. She was built like a defensive tackle and had a scowl to match. All she needed was a swipe of eye black on each cheekbone and she'd be ready to go in for the goal line stand. But I was pretty sure about the orange juice, so I held my ground. Stupid me, I got so nervous I didn't even think to look in the recipe book, which would've backed me up. As it turned out, I got rescued by another waitress of a certain age, Harriet, who overheard and said, "Oh yes, there's orange juice in a Golden Dream, Gladys."

"Well, all right," Gladys huffed, giving me the dirtiest look I'd gotten all week, worse even than Mr. Simons' Brandy Alexander glare.

One good thing was I got kind of a friendship going with Leroy, the chef, on my trips back and forth to the ice machine. I liked to stand in the kitchen and watch the cooks and waitresses go through their daily paces, and everything at the King Richard was on a much bigger scale than the steak house I'd worked at before. The thing was, if I stood there watching too long, Leroy would yell, "Coleman, get that ice outta here 'fore Fauntleroy and Queen Trish skin you alive!" That always got me hustling back to the courtyard. Another thing, this one not so good, was that there were all sorts of rules about where we employees could go in the hotel after our shifts. We were allowed to go to the downstairs bar, the Tower, because that was supposed to be the informal place for young people and all, but the rest of the hotel was strictly off-limits.

I think it was my fourth night at King's Court when, just after my shift, I was starting to head back to the BI. As I walked past the front of the hotel, through the open windows, I heard the piano player in the little salon just off the reception area. He was there almost every night, and he was really good. He played mostly jazzy stuff, but every now and then he'd work his way into something more serious, like Bach. As it turned out, classical music was a pretty big deal in Pierrevert because there was an orchestra, the East Coast Philharmonic, that played there all summer at a place a few miles out of town. I didn't even know about it until I saw a big ad in the local paper that had the week-by-week schedule.

Anyway, on this particular night, I couldn't resist going back inside the hotel when I heard the guy playing. I felt like I was about to commit armed robbery when I opened the big front door, and I kind of tiptoed over to the salon as if walking quietly would make me invisible. The pianist looked like he was maybe in his fifties or sixties, kind of thin and tall, but it was hard to tell because he was sitting down. He was dressed all in black, real cool-like. I'd never heard the song he was playing, but even someone at my kiddie level could tell what he was doing was pretty sophisticated. A lot of the chords sounded out of whack, like they weren't quite right, but they were if you just kept listening.

"Hi there!" he said, friendly as could be, when I got close to the piano.

I returned the greeting and stood there staring at his hands. They were moving all over the place, kind of *gliding*. He had a very soft touch on the keys, not like some guys who bang the hell out of the piano and drive you half crazy. After maybe half a minute he looked up and said, "It's called 'Lush Life.' Written by Billy Strayhorn. A real lesson in harmony."

Then he started playing a different song, another one I'd never heard. He even started to sing, something about someone's foolish heart, as I remember. He had one of those scratchy voices that make you feel like you're in a seedy bar in Greenwich Village, and it drew maybe five or six people over from the reception area. The song went on a while longer, and we all clapped when he was done. He moved into another tune without missing a beat.

"You work here?" he said, looking at me, not his hands, which seemed to have a mind of their own. I figured he'd noticed my standard-issue black pants and white shirt, because I'd taken the blue vest and tie off. The shirt had a cherry-juice stain on it from when I'd had to make five whiskey sours fast for one of Harriet's tables.

"I started this week, tending bar in the courtyard," I said. Heart in hand, I added, "I try to play a little piano myself."

"No kidding! What do you like to play?"

"Oh, nothing really. Stuff I hear on the radio. I still kind of like the Beatles."

"Nothing wrong with Lennon and McCartney, man. Personally, I'm more into stuff from the thirties, forties, and fifties. Great American Songbook, Broadway shows, you know. But I'm an old guy. And your name is?"

"Coleman."

"Like the Hawk!"

When he saw my clueless look, he said, "Coleman Hawkins was a sax player. Everyone called him 'the Hawk.' I got to jam with him once in New York."

Still playing with his left hand, he held out his right hand and said, "I'm Skip. Skip Jones. Nice to meet you."

I shook his hand and was about to say "Likewise" when I caught a glimpse of Mr. Simons striding across the reception area, face glowering. The next second, he was in my face.

"Coleman," he spat. "Are you retarded? Didn't I tell you this part of the hotel is forbidden to off-duty employees?"

I opened my mouth but nothing came out. He eyed my shirt.

"And it would be nice if you could do your job with a little class, not spilling things all over yourself."

"Hey, Jeff," Skip said, without interrupting his playing. "It's OK. I asked Coleman to bring me some club soda. So, it's my fault."

There was a tall glass of club soda with a slice of lime in it sitting on a small table next to the piano, but I hadn't put it there.

"Did you know Coleman here plays the piano?" Skip added. "Maybe if I can't make it one of these nights, he's your man."

Mr. Simons looked at Skip, then back at me. I stared at the wall to avoid his glare and happened to notice a little frame hanging behind the piano. Inside was some pink stitching that spelled out "In Memory of Pearleen Porter." It was the same name Dr. Nelson mentioned on the day I was admitted to Buchanan. The girl who'd committed suicide, much to Nelson's irritation.

"That's strike one, Coleman," Mr. Simons said. "Three and you're out. Now go back to your nut farm."

Skip shot me a wink as I left. I hustled back to the BI and went straight down to the piano room.

16.

Excerpted from the book *The Maine Murders: What Really Happened in Pierrevert*

By Hayley Blossom
Originally published in the United Kingdom.

The Cauldron Café was owned and operated by two first cousins who, oddly enough, had the same name: Beverly Breen. They'd both been born in 1943 at Hargrove Hospital and had grown up in Pierrevert as Beverly Stewart and Beverly Murphy. Barely out of high school, they'd married two brothers, Bud and Bart Breen, who ran a house-painting business in town. But while they bore a strong family resemblance—their mothers had been twin sisters—and were of similar height and weight, they had one strong differentiating characteristic: the former Beverly Stewart had very large breasts, which occasionally got in the way of carrying a tray or serving food, while the erstwhile Beverly Murphy was rather flat-chested.

Pierrevert being the type of place it was, and the two women both being pretty and quite well known—the café was popular, renowned for its homemade soups that changed with the seasons—the variation in the Bevs' breast sizes had sparked a good deal of discussion among males at watering holes such as Erin Go Bragh's and the King's Court. Indeed, as a means of telling the Bevs apart in conversation, not only the men but most of the women in town had long referred to the cousins as "Bev A" or "Bev D," in reference to the respective cup sizes of their brassieres. The Bevs didn't mind the nicknames and, having similar voices in both tone and timbre, sometimes referred to themselves that way over the phone, saying, "Hi, it's Bev A," or "Hello, it's Bev D," to ensure the listener knew exactly who was speaking.

It was Bev D who happened to be serving at the café on a Saturday morning at ten o'clock, roughly two weeks after the murder of Dr Gregory Frazier. The Cauldron was also known for its pancakes and home fries, which is what both Chief Cody and Officer Kincaid had just ordered. The steaming plates arrived, and the two officers settled in for a rare moment of relaxation amid the pressure to find anything that could provide a lead on the two murders that had shaken their little village to its core.

The trail was as frigid as a January night in Pierrevert: two brutal stabbings, no fingerprints, no murder weapon, and no motive that anyone could think of. Nor was there a thread of information that could link the two victims together. So far as anyone could tell, Ronald Sanders and Gregory Frazier, while acquainted (like just about everyone else in Pierrevert), had nothing in common personally or professionally. Sanders was a lawyer, Frazier a psychiatrist. Sanders had been single and childless, Frazier a widower with children. They were not known to spend time together or have mutual friends.

Cody and Kincaid had interviewed just about everybody who knew either victim well, along with those who had been at the Tower the night Frazier was killed and the joggers who'd found his body the following morning. The state of the corpse was virtually identical to the way Sunny Singhaboon had found Ronald Sanders in his den the previous October—the torso savaged by multiple thrusts, far more than required to kill anyone. This modus operandi implied a high degree of fury, psychopathology, or both. The apparent murder weapon was a hunting knife with a jagged edge.

The two policemen had been over both crime scenes with a fine-tooth comb, aided by forensic experts sent in by Zeke Murkowski, the state police's head man in the county, who was based in Hargrove. The problem was that even the forensic specialists had come up with exactly zero—or as Marvin Glickman, Pierrevert's chief selectman (and Cody's boss) was fond of saying with no small dose of derision, "bupkis."

First and foremost on Cody's mind as he dug into his breakfast was an article that had appeared on the front page of that morning's *Northeast Telegram*. The first few paragraphs were all he could bear to read.

No Leads in Pierrevert Murders
By Hayley Blossom
Telegram Staff Writer

PIERREVERT—Nine months after the murder of Ronald Sanders and two weeks after the killing of Dr. Gregory Frazier, Pierrevert police say they have no leads in either case.

"We're very disappointed at this stage," said
police chief Chester Cody in an interview Friday.
"The investigation is ongoing, and we'll get to the
bottom of these terrible crimes. The townspeople
should know we are still on the case and they have
nothing to worry about."

Cody said that anyone with information
potentially relevant to the investigation should
come forward, and that all interviews would be
treated as strictly confidential.

The rest of the article was just warmed-over accounts
of each incident—material journalists refer to as "B matter" that provides background and makes the article longer
when the page layout calls for more text. Of course, this
particular piece was a rarity in that the news it claimed
to report was that there was, after all, no news. That's
why there'd been a heated debate in the *Telegram* newsroom over whether to run the story at all. Martin Taft, the
paper's gray and grizzled editor, and Jerome Kolner, the
young publisher who'd succeeded his father several years
before at age thirty-five, had green-lighted the article on
the grounds that the public needed an update, even if it
was of the no-news variety. They had done this over the
cries of more than a few old-school reporters whose atti-
tude was basically, *We're a newspaper and the lead story
on the front page says there's no news—beautiful.*

"Glickman called me this morning," Cody said, taking
a forkful of pancakes that dripped with hot maple syrup.
"He's not happy."

"What the fuck we supposed to do?" said Kincaid, cutting an admiring glance at Bev D's bustline as she leaned
over a table on the other side of the dining room. "He's an
old buzzard. What's he pushing, eighty by now?"

"Shhh," said Cody, who rarely used vulgarity and disdained Kincaid's lack of manners. "He's seventy-two."

"Whoever we're looking for is one goddamn smart dude—or girl," Kincaid said. "We got nothing 'cause nothing got left behind. Still think you're giving the Thai chick a pass on Sanders."

"I've spoken to her at length," Cody said patiently. "She's not involved. Accept it."

Kincaid sat back in his chair and took a sip of coffee.

"I understand where Glickman's coming from," Cody said, passing the maple syrup over to his deputy. "He got reelected last fall. No one's arrested, they'll say he's incompetent or soft on crime. I might feel the same way."

For the chief, the Bevs put the syrup in a small thermos to keep it hot. They never did that for Kincaid when he was in the café alone or with his best mate, Jason Mason, although both were regular customers. In truth, the Bevs did not care for either Kincaid or Mason, whom they saw as bullies who'd never grown up. Both men, now in their early thirties, had graduated in the same class from Two Rivers Regional High School and been teammates on the hockey team. They referred to each other as "wingman"—as in "Hey, wingman, pass the sugar"—a means of address that annoyed the Bevs to no end. When Kincaid was with the chief, however, whom the Bevs adored for his natural friendliness and the way he treated everyone from Patricia Sorensen down to the dustbin man with the same degree of respect, even the deputy got hot maple syrup.

"Glickman said the whole thing's keeping him up nights," Cody continued. "I told him I wasn't sleeping too well either."

Cody shot a look at Kincaid's plate, which his deputy had barely touched.

"Hey, what's with you?" the chief said. "You usually wolf this stuff down."

"Yeah, I wasn't sleeping too good myself last night, so I got up around five and made some eggs," Kincaid said. "Guess I'm just not that hungry."

The deputy looked across the table to gauge if there were any chance at being caught in the lie, but Cody's face showed no sign of suspicion. He just nodded and gazed out the window at the King Richard Inn across the street. Kincaid relaxed and took another swill of coffee.

"Maybe things will take a turn for the better," Cody said, snapping out of his reverie and returning to his pancakes.

***

Kevin Kincaid had been only partly lying to his boss. He had indeed slept poorly the previous night and gotten out of bed at five o'clock. He'd even eaten some scrambled eggs before meeting Cody at their office at about nine thirty. But the eggs had not been prepared by Kincaid in his small apartment on Cheshire Street, about a mile from the center of town, where he lived alone. They'd been cooked by Sunny Singhaboon in her own kitchen.

Ever since the night the previous month when Kincaid knocked on Sunny's back door for the first time, he'd been stopping by regularly. He used his own car, an old Volvo that fit perfectly into a cluster of trees about twenty-five yards from Sunny's house, the last structure on an isolated dead-end street called Lilac Lane. The car was invisible to any passerby who did not stop and squint.

That first evening, the same one that had earlier found Sunny evaluating her naked reflection in her bathroom mirror, it was under the guise of checking in to make sure she was all right—what with the tension in town and people whispering unkind things about her—that Kincaid paid a visit. The truth was that he'd wanted to see how she'd be dressed at that time of night and throw his police officer weight around a bit. He did not truly suspect her of involvement in the murder of Ronald Sanders, a claim he'd made to Chief Cody out of spite for a woman he'd lusted after since the day she arrived in Pierrevert. More recently, as he'd observed her comings and goings from the King Richard Inn, where she'd been hired as a cook, she'd become an obsession.

Sunny let Kincaid in the door that first night because she'd had to—he was, after all, a copper. Being naturally polite and wanting to appear relaxed, she'd even offered him a cup of herbal tea (although she'd quickly excused herself while the water was boiling to change out of her silk bathrobe into a pair of jeans and a baggy jumper). As the two sat at her kitchen table, Kincaid had offered his sympathy for what an ordeal it must have been to come upon Sanders' ravaged body, then have to deal with people's suspicions. Sunny had replied that people had a right to think whatever they pleased, however hurtful the rumours might be to her and her daughters. Kincaid quickly ran out of things to say, so to keep the conversation going he'd asked Sunny how it was that such a pretty girl from the other side of the world had ended up in a backwoods burg like Pierrevert in the first place.

And that was when the young Thai beauty, normally as cool and self-assured around men as women came, showed her Achilles' heel.

No matter how you sliced it, Sunny knew she'd obtained her visa under dodgy circumstances. Moreover, the US diplomat who'd been her customer and benefactor had died of complications from a massive coronary only a month after she'd arrived in Pierrevert, having never provided her with a backstory. The man's brother, with whom he'd shared an apartment in Alexandria, Virginia, had informed her in a short letter, explaining that his dying sibling had asked she be notified.

Indeed, Sunny's customer had provided his mailing address during their last meeting in Bangkok and asked that she do the same once settled in America—a favour she'd granted out of gratitude. Yet while somewhat relieved by his death—Sunny no longer had to worry that he might come knocking in Pierrevert—she also knew that his demise meant there was no one to take charge when her visa expired. She'd have to go to the state capital and deal with a faceless official who would leer at her across his desk and ask pointed questions about how she had obtained the visa in the first place. Her former profession was an illegal one in America, she knew that, and governments had ways of finding out about one's past, didn't they? Could they put her in jail in Maine for things she'd done years before in Thailand? On the night Kevin Kincaid showed up at her back door, this reckoning was less than two years away.

The notion of being sent back to her native country—or in the worst case, arrested—introduced raw fear to Sunny's otherwise calm, self-possessed equilibrium. So when Kincaid, quite by chance, asked Sunny about her path to the United States, she became unglued. She giggled nervously. She said she'd won a visa in a lottery. Then she changed her story to having a great grandmother who'd been American. Noticing her skittishness, Kincaid pressed on with a few specific hows, whys, and whens. She became even more anxious, stammering out one silly explanation after another. And that's when the deputy police chief knew he had something unspeakably precious: leverage over this rare Asian bird to extract what he wanted.

So Kincaid made a promise to Sunny: if she did not become his mistress, he would have her visa investigated. At the very least, he would make sure it was not renewed. This was pure bluff on Kincaid's part, but Sunny, all too aware of her tenuous situation, was scared both for herself and her daughters, who had settled so happily into their new American lives. Kincaid added that if she said anything to anyone, especially to Chief Cody, well, she didn't want to think about what he might do under those circumstances.

With female antennae that were highly attuned to the male psyche, Sunny had already sensed that Kincaid could be violent with women—although she had no way of knowing that the two girlfriends with whom he had cohabitated during his adult life had both left him for that very reason. The apple did not fall very far from the tree.

After that night, Kincaid's visits came early in the morning before the girls were awake. He limited the meetings to once per week—in his mind, a sustainable frequency both for Sunny's capacity to acquiesce and his own ability to avoid detection. Breakfast was part of the deal and provided an excuse, or so he hypothesized, in case he were ever noticed. He'd just say he and Sunny were friends and that he loved the Thai spices she put in the eggs.

Sunny dealt with the situation as stoically as she could. She had the advantage that, with her background, she was able to compartmentalize her life better than most women. And she provided Kincaid the most basic service possible: purely missionary, nothing oral, no heels or lingerie, no makeup, her luxurious jet-black hair tied back demurely. She was utterly passive during the act itself, which was always finished in less than thirty seconds. Kincaid, who did not push his luck by refusing her insistence on a condom, did not feel slighted. It was the only type of sex he had ever known.

**

Chief Cody finished his pancakes and left enough cash on the table to pay for both breakfasts, adding his customary 20 percent tip for the Bevs. Kincaid eyed him again for any sign of suspicion and decided to continue the ruse that he thought Sunny had played a role in Ronald Sanders' death. How could Cody suspect him of having a relationship with her if he, Kincaid, was always accusing her of murder?

The deputy needn't have bothered. Cody no more imagined his charge having sex with Sunny Singhaboon than he imagined him having a secret life as a ballet dancer.

"By the way," Cody said, rising from the table. "There's a dinner for the Pierrevert Historical Society coming up on Labor Day weekend at the King Richard. The selectmen will be there. We're both invited. They want us to lend a hand with the fund-raising. Try to watch your language at the table, OK?"

"Sure, Chief," Kincaid said. "Sorry 'bout that. And thanks for the breakfast."

17.

Amy and I were sitting at the bar at Erin Go Bragh's. It was the first time I'd been back since the night I met Cheryl a couple of weeks before, and we were talking about how weird things were at the BI. I know that sounds dumb, because the place was a loony bin. How could things not be weird? What I mean is a lot of people were still pretty shaken up about Dr. Frazier getting killed. I'd even heard that a few patients were leaving Buchanan because they were too scared to stay or their parents didn't think Pierrevert was safe anymore. For me it was still summer, the symphony was playing even though I hadn't heard it yet, and the hotel was full. People might be a little skittish—I knew that from the conversations I'd overheard at King's Court—but they weren't packing up and heading back to wherever they came from.

Amy and I had gotten to be pretty good friends, and I'd figured out that her main source of calories was cocktails. She thought a sandwich or even a salad would make her fat, but she liked to drink, especially apricot sours, and she liked bars. Whenever she came over to King's Court, I'd try to load up her drinks on the sly, mixing them in the blender—which was under the counter, out of sight—and sneaking in some extra sugar and a raw egg, which made for a nice froth on top. She never knew the difference. I thought I should do whatever I could to fatten her up, especially since she had the bad luck of having Dr. Nelson for a shrink.

Amy had ideas about what'd happened to Dr. Frazier.

"Nelson knows something about it," she said, taking the first sip of an apricot sour that Seamus had just put in front of her. Not that I had any confidence as a bartender, but I was pretty sure Seamus' sours weren't as good as mine. He'd just thrown Amy's drink together without a thought, or at least it looked that way. Never mind that the sour mixes and cordials at Erin Go Bragh's were the bargain-basement type, not like the premium brands at the King Richard.

"She didn't like him, I know she didn't," Amy said. "She doesn't like men, period. Frazier was against her getting the admissions job, but Bellino thought the BI needed more diversity, so she got it anyway. And he thinks she's good with women."

"How do you know this stuff?" I said, sipping from my bottle of beer.

"I've been here a *year*, Coleman. I hear the nurses talking. Nelson hangs out over at the Tower on weekends, and I've heard some stuff about that too. Frazier was there the night before he died."

"What's she like as a shrink?"

"The truth? Bellino's right. She's been really nice to me. But she's got a dark side. I can feel it."

Amy knew how to wear loose clothes to hide her skin-and-bones frame, and she was good with makeup and naturally pretty. So I guess it wasn't so strange after all that someone might try to pick her up at a bar, which is exactly what happened next. I didn't care for the look of the guy—goatee, tattoos on his arms, biker vest—but she gave him a big smile, and it seemed like they knew each other, so I took that as my cue to take a walk. I wandered over to the room where they had a pool table and watched two girls play eight ball for a couple of minutes, then toddled back to the main room to see what was on the jukebox. I was leaning over it, giving the songs a good look, when someone tapped me on the shoulder from behind. I turned around to see a sharp-looking Black fellow, maybe thirty-five or forty years old, smiling at me. He was heavyset, had a closely trimmed Afro and a thick, full beard, and was dressed in tight-fitting clothes. I caught a big whiff of cologne. Like me, he was holding a bottle of beer.

"'Scuse me, bro," he said. "I just wanna put somethin' on."

He dropped a couple of quarters in the slot, pushed some buttons, leaned back against the jukebox, and took a big gulp of beer. There was a group of maybe eight girls dancing together.

"Not much out there tonight, man," he said with an air of authority. "Nope. What we got ourselves here is a *poverty* of *pulchritude*." He shook his head grimly from side to side as if to say, *The world's just not a fair place, is it?*

He took another swill of beer and looked toward the bar.

"Damn," he said. "Linda's here."

"Who?"

"Over there." He gestured with his head. "In the blue tank top."

Leaning over the bar was a good-looking fortyish woman with dark hair. Seamus was handing her a drink, which looked like a gin or vodka and tonic judging from the clear color and slice of lime he'd just squeezed into it.

"Linda's OK," said my new acquaintance, "and she likes guys with my complexion. I don't feel like hangin' out with her tonight, though."

He paused for a moment and chuckled to himself.

"Coupla weeks ago, me and my friend Earl was here, and Linda, well, she made it clear she was up for some fun, know what I'm sayin'? We hesitated 'cause . . . well . . . she got a lot of miles on her, you know? After a few drinks, we said what the hell. We put a few more on."

It was the first time in my life that another male had considered me worthy of banter about women.

"I've only been here once," I said. "I don't know anybody."

He thought for a second and slapped his hand to his thigh. "*That's* where I seen you before!" he said with a wide grin. "Right here! You was dancin' with *Cheryl*. Whole place was checkin' you out 'cause nobody know you and everybody know her. You new in town?"

"I'm a patient at Buchanan."

"That's cool, man. Lotta people I know been to Buchanan." He gave me a mischievous look. "Saw you *leave* with Cheryl too, man."

I tried to manage a knowing smile, something I knew nothing about.

"Word of advice?" he said.

"What?"

"Mind if I give you a word of advice?"

"Sure. I mean no, I don't mind at all."

"None of my business, man, but be cool with Cheryl. She look at you with that face and that blonde hair, and she know she got that Playboy Bunny body, and you think you died and gone to heaven. Maybe you did too. One day you wake up with her thinkin' everything be fine, and she drop you cold and heartless. I seen it happen time and again."

He continued to survey the room as he spoke. "S'another reason to be cool with Cheryl," he said. "See the dude in the black T-shirt? The one with the muscles?"

I followed his gaze toward the other side of the bar. It was the mountain man who'd given me the evil eye when I was dancing with Cheryl. He was leaning against the wall with a beer in his hand.

"That's Jason, works in the forest. Been off and on with Cheryl since she been 'bout sixteen. Motherfucker's crazy, man. Walk around half the time with a huntin' knife on his belt. Hangs out with a cop, Kincaid. He crazy too." His tone suddenly changed. "Hey, speak of the devil."

I looked toward the side door and saw Cheryl breeze in. She was wearing a turquoise halter top—her perfect flat tummy on full display—and very short white shorts. She was with her roommate Kim, and they headed straight for the bar. Cheryl gave Seamus a big smile and leaned in to order a drink.

"Looks killer, as usual," said my new friend. He tipped his beer bottle high and drained the last few drops.

"Hey, I gotta split, man," he said. "Nice meetin' you, though." He extended his hand. "I'm Fontaine . . . Fontaine Perkins."

"Coleman Cooper," I said, shaking his hand in the two-step, playground-basketball way of the day. At least I knew how to do that. Harold Cherry taught it to me in high school when he wasn't screaming at me for blowing layups.

I watched Fontaine leave out the side door and took up his post, leaning on the jukebox. As far as I could tell, Cheryl hadn't noticed me. The thing was, the beer was already going to my head. I'd hardly eaten anything that day, as usual, and when I drink on an empty stomach it only takes one to get the room spinning. The mixture of the alcohol, the thumping music, Fontaine's advice about Cheryl, and the sight of her across the room was making me feel pretty weird, like I'd just had a hefty shot of Thorazine. I was tired and suddenly struggling to keep my eyes open. Drifting . . . drifting . . .

"Coleman."

I snapped to, and Cheryl's face was no more than six inches from mine. The perfume and lipstick were different, the warm, cinnamon-scented breath the same.

"Are you all right?" she said. "You were listing to port. I thought you were gonna capsize."

"Fine."

"I can't talk to you now, but you were wrong about what happened." She handed me a book of matches. "My number's inside. Call me."

As she turned and walked back to the bar, I caught sight of the mountain man again. He was staring, looking like he wanted to kill me.

18.

Hey, Coleman," said Skip Jones. "Anyone ever say you got big hands?"

I was sitting at Skip's grand piano in his second-floor apartment across from the Pierrevert Wine Cellar on Acorn Street, a few blocks away from the King Richard Inn. It wasn't like me, but I'd found the nerve to ask Skip if he'd give me lessons. I figured maybe I could make up for lost time if I had a teacher like him, and I could afford the twenty bucks an hour he charged because I was making money tending bar and wasn't paying any rent. With my room, board, and therapy at the BI taken care of by my mother's insurance, I was saving money for the first time in years. Skip's piano was a Steinway, a big one too.

"Put your left hand on the keyboard," Skip said. He was standing behind me, looking over my shoulder. "Put your pinky on the C below middle C, and stretch out your hand as wide as you can."

I did as I was told.

"Damn," he said. "You can reach a major tenth, no sweat."

A major tenth is ten whole steps. I could reach some pretty easily, depending on the key.

"Now put your pinky on D and reach up to F-sharp with your thumb."

I did it with no effort.

"OK, put your pinky on B-flat and reach up to D with your thumb."

That one I couldn't do, but it was close.

"Tell you something, man," he said. "I had hands like yours, I'd sound like Oscar Peterson."

Mr. Glover, my high school basketball coach, had pointed out the size of my hands to the whole team more than once. Everyone used to say what a waste it was that someone as uncoordinated as I ended up with such a pair of mitts. So what if I could palm the ball? I didn't know what to do with it once I had it, which explains why I never got it. It was just one more thing the guys made fun of me for.

I figured my big hands wouldn't do much good for me at the piano either, given that I had no talent. Even so, listening to Skip play at the hotel had given me motivation I hadn't had in years, and I'd been working on major and minor scales down in the piano room at the BI. I'd try them first with one hand, then with both, which was a lot harder because you had to get the fingering right for things to come out even. Lucky for me, the little room was soundproofed, so no one complained about the noise. I'm pretty sure anyone at the BI who wasn't crazy already would've been driven that way fast if they'd listened to me hacking away for a couple of hours.

Sure enough, Skip finally got around to the question I dreaded.

"So, Coleman, let's hear you play something, man!"

The thing was, after hearing Skip at the hotel and then listening to some jazz records with Amy up in her room, I'd tried to imitate something I'd heard. It started with a bass line in the left hand. Then I'd tried to add some chords in my right. It was pretty difficult, at least for me, but after playing it about a hundred times, I thought I'd got it to where it wouldn't make people cover their ears.

"I'll just try this," I said to Skip, between nervous throat clears. "I know it's terrible."

"Don't be so hard on yourself," he said, taking a seat on the sofa across the room.

Typical me, once I put my hands on the keys, I couldn't play a note. My fingers stiffened. I started to sweat.

"Coleman," Skip said calmly but sternly. "Sit up straight."

I'd been all hunched over the piano, tense as hell.

"Now take five slow, deep breaths. I'll do them with you."

We did them together.

"Take it one hand at a time," he said. "Start with the left. Play whatever you'd like. And take it slow."

So I tried to go into my little bass line at a snail's pace. I was getting some feeling back in my fingers, and the notes were coming out. Skip looked like he was listening carefully, so when I got to the end of the pattern I just repeated it. After the second go-round, I stopped.

"Where'd you hear that?" Skip asked.

"I heard you play something like it at the hotel, and I've heard it on a record too."

"Do you know what that's called, what you're doing?"

Clueless, as usual.

"In a word, it's blues," he said. "Twelve-bar blues. There's a million songs written in that form. Do you know what key you're in?"

"Well, I started on F."

"That's right, you're in F. Let's try something."

I'll never forget what happened next.

"Start your bass line up again," Skip said, taking a seat next to me on the piano bench.

He let me go through the pattern once. Then as I came around to the beginning, he started playing along with me, chords in his left hand and improvising solo notes with his right. I don't know how else to describe it except to say that, kind of like magic, what he was doing made what I was doing actually sound good. I realized I had a huge grin on my face but wiped it right off. None of the guys in the black-and-white photos on Skip's wall were smiling like eight-year-old dorks. I figured they must be old-time jazz stars or something. After a few more times through, Skip pulled his hands up from the keyboard.

"That's not bad, Coleman," he said. "You've got decent rhythm, and you held it steady. How many years of lessons did you have as a kid?"

"Five, but I never got any good."

"What kind of pieces did you play?"

"A little Bach, a little Mozart. Just the easy stuff."

"Never played any blues or jazz?"

"Just trying to copy stuff I heard on the radio."

"You know your scales? Major, minor, diminished?"

"Just major and a few minor."

"Ever hear of scale-tone triads? Scale-tone seventh chords?"

"No."

"Then that's where we'll start."

For the next half hour, Skip showed me scale-tone triads, with three notes each, and scale-tone seventh chords, with four notes each, in the key of C. Anyone could do them, really. All you had to do was put your hand in the right position and move it up and down. There weren't any black notes. Then he showed me a blues scale, which sounded really cool when he did it and terrible when I did, because I kept hitting wrong notes.

"Let's call it a lesson," Skip finally said, getting up and stretching. He went into his kitchen, and I heard a fridge door open.

"You want a beer?" he shouted.

"Sure."

It was only four in the afternoon, and I was going to work just afterward, but I wasn't going to refuse a beer from Skip Jones. We took a seat in the two easy chairs he had in the small living room.

"How well can you read music?" he asked, sipping from his bottle.

"Really slow."

"But you can read, right? If I give you something to work on, it's not gonna look like Greek?"

"No."

He got up, walked over to a bookshelf, peered around, and pulled out a thin volume. "Let's see if those hands of yours can deal with this," he said, tossing the book onto my lap.

On the cover it said, *Three Preludes: George Gershwin.*

"It's the second prelude I think you can do," he said. "Here, listen."

He sat down at the piano and started to play from memory. It was a slow, kind of haunting piece, the type you could really let your imagination run away with. I didn't think for a second I could ever play it. It ended with a stray, single note, followed by a deep bass note.

"That's genius," Skip said quietly.

He meant Gershwin, not himself. Then he looked at his watch.

"Damn!" he said, jumping up. "I'm supposed to be someplace! Sorry, gotta go."

We walked down the stairs together and out onto the street. It was there that something occurred to me.

"Hey, Skip, can I ask you a question?"

"If it's quick."

"Did you know Pearleen Porter?"

At the mention of the name, his face just changed. He looked down at the ground and shuffled his feet around.

"Why do you ask?"

"I saw a little frame on the wall at the hotel near the piano, that was all. I just thought maybe—"

He took a deep breath and looked into my face. "She was a waitress at the inn, a friend of mine. If there was no one around, she'd sing. Man, what a voice. She died very young. That frame just showed up one day. I never asked who put it there."

"I'm sorry, I'm really . . ."

Leave it to me.

Skip smiled sadly and reached into his pocket for a cigarette. He lit up and gave me a friendly clap on the shoulder.

"Practice that prelude," he said, turning away. "Nothing like Gershwin."

19.

Excerpted from the book *The Maine Murders: What Really Happened in Pierrevert*

By Hayley Blossom
Originally published in the United Kingdom.

In the 1950s, professional football was just coming of age in the United States. One match in particular, the 1958 National Football League championship between the Baltimore Colts and the New York Giants, won by the Colts 23–17, has been cited by sports historians as the game that broke a barrier. Viewed by millions on television, the contest represented a turning point in pro football entering the mainstream of American culture. And in the mud-soaked gridiron lore of that day and age, no player epitomized old-school, blood-and-guts machismo quite like a journeyman linebacker who hailed from Hargrove, Maine. His name was Henry Porter.

In a ten-year career that began in 1955, following his graduation from all-Black Grambling State University in

Louisiana, Porter had stints with the Cleveland Browns, Philadelphia Eagles, Detroit Lions, San Francisco 49ers, and Green Bay Packers. Owing to the number of quarterbacks, running backs, and receivers he knocked out of games, sometimes ending their seasons (and occasionally their careers), he was one of the most feared players in the league, known especially for his unorthodox style of tackling.

When Henry moved in to bring down an opponent, he first extended his arms. That at least looked correct. But his signature was hitting ball carriers not with his shoulders, as proper technique dictated, but with his head, more often than not targeting the head of the opposing player. Hence the nickname that followed him throughout his career: Henry the Helmet. Fans were so enthralled with Henry's daredevil tactics that TV networks would turn up the volume on their sideline microphones when he was on the field so that viewers at home could hear the astonishing helmet-to-helmet crunch of Henry's hits.

"You know, Henry," one of his Packers coaches, Bruno "Cookie" Cutter, said to him one day after practice within earshot of a national reporter, "I think you'd slam that helmet of yours into your grandmother if you had to."

"Not unless she was about to score for the other team, Coach," was Henry's unflinching reply.

Yet off the field, belying his six-foot-three, 240-pound frame, Henry was rather a lamb—the gentlest, most soft-spoken friend anyone could ask for. His former teammates said he would do anything for anyone, usually with a smile. His personal warmth, they speculated, could be explained by the fact that he had a happy home life. He'd married his Hargrove High sweetheart, Pamela Gilmore, in July 1954, just before his senior year at Grambling. The couple had wanted children, but Pamela, whose own mother had died giving birth to her, had a phobia about pregnancy. So, in June 1955, when Henry was twenty-three and Pamela twenty-two, they adopted an infant, light-skinned Black girl from a small orphanage nestled in the hill country just west of Hargrove. They called her Pearleen.

Pamela and Pearleen lived in Hargrove year-round, with Henry, during the football season, taking a hotel room in the city of whatever team he played for. Although this arrangement kept him away from home from July through December, the couple felt that stability for Pearleen was preferable to constant house moves and switches of schools and friends. Henry would sneak home for a couple of days during the season when he could. In the off-season, he worked at Hargrove High as co-head basketball coach in the winter, joining the team in January, and head track coach in the spring. The school board was thrilled to have a real-life professional football player mentoring the town's youths. Even better, Henry was an understanding coach, not the type who screamed at young boys when they missed a key shot or lost a race. He might ride his athletes hard, but after practice he'd muss up their hair and tell them how much progress they'd made. In later years, many of Henry's athletes said he'd been like a second father to them.

Pearleen was ten when Henry finally retired from pro football and returned to Hargrove to live year-round. Since he was now free in the autumn, the school board made him head football coach straightaway. One result was that the Hargrove Hornets went undefeated in 1965, Henry's first season on the sidelines.

As a mentor, Henry made a point of teaching his defensive players the proper tackling style. "Do as I say, not as I did!" he'd shout in practice as his charges slammed their shoulders into blocking sleds. More than a few went on to be successful football players in college, several at Grambling, although none ever broke into the professional ranks.

Henry had saved money during his NFL career and now had a full three-season coaching salary to complement Pamela's earnings as the high school librarian, a job she'd taken when Pearleen was eight. The future seemed bright. But in the winter of 1967, Henry began to complain of severe headaches. Not only that, his affable demeanor began to shift, with flashes of unprovoked anger erupting both at home and at work. Even worse, these symptoms coincided with the dreadful news that Pamela had been diagnosed with breast cancer.

Henry was still functioning as a coach at the high school and a father to Pearleen when Pamela passed away two years later, in the summer of 1969. But the enormity of the event triggered a fundamental change in his personality. Grieving profoundly, and after spending his entire adult life as a teetotaler, Henry began to drink. He also, as Pearleen's own diary recovered after her death revealed in agonizing detail, began to beat his daughter.

Henry would start drinking every morning with vodka in his orange juice. After breakfast, he'd pour a four-to-one mixture of coffee and dark rum into a thermos, which he'd toss onto the back seat of his fire-engine-red GTO for the ten-minute ride to Hargrove High, where Pearleen was beginning her freshman year. The drive was typically a silent one, Henry ruminating on the various problems his teams faced and Pearleen afraid to let out a peep. He'd drop her off at the side door next to the cafeteria, drive around back and park the car, then walk to his office near the gym and locker rooms. Students he passed on the way would offer deferential smiles to Coach Porter, and Henry would try to return them.

It fell to Pearleen, at age fourteen, to do the shopping after school and all the cooking. If she caught the buses right, she'd make it home by four thirty. That left two hours to do her homework and prepare the evening meal before Henry returned from practice.

It was usually as Pearleen cleared up the kitchen after dinner that Henry, brooding at the table with his third or fourth glass of cheap brandy, began to transform. It would often start with tears, followed by a stumble across the kitchen to hug Pearleen from behind as she stood at the sink rinsing dishes. Lost in his own swirling thoughts, out of nowhere, Henry would feel a powerful impulse and shove Pearleen to the floor. He'd then lift her up gently, his eyes full of remorse, before his gaze would darken again and he'd slam her back down. Slaps to her face and punches to her sides and midsection would follow as he pinned her to the floor with his knee.

Pearleen always managed to extricate herself and dash out of the kitchen, but Henry would pursue her, still fleet of foot even when stone-drunk. The session typically ended with the ex-linebacker's collapse, wherever in the house he happened to be when his will gave out, then three or four hours of heavy slumber on the floor. When he eventually came to, he would stagger to bed, sleep for another few hours, and have no recollection of the episode when his alarm clock rang the next morning. His day would begin anew, the vodka and orange juice turning his motor over for another day on the sidelines.

The beatings did not occur every night or even every week, necessarily. But over the course of the next four years, the violence happened often enough to erode the soul of Pearleen Porter. Timid and yielding by nature, she still loved her father and could sense what her mother's death had done to him, even if she couldn't articulate it. She never said a word to anyone about the beatings, the evidence of which she hid with careful placement of clothing until long after the fact. If body bruises were evident on a day when Pearleen had physical education class and was obliged to wear a revealing gym suit, she would either feign illness at school or stay home altogether. Henry never punched her in the face, only slapped her there with an open hand, leaving no marks after the initial redness subsided.

Pearleen kept her grades at an acceptable level despite the physical and emotional toll the beatings took on her, but she had few girlfriends and never had a boyfriend—not that she didn't have suitors. Slim, bronze-skinned, fine-featured, nearly five foot ten, people said she looked like a model. Her appearance and the fact that she was Henry Porter's daughter assured plenty of phone calls, hallway chat-ups, and wistful glances from male teachers. But no one ever got anywhere with Pearleen, who was petrified that any visitor to her home would sense that something was terribly wrong.

Henry, for his part, managed to hide his alcoholism from colleagues, players, and friends, aided by constant gum chewing that both cleansed his breath and fit right in with the coaching persona. His deepening cognitive problems were tougher to conceal, but he largely pulled the act off until just after Pearleen turned eighteen and graduated from Hargrove High. Perhaps that had been an unconscious goal, to witness the milestone. The summer just after, as Pearleen began work at Fegelmann's Department Store in downtown Hargrove selling perfume, Henry's dementia picked up speed—chasing him as relentlessly as he'd pursued opposing ball carriers before bringing them down with a sickening, helmet-to-helmet thud. One August night in Pearleen's second month on the job, she returned home to find her father facedown on the sitting room floor, clad only in a pair of Hargrove High gym shorts. An empty half gallon of vodka lay next to his lifeless body.

Half the town turned out for Henry's funeral at the First Baptist Church. In addition, there among the legions of men that Henry had coached over the years were at least fifteen former National Football League players, several from each team he'd played on. The eulogy was given by Homer Taylor, Henry's former Grambling teammate and a second-team All American at tight end who'd chosen the law over football and gone on to a successful litigating career in Charlotte, North Carolina. Mabel Prescott, the athletic department secretary at the high school, sat next to Pearleen in the front row and held her hand.

Both Henry and Pamela had pensions from the Hargrove school system that reverted to Pearleen, as did Henry's NFL retirement income. The small family home was paid for, and Pearleen had a job, however modest the wages. In the short term, at least, she had enough to live on. And in the weeks following the funeral, she tried to reassemble what was left of her emotional stability. She was not up to the task.

Being the type of person she was, Pearleen had always felt deep down that *she* was responsible for Henry's beatings. Maybe if she'd somehow been a better daughter, her mother would never have fallen ill and her father would never have transformed from a teddy bear into a monster. She shared a few of these self-recriminations with Homer Taylor, who made a point of calling her every week from Charlotte, where he lived with his wife and two teenage sons. But Homer's reassurances didn't help, nor did his urgings that she seek out a therapist—advice she ignored.

What Pearleen did not know, and what Homer Taylor did not find out until it was too late to tell her, was that the coroner of Hargrove County, Dr Jonathan Monroe, had ordered an autopsy on Henry's body, one that was never publicized. Dr Monroe, the unofficial team physician for Hargrove High's football team (on his own time), had quietly noticed the slow but sure alteration in the coach's mental and emotional state. He'd possessed the legal authority to order the autopsy and had performed the procedure himself. His findings, a matter of public record open to anyone who cared to peruse the Hargrove County Health Department's voluminous files, were dramatic.

Dr Monroe discovered that Henry's brain was severely atrophied and darkly stained, with ventricles far larger than normal. It reminded him of a boxer's brain that he had examined early in his career. His opinion was that the damage must have resulted from the hundreds of high-speed, helmet-to-helmet hits that Henry sustained during his football career, collisions that must have caused multiple head concussions. The physician found it a small miracle that Henry was still functioning at all when he died.

Whether knowledge of her father's condition and the logical conclusion that his violent behaviour had been the result of profound illness—rather than of something she had done to provoke it—would have helped Pearleen's own mental health is something we will never know. What we do know is the series of events that befell her in the year following Henry's death.

20.

I'd kept the matchbook that Cheryl gave me at Erin Go Bragh's, but it took maybe a week to find the nerve to call her. I finally did it from the phone booth at the Manor, and take my word, you can't imagine a less cool place to call a girl from. My friend Lenny was standing outside the booth, gut poking through his shirt, swilling a diet soda. Another patient, a new guy called Richard, was standing in a corner mumbling something to himself. The scene didn't do any wonders for my self-confidence, not that I had any to lose.

Cheryl answered after about five rings and said she'd pick me up at seven that evening. I was nervous all afternoon, meaning more than usual, and the fact that it was a day off from bartending meant I had nothing to take my mind off messing everything up. I'd also forgotten that seven o'clock, being right after dinner, was the hour when a lot of patients and staff hung out on the front steps of the Manor, exactly where we agreed she'd stop by. Sure enough, when the time came, Freddy Cruz and April were out there along with Lenny and Amy and another new guy called Daniel, who was pretty out of it. Amy, fountain of inside information she always was, told me that Daniel had been a cocaine addict and had sniffed some powder that turned out to be rat poison. Even Ruby Calhoun, who gave out the night meds at ten, had moseyed outside to see how everyone was doing.

Ruby had just turned toward me to say something—I was hanging back, leaning against the front of the building—when the sound of a car got everyone's attention. It was off in the distance, passing through the parking lot of the doctors' building toward the Manor, but you could tell from the noise that it was no run-of-the-mill sedan. As it got closer, the form of a white convertible, built low to the ground, took shape.

When the sleek vehicle screeched to a halt in front of us, everyone could see that the driver was a young woman with blonde hair—but she was looking away. It wasn't until she yanked up the parking brake, pushed her sunglasses to the top of her head, and got out of the car that the full Cheryl effect hit home. She was wearing a white denim miniskirt and a tight purple top that she'd pulled down off her left shoulder to show a matching bra strap. When she sashayed around the fancy taillights, you could see that her platform sandals and toenail polish were the exact same shade of purple. I figured you could bet the national debt on the color of the panties she had on underneath. She gave us one of her patented, dazzling smiles, the perfect teeth as white as the skirt, and said, "Well! This looks like quite a gathering!"

I thought Freddy Cruz was going to have a heart attack. Lenny froze too. He couldn't even manage another slug of diet soda. Ruby had one hand over her mouth in the *oh-my-goodness* fashion. April and Amy were just as riveted, but their eyes were narrowed, sizing Cheryl up as only young females can. April was the only person who found the nerve to speak: "Can I, um, help you?"

"Oh, I don't think so," Cheryl said, picking up on the chill in April's voice. She opened the passenger door, made one of those swirling gestures with her right arm that kind of means "at your service," and looked me straight in the eye. "Sir Coleman," she said, "your carriage awaits!" Boy, that did it. This creature from another planet, a *Vogue* cover girl and *Playboy* centerfold rolled into one, had come for *me*, Coleman Cooper, the furthest thing from a "sir" anyone could imagine—more like the Duke of Dorks or Prince of Pimples, not to mention a career mental patient with maybe a few bucks to his name. All heads swiveled toward me, but I didn't look up, not even at Cheryl. I just focused on the skyblue bucket seat she was beckoning me toward. Small victory, I made it down the wooden steps and slid in without tripping. Cheryl slammed the door with her usual flair, sauntered slowly around the front of the car to give everyone a parting view of her backside, hopped in, and flashed me a conspiratorial wink. Everyone got a load of that. And when she fired up all that horsepower, sending loud kicks of exhaust out the chrome tailpipes, I couldn't help myself: I smiled almost as widely as I did that day in the gym against Malvern. I probably looked ten years old.

I spent that night at Cheryl's house, and this time she was still in bed next to me when I woke up in the morning. She even made scrambled eggs for breakfast. Part of me was still waiting for her to burst into laughter, call in a horde of friends that must be hiding nearby, and between gasps of delight, say in staccato:

Oh . . . my . . . GOD . . . he . . . really . . . thought . . . this . . . was . . . for . . . REAL! Then everyone would explode in hysterics.

But it didn't happen that way. If anything, it was the opposite. She even gazed at me across the kitchen table, dressed in an old flannel bathrobe she'd thrown on when we got out of bed, with what looked like some variation of affection. Her face was just as flawless first thing in the morning as it was made up at night, if a little pale, and I stared at it with wonder.

As I was eating the eggs, she did the types of things girls tend to do: pushed her hair off her face, examined her fingernails, mused that one of her friends was mad at her and she didn't know why, stuff like that. At one point, she took too big a sip of coffee and let out a little burp, which made her eyes go wide with mock horror. She covered her mouth and started to giggle, and I got a flash of what she must have looked like as a little girl. I found it touching beyond belief. As she chattered on about this and that, I noticed a stack of mail on the other side of the table, which gave me my first glimpse of her full name: Cheryl Beringer. It struck me as a perfect name for a girl like her. I asked about it and she said her father's side was French, her mother's Swedish. She said she'd been to Paris as a teenager and that maybe she'd want to live in Europe someday. All of which made her more exotic in my eyes than she already was.

She dropped me off at the BI after breakfast and said she'd be in touch. Watching her drive away, zooming through the parking lot of the doctors' building and out toward Main Street, I felt like a dog watching his master leave for a month's vacation while he stayed behind at the kennel with all the other animals yapping inside. That's pretty much what I had to go back to, at least it seemed that way.

Looking back, I think it was the burp and giggle that finished me. It wasn't the gorgeous face and figure, the sexy clothes, or the supreme bar-and-bedroom confidence. I may have been mesmerized by that side of Cheryl, but I was also scared to death of it. It was more the way she let me into her life with her guard down, if only for a few minutes, that morning in the kitchen: the ratty bathrobe, the mindless chitchat, the look on her face when she realized she'd done something unladylike, the story about her family. It was all another gift she'd given me, something called intimacy, and I was a most unlikely recipient. Of that I was sure.

Fontaine Perkins was not going to be happy, and of course neither was I. Because there was one more thing I was sure of: for the first time in my life, I was in love.

21.

kip Jones was sitting next to me on the folding chair he used for lessons. He'd just listened to my rendition of Gershwin's second prelude and seemed deep in thought. I figured he was searching for a nice way to tell me I had no talent, but I couldn't help hoping for better because I'd spent a ton of time working on the piece. I'd been getting up early, going down to the piano room in the basement of the Manor, and practicing it for several hours. By then it would nearly be time for therapy. After that I'd have lunch in the dining room with April or maybe Lenny, go to my room and lie down for forty-five minutes or so, then go back down to the piano room for another couple of hours before going to work over at the King Richard. The half-mile walk always helped clear my head.

"Coleman," Skip finally said, "that wasn't half bad. You're hitting some wrong notes, but your tempo is good and I think you can feel how it's supposed to sound."

I knew I was hitting wrong notes, but I'd just kept going because that was one of Skip's rules. If you started a piece, you finished it even if it ended up being a disaster. You couldn't stop and start again because you couldn't do that at a real performance, or at least you shouldn't. So you tried to keep your cool and get back on track.

"You keep working on this, I think you'll be able to play it pretty well," he said. "You game?"

"Sure."

"Since we're in Gershwin mode, why don't we try one of his popular songs?" Skip said. "He wrote symphonic music— you know, *Rhapsody in Blue, American in Paris*—and an opera called *Porgy and Bess*. Ever hear of it?"

"Of course," I lied.

"And a lot of show tunes and popular songs."

He reached for a volume that was sitting on top of the piano. On the cover, in kind of fancy letters, it said *The Real Book.*

"Ever see one of these before?"

I thought of lying again but shook my head no.

"It's called a fake book. It's a collection of songs that someone pulls together, just the chords and melody lines, slaps them between two covers, and sells it. It's illegal because you're not paying royalties to the copyright holders, but these days you can find them pretty easily. This is the one everyone uses."

He turned to a page with a song called "But Not for Me."

"See if you can pick out the melody," he said.

I tried but kept screwing it up. The other problem was that I didn't understand all the notations on the page. I knew a "G" meant a G chord, but some letters had triangles or circles, or circles with lines through them, or abbreviations like "dim" and "alt" next to them.

"That's not bad," Skip said again. It was his favorite expression, and it pretty much meant "that was terrible." But being a nice guy, he didn't want to discourage me.

"I don't understand the symbols," I said.

"Ah . . . sorry . . . thought we'd covered some of that." He went over to his bookshelf, pulled out a sheet of paper, and stuck it in front of me. "Meet the chord bible."

For the rest of the lesson, and we even went half an hour overtime that he didn't charge me for, we went through Skip's chord bible. It wasn't from a book but something he'd written out himself by hand and fit onto one page. And it was just in the key of C, so you'd have to transpose the rules onto other keys, which meant you'd have to know your major and minor scales. But that was all part of the game, Skip said. For each chord, he'd drawn a little keyboard with black dots on it so you'd know exactly where to put your fingers. Even an idiot like me could follow that. So I learned what CΔ7 meant and Cm9 and C9+5 and C7 alt, and a bunch of other stuff. Not that any of it stuck with me, but I could keep the piece of paper to look at.

"Your homework is to learn all these chords in C *and* in G for next week," he said as I took out my backpack and prepared to leave. "Keep plugging on the prelude, and see if you can add the chords in your left hand to 'But Not for Me' with the melody in your right. Not easy, I know. Unfortunately, if you want to play, the work's not negotiable."

I was about to shake his hand and head down the stairs when he said, "Hey, sorry about last time."

"What?"

"You asked me about Pearleen Porter, and I probably wasn't very nice about it."

He'd been perfectly nice, as usual. I was the one who'd brought up something I shouldn't have, at least in my mind.

"Like I said, she was a friend of mine," Skip said. "She worked as a cocktail waitress at the King Richard. Sometimes after her shift she'd come in and sing. If there were customers around, she'd stop the place cold, man. Her favorite tune was 'Body and Soul.' Another was 'Stars Fell on Alabama.' You closed your eyes, you'd swear it was Billie Holiday right there in that room. Never heard anything like it, and I've accompanied some damn good singers. I tried to make some contacts for her down in Boston, but she wasn't interested. Didn't want to sing in the bar downstairs either, even though Mrs. Sorensen said she could if the two of us got a program together. All Pearleen wanted to do was mosey over to my little room when things were quiet. She felt safe there. She'd do maybe three tunes, max. She could swing too. She could bossa nova. Sometimes I'd call her 'The Girl from Ipanema.' She sure looked like one."

Skip looked down at the floor. I thought he might cry.

"She was a tortured soul," he said. "Then she died."

I couldn't bring myself to ask him what exactly had happened, even though I really wanted to know. Dr. Nelson had said she committed suicide, but I didn't think Nelson was the most reliable person I'd ever met.

Skip clapped me hard on the shoulder, his standard gesture for signaling a lesson was over.

"Don't forget," he said. "You want to play, the work's not negotiable."

22.

Excerpted from the book *The Maine Murders: What Really Happened in Pierrevert*

By Hayley Blossom
Originally published in the United Kingdom.

Everyone at Fegelmann's Department Store adored Pearleen Porter. Her skills as a salesgirl were superb and seemed to come naturally. She also made it her business to study the components of the perfumes sold by the store so she could explain them and help women choose appropriately. She was impeccably polite, projecting just the right balance of authority on which scent she thought each customer *should* wear, and deference to what the lady herself *wanted* to wear. With her stylish Afro perfectly complementing her height, figure, and facial structure, a few coworkers had started calling her "Cleo," short for Cleopatra. All outward appearances suggested a self-possessed young woman successfully coping with a double dose of hardship—the

loss of both parents as a teenager—and taking the bull by
the horns to move forward in life.

What no one could see or sense, but what became crys-
tal clear from Pearleen's diary, was that she was haunted
by guilt, anxiety, and nightmares, some of which were
recurring. In one dream, she would return home from
school, open the front door, and see her father dressed
in a Hargrove Hornets football uniform. Henry would be
crouched in a defensive stance, the stylized silver "H" on
each side of the helmet glowing against the maroon background. He'd fix his killer linebacker's stare on Pearleen
and launch himself like a rocket, just as she'd seen him do
countless times in old films of his football career. The top
of his helmet would smash into her face and she'd wake up
screaming.

In another dream, she'd be standing at the kitchen
sink, washing up after dinner. She'd hear the clinking of
glass, like wind chimes, and turn to witness her father on
the floor, flailing wildly underneath a small mountain of
empty liquor bottles. She'd know he was underneath the
pile, but all she could see was his baseball-style coaching
cap swaying from side to side as he struggled, the big letter
"H" once again glowing against the maroon background.
Documents viewed years later concerning Pearleen's medical treatment revealed that she had interpreted the dreams
as a signal her father was sending from beyond the grave
to relieve her pain. She gave particular significance to the
letter "H," which she took to stand for something other
than Hargrove.

Indeed, despite Hargrove's location in a picture-
postcard area of Maine, the town was rather a hardscrab-
ble place—especially since many of the once-thriving paper
mills and chemical companies had downsized or left Maine
altogether in search of a more favourable tax climate. With

a year-round population of just under 100,000, the city was no stranger to high unemployment, teenage pregnancy, and crime. It was also no stranger to hard drugs, in particular a remarkably pure strain of heroin originating in Thailand and distributed at the wholesale level through Asian restaurants in the northeastern United States. It was this substance, sold on the streets of cities and towns all over New England in small packets bearing the stamp "Bad Payback," that began to ensnare Pearleen. It was at the suggestion of a coworker who managed the luggage department at Fegelmann's, Bonita Jackson, that she first sniffed it.

"You try this, girl," Bonita said at a party one night after work. "It's like a thousand orgasms."

Being inexperienced when it came to sex, Pearleen may not have had any idea what an orgasm felt like. But she'd read about them, as evidenced by more than one entry in her diary, and figured even one had to be good. A thousand must be like the way her father had felt crashing into a fullback, scooping up a fumble, and rambling sixty yards for a touchdown.

That night with Bonita began Pearleen's dependence on Bad Payback, which seemed to magically remove the bad feelings that had been plaguing her. She never used at work, but often snorted immediately after leaving—usually alone in her car before driving out of the store parking lot.

It was nearing Christmas, a few months after Henry's death, when the flow of Bad Payback through Hargrove suddenly dried up. The drought was brought on by a federal sting that nabbed 150 pounds of pure heroin aboard a cargo vessel that had sailed from Surat Thani, Thailand; passed through the Red Sea and Suez Canal; stopped in Naples (to pick up Italian olive oil) and in Marseille (to pick up French cheeses); and eventually arrived in Boston.

Although Pearleen was not yet a hard-core addict, she had become dependent enough that when her "saviour" (as she referred to the substance with Bonita) was not available for the fourth night in a row, she panicked. It happened at Fegelmann's, after closing time, when the only other person in the store was the night watchman, Otis Ellis. Fifteen years earlier, Otis had been a starting forward for Hargrove High's basketball team under the tutelage of coach Henry Porter.

It was shortly after nine p.m. when Pearleen, the last salesperson on duty, finished tidying her counter. But instead of heading down the back stairs and into the parking lot as usual, she hid in the ladies' room, her mind racing. And she had a plan. Most rank-and-file employees knew that Otis kept whiskey hidden in the filing cabinet next to the old desk in the security office. When passing by less than a week before, Pearleen had seen him stash several bottles in the bottom drawer. So that's what she'd do—she'd get Otis' whiskey. It would be a departure for Pearleen, who, having seen the dramatic effect of alcohol on her father, never touched the stuff. But it was a desperate moment and she needed something, anything, to tide her over until Bad Payback hit the streets again. On this particular night, Otis' stash seemed the best option because she had no alcohol at home, the local liquor stores closed at seven thirty, and she loathed bars (the primary reason being that men always tried to chat her up).

Fifteen minutes later, as she sat in a pitch-black ladies' room stall, Pearleen heard Otis pass by and head upstairs. As his footsteps became fainter, she tiptoed back out into the darkened store, through the men's department, down a rear corridor, and into the security office where the small television that Otis kept going all night was blaring a Boston Celtics basketball game. The filing cabinet drawer was unlocked, and underneath a smelly old jumper were two bottles of Old Chaffinch whiskey, one nearly full, the other still unopened. Pearleen snatched them both, closed the drawer, and ran down the hallway. When she banged through the set of padded double doors that led back out to the men's department, Otis was nowhere in sight. But with the temperature in Pierrevert that night hovering at ten degrees Fahrenheit, Pearleen couldn't face drinking alone in her car, and driving home first would take too long. That made the immediate problem one of finding a place inside the store to down the whiskey.

It occurred to Pearleen that the last area Otis was likely to check when making his rounds was near the huge display windows that faced Grant Avenue. There was so much light from the lampposts on the street that no burglar in his right mind would choose that part of the store to break into. But where to hide?

With Christmas near, one of the two windows featured life-size Santa Claus and reindeer dolls (each with a red nose) and a huge sleigh that Felix Fegelmann, the store's patriarch, had bought at an antiques auction in Boston in the late 1950s. Behind the sleigh, Pearleen noticed, was a cozy corner just big enough for her to snuggle into. So she stepped up into the window with her two bottles and got comfortable. No one outside could see her, but she could see the street through gaps in the wrought iron structure of the sleigh. It had started to snow, and Pearleen's view as she pulled at the first of the two bottles—initially gagging at the taste and the afterburn—was pleasantly wintry. A few pedestrians and car headlights enlivened a bucolic scene that included the town square across the way with its huge bell tower in the middle. She might have been gazing at a Norman Rockwell painting.

It took Pearleen about half an hour to down the first bottle, and there was no need to open the second. Having never drunk alcohol in her life, she felt as if she'd been run over by a lorry—except the road she was lying on was spinning at a dizzying speed. She felt dreadfully sick to her stomach and in dire need of the ladies' room. It was when she decided to make that trip that her life took a turn.

Pearleen stood up, using a bar on the sleigh for balance, and remained stationary for perhaps half a minute trying to find an equilibrium that would allow her to walk. But just as she turned toward the inside of the store, preparing to step gingerly down from the window, three teenage boys passed by on the sidewalk. They saw Pearleen plain as day. Not only that, being former classmates of hers at Hargrove High, they recognized her instantly.

"Hey Pearleen!" shouted one. "What the fuck! What you doin' in there?"

Another cried, "Let us in, Pearleen!"

The third, taking note of the deer-in-the-headlights expression on her face, yelled, "You all right, Pearleen?"

It was the first boy, apparently drunk himself, who turned nasty.

"You don't let us in, we gonna *bust* in!" he screamed. "We gonna git you right front o' Santy Claus! Maybe Rudy the reindeer, he want some pussy too! You'd like that, right Pearly?"

When Pearleen was a youngster, Henry had taught her how to throw a football. He'd even hung an old spare tire from a tree limb in their garden so she could learn how to thread the needle. According to several of Henry's NFL teammates who visited the family house during Pearleen's youth, her throwing motion gradually became more like that of a boy than a girl, and she could toss a nice, tight spiral. Henry, in fact, had occasionally joked that if the

Hargrove Public Schools Department had allowed females to play on the varsity football team, she would have been his starting quarterback.

The coarseness of Pearleen's former high school classmate offended her. It also prompted an old reflex to kick in. Having perhaps momentarily forgotten that there was a plate of heavy glass between herself and the boy, she picked up the unopened bottle of Old Chaffinch that sat at her feet and hurled it at him with everything she had. Her aim was straight and true.

When the bottle smashed through the store's display window, shattering it and sending daggerlike shards onto the sidewalk, all three boys scarpered at full tilt. The burglar alarm howled at full blast. Otis Ellis, who'd been making his rounds on the third floor where the housewares were sold, came sprinting down the stairs. With the alarm triggering an alert at the police station on the other side of the town square, a cruiser screeched up within two minutes. What Otis and then the two officers came upon was a hysterical Pearleen Porter writhing on the carpeted floor near the men's shirts counter. She reeked of whiskey, and her bladder had emptied. They tried to talk to her, but she was incoherent. Vulgarities spewed from her mouth.

"Was like someone else talkin' through her," Otis said later. "Was like her daddy cussin' out a referee."

It took the three men twenty minutes to calm Pearleen, at which point she turned silent. She would not respond when spoken to, and did not seem to understand their questions. The term the doctors would later use was "psychotic episode."

Hargrove General Hospital did not have a psychiatric unit. The only licensed mental health facility in the county, for hundreds of miles, in fact, was the Buchanan Institute a few towns away in Pierrevert. After a phone call to the

institute, answered by the night supervisor Frederico Cruz,
that's where the officers took Pearleen. She was admitted on a five-day observation basis, pending verification
that she had sufficient insurance to pay for treatment at
Buchanan. If not, she would be taken to the state psychiatric hospital near Augusta. As it happened, her coverage
was minimal, provided by her job at Fegelmann's, and not
even close to the required level.

Ironically enough, what helped enable Pearleen to stay
at Buchanan for a much longer period of time was the fact
that she had thrown the bottle of whiskey through the store
window. Despite her medical condition, that was a crime.
As such, when *The Northeast Telegram*'s police reporter,
Timmy Walsh, made his daily call to the Hargrove station
house the next morning, he found out about the events at
Fegelmann's. The day officer, Vito Petrello, noted that the
perpetrator had been taken to the Buchanan Institute.

The story in *The Northeast Telegram* the following day
was short, no longer than four hundred words. But the
fact that the person in question was the daughter of Henry
"the Helmet" Porter prompted the editors to play it on the
front page, below the fold, next to the "In Today's Edition"
box. The workmanlike headline read "Late Football Star's
Daughter Arrested." Given the circumstances, Fegelmann's
later decided not to press charges.

But someone with financial resources, perhaps one
of Henry's former NFL teammates who had been successful in business, must have seen the story. Because
the following week, as preparations were being made
for Pearleen's transfer to the state mental hospital, the
Buchanan Institute received a certified check for $30,000
drawn on a bank in Boston. There was no name attached,
and the accompanying letter from the bank—addressed to
Buchanan's medical director, Dr Angelo Bellino—specified

that the donor wished to remain anonymous. The check was intended to pay for the care of Pearleen Porter for a period of six months at Buchanan's published, all-inclusive rate of $5,000 per month. In the event that Pearleen needed to stay longer, the donor would find out and additional funds would be forthcoming. If Pearleen was "cured" and left the hospital before six months had expired, the balance of the money could be considered a donation.

Now that Pearleen was a patient in full standing at Buchanan, she was assigned a physician who would supervise her treatment and see her four times per week in fifty-minute psychotherapy sessions. This particular clinician was a man who had grown up in Hargrove before being the first local boy ever admitted to Harvard College, where he was a starting point guard on the varsity basketball team. Following his undergraduate work in biology, he'd stayed in Boston to attend Harvard Medical School, where he'd become interested in psychiatry. After his residency, he'd returned to Hargrove County to establish a practice because he loved the area and many of his old friends still lived there. Among the fondest memories of his growing-up years had been playing basketball at Hargrove High, where he'd been a teammate of Henry Porter. The doctor's name was Wilson Haynes, but to friends he was always known, quite simply, as "Willie."

23.

It was a late-August night when I got a ride to Bra's from Benny, one of the other bartenders at the King Richard. He had dark, curly hair, and worked in the tavern next to the main dining room. I'd had to go there near the end of my shift in the courtyard because I ran out of a cordial called Grand Marnier.

I didn't care much for cordials myself—they tasted like cough syrup with a kick—but a lot of people drank them after dinner. The kitchen would use Grand Marnier on desserts too. The waitresses would pour it over crepes and light it on fire, and the customers would *ooh* and *aah* over that. I knew they had a few extra bottles in the tavern, and when I asked Benny if I could have one, he said, "Hey, I'm going to Bra's after work, wanna go?" It took me by surprise because nobody ever asked me to go anywhere. Then when I got back behind the bar at King's Court, it dawned on me why people seemed to be treating me more like a real person and not just another local loony. At least it seemed like they were.

A few nights before, a bunch of waitresses and bartenders had gone downstairs to the Tower after their shifts. I'd gone too but sat by myself at the bar because nobody asked me to join them. Being a patient at Buchanan can be kind of off-putting to a normal person, no matter how you slice it, so I understood.

Anyway, I was sitting there sipping my beer, listening to the legendary Charlie Biggs work his way through a real gem called "Bar Room Buddies," when all of a sudden, poof, there was Cheryl. She'd come down the staircase from reception, and when somebody does that, the whole room sees them enter because the doorway is right next to the stage. She was wearing jeans, high-heeled black boots, and a tight black T-shirt. Poor Charlie fluffed about five chords in a row staring at her. I had no idea she'd be there, and as usual the first thing I felt when I saw her was fear. The thing was, she sashayed across the room, came straight over to where I was sitting at the bar along the back wall, leaned in, and planted one right on my mouth. Everybody in the place nearly fell off their chairs when they saw that. It was like Miss August kissing *Bartending Magazine*'s Glass Washer of the Month.

"I decided to surprise you," she said, her breath all warm and cinnamony. "I went to the courtyard and somebody said you might be down here. Come on, drink up. Let's go."

The whole room was watching, and don't think she didn't know it. She played to stuff like that. So I got up from my barstool, and that's when I noticed the front of my shirt had potato-chip crumbs all over it. I'm always eating potato chips, to this day, which is probably why I look so unhealthy, and they used to put baskets of them on all the bars at the hotel so people would sit longer and drink more. They didn't make them every day, just when Leroy up in the kitchen felt like it. Cheryl saw the crumbs at the same time I did, but she didn't roll her eyes and say "you disgusting pig" or "how revolting" or something like that. Instead, she just giggled and brushed them off, giving everyone in the bar one more thing to marvel at. Maybe they thought she worked for Hargrove County Social Services and was getting paid to look after me. She reached for my hand, wrapped her fingers in mine, and we left through the door that led out to Main Street.

It was that little episode that popped into my head a few nights later—the night I got the bottle of Grand Marnier from Benny—as maybe the reason why people at the hotel seemed to be treating me better. Up to then I'd just been Coleman the Head Case, community project, an example that the King Richard Inn doesn't discriminate against screwed-up losers. Now I was getting a little . . . I don't want to say "respect," because that's going too far, but at least something I didn't have before.

So Benny drove us to Bra's after we'd finished our shifts, and we had a beer. Then he went to play pool in the back room, and I noticed Fontaine leaning against the jukebox.

"Yo, Coleman, my man, what's hapnin'," he said, giving me a big smile as I ambled over.

"I'm OK," I said, always a master of repartee.

"So what's up with Cheryl, man? You hangin' out with her?"

"I've seen her a couple of times."

"Like I said."

He left it at that, so I asked him a question I'd wondered about. "Where do you work, Fontaine?"

"In Hargrove, for the city. I'm a drug counselor. They got a whole buncha heroin addicts up there. Never touched it myself, but lotta folks need help."

At that moment, the side door of the bar flew open. Two handsome guys half staggered in, both of them trim and athletic looking. Trailing behind was Cheryl, dressed in a pair of shiny silver shorts with cuffs at the bottom.

"Good God," said Fontaine, who like half the people in the bar stopped and stared. "She's wearin' hot pants. Have *mercy*."

I watched as Cheryl cupped a hand to her mouth and whispered something to her friends. I imagined her saying, *Look over there. That's the doofus who thinks I like him.*

I was about to take a powder out the front door, but the three of them came strolling over to the jukebox, Cheryl not so much as glancing at me. Instead, she held her hand out to Fontaine and gave him a smile that pretty much broke my heart.

"Let's go, Super Fly," she said, pulling him onto the dance floor.

"Gotta use whatcha got, right Cheryl?" he said, and off they went.

There was a fast song playing, and believe me, they put on quite a show. Fontaine danced like one of the people on that Saturday morning TV program, every gesture in perfect time and as cool as it got. He was leading Cheryl all over the place, and she was matching every move. The two of them looked like they'd been at it for years. The thing was, I got so wrapped up watching that I didn't notice Cheryl's two friends staring at me from about six feet away. When it registered, they were nodding their heads like they were having some sort of serious discussion. Then the record changed to a slow song, and I watched Fontaine put his arms around Cheryl. But the song wasn't as loud as the one before, so I could overhear what her friends were saying. They either didn't realize that, or didn't care.

"What do you *really* think?" said one.

"Kind of cute in a funny way," the other replied. "*Desperately* needs a makeover. I've got some creams that may help the skin . . . well . . . *problem. No* fashion sense, but she warned us about that. His hairdresser ought to be *shot . . . on . . . sight.*"

I listened to them go on for a couple of minutes, losing sight of Fontaine and Cheryl amid the crowd, until she suddenly breezed in between us, drink in hand. Her eyes met mine, finally, and they were full of mischief. She kissed me on the cheek, and I got a strong whiff of whiskey and cigarettes. Her friends moved in closer, big smiles on their faces.

"OK, guys," she said. "Let's have it!"

"Split decision," said the one who took issue with my hairstyle. "I'm actually in favor, with *obvious* caveats. I think Gary is . . . well—"

"I'm not trying to be *unkind*," said the other. "James has a right to his opinion. It's just that . . . one *does* have to be truthful, doesn't one?"

"Right," said Cheryl. "James is *for*, Gary is *against*. That leaves *me* with the deciding vote. Hmmmm." She started silently counting things off on her fingers. "I vote *for*," she said, slapping her knee and losing herself in high-pitched giggles.

Her friends immediately joined the laughter. I tried to smile, but it wasn't coming out right.

"Sorry, Coleman," she managed to say. "I couldn't resist."

"We've got all *sorts* of things planned for you, young man," James said archly.

"Let's go to your place," Cheryl said to the two. "We'll have a nightcap there. God, I've gotta stop drinking scotch. Can we all fit in my car?"

"Coleman can sit on my lap," said James.

"*I'll* sit on your lap," Cheryl replied. "I'm too drunk to drive." She fished around in her purse, tossed me her keys, and said, "Ever drive a Porsche?"

The four of us left through the side door, Cheryl still toting her drink, and turned left toward the rear parking lot. It was pretty dark back there, but it looked like someone was leaning against her car, smoking a cigarette. Just a shadow, though. Then we got closer, and the bottom fell out of my stomach.

"Go play with your jerk-offs, Cheryl," said the mountain man. "I wanna talk to your boyfriend."

"Jason!" Cheryl shouted. "What are you doing here? Get back inside!"

From her tone, she might've been yelling at a dog who'd dashed out of the house.

"Shut up, bitch. I wanna see *this* guy."

He grabbed me by the shirt collar and pinned me up against Cheryl's car. I never saw it coming.

"Jason, STOP it!" Cheryl cried. "Gary, get Seamus NOW!"

I heard Gary run off with James but didn't see them because Jason's sweating, bearded face was an inch from mine. A sour gust of beer and cigarettes hit my nostrils.

"What's your problem, mental boy, huh? I know all about you."

"Jason!" Cheryl shouted again.

"You doin' her? You doin' her?" His grip tightened around my collar.

"Jason!"

I remember Cheryl jumping onto his back and trying to pull him off me. And I recall the feeling when his fist met my jaw. Then the lights went out.

24.

Excerpted from the book *The Maine Murders: What Really Happened in Pierrevert*

By Hayley Blossom
Originally published in the United Kingdom.

Pearleen Porter had as much emotional baggage as any patient at the Buchanan Institute: a father who'd abused her over a number of years, pitifully low self-esteem, and a fresh addiction to heroin. Fortunately, the properties of the drug had not had time to become fully engrained in her physiology or psychology, enabling her dependence to ebb away during her first few weeks at the hospital without major withdrawal symptoms. The therapeutic environment likely helped, as did the absence of Bad Payback on the streets of Pierrevert. Her sessions with Dr Haynes centered, naturally enough, on her father and her continuing conviction that she, not Henry, was responsible for the beatings she had endured.

Pearleen knew she'd been adopted, of course. Pamela had told her the story when she was twelve. Dr Haynes noted in Pearleen's treatment records that some adopted children feel a sense of guilt over the fact that their natural parents chose to discard them. Pearleen herself hypothesized in therapy sessions that she must have done something dreadful as a baby to merit being cast aside. Dr Haynes had replied that babies were not bad people and that couples sometimes could not cope with a child—*any* child—because they weren't in love, had no money, or just weren't cut out for parenthood, among other reasons. But Pearleen held fast to her culpability both in regard to her natural *and* adoptive parents. As such, hers was a somewhat puzzling case.

Nonetheless, Dr Haynes felt that long-term therapy would unravel the deep-seated roots of Pearleen's guilt and prepare her to live a happy and productive life. His optimism was bolstered by the fact that two months after being admitted to Buchanan, she responded to a newspaper ad and got a part-time job as a cocktail waitress at the King Richard Inn, working the main reception area and Bosworth's Tavern. The inn's proprietor, Patricia Sorensen, had always been open to hiring Buchanan patients, more so than most local business owners. She felt that if Buchanan patients performed well on the job, hiring them was her way of giving something back to the community. In Pearleen's case, it didn't hurt that she was tall and striking.

Much as she had been at Fegelmann's Department Store, Pearleen was a hit with hotel coworkers and customers alike. She was courteous, well spoken, and made an effort to learn about cocktails: their recipes and garnishes, the type of glassware required, even the preferred type of ice (cubed or crushed). She did not feel tempted by her proximity to alcohol, her one encounter with Old Chaffinch being enough to put her off liquor for the rest of her short life.

On occasion, Pearleen would sing a few songs with the hotel pianist, Sebastian "Skip" Jones, who played in the side parlour just off the reception area. Her vocal talents only enhanced her popularity. She also struck up a close friendship with the executive chef, Leroy Little, who seemed to feel unusually protective, taking her under his wing and passing on the finer points of the restaurant business. After just three months on the job, Pearleen won the hotel's coveted Employee of the Month award, voted on by all department heads and by Mrs Sorensen herself. Unheard of for a part-timer, the honour meant a $250 bonus and Pearleen's photo mounted on a plaque behind the reception desk. Back at Buchanan, her therapy sessions were going well: no major breakthroughs, but a gradual lessening of her anxiety.

Pearleen and Dr Haynes eventually decided that she would leave the hospital during the final week of the six-month period financed by her anonymous benefactor, and return to her house in Hargrove. The hotel had offered her a full-time waitress position, so she would commute from Hargrove to Pierrevert on workdays—a manageable twenty-five-minute drive or bus ride each way—and continue to see Dr Haynes twice a week as an outpatient. Everyone in Pierrevert who knew Pearleen was happy for her, and the Buchanan Institute was ready to chalk up another success story of a once-disturbed patient moving on to a productive life.

It was on the Friday night just before Pearleen was scheduled to depart Buchanan when, exiting the King Richard by the front walkway, she heard a familiar voice.

It came from a young woman who was leaning against a car parked just in front of the inn on Main Street.

"Hey there, girl," said Bonita Jackson.

***

We have no record of where the two young women went to snort Bad Payback that night. Nor do we know how difficult it may or may not have been for Bonita to convince Pearleen to use again. What we do know, from police records, is that a fresh shipment of the drug had arrived in Hargrove the previous week and that Bonita Jackson was dealing it. We also know that when Pearleen returned to the Buchanan Institute later that night, a significant dose was coursing through her system. In the very last diary entry of her life, she wrote down the words to a song she'd been working on with Skip Jones:

> I make a date for golf
>> and you can bet your life it rains,
> I try to throw a party
>> and the guy upstairs complains,
> I guess I'll go through life
>> just catching colds and missing trains,
> Everything happens to me.

Underneath the verse of lyrics, she wrote something similarly plaintive. Dr Wilson Haynes would later say the entry indicated that Pearleen had realized, on some level, what she had done and deeply regretted it.

> Why, why, why . . . have to sleep, have to
> sleep, have to sleep.

Sometime between ten and ten fifteen p.m., Pearleen wandered out of her room on the second floor of the Manor and walked down the hallway. Her destination was an alcove, located up on the recreation-room floor, where Ruby Calhoun, the head nurse, dispensed pills from a heavy steel locker between ten and ten thirty. When Pearleen mounted the stairs and arrived at the alcove, she could see that the upper doors to the locker, as well as the large drawers that made up the bottom half, were all shut firmly. This was as it should have been, at least at a glance. Maine state law required all accredited hospitals to keep prescription medications under tight security, and the Buchanan Institute had always scrupulously complied. The locker in the alcove required two separate keys to open it. Yet there were several unusual circumstances in play on this particular night.

The first was that the recreation room was deserted, which never happened at that hour. Ruby Calhoun, who typically sat at a small table in front of the locker to give out the pills, was nowhere in sight. The second was that when Pearleen pulled the handle on the top half of the cabinet, the doors opened right up. The third was that, at that very moment, there was a major disturbance in progress downstairs. Simply put, Dr Samantha Nelson, Buchanan's director of admissions, had gone off her trolley.

Dr Nelson had entered the Manor by the front door, heavily inebriated, brandishing a hunting knife. She'd run through the front hall, surprising a few bewildered patients who were sitting on the sofas, and barged into the sitting room, where she'd thrown the knife down and begun upending most of the furniture. Chairs, tables, and lamps crashed loudly onto the hardwood floor as she stomped about in a fury. Hearing the ruckus from the basement TV room, the night supervisor, Frederico Cruz, came running. When he reached the sitting room and peered in, he shouted, "CODE BLUE!" four times at the top of his lungs. Patients knew this meant to return to their rooms immediately. The staff knew it meant all hands on deck, straightaway, and urgent calls both to Dr Bellino, the medical director, and to the police. April Adams, a nursing assistant, ran up to the hospital switchboard on the second floor.

When Cruz entered the sitting room, followed closely by Calhoun, who had dashed all the way downstairs from the recreation room—closing the medicine-locker doors but forgetting to lock them—Dr Nelson grabbed the knife and brandished it at them.

"I know how to use this!" she screamed.

Both Cruz and Calhoun had been trained to deal with violent situations, although in the past such problems had always involved patients, not doctors. They tried to calm Dr Nelson by talking to her. She cursed at them, wielding the knife, a standoff that lasted for roughly five minutes. When Chief Cody and his deputy, Kevin Kincaid, arrived in the sitting room, she threw the knife—barely missing Calhoun, who fled into the hallway. Both policemen rushed the physician and held her steady, one on each side, as she struggled to free herself and continued to spew expletives.

Pearleen, who had neither heard the Code Blue call nor noticed that other patients were scurrying back to their rooms, knew exactly what she wanted in the meds locker. Although she had been off all medications for quite a while, she'd been given a powerful prescription drug called Dorbien during her first couple of months at Buchanan to help her sleep. It had worked well, without noticeable side effects. As the staff dealt with Dr Nelson downstairs, Pearleen quietly helped herself to a clearly marked jar containing nearly two hundred capsules of Dorbien, and carried it back to her room.

Later that night, Dr Nelson was in police custody, no longer drunk or unhinged. She tried to explain her behaviour by saying it stemmed from a lovers' quarrel at the Tower, the bar where she'd been drinking. Dr Bellino struck a deal with Cody at the police station stipulating that so long as Dr Nelson was remitted to a psychiatric hospital in northern Vermont—he'd already made the arrangements with a quick phone call—the entire matter could be kept in-house. Cody agreed, over strenuous protests from his deputy, but only because it was Dr Bellino, whom he liked and respected, doing the asking. This arrangement did not last for long.

The next morning, Ruby Calhoun found Pearleen Porter, who'd had the presence of mind to close the doors to the medicine locker when she left it, dead in bed. The combination of heroin and Dorbien—Pearleen had ingested forty-two capsules of thirty milligrams each—had easily proved fatal. But as Homer Taylor, Henry Porter's former Grambling teammate, later argued in court—backed up by the testimony of a physician who specialized in sleep medication—the amount of Dorbien that Pearleen swallowed would have killed her *regardless* of the heroin in her system that was detected during a postmortem examination at Hargrove General. For that reason alone, Taylor implored, the hospital was responsible for her death and had been negligent in leaving the doors to the medicine locker unsecured. He further argued that the hospital staff, in particular Pearleen's therapist, Dr Wilson Haynes, should have known she was vulnerable to narcotic drugs available on the street and taken steps to protect her from falling victim. Taylor, in the lawsuit he personally brought against the Buchanan Institute, was seeking $750,000 in damages, the funds to be used to open a new facility in Hargrove dedicated to the care of young adults with drug problems.

Ronald Sanders, the attorney representing Buchanan, countered that the circumstances at the hospital on the night Pearleen died were extraordinary to the extent that the institute could not be held liable or negligent. He also argued that Pearleen, in all probability, would never have gone near the medicine locker if she hadn't snorted heroin first, a claim backed up both by the testimony of Dr Haynes and that of a Portland-based expert on the effects of narcotics. Being a legal adult, she alone was responsible for that, Sanders said. Buchanan was an open facility, not set up to babysit patients.

Sanders concluded, in front of a rapt jury and a full courtroom in the Hargrove County Municipal Building, that the case amounted to a confluence of events that was tragic on many fronts but did not constitute legal grounds to find Buchanan at fault. After two days of deliberation, the jury unanimously agreed. Local reaction, as evidenced by an editorial in the *Telegram* and numerous letters to the editor, clearly supported the decision.

Pearleen's funeral at the First Baptist Church, although not as large as her father's, attracted at least a hundred neighbours and friends in Hargrove, mainly people who had been close to Henry and Pamela. There was also a collection of her high school mates, a contingent from the King Richard Inn—a stoic Patricia Sorensen and a tearful Skip Jones among them—and a group of former coworkers from Fegelmann's (not including Bonita Jackson). Quite a few patients and staff from the Buchanan Institute were also present, including Doctors Bellino, Haynes, and Frazier, as well as Ruby Calhoun. Homer Taylor himself gave the eulogy, just as he had for Pearleen's father. A recording of the proceedings was made on a small cassette machine by Mabel Prescott, the athletic department secretary at Hargrove High, who'd held Pearleen's hand at Henry's funeral.

"Pearleen was a beautiful person," Taylor eulogized. "She faced many difficult problems in her life, none of which were her fault. But she persevered, yes she did."

A few cries of "Amen!" pierced the silence.

"Don't ever let it be said, as I've heard some people opine, that she took her own life. She did not. Her death was a terrible accident that should never have happened. She had everything to live for. A bright future lay ahead of her."

He seemed to hesitate there, a funeral not the place to make legal arguments that would come later—and prove unconvincing in court. But Taylor continued on for ten more minutes remembering Pearleen's childhood, which he had been a part of when the Porters visited North Carolina and when he and his family had come to Hargrove. He asked everyone to remember that Pearleen was now in a better place and urged them to say a little prayer that night to wish her well in her future journeys. He concluded that her passing was "just a change of address, one we'll all experience someday."

Skip Jones then sat down at the upright piano situated to one side of the altar, and played "Body and Soul." The church organist followed up with "Amazing Grace" as the recessional.

As for Dr Samantha Nelson, following three months of hospitalization in Vermont and nine additional months of intensive therapy, she was permitted to reclaim her job as director of admissions at Buchanan. Her return perplexed a few Buchanan clinicians who, according to interviews conducted long after the fact, felt that she was still a potentially violent person.

25.

It was just before five in the afternoon, and I was getting ready for my shift at King's Court, cutting up the limes and slicing the lemon skins to make twists. All the bottles in the speed rack were full and ready to go. Most bartenders have a certain order they like—mine, left to right, being vodka, gin, scotch, bourbon, rye, tequila. If someone ordered a gin and tonic or scotch on the rocks, you gave them the rack brand. The expensive stuff that people asked for by name like Beefeater or Chivas or Jack Daniel's was all on the shelves behind the bar. The rack brands at the King Richard were still pretty good, though, not like at Erin Go Bragh's, where they had names like Frozen Toes vodka and Swimmin' Hole bourbon. You could make that stuff in your garage.

The bruises on my face were healing, but my jaw still hurt like hell. At least it wasn't broken. The main injury after being decked by the mountain man was to my ego. Not that I didn't think almost every guy at Bra's was afraid of him—they probably were—but the whole thing couldn't have made me look very manly in Cheryl's eyes. He'd knocked me out cold, and she'd thrown her watered-down drink on my face to bring me around. I wondered if she hadn't been thinking, *What a wimp,* and done it with scorn. She'd driven me back to Buchanan, not to her house, and I figured that meant something. I told Dr. Haynes about the whole thing, and he listened quietly but didn't say much or give me any sentences to repeat. Lucky for me, I'd had three days off in a row, so I looked OK when I came back to work.

Just as I finished getting the fruit ready, the bar phone rang.

"Is that you, Coleman?"

It was a woman's voice, one I'd heard before but couldn't place. It wasn't my mother, that much I knew. But it wasn't one of the waitresses either.

"It's Mrs. Sorensen."

Any time someone in authority says something to me, I get anxious. I'm still that way to this day, but the shrink I'm seeing now tells me to just accept it and go with the flow.

"Hello, Mrs. Sorensen."

"Is the bar busy yet?"

"No, there's nobody here."

"All the better, then. I'm in my suite on the fourth floor, number 400. Would you mind terribly bringing me a glass of Grand Marnier on the rocks in one of the large snifters? I'd be very grateful."

"Sure, I'll be right up."

It crossed my mind that Mr. Simons might come by King's Court and see my post abandoned, but I had a great excuse: the boss.

"Thank you, Coleman," she said, and hung up.

I poured the Grand Marnier into one of the snifters, the kind that were always getting broken because the glass was so thin, plunked in a couple of ice cubes, and grabbed a round cocktail tray. I'm a little embarrassed to say this, but I draped a white bar towel over my forearm as I carried the drink across the courtyard and into the reception area toward the elevator.

I'd seen waiters do that in movies and thought it looked kind of cool. A little subservient maybe, but my station in life couldn't get much lower than it was.

There was only one elevator in the whole hotel, just past the side piano parlor, and it was a new model, all shiny and steel and glass. The only problem was that it broke down about twice a week. Typical me, I went into the film-noir thing again as soon as I entered it, pretending it was 1948, that somebody was going to get stabbed in the reception area, and that I'd be the only witness—which of course meant curtains for me. I didn't have one of those snappy 1940s waiter costumes that looks like a tuxedo with the jacket cut off at the waist, but I *did* have my blue King Richard vest and necktie on, which were better than nothing. Still, it took a little imagination to turn the homey reception area into a place called the Hotel Metropolitan with sharpies in suits and fedoras peering over the edge of their newspapers to see who's coming and going. All I really saw was an old lady sitting in a rocking chair reading *Yankee Magazine*.

"Come in, Coleman!" Mrs. Sorensen yelled when I knocked on the door of room number 400.

It was the first time I'd seen her apartment: a big living room, a bedroom, and a small kitchen. A picture window looked out onto Main Street, giving a view of pretty much the whole town. Not that Pierrevert was like looking at the New York skyline, but the scene was impressive enough in its own little way. There was a big white church across the street from the hotel with four columns out front and a steeple on top, and I always found it comforting when the bells rang the hour starting at six in the morning and stopping at midnight. Not everyone did, though. I'd seen an article in *The Northeast Telegram* saying that some guests at the hotel had complained the bells were either waking them too early or keeping them up too late.

Mrs. Sorensen was sitting at a small table next to the picture window, the kind of place where she might have breakfast every morning and read the paper. On the floor underneath the window, placed on an old magazine, was a pair of high-top, lace-up gumshoes, the kind New Englanders wear in the rain and snow. It was hard to imagine a classy lady like Mrs. Sorensen putting on boots like that, but I think just about everyone in Pierrevert had a pair. Everyone except me, that is.

"Please have a seat," she said, offering me the chair just across from her. I was happy to sit down, but before I did, I held the tray out so she could take her drink. Once I was settled, she took a long sip.

"I do *so* love Grand Marnier," she said. "Just the right balance of orange, sweetness, and whatever it is that gives you a little jolt when it hits bottom. I'd offer you some, but I know you're on duty."

I was glad she didn't offer me any. Like I said before, I'm not big on cordials. Not that I have anything against sweet drinks in general, though. I pretty much grew up on root beer and potato chips. Well, and cinnamon doughnuts.

"Yes ma'am," I said.

To this day, I have no idea where that came from. I'd never said "yes ma'am" to anyone in my life. I'm from the Northeast, not South Carolina.

"Tell me, Coleman," she said. "You've been with us awhile now. How are things going? Are you happy working here?"

"Yes, very much."

"I've heard good things about you from a few of the waitresses, and some of them aren't so easy to please. They say you're a good worker and know your drinks."

"I do my best, ma'am."

"You're a patient at Buchanan, aren't you?"

That one caught me by surprise. "Yes, I am."

"And how are things over there?"

My nervous throat clear started to rouse itself. "OK, I guess."

"Do you like your therapist?"

"He's all right."

"Who is he?"

"His name's Dr. Haynes."

"Ah yes, Willie Haynes. I remember when he was an athlete up at Hargrove High, a real star. That was a long time ago. He's come a long way since then."

She took another sip and looked out the window. The silence lasted for quite a while, and I remember starting to wonder if maybe she was losing her marbles.

"Forgive me, Coleman," she finally said. "This is none of my business. But someone on the staff told me you've been seeing Cheryl Beringer."

I didn't expect that one either. My nervous throat clear shifted into second gear.

"I like you, Coleman," she continued. "Not every Buchanan patient wants to get back on his feet. Some sit around feeling sorry for themselves, waiting for the doctors to come up with a magic potion. You don't seem to be like that."

She took another sip and stared out the window again. Then she turned and looked me in the eye.

"I've known the Beringers since before Cheryl was born," she said. "Her father was a dreadful man, and her mother could never stand up to him. I've no *idea* what went on in that house. Cheryl was always a very precocious child."

"Yes ma'am."

"I just want you to be careful, as beautiful as she turned out to be."

I knew she was right. She and Fontaine Perkins. Now *there's* an unlikely pair.

The truth was I'd have done anything for Cheryl by then. If she'd told me to stand in a corner and bark like a dog, I'd have done it. I'd have pretended it was all for fun and that I was just playing along with whatever silly game she had in mind, but I'd have been afraid to disobey her. Over the past couple of months, little by little, I'd told Dr. Haynes about her but had held back the details. That was a flicker of hope for me, I thought, being able to hide things from my shrink and not feel guilty about it. I was sure he'd heard about the time she picked me up in her hot car at the Manor, but he never said anything. One thing I *had* said to him was that, go figure, it'd gotten to the point where I'd almost rather *not* see Cheryl because when I was with her all I did was worry about doing or saying the wrong thing and getting dumped. How screwed up is that? Par for the course if you're me.

"Coleman," said Mrs. Sorensen, "there's an event coming up for the Pierrevert Historical Society this Friday. It's an annual dinner, always the beginning of Labor Day weekend, and I'm the chairwoman. We're going to close off the back half of the main dining room and install a bar there to serve the guests. The Board of Selectmen will be there along with other important people. I'd like you to be the bartender. Would that be all right with you?"

"Yes ma'am, of course."

"Well, good then. You'll receive your usual wage plus a fifty-dollar gratuity. I'll let Jeffrey Simons know."

"Thank you, Mrs. Sorensen."

"You're very welcome, and I apologize if I was getting nosy earlier. It's one of my faults."

Looking like a very sweet grandmother, if a lot more stylish than most, she held out her hand for me to shake. Like the first time I met her, her grip was firm.

26.

Leroy put on quite a spread for the Pierrevert Historical Society dinner. When I got to the hotel at about five o'clock that afternoon to set up the bar, the dining room was already decked out with flowers on every table, name cards, and menus at each place printed just for the occasion. I saved one and have kept it in a drawer all this time. It's gone kind of yellow by now.

&

Hors d'Oeuvres and Cocktails

King Richard Inn Clam Chowder

Broiled Lobster Tail in Drawn Butter
Château de Puligny-Montrachet 1966, Bourgogne

Roast Rack of Lamb with au Gratin Potatoes
Château Lynch-Bages 1967, Pauillac

Hot Cinnamon Apple Crisp with
Riverbrook Farms Vanilla Ice Cream

❧

After-Dinner Drinks and Homemade Chocolate Truffles

❧

Each place had to have three glasses: one for white wine, one for red, one for water. That was my job, so as I moved among the round tables—there were six with six places each—I eyeballed the name cards to see if there was anyone I knew. There was, as it turned out: Dr. Bellino and Ruby Calhoun for starters. I guess that made sense since they were both pretty old and had lived in Pierrevert a long time, or so I'd been told. One name caught me by surprise: Hayley Blossom, the reporter for the local paper who was my bar customer at King's Court and at Bosworth's Tavern when I worked there, which I was starting to do a lot more. The weather was turning chilly, and the courtyard was open only when it was warm enough. Pretty soon it would close for the season.

The best surprise came at about six o'clock when one of the maintenance guys, Kenny, wheeled in an upright piano and set it just a few feet from the bar.

"What's that for?" I asked.

"You didn't know? Skip's playing tonight for the bigwigs."

Half an hour later Skip came sauntering in, and I figured it would be a fun evening: making drinks for the local VIPs with Skip playing close by and cracking a few jokes between songs. Plus, I'd make more money than usual.

"Looks like you've hit the big time, Coleman," Skip said. "You wanna sit in for a couple of tunes?"

He'd been pushing me pretty hard in our lessons, making me do stuff I really didn't want to do. Like he'd show me an exercise or a sequence of neat chord voicings, and then say,

"You try it." It was always really hard, at least for me, so I'd meekly reply, "Can I work on it by myself and play it for you next time?" He'd give me a look like a principal staring down a fourth grader, and say, "Try it *now*." So, I'd have to do it. Then I'd sweat and struggle and *always* screw it up. The funny thing was, when I got back to the BI to practice, I was glad he'd forced me. It was easier the second time around.

"I don't think Mrs. Sorensen would let me," I said.

"Your day's comin', man. Hey, how's about a glass of the house red?"

So I poured him the wine, and he sat down to play. As always, the ambience in the room warmed right up. He played with such authority but still had a light touch. The first tune he played that night was a ballad called "That's All." It's one of those tunes that's so pretty you can hardly even listen to it without getting a little choked up. I think of him every time I hear it.

It was right after Skip got started that the first few guests began filtering in, the men in ties and jackets and the ladies in dresses. I thought I looked kind of natty in my blue King Richard Inn vest and necktie, or at least as slick as someone like me can look, and my white shirt and black pants were freshly pressed. That's one thing Mom had taught me how to do as a kid, and I'd bought a small iron I could use in the downstairs laundry room at the Manor.

I admit I was kind of excited about the big evening. Mrs. Sorensen had asked *me* to work it, not one of the other bartenders, and plenty of them had been at the hotel a lot longer than I had. I'd set up the bar on a long, rectangular table, with all my bottles in front of me. The fruit tray, everything freshly cut, was off to one side. A fancy silver ice bucket with a matching scoop was off to the other. The deal was that people would come up to the bar during the cocktail hour and I'd serve them directly. Then after they sat down to dinner, the waitresses would take their orders and come get the drinks from me, service-bar style.

My first customer was a lady who looked about Mrs. Sorensen's age but wasn't nearly as polished. She made me think of something Mom used to say when I was young: "Coleman, you look like an unmade bed." This lady had a great accent, though. I'd never heard anything like it.

"I dunt suppose ya'd have any Old Chaffinch, would'ja, lad?"

"Do you mean the Irish whiskey?"

"That's the one. On the rocks, if ya please."

As I was pouring out the drink, she said, "I've seen ya before, I have, over in my place with the Beringer girl. Oh, she's a fine thing." She took the glass, knocked back a healthy swill, and gave me a warm smile. "Tis me owns the bar o' ill repute outside o' town. Had it fer donkey's years. Erin O'Brien, pleased ta meet ya." She extended her hand, which I shook.

It was *the* Erin, of Erin Go Bragh's. Live and in color.

"I might be able ta use ya behind me bar one a these days," she said. "Always lookin' fer experience." She downed the rest of her whiskey in one gulp and held out the glass for a refill. "Just one more, lad," she said. "If I have three, I'll be langers 'fore we ever sit down at all."

I poured Erin another, and just as she turned away—poof— there was Hayley Blossom all decked out in dangly earrings and lipstick.

"Well!" she said. "Only the best barman to serve the nobility?"

"I didn't know you were in the historical society, Hayley."

"I'm not, but they like press coverage. That's how the likes of me gets in."

"Ah."

"I don't *have* to write something, but you can't accept the drinks party and dinner and then stiff them, can you? Against my principles, but *The Northeast Telegram* isn't *The Daily Telegraph*, is it?"

I wondered what *The Daily Telegraph* was but didn't say anything. I thought of something else I'd been meaning to bring up, though.

"Hope you don't mind me asking, but how'd you end up in Pierrevert, anyway?"

"Mum's from here, Dad's from London. Great Missenden, actually. Buckinghamshire. Divorced when I was a baby, so I've gone back and forth like a tennis ball my whole life. I'm like a pet dog on the Boston–Heathrow flight—everyone wants to scratch behind my ears. I'll probably go back in a few years."

"What can I get you?"

"I'd sure fancy one of your cracking Beefeater and tonics."

"Coming up," I said, mixing it quickly and handing it to her.

"I'm a bit peckish, so I'm stealing one of your cherries." She reached into the fruit tray, picked up two maraschino cherries, and popped them into her mouth. "Oops, more than one!" She giggled and turned away.

The room was filling up, and I started getting busy. I recognized the two policemen I'd seen in town, the same ones who'd been at the Manor after Dr. Frazier got killed. They weren't in uniform, though. Mrs. Sorensen, who'd been in the kitchen earlier talking to Leroy, was making the rounds, and boy, you could really tell she'd been in the hotel business a long time. When she talked to someone, she smiled right into their face like they were the most important person in the world. She was all done up in a navy-blue gown that went down almost to the floor.

A couple of Asian girls came in from the kitchen carrying trays of spring rolls that they walked around offering to everyone. They looked a little young to be working, and I'd never seen them before, but I found out later they were Sunny's daughters, the lady who worked in the kitchen with Leroy. I remember thinking I wouldn't mind one of those spring rolls, but there was a big sign in the kitchen saying employees weren't allowed to eat in front of customers.

Dr. Bellino and Ruby might've been the last people to arrive, because the room was really buzzing by the time they made it over to my table to get a drink.

"Congratulations, Coleman," Dr. Bellino said, extending his hand. "Great to see you working. Dr. Haynes tells me things are going well."

"OK, I guess."

He was being pretty friendly for someone who'd said hello to me maybe once or twice since I'd been at the BI. He always seemed so distant and unapproachable. Ruby smiled at me but didn't say anything, which was kind of unusual for her, but I knew she didn't like a lot of noise. It was getting pretty loud in there with everyone standing around drinking and laughing and Skip playing in the background.

"Do you have any sweet vermouth, Coleman?" she asked.

"Sure."

"I'll just have a little of that, please. With some ice."

"A Sidecar for me," Dr. Bellino said. "On the rocks."

Half an hour later, nobody had sat down to dinner yet. That meant most of them were getting pretty looped, and my bottles showed the damage. More than a few people, including the young policeman, had come back for several refills. Then someone started tapping a spoon against a glass, and everyone hushed up, including Skip at the piano.

It was Mrs. Sorensen.

"I just want to welcome you all," she said, beaming. "This is *such* a special group. We get together just once a year, and I always look *so* forward to it. As you all know, we have business to attend to: the fund drive for the book we're planning on the history of Pierrevert. Many of you have worked hard to collect old photographs from your families and friends, and we're *so* grateful. Combined with the archives at the public library and the collection my father left me, they should shape the book up *very* nicely. We're still looking for a writer for the text."

I happened to look over at Hayley just then, and she jiggled her eyebrows at me as if to say, *This sounds like a job for you know who.*

"I've been speaking to Hargrove Editions," Mrs. Sorensen continued, "and the planning is going well. But there is one small glitch: we need *money.*"

Her smile got even bigger when she said "money," and everyone laughed.

"But that's a topic for after dinner. Our chef has prepared a wonderful meal that I hope you'll all enjoy. So please find your places and be seated. Above all, keep having a *good time!*"

Everyone gave her a big round of applause, and Skip started playing again, working his way into "Satin Doll." Then the waitresses, including my favorite defensive lineman, Gladys, started serving the chowder. Twenty minutes later came the lobster. Twenty minutes after that came the lamb. I could see from watching the trays go by that the portions weren't huge, but everything looked really good, and the service was quick.

I guess Mrs. Sorensen wanted to get back to the money thing. I don't remember exactly where everyone was sitting, but I do recall that Mrs. Sorensen was at the same table as the police chief, Erin O'Brien, and Ruby. Dr. Bellino was at a table with the younger policeman, right next to him, in fact, with Hayley across from both.

One thing about this crowd: even though they had wine with each plate, they kept ordering cocktails. By the time they got through the two main courses, they all had to be blitzed. Even the police chief was knocking back the wine. The only person who wasn't drinking was Hayley. After her one cracking Beefeater and tonic, it looked like she was sticking to water.

It was just after the waitresses cleared the plates from the lamb that Gladys came over to order more drinks. She wanted two Grand Marniers, straight up, and three other drinks on the rocks: a Manhattan, a bourbon Old-Fashioned, and a Sidecar. I figured the Sidecar had to be for Dr. Bellino—he was the only one drinking them—and maybe one of the Grand Marniers for Mrs. Sorensen. Gladys said she'd be back in a couple of minutes, and off she went.

I'd finished pouring out everything except the Manhattan when I ran out of ice. I'd already refilled the bucket a few times that night, but like I said, these people were drinkers. Gladys was nowhere in sight, so I put the four drinks I'd finished on a round serving tray in case she passed by and wanted to deliver them. Then I headed into the kitchen, ice bucket in hand. Leroy was clowning around with the waitresses, yelling, "Come on, let's crisp these folks and get outta here so's I can get my beauty sleep!" That's when I noticed he'd put some dishes of apple crisp on a side counter for the staff. He was always doing stuff like that with desserts, and apple crisp is about my favorite thing in the world—especially when it's all soft and gooey and cinnamony, which is just how Leroy made it. I couldn't resist, so I put the bucket down for a second and scarfed down one of the portions. When I got back to the bar, maybe five minutes after I'd left, the four drinks were still sitting there on the tray. So I made the Manhattan on the rocks and started looking around for Gladys. Here she came, scowl intact, ready to sack the quarterback. She grabbed the tray and went off without a word. No penalty flags on the play.

I remember thinking, as the waitresses served out the apple crisp, that this was one of the happiest parties I'd ever seen. Not that I'd been invited to lots of fancy evenings, or even worked at them, but everyone was smiling and laughing, Skip's music filled the room, and the place just seemed full of good cheer. The lighting was just right, not too bright, not too dim. Mrs. Sorensen, who'd popped in and out of the kitchen a couple of times to check on things, was in top form, gabbing away with the police chief and Erin O'Brien and moving from table to table to chat with other people. Ruby didn't seem to be saying much, but she was over seventy and maybe had a little too much wine. At one point Skip started playing "A Foggy Day," which he'd played for me during one of our lessons. He was doing it real up-tempo with a walking bass line in his left hand. Like he used to say, there's nothing like Gershwin.

A bonus was that one of the waitresses, don't know who to this day, left a half-full bottle of Château Lynch-Bages on the edge of my table and forgot about it. So when no one was looking, I emptied it into two tall juice glasses, slipped one over to Skip, and kept the other for myself. I know it sounds stupid, like I always sound, but I remember thinking that maybe stealing the wine could be a turning point for me. I'd never had the nerve to do anything like that before, and I risked getting fired, which is exactly what would happen if Mr. Simons ever found out. But I hadn't seen him all night, and something inside me just said, *What the hell?* Dr. Haynes would probably say it was a dumb thing to do, but underneath I bet he might have been just a tiny bit proud of me for showing a little daring. And I got two benefits right away: the wine itself, which was like velvet but gave you a little fire in the belly, and the look on Skip's face when he took his first sip. Almost as good was the fact that Skip tasted it while still playing, moving into a few bars of old-fashioned stride piano with his left hand and gripping the glass with his right, of course not missing a beat or a note.

I know some of what I was feeling was the effect of the wine, because the room was starting to take on sort of a glow. Some of it was Skip's playing too, which always put me in a good mood. But I remember getting a sense that maybe things were going to be OK after all, and maybe I'd found kind of a home, and maybe someday I'd be able to make something of my life that wasn't all shrinks and loony bins. Standing there in my King Richard Inn vest and tie surveying the scene, I remember thinking to myself, *This is where I belong.* Like I felt a *part* of something.

That's when I heard a loud gagging noise. It reminded me of how my dog Frosty used to sound when he got something caught in his throat, meaning it wasn't quite human. Everyone else heard it too, and the buzz of conversation in the room quieted down fast even though Skip kept playing softly. That's what piano players are supposed to do when something weird happens at a fancy dinner: just keep playing to keep the mood going so people won't get upset and the staff can take care of the problem. I didn't know that then, but I know it now.

I looked over to where the noise was coming from, and what I saw haunts me to this day. It was coming from Dr. Bellino. He'd stood up, and his face was turning red. His eyes were bugged out, and he was gasping for breath. The young policeman who'd been sitting next to him jumped up and started giving him that thing they call the Heimlich maneuver, but nothing came out. Skip finally stopped playing, and Ruby, fast as she could for a person her age, rushed over to the table. The thing was, and I know because I could see clearly, there wasn't anything at Dr. Bellino's place that he could've choked on. The only thing there was his dish of apple crisp, which it didn't look like he'd even touched, and that wasn't the type of thing that would get caught in your throat anyway. I'd had some myself. He'd only been sipping his Sidecar, and the glass was still half full. His water glass was nearly empty, and his wineglass had already been taken away.

The police chief ran out to the front desk, and the other policeman lowered Dr. Bellino to the floor. Ruby kneeled over him. Mrs. Sorensen stood off to one side, white as a sheet. The others either sat quietly or started wandering around looking confused, not knowing how to act with something like this happening. Hayley moved over to a table as far away from Dr. Bellino as she could get and started scribbling into a little notebook. With such a heavy pall settling over the room, I remember thinking, *There's a good reporter for you.* Within about a minute we heard a siren outside, and that's when the police chief came back into the room.

"I'm sorry, but I have to ask you all to leave the room for a few minutes, and that includes the staff," he said. "The rescue squad is arriving, and we have to take care of the situation. Thank you all very much."

All eyes seemed to gravitate toward Mrs. Sorensen, looking for some direction on where the evening was going to go from there.

"I don't see how we can continue with the fund-raising under these circumstances," she said, her normally strong voice barely audible. "I'll be in touch with you all. I'm so very, very sorry."

***

Twenty minutes later I was standing in a crowd on the front lawn of the hotel, watching the rescue squad carry Dr. Bellino out. They'd pulled a sheet over his head, so we all knew that was that. The red light on the ambulance was swirling away, and you could hear the scratch of walkie-talkies. People were muttering that it must have been a heart attack, and how strange it was because Dr. Bellino looked so fit and seemed in such good health. A group of gawkers had gathered on the other side of the street in front of the big white church, and I saw Lenny, bottle of diet soda in hand, talking to Amy. I waved but neither noticed me. Amy was looking more skeletal than ever, her cheekbones and forehead really jutting out, and I remember feeling guilty that I hadn't spent any time with her in a while. It wasn't like she'd asked me to hang out and I'd said no—more like I hadn't made an effort to drop by her room and see how she was doing. I'd been on a treadmill of work, piano practicing, and obsessing over Cheryl. I made a mental note to invite Amy over to the tavern for drinks so I could sneak some fattening stuff into them without her noticing.

The rescue squad guys loaded Dr. Bellino into the ambulance, and I glanced over at Skip, who was standing about twenty feet away. He gave me a rueful smile that as much as said, *What can you do? People live, people die. That's just the way it is.* I was about to trudge back inside to clean up my bar table when I felt a hard tap on my shoulder. I turned around and got the same feeling in my gut as the moment I'd recognized the mountain man leaning against Cheryl's car in the parking lot at Bra's.

"Coleman?" Mr. Simons said sternly.

So much for my sense of belonging and starting a new chapter in my life. At least it was quite a night to go out on.

"Yes?"

Here it came. Fired for drinking the Château Lynch-Bages.

"Benny just went home sick in the tavern. I'll get someone to break down the bar in the dining room. I want you to finish Benny's shift. We're still busy in there."

"Um . . . sure."

"Thanks," he said, for the first and only time.

Needless to say, the events in the dining room were the main topic of conversation in the tavern for the rest of the night. I ended up getting into a conversation with one of my bar customers, a distinguished-looking Black man, about jazz. He'd been sitting there when I came in and had made a comment about the piano music that was wafting through the hotel, Skip having gone back to his usual post in the side parlor. So I told the guy that the piano player was my teacher, and we talked about favorite songs and stuff. I finally got around to

asking if he was a musician. No, he said, a lawyer. After downing a third vodka Gimlet, he got up to leave.

"Just put it on my room, 402."

"I'll need you to sign," I said, punching the last drink into
the register and handing him the bill and a pen. I do things like
that all night long with a hundred different customers, but for
some reason I remembered this one because he seemed like a
cool guy and had kind of a cool name: Homer Taylor.

27.

Excerpted from the book *The Maine Murders: What Really Happened in Pierrevert*

By Hayley Blossom
Originally published in the United Kingdom.

The news story in *The Northeast Telegram* reporting the death of Angelo Bellino was phoned in to the county desk in Hargrove from the paper's small bureau around the corner from the King Richard Inn. It barely made the nine p.m. deadline for the next morning's edition. As such, it was relegated to a briefs column on the bottom-left side of the front page reserved for late-breaking items. The two-paragraph account was matter-of-fact, other than it happened to be about the top man at a well-known facility dropping dead in a very public manner at a hotel everyone in the county knew about. The cause of death was reported as unknown.

A full obituary of Dr Bellino was published on an inside page the following day, in the Sunday paper, penned by the paper's chief obit writer, George Hammond. Given Bellino's position in the community and the fact that he was in his midsixties, the obit had been written in advance and kept in a folder that contained the death stories of other local notables who were still very much alive and might be for some time. The story recounted the tale of Bellino's family emigrating from Genoa, Italy, to Boston's North End in the early 1900s, young Angelo's medical training at the University of Rhode Island, and his hiring in 1939 by the founder of the Buchanan Institute, Dr Hamish Buchanan.

Bellino's subsequent rise through the ranks at the institute had been rapid, spurred by the fact that he was both a fine theorist and a skilled writer—the result being numerous articles published under his byline in medical magazines and journals. According to several of his former patients, he was also a gifted therapist. Bellino and his wife, the former Luciana Morello, who had predeceased him by ten years following an auto accident on an icy back road in Pierrevert, had no children.

Both the brief news item and the full obituary were widely read, but no more so than articles concerning the deaths of other prominent people in the county. It was the third Bellino story, which ran in a box atop the front page three days after the obit, that caused a major stir.

Hospital Chief May Have Been Poisoned
By Hayley Blossom
Telegram Staff Writer

PIERREVERT—An autopsy on the body of Dr. Angelo Bellino, the former medical director of the Buchanan Institute, revealed a strong and clear presence of potassium cyanide in the bloodstream, a county official said Tuesday.

"In my opinion, the cause of Dr. Bellino's death was acute toxicity, enough cyanide to kill a lot more than one person," said Dr. Jonathan Monroe, the Hargrove County coroner, in a phone interview with the *Telegram*. "I can't recall ever being so surprised at the results of an autopsy."

Bellino, whose death occurred last Friday night at a fund-raising dinner for the Pierrevert Historical Society at the King Richard Inn, had been widely thought to be the victim of a heart attack, although no official determination had yet been made.

It was toward the end of an elegant dinner, an event attended by the *Telegram*, when Bellino rose from his chair, apparently choking. Kevin Kincaid, a Pierrevert police officer who was also a dinner guest, performed the Heimlich maneuver in an attempt to dislodge whatever was apparently caught in the physician's throat. But it soon became evident that the choking was being caused by something other than a food blockage. The Pierrevert Rescue Squad was called in immediately, and Bellino was pronounced dead at the scene.

Both the state police in Hargrove and local police in Pierrevert, contacted by the *Telegram* late Tuesday, declined comment on the possibility of poisoning. Patricia Sorensen, owner of the King Richard Inn, and Dr. Wilson Haynes, a spokesman for the Buchanan Institute, also offered no comment.

Marvin Glickman, Pierrevert's chief selectman and a guest at last Friday's dinner, called the possibility that Bellino was poisoned "bizarre."

"I've known Angie Bellino for over thirty years," he said in a phone interview Tuesday night. "Knew him as a young man. He was a fine physician and administrator. I wish I could tell you what's going on in this town. It's the most awful thing we've ever lived through."

About 20,000 households in Hargrove County had daily home-delivery subscriptions to *The Northeast Telegram*. On a typical day in late summer, the paper sold roughly 1,200 additional copies at variety stores, pharmacies, supermarkets, and coin-operated newspaper machines. The story about Angelo Bellino's possible poisoning lifted sales of nonsubscription copies to nearly 2,500, more than double the average.

As for the story itself, it took a narrow angle. It did not directly mention that Dr Bellino's demise was the third violent death to take place in Pierrevert within less than a year. Nor did it note that Dr Bellino was the second senior physician at the Buchanan Institute to die under extraordinary circumstances within a period of two months. These omissions were not intentional, but the result of human error and deadline pressure. The reporter, calling from the Pierrevert bureau, had reached the coroner at his home at 8:20 p.m., forty minutes before the paper's deadline, merely fishing for a story. The question of an autopsy on Dr Bellino was still an open one, at least publicly. Dr Monroe, not known for speaking freely with the press, was caught off guard. He had completed the autopsy that very day and was sitting in a recliner nursing his second scotch whiskey of the evening when the reporter phoned. For whatever reason, he decided to share his findings. He did not ask to go off the record.

Following a subsequent flurry of comment-seeking phone calls, the story was written in ten minutes from the Pierrevert bureau and faxed to the newsroom in Hargrove. When it arrived, it was handed to Marge Branning, a seasoned support staffer who quickly typed it into the paper's computer system. Despite the risk of making the edition late to press, the night editor, Steve Wilkinson, decided to redraw the front page and run the piece as the lead. Under the tension of the moment, no one at the paper— not the reporter, not Branning, not Wilkinson—thought to include in the story the names of the two men who had been stabbed to death in Pierrevert in the months before Bellino died at the King Richard Inn.

The next day, after the Wednesday paper had hit local driveways and newsstands, there was more than enough embarrassment to go around at the *Telegram* when the omissions were noticed. That said, the gaping hole in the story focused the newsroom's attention on all three alleged murder victims: Ronald Sanders, Gregory Frazier, and Angelo Bellino. The link between Frazier and Bellino was obvious: they were both senior physicians at the Buchanan Institute. But what about Sanders?

It was the *Telegram*'s editor, Martin Taft, who decided to "check the clips," journalist parlance for delving into the paper's archives where old articles—literally clipped with scissors from previous editions—were kept in folders with subject headings. What Taft found, in a folder marked "Buchanan Institute," gave him a start. Then it brought a calm smile to his face, the kind journalists get when the fog over a story begins to lift.

The discovery was a photograph taken inside the Hargrove County courthouse during the negligence trial concerning the death of a former patient, Pearleen Porter. The wide-angle shot had been taken by Paul Gordon, the paper's top photographer, from a corner of the courtroom behind the judge. Angelo Bellino was on the witness stand being questioned by Ronald Sanders. In the front row, side by side, sat Gregory Frazier, Wilson Haynes, and Ruby Calhoun. To their right, sitting behind a counselor's table, sat Homer Taylor, the North Carolina attorney who had brought the unsuccessful lawsuit forward.

When Gregory Frazier was murdered, no one had made a connection between the psychiatrist and Ronald Sanders, who had been killed many months prior. Sanders had worked for scores of clients in Pierrevert and throughout Hargrove County. The fact that he had represented Buchanan in the Pearleen Porter case did not immediately stand out. But Angelo Bellino's alleged murder, along with the newfound photograph, made it difficult not to connect the dots.

Still, said Taft at the special news meeting he called just after unearthing the photo, the fact that all three victims were connected to Buchanan did not necessarily mean the murders had anything to do with the Pearleen Porter case. It *could* mean that, he stressed, but it did not *have* to. The photo was a viable lead, not proof. Maybe the killings were being carried out by a disgruntled Buchanan patient, present or past, who simply wanted to eliminate the big shots.

But Steve Wilkinson came up with another theory. Sanders had frequently been active in the annual recertification of the Buchanan Institute as a nonprofit organization, meaning that it paid no property taxes. How many times had locals raised a major kerfuffle at weekly selectmen's meetings—which were open to the public—over the fact that Buchanan, situated on five acres of prime land half a mile outside Pierrevert, got off scot-free from the taxman? The possibility that an angry (and deranged) local taxpayer was getting his own back against Buchanan seemed more plausible than anything related to the Pearleen Porter case, Wilkinson hypothesized. The night editor had a point. It was easily verifiable from the *Telegram*'s coverage over the years that many townspeople felt the institute's tax status hung a fiscal anvil around their necks. They couldn't make ends meet, they argued, because the Board of Assessors nailed *them*, not Buchanan, every year to pay for Pierrevert's schools, police department, fire department, sanitation services, water from the reservoir, and everything else. Not only that, but plenty of the chronic complainers were gun-owning, knife-toting yokels whose elocution made Officer Kevin Kincaid sound like the host of a BBC documentary on Queen Victoria's wardrobe.

The fourth story concerning the death of Angelo Bellino, which ran the following day, on Thursday, was written very carefully and "lawyered"—set before the paper's legal counsel to gauge the possibility of libel. Smithson & McKinney, the venerable Hargrove firm that had represented the *Telegram* for over fifty years, cleared the piece, which occupied the top right-hand side of the front page, the lead position. The story was accompanied by the photo that Martin Taft had fished out of the clips. That day's paper broke all records for nonsubscription sales at just over 3,300 copies.

Where the Murdered Met: The Buchanan Institute

By Hayley Blossom
Telegram Staff Writer

PIERREVERT—The victims of the three alleged murders that have rocked Pierrevert over the past year all had something in common: a link to the Buchanan Institute, the mental-health facility located outside of town, an investigation by the *Telegram* has revealed.

The connection between Dr. Angelo Bellino, the alleged victim of cyanide poisoning at a Pierrevert Historical Society dinner at the King Richard Inn last Friday, and Dr. Gregory Frazier, found stabbed to death roughly two months ago in a parking lot behind the same hotel, has been clear since Bellino's death. Both were senior physicians and administrators at the institute. Yet the tie to Ronald Sanders, fatally stabbed at his home on Daffodil Lane last October, has gone unnoticed by law enforcement officials.

Sanders, in fact, was the hospital's general counsel and had represented the institute in a number of legal matters over many years. Among those occasions were the annual certification of Buchanan's status as a nonprofit organization that pays no property taxes and a negligence suit brought against the institute nearly two years ago. The suit concerned the death of a young woman, Pearleen Porter, who died of an overdose of sleeping pills while a patient at Buchanan. The institute was deemed not at fault by a jury in Hargrove.

The rest of the story, which went on for eight additional paragraphs, was just B matter—rehashing details of the three deaths that the *Telegram* had already covered. The paper decided not to contact Pierrevert's police chief, Chester Cody, for comment, nor did it call Zeke Murkowski, the state police's senior officer in Hargrove. The editorial decision was simply to run the piece as the result of the paper's own investigation—which, in fact, amounted to nothing more than Martin Taft happening on the photo from the Pearleen Porter case. Most important to Taft was that the story was a scoop by any standard, guaranteed to embarrass the police who'd come up with exactly nothing since the first alleged murder took place. Or as Marvin Glickman, the town's chief selectman, might say: *bupkis.*

28.

In my very first therapy session with Dr. Haynes, he'd suggested I join the local gang that he played basketball with over at the town gym a couple of times a week. It wasn't until the week after Dr. Bellino died that he brought it up again. I thought I was getting a little flabby, more than usual even though I still had a skinny frame, and I knew the exercise wouldn't hurt.

So on my one night off from work the following week, I think it was a Monday, about ten days after the historical society dinner, I found myself back on the hardwoods for the first time in nearly a year. I was wearing gray Bermuda shorts that fell below my knees, a white T-shirt, brown socks, and a pair of dirty Converse All Stars high-tops. Except for the sneakers, this particular outfit sent my grade on the dork scale off the charts. Dr. Haynes, of course, looked as cool as any basketball player ever could: gym shorts at just the right length, toned legs, a gray Boston Celtics T-shirt, white socks that came halfway up his calves, white Adidas Superstar low-tops. The other guys in the gym were a pretty ragtag lot, all in their twenties and thirties, some not much better off than I. Sartorially speaking, that is.

Dr. Haynes and I didn't end up on the same team, and I couldn't decide whether that was a good or a bad thing. What'd be weirder, passing him the ball or trying to block one of his shots? High-fiving him or jostling him for a rebound?

I'll tell you this, though: once we got started, I could see what a great player Dr. Haynes must've been when he was young. I'm not saying the group of housepainters, shelf stockers, produce-aisle managers, and construction workers in the gym that night represented anything close to what you'd call high-level competition, but Dr. Haynes dribbled circles around everyone. He ran the floor. He set picks. He rebounded. He played defense. He passed, sometimes the no-look variety. And he had as sweet a jump shot as I've ever seen, all fingertips and backspin. He was twice the age of at least half the guys there and by ten miles the best player in the gym, no contest. I wondered if he ever traveled around, maybe to Portland or Augusta or even Orono, where the state university was, to play with people at a higher level.

Anyway, early in the game someone passed me the ball, and I had a clear shot from the corner. As I raised my arms to let fly, a guy on Dr. Haynes' team called Scotty came running over to me, waving his arms in the air and screaming, "He can't do it, he can't do it!" Don't ask me how, having not touched a basketball for so long, but I sank the shot. I felt like grinning from ear to ear as I ran back down the floor, but instead tried to clamp a nonchalant, nothin'-to-it expression on my face, the kind Harold Cherry used to give us in high school when he swished a thirty-footer.

Then later, when my team was losing something like fifteen to ten, one of my teammates got a defensive rebound, and I broke for the other end of the court. He chucked me the ball, quarterback style, and I drove in for the layup, expecting to blow it as usual. That's when Scotty, who was maybe six feet tall and pretty strong, came running up behind me to try to block the shot. At least that's what I *thought* he'd do. Instead, he shoved me hard, straight into the wall behind the basket. If there hadn't been a gym mat hanging from some hooks to soften the blow, I don't know what would've happened. I remember lying there trying to figure out where I was. My right ankle felt like someone had shoved a knife through it. Dr. Haynes was suddenly leaning over me.

"Coleman, are you all right?"

He put his hand on the back of my head and felt around a little. Then he reached for my arm and checked my pulse. I could hear people shouting in the background but couldn't figure out what it was about. I learned later that one of the bigger guys had grabbed Scotty by the collar and pinned him up against the bleachers.

"Know who I am?" Dr. Haynes asked.

"Yes."

"Move your legs around, OK?"

As always, I did as I was told. The pain from my ankle was awful, but I didn't say that.

"Wiggle your fingers. Try to make a muscle in each arm."

I tried.

"Just lie still for a minute."

The next thing I remember is Dr. Haynes holding a cup of water to my mouth. Then more shouting in the background. Then a blank. I passed out. Then I was awake again, still lying there, with a few other people gathered around.

"Guys, let's call it a night," I heard Dr. Haynes say. Then, sharply and loudly: "*That's not how you play the game, Scotty!*"

A few minutes later he helped me to my feet, and I told him about the ankle. They say a bad sprain hurts worse than a break, and I believe them. I knew that's what it was because I'd had the same thing before, just not for the same reason. Dr.

Haynes brought me to his car, my arm around his shoulder for support, and drove me over to the Manor. He briefed Freddy Cruz and Ruby on what'd happened, told them to put some ice on my ankle, and left.

"See you soon," he said.

"Thanks, Dr. Haynes."

Freddy said he'd bring an ice bag and some crutches up to my room as soon as he could, so I started to limp upstairs, passing by Amy's room on the way. I heard her moving around inside, and I stood there silently, wondering whether I should say hi. At one point I thought I heard her crying, or something close to it, but I decided not to knock on the door—just leave her alone and respect her privacy.

The thing was, standing there like an idiot, I noticed the lock inside Amy's doorknob. All the doors to the patients' rooms at the BI had locks, which is a little strange for a loony bin, I know, but the staff all had master keys—so who was kidding who, if you know what I mean. I think it was a patients' rights sort of thing.

Anyway, looking at the lock made me think of something that happened when I was about ten years old. My stepfather, Terry, had come into my room one morning and said he needed me to do something for him. He told me to go downstairs to the drawer in the kitchen where we kept a few tools, fetch a screwdriver, and meet him in the bedroom where he and Mom slept. When I made it back upstairs, a little out of breath, he was standing just outside the door to their bathroom. The shower was running, so I figured Mom was inside washing her hair or something. Terry said he needed to get inside to brush his teeth but didn't want to get Mom out of the shower. He told me to jimmy the lock inside the doorknob. I knew how to do it, so I stuck the screwdriver in, wiggled it around a bit, and twisted. *Click.* Presto, the door slowly swung open. And there was Mom standing right in front of us, stark naked, about to step into the shower. On her face was the most mortified look I've ever seen on anyone. I dropped the screwdriver and ran. I can still hear the sound it made bouncing on the bathroom tiles.

I hadn't thought of that day in years, until I passed by Amy's room on the night I sprained my ankle. I think I'd tried pretty hard to forget it. Like I still try to forget that I didn't knock on Amy's door.

29.

Excerpted from the book *The Maine Murders: What Really Happened in Pierrevert*

By Hayley Blossom
Originally published in the United Kingdom.

The futility of the Pierrevert police force did not mean that Chief Cody and his deputy Kevin Kincaid had not been trying. Since the cyanide story broke, the two had begun the process of interviewing King Richard Inn employees who had been on duty the night Angelo Bellino died, as well as invited guests. They had also examined the chronology of the Pierrevert Historical Society dinner in meticulous detail. Their working assumption was that the *Telegram* was correct, that Bellino had indeed been poisoned. But how had he ingested the chemical? Everyone at the dinner had eaten the same things.

Cody had called Dr Monroe and, after expressing consternation that the physician had spoken to the press before coming to him, asked precisely how cyanide kills.

The answer was by inhibiting cellular respiration, essentially causing death by suffocation. Cody had also asked how fast the chemical acts, which turned out to be *very*. All of which led to the conclusion that the cyanide must have been present either in Dr Bellino's plate of apple crisp, his glass of water, or the cocktail he'd been imbibing. Those were the only three items in front of him when he'd started to choke.

Another question concerned the difficulty of obtaining potassium cyanide in the first place. According to Monroe, any proper chemist or someone working in an industry that used cyanides—such as paper, plastics, and textiles, all present in Hargrove County—could easily obtain or concoct enough of the substance to get the job done.

All things considered, the first determination to be made was whether the food or drink had been contaminated *before* or *after* being served by one of the two waitresses who'd looked after Bellino's table: Gladys Plotkin, a King Richard old-timer, and Beverly Breen, co-owner of the Cauldron Café who occasionally moonlighted at the hotel.

The *after* hypothesis seemed improbable: there were simply too many people watching. That said, the elephant in the room was that just about every guest had been three sheets to the wind on liquor and wine. Who could recall any details? Officer Kincaid had been so drunk himself, not to mention blissfully absorbed in admiring Beverly Breen's bustline at every opportunity—this was Bev D, after all—that Lucrezia Borgia could have waltzed in and dumped a fistful of cyanide crystals onto the table without so much as a blip on his radar. Yet it was also true that when Bev D leaned over in front of anyone, the outline of her breasts was all they could see for a few moments—certainly long enough for someone to slip a pill into a drink.

Ultimately, the officers decided to concentrate on the *before* hypothesis—the idea that the fatal drink or dish was already lethal when it was served to Bellino. Both seemed to recall that everyone's water had come from the same pitcher, poured at the table. The same principle applied to the wine: the bottles had been opened at the table and served to everyone. That left the apple crisp and the cocktail as potential culprits. Where had each item come from?

The apple crisp had come straight from the kitchen, and the cocktail directly from the service bar at the back of the dining room. Kincaid thought he remembered that Bellino's drink and apple crisp had both been served by Gladys, whom he knew because she was the mother of a childhood friend, Mark Plotkin. But he had no idea whether it was immediately after a sip of the drink or a bite of the apple crisp that the psychiatrist had risen from the table gasping for air. At that moment, the deputy had been lost in reverie staring at Bev D, who was bending over a table across the room.

Yet the most exasperating part, in addition to being out-investigated by the local paper, was the absence of any evidence. Since everyone at the dinner, the officers included, had assumed Bellino died of a heart attack, the dining room had not been treated as a crime scene. Every glass, plate, or piece of cutlery in the room had been sterilized ten times over in the King Richard's industrial dishwashing system, a new model of which had been installed in the kitchen just six months prior to the tune of $7,500, an invoice paid promptly, as always, by Patricia Sorensen.

It was on the Sunday after *The Northeast Telegram* ran the story establishing a link between the victims and the Buchanan Institute that Cody raised another theory, albeit one he considered a long shot. He was sitting behind his office desk, sipping coffee from a Styrofoam cup, as

Kincaid slumped in an easy chair he'd bought at a yard sale and transported to the office the previous year.

"You know," Cody said, "we're making a pretty big assumption."

"What's that, Chief?"

"With everyone so plastered, I'm ashamed to say myself included, we're—"

"You're fucking allowed to have a good time too," Kincaid broke in. "Fuck it."

Cody sighed. Perhaps Kincaid meant well at times, but his crudeness could be supremely annoying.

"Ever stop to think that maybe Bellino wasn't the intended victim?" Cody said. "With all the plates and glasses and people moving from table to table, who says the poison didn't get put in front of the wrong person? We've got a small town here. People hold grudges for fifty years. Maybe someone planned the whole thing *knowing*, or at least *assuming*, that everyone would be smashed. Too many suspects, nobody remembers anything, impossible to pin down. Maybe it has nothing to do with Buchanan at all."

"You're thinking too much, Chief. Glickman must be get—"

"Maybe someone's after *me*."

"Listen," said Kincaid, jabbing a finger in the air. "The guy we gotta talk to is that kid who was making the drinks. He's one of the crazies over at Buchanan—was there the same day we were after the first doctor got offed. Came in late. You never know what those jerkoffs'll do."

"I agree we should talk to him," Cody replied. "He's on my list. But I've gotta go to Augusta tomorrow for a few days. Regional chiefs meeting. Just sit tight until I get back. Then we'll talk to everybody we need to."

"I don't like those loonies," Kincaid said with disgust. "Not one of 'em. Why'd they have to put a fucking crazy house in *my town.*"

"It was here before you were born," Cody deadpanned. "And there's nothing wrong with people getting help they need. I could've used a stint over there myself after Darlene died." He paused for a few moments. "Like I said, take a time-out. It'll do you good."

The chief sat back in his chair, and the two men fell into silence, Kincaid brooding away. That's when Cody decided to lighten the mood and have a little fun with his hotheaded deputy.

"Hey, Kevin, you're not the most popular guy in town," Cody said with a grin. "Come to think of it, *you* were sitting next to Bellino. Maybe our killer missed the target by just *one place.* All those cheerleaders you jilted in high school? I bet a few of 'em work right there at the hotel, maybe even in the *kitchen.* There must be at least *one* who'd like to put you six feet under! Am I right? Am I right?"

Cody was doing his best not to laugh directly in Kincaid's face, but the colour drained from the deputy's swarthy cheeks so rapidly that the chief noticed.

"Hey, Kevin, I'm only kidding."

"I know, I know," said Kincaid, weakly. "It's just that this case has really got me down."

30.

The morning after the basketball game, the Manor seemed quieter than usual. Most days you could hear people heading this way or that, or the maintenance guys crashing around for one reason or another. But all I heard when I woke up was a dead silence.

I hopped out of bed in my boxer shorts, then fell right back in once I tried out the ankle. Freddy had brought up a pair of crutches late the previous night, so I grabbed them, hobbled over to my door, and opened it. The hallway was deserted. I got dressed as quickly as I could and made my way downstairs on the crutches.

The first person I saw in the front hall was April. She was sitting on one of the sofas, dabbing at her eyes with a tissue. Lenny, Marie, Ruby, and Dr. Nelson, were there too, looking dazed. That's when I saw two people wearing Pierrevert Rescue Squad uniforms wheeling a gurney down the first-floor hallway, off to my left. They were coming right at me, so I inched backward to get out of the way. There was someone on the gurney, and a sheet had been pulled up. It was when they passed by and turned to go out the back door toward the parking lot that I saw the locks of long, straight red hair sticking out from underneath the sheet. I looked over at April, who was nodding at me through her tears. Everyone stared as Ruby and Dr. Nelson followed the rescue workers outside. Once they were gone, I made it over to the sofa to sit next to April.

"We didn't think she was in danger," she whispered, barely able to get the words out. "Her heart just stopped."

We sat there for maybe half a minute, April blowing her nose a few times. Then my guilt complex kicked in.

"Maybe if I'd—"

"*Don't*, Coleman," April said firmly. "Amy wasn't your responsibility."

I suddenly wanted to scream, destroy things, break all the furniture in the front hall. Run into the kitchen and smash the dishes against the walls.

Instead, I got up and hobbled toward the staircase that led to the basement. The stairs were circular and hard to manage with the crutches, but I made it down and went over to the piano room. I thought for a second about going in, but realized that banging on the keyboard in a crazed fury would ruin it. A glance into the TV room revealed two new patients staring at the screen, absorbed in an old movie. So I stumbled over to the little exercise room, which had some barbells, dumbbells, and mats lying around—and closed the door behind me.

"AAAAHHHHHHHHHHHHHHHHHHHHHHHHHHHH! AAAAHHHHHHHHHHHH! AAAAHHHHHHH!"

I let fly at the top of my lungs, smashing the crutches against the wall.

"AAAAHHHHHHHHHHHHHHHHHHHHHHHHHHHH! AAAAHHHHHHHHHHHHHHHHHHHHHHHHHHHHH! AAAAHHHHHHHHHHHHHHHHHHH!"

I grabbed a free weight, a twenty-five-pounder, and slammed it down.

"AAAAHHHHHHHHHHHHHHHHHHH!"

I threw anything I could get my hands on for the next couple of minutes, then paused, dripping with sweat, and looked around the room like the madman I was. A loud knock came at the door.

"LEAVE ME THE FUCK ALONE!"

The door opened and it was April. She wasn't crying anymore, but her face was all red and puffy. A cop was standing behind her, one of the two who'd come to the Manor after Dr. Frazier got killed. He'd been at the King Richard the night Dr. Bellino died too. But he wasn't dressed in a sport coat and slacks, like at the dinner. He was wearing his blue uniform.

"Coleman?" he said. "I'm Officer Kincaid. I'd like to ask you a few questions."

***

I figured the cop had come to arrest me for disturbing the peace or something, which wouldn't have been all that strange. I'd been tossing things around and screaming at the top of my lungs like a card-carrying mental patient. So I picked up my crutches and we went into the little TV room, vacant by then, my impersonation of a true psycho having driven away the two new patients. We sat down, April at my side.

"I'm here to talk about the dinner at the King Richard," the cop said, and none too friendly either. "I'm investigating Dr. Bellino's death."

"Okaaaay," I said, my nervous throat clear instantly starting up. I cut a side glance at April, and she might've looked worse than I did. First, a patient dying on her. Then another, that would be yours truly, going berserk. Now the police.

"You were the bartender, weren't you?"

"Yes."

April suddenly broke in. "Officer, are you aware that one of our patients passed away this morning?"

"Oh yeah," Kincaid said, as if April had just mentioned the weather forecast. "I heard it on the scanner. Gee, that's too bad. Guess there's one less of you to worry about now."

April's mouth opened in astonishment, but nothing came out. The cop turned back to me and plowed on.

"Well, what was Bellino drinking? Come on, I haven't got all day."

"A Sidecar."

"What's in that?"

"Cognac, triple sec, and lemon juice."

"Did you use any of those bottles to make other drinks?"

"Yes."

The cop reached into a black leather purse he was wearing on his hip and pulled out a little note pad and a pen. My nervous head jerk started revving up to join the throat clear. I noticed he wasn't wearing a gun holster.

"Where're those bottles now?" he asked.

"Long gone," I answered. "All the bottles from that night went back to the bar in the tavern."

"All right," he said. "Which waitress served Bellino's table?"

"It was Gladys. I remember 'cause I ran out of ice and had to go get some to finish her order. I left a few drinks on a tray, and when I came back from the kitchen they were still there. So I made the last drink, and she came and took the tray."

"I knew it was Gladys," the cop said. "And I knew Bellino was drinking Sidecars—I was sitting next to him." He paused for effect. "Just making sure you're telling the truth."

April finally found some words.

"*Excuse me*, but why would Coleman tell you anything but the truth? He has nothing to hide!"

"Did I ask you a question, little lady?" the cop replied sharply. "Why don't you keep your mouth shut till I ask you to open it?"

April's face reddened. But this was a cop, so she couldn't let fly. Kincaid turned back toward me.

"How long were the drinks on the tray when you went to the kitchen?"

"Maybe five minutes."

"That'd give you a pretty good alibi, wouldn't it?"

It took a few seconds for me to get what he was implying. "What do you mean?" I said, witty as ever.

"You can say you weren't in the room when the doc got poisoned. Maybe you'd already made the drink that killed him—at least that's how it looks to me. Hey, remind me, what's your last name?"

"Cooper."

"How long you been here at Buchanan?"

"It'll be a year in October."

"What'd you think of Bellino before he croaked? Big boss, huh? Easy guy to hate?"

"I didn't really know him."

He stopped to write something down in his pad, then looked up again. "Lemme put it to you this way, Coleman Cooper. If the doc gets poisoned, and you're the guy who made his drink, what's that make you?"

"I don't know," I said weakly, my nervous throat clear and head jerk moving into high gear.

April leapt to her feet. "You have NO RIGHT to say these things!" she cried. A look of determination came over her face, but there was plenty of fear in it too. She lowered her voice and said, "I'm afraid I'll have to ask you to leave."

"I'll decide when I leave, little lady," the cop said. "Unless you haven't noticed this badge." He nodded down at his chest.

"Coleman, I'll be RIGHT BACK!" April shouted, dashing out of the room. "Don't say anything more to him!"

"Who's she, your lawyer?" the cop asked as April broke into a run down the hallway. "You're gonna need one, Cooper. Now stand up and put your hands behind your back."

***

Two minutes later, Officer Kincaid was leading me out the front door of the Manor toward his squad car. My hands were bound tightly behind me, and don't ever let anyone tell you that handcuffs don't hurt. Never mind that I was hobbling like crazy on one foot and one heel because my ankle was killing me. When I'd told the cop I needed my crutches to walk, he said, "You need the handcuffs more."

There hadn't been a soul in the front hall—not even Lenny swilling a diet soda—I guessed because Amy's death had knocked the wind out of everyone and they were all in their rooms. So no one saw the spectacle of Coleman Cooper being led away by the police. They probably would've thought it meant *I'd* killed Amy. Just what my guilt complex needed.

The cop was pushing my head under the doorframe, trying to get me into the back seat of the squad car, when out of the corner of my eye I saw two people running toward us from the direction of the doctors' building. Within a few seconds I could make out Dr. Haynes, necktie flying in the air, in full sprint. April brought up the rear. The cop stopped trying to push me into the car, and we both stood there. Dr. Haynes was upon us in no time, and not even out of breath.

"NOT SO FAST, KINCAID!" he shouted. "WHAT THE HELL'S GOING ON?"

"I'm taking this kid down to the station house for more questioning—maybe even for a night or two—until we figure out what happened over at the King Richard," the cop said. He was trying to sound defiant, but his tough-guy veneer was already cracking face to face with Dr. Haynes. My therapist could be very intimidating even when he wasn't angry, and at the moment he was livid. He looked like he wanted to break every one of the cop's bones.

"WHERE'S CODY?" Dr. Haynes demanded.

"Out of town."

"*WHERE* OUT OF TOWN?"

"Augusta."

"DOING WHAT?"

"He's at a meeting."

April pulled up just then, breathing hard. Dr. Haynes lowered his voice, but his tone was no less commanding.

"Get those handcuffs off Coleman *this instant* or I'll be on the phone to the Augusta PD in one minute. I'll find Cody and you'll be off the force *tomorrow*. We'll file a complaint and *you'll* be the one in court."

I'm not sure whether it was the job thing or the complaint thing that got to Kincaid, maybe both. But he slowly reached into his black purse and pulled out a small key.

"OK, Haynes," he said as he unlocked me. "You haven't heard the end of this. Maybe *you're* the one who wanted—"

"Oh, I wouldn't threaten me, Kincaid," Dr. Haynes broke in. He said it quietly, but as menacingly as I'd ever heard him sound.

The cop held his tongue, got into his squad car, and started up the engine. Just before screeching off, he stuck his head out the window and looked straight at me. I'll never forget what he said:

"I'm not through with you neither, Coleman Cooper."

31.

Excerpted from the book *The Maine Murders: What Really Happened in Pierrevert*

By Hayley Blossom
Originally published in the United Kingdom.

Journalists and law enforcement personnel are not known for mutual affection, especially when it comes to investigating crime. They often see each other as adversaries or, at best, nuisances that must be dealt with if any progress is to be made.

Nonetheless, one week after the *Telegram* ran the "Where the Murdered Met" story, a meeting took place in a small office just off the newsroom at the paper's headquarters in downtown Hargrove. It was the same venue where thrice-daily news meetings took place, Martin Taft working his way around the oval-shaped table asking the editors responsible for various sections about the contents of their skeds for that day, then deciding which stories would be played on the front page. Such meetings provide the pulse of any daily newspaper's life, a place where events of the moment are bantered about, often in irreverent terms, and considerable energy is devoted to finding a good story that no other newspaper has, that holy grail known since time began as "the scoop." These were harder and harder to come by in the dawning era of pack journalism and round-the-clock, global wire-service coverage, but the *Telegram* had a big one with the alleged serial murder case that was riveting the small county it served.

The police had been duly humbled. Even better, here was the chief at the *Telegram*, cap in hand, asking the paper to share whatever information it possessed—which, in fact, was nothing more than the newly unearthed court-room photograph from the Pearleen Porter negligence trial. In Taft's view, the police did not have to know that this was all the paper had.

It was Pierrevert's police chief, Chester Cody, a modest man not afraid to ask for help when he needed it, who had requested the meeting. On one side of the table were Cody and state police sergeant Zeke Murkowski. On the other side were Taft, publisher Jerome Kolner, night editor Steve Wilkinson, and the reporter who had written the stories about the Pierrevert murders. Also seated at one end of the table was Dr Wilson Haynes, recently named acting medi-cal director of the Buchanan Institute following the death of Angelo Bellino. Cody had asked that Dr Haynes attend, provided Taft had no objection. Taft, on the contrary, was more than happy to have a potential newsmaker in his lair.

"There's no way to know if this means anything," said Cody, holding up a print of the courtroom photo in which Ronald Sanders, Gregory Frazier, and Angelo Bellino were clearly visible. Taft had asked the photo lab for prints made from the original negative and had placed one in front of each chair.

"Exactly what I said before we ran the story," Taft said with his usual bluster. "The first two victims were stabbed to death, the third poisoned. I'm a newspaperman, not a detective, but that's not a typical MO."

"But why choose such a populated place?" said Wilkinson, a small-town-journalism lifer in his early fifties. "A roomful of witnesses? Makes no sense."

"Unless the killer wanted Bellino to suffer in a public manner, which implies vengeance," Cody said evenly.

"Then why only him in public and not the others?" Wilkinson replied.

The police chief sat back in his chair and took a professorial tone. "Let's assume for the moment that we're dealing with one person who has a pathological ax to grind against Buchanan. The question is *why*, which is the reason I asked Dr Haynes to join us."

All heads turned toward Haynes, who, although close to fifty, appeared to be in the kind of physical shape associated with much younger men.

"I've been a therapist at Buchanan for over twenty years," the psychiatrist said. "I've seen more patients than I can count and cannot think of one, in my medical opinion, who would be capable of serial killings. That's not the kind of person we treat."

"Hell," said Murkowski, who in his early sixties still wore a crew cut atop a blotchy, pockmarked face. "I seen plenty of people from that joint come up to Hargrove and raise hell. I should've arrested some."

Cody glanced over at Murkowski, who appeared to be nursing a hangover, and immediately regretted inviting him to the meeting. He'd not had much choice, though, needing to show at least a token effort to keep the state police in the loop of the investigation. Taft, ignoring Murkowski, looked at Haynes.

"How about your colleagues?" Taft asked. "Other doctors? Someone's getting stiffed on salary? Passed over for promotion a few times?"

"I've thought about that," Haynes answered. "We did have one instance in which a therapist had a psychotic episode a while back. She was intoxicated and demonstrated violent tendencies. We required her to take a long leave of absence and receive intensive treatment. Following that, we permitted her to return. She's still with us and doing fine. Her name is Samantha Nelson."

"My deputy and I were there the night she went off the rails," Cody said. "I was surprised to hear she'd been taken back."

"I don't think she's our man, so to speak," said Haynes. "Of course, psychiatry is an inexact science."

Wilkinson interjected: "I've covered enough selectmen's meetings to know there's plenty of people who hate Buchanan. It jacks up their taxes."

"Indirectly, yes," replied Cody. Then his thoughts seemed to switch gears.

"I can't say for sure," he continued. "But I think whoever's doing this was personally acquainted with the victims. Maybe not close friends, but enough to say hello on the street."

"What about the guy who brought the negligence case," said Taft. "The lawyer. Gave the eulogy at the girl's service. At the father's too, come to think of it."

"I had a few conversations with Homer Taylor in the weeks following the trial," said Haynes. "We'd both known Pearleen's father, and I called him in North Carolina to try to mend fences. He said he had other friends in Hargrove whom he occasionally flew up to see, and I asked him to call if he ever had time to meet. Eventually, we became friends. He told me that in retrospect he thought the verdict was the correct one. In terms of Homer being a suspect, that's a nonstarter."

Cody added that although he was well into the process of interviewing everyone who'd been in the hotel dining room and kitchen the night Bellino died, the task would now take longer because he'd taken his deputy, Kevin Kincaid, off the case. Murkowski, who looked as if he were nodding off, did not offer the assistance of the state police, and Cody did not request it.

"What happened with your deputy, if I may ask," said Taft.

"It's off the record."

Taft nodded.

"He falsely accused a Buchanan patient, cuffed him and everything, way out of line. To be clear, Kevin's not a suspect, but he does have a thing against Buchanan. His excuse was he 'just wanted to show them who's boss'—his words. Totally unprofessional, and he's on probation. Dr Haynes made me aware of what happened."

And that was that. The entire meeting lasted no longer than thirty minutes, and all involved agreed to stay in touch. Just before everyone rose to go their separate ways, Cody brought up a point that no one had mentioned. He again looked across the table at Haynes.

"Sorry to bring this up, Willie," he said. "There's plenty of 'ifs.' But *if* we're dealing with a serial killer, and *if* it all has to do with the Porter case, and *if* the photo means something, then there's two targets left: you and Miss Calhoun."

"I'm aware of that," Haynes replied soberly, "and I'm taking precautions." He paused for a moment, letting everyone wonder exactly which measures he had in mind, before deadpanning: "I've asked my wife to start my car every morning."

When everyone laughed, Murkowski jerked awake.

32.

It was a few days after the cop had tried to arrest me, and I hadn't had a therapy session since late the previous week. Dr. Haynes had canceled a few of my appointments. I'd only seen him once since he rescued me from Officer Kincaid, and that was at a special coffee club he called the next day to give everyone a chance to talk about Amy's death.

I did my share of talking, I can tell you that. No matter what April said, I still thought if I'd taken the time to stop by Amy's room more often instead of mooning over Cheryl all day, or maybe pushed her to come over to the King Richard where I could've loaded up her drinks with extra calories, she might still be alive. At the meeting, Dr. Haynes said several times that Amy's death had nothing to do with any of the other patients, and that was very kind of him, but you know me. Give me a chance to feel guilty about something and I'll grab it with both hands, like a rebound high off the rim.

Anyway, Dr. Haynes was giving me the smirk again when I walked into his office. It was my first day off the crutches.

"You're still limping," he said.

"I'll be OK." What a trooper.

I have to admit I had a new respect for Dr. Haynes, though. Mainly for the way he'd treated me after the basketball game and for the way he'd stood up to Officer Kincaid. I'd even found myself wondering about his life outside the Buchanan Institute. My friend Lenny, between swigs of diet soda one morning at breakfast, told me Dr. Haynes' wife was a model-type lady from the West Indies, that it was the second marriage for both, and that there were no kids. I didn't bother asking Lenny how he knew this stuff, but I figured it was because he spent so much time hanging around on the sofas in the front hall of the Manor. That was a pretty gossipy place.

The thing was, all Dr. Haynes wanted to talk about on this particular day was how I felt about being pushed against the wall by the guy named Scotty in the basketball game. He said that when you got right down to it, people like Scotty and Officer Kincaid were just bullies, and that to deal with them you had to stand up to them in one way or another. *Easy for him to say,* I remember thinking to myself. Dr. Haynes had more self-confidence than anyone I've ever known, and I was sure he knew how to fight. All you had to do was look at him. But he was smart enough to know that fighting should be the last resort, that nothing good comes from it most of the time, and that you should try to avoid it if you can. That kind of tough guy doesn't come along every day.

So how would anyone feel about getting pushed into a wall? That's what I told him. Sure, I'd wanted to punch out Scotty but hadn't had to face him because I'd been lying on the court and couldn't get up. By the time I came around, he was long gone, not that I was in any shape for a fight even if I'd had the guts, which I didn't.

Then Dr. Haynes asked if the experience brought back any old memories that involved sports. He must've had a sixth sense, because it brought back a ton of stuff, all of it pretty embarrassing. But I'd been in therapy long enough to know you were *supposed* to talk about stuff that makes you uncomfortable. So I told him about this thing that happened when I was eleven years old.

I'd gone out for the seventh- and eighth-grade football team at my school. They called us the bantams. There was the varsity, the junior varsity, and the bantams. Tryouts were held in the gym one afternoon at the beginning of the year, and there were about twenty-five of us. All we had to do was slam into a foam-rubber tackling dummy, one by one. That was it. After we were done, the coach, Mr. Reilly, said, "OK, I want to see Cooper and Steinberg one more time." Steinberg was even scrawnier than I was, but we both hit the thing again and the tryouts were over. Mr. Reilly looked down at a notebook he'd been scribbling on and read off the names of the boys who'd made the team. Steinberg was on the list, I wasn't.

"OK, everybody get a shower," Mr. Reilly said. "I'll see the guys whose names I called right here tomorrow at three o'clock."

The thing was, that morning, the varsity coach, Mr. Price, had brought one of the bantam football uniforms into the homerooms to show us. The jersey was light blue with white numbers, and the helmet was white with a light-blue stripe coming over the top. I don't think I'd ever wanted to wear anything or belong to something so badly in my life. Just the idea of being on a team and spending afternoons on a football field instead of trudging home and waiting for Terry to show up and punch me seemed like paradise. I couldn't bear not having it. So as the other guys were leaving the gym, I walked up to Mr. Reilly.

"Sir," I said, my voice cracking. "Could you tell me why I didn't make the team?"

He stared down at me, clearly annoyed.

"I mean, when you called me and Steinberg up?" I added.

Mr. Reilly was maybe around fifty at the time, I think. Gray hair, medium height, in good shape.

"What can I say?" He shrugged.

So, what did I do? As usual, the worst thing possible. As I searched for more words, some way to convince him to give me another chance, I started to choke up even more. Mr. Reilly shook his head in disgust and walked away.

But you won't believe what happened next: a few days later they decided to have new tryouts. We were all going outside to hit the real blocking sled, the one the varsity players used, and when I got out there I was a boy possessed. We had to run in place in groups of five in front of the sled, which had five big pads on it, and when Mr. Reilly gave the command, we slammed into it with our shoulders. WHAM! I gave it everything I had. WHAM! Again. WHAM! WHAM! WHAM! That's when the assistant coach, Mr. Fuller, yelled out to everyone, "Hey, look at Cooper! *That's* the way to do it! Cooper's the only one hitting out here! Now let's *go!*" After a few more groups of boys hit the sled, Mr. Reilly blew his whistle.

"Listen up!" he shouted. "I'll put a list on my door after lunch tomorrow! The guys on the list come back out in the afternoon! Now hit the showers!"

On the way home in the bus, I was the happiest eleven-year-old in the world. How could I not make the team when Mr. Fuller had singled me out? I didn't sleep much that night, my head full of vivid images: sprinting down the sideline, leaping up to make a circus catch, tumbling into the end zone for a touchdown, being mobbed by my fellow warriors of the gridiron.

So after lunch the next day, I hustled down to the coaches' offices. There was a yellow legal-size piece of paper taped to the door. I stared up at it and scanned. It was in alphabetical order, but the name after "Bloom" was "Davis." Maybe Mr. Reilly just couldn't spell. So I read up from the bottom. Maybe he'd just forgotten until the last minute or until Mr. Fuller reminded him of what a terror I'd been on the blocking sled. After reading up and down maybe five times, I had to face a fact: there was no "Cooper" anywhere. And it hit me then and there that if I hadn't started to choke up in front of Mr. Reilly, I would've made the team. In his eyes I wasn't man enough, at age eleven, to play bantam football.

"That's a terrible story, Coleman," said Dr. Haynes, and we let that hang in the air for a while. Finally, he spoke again. "How does all that make you feel today?"

"It feels like it happened yesterday. I'd still like to punch Mr. Reilly."

"That's understandable. Anything else like that ever happen with a coach?"

The answer was yes. So I told him about the very next fall when I was twelve. I made the bantam football team that year because I'd gotten tall for my age. Mr. Reilly had left the school, and there was a new coach, Mr. Leblanc, who didn't have anything to hold against me. He was really tall, maybe six foot six, and really strong. Sometimes we'd see him in the weight room, dinky as it was, and you wouldn't believe how much he could bench-press. The thing was, he was a pretty mean guy, maybe even meaner than Mr. Reilly. In phys-ed class we all had to line up in our gym uniforms, and when he called your name to take attendance, he'd give you this evil look all up and down to make sure your shorts and shirt were clean and that everything was just the way it should be. God help you if it wasn't. We were all shaking in our sneakers.

Anyway, one Friday afternoon we had a game against the bantam team from Spring View, just a couple of towns over, and I was playing wide receiver. We had a big, red-haired kid playing quarterback, Bo Brunson, and boy, could he throw the ball. I don't know what happened to him because his family moved away the next year, but it wouldn't surprise me if he'd been a college player when he got older. He threw it like a rocket when he was only thirteen years old.

It was the third quarter, and we were losing by three points when we ran a pass play. I was all alone on the sideline, nobody on the other team between me and the goal line about fifty yards away. Bo saw me and drilled one in my direction. He couldn't have thrown it more perfectly or any harder. So hard, in fact, that like the uncoordinated idiot I am, I didn't react in time. The ball hit me square in the chest between the two eights on my jersey and dropped to the ground, my arms grasping thin air a second too late.

There were a lot of people in the stands, mostly students and parents of the boys who were playing. Mom wasn't there because she was working, and Terry never came to stuff like that, not that I'd have wanted him to. So with all those people in the bleachers, maybe around two hundred, Mr. Leblanc came running out onto the field straight at me. He put his face about an inch away from mine, just like that crazy shrink did when I got older, and screamed, "COOPER! THAT WAS A TOUCHDOWN!" Then he stormed away. Mr. Fuller, who was still there that year, came over to me later and said, "You'll get it next time, right?" He was a pretty good guy.

"That's quite a memory you have, Coleman," said Dr. Haynes. "If it's any consolation, I've seen lots of coaches behave badly with children. They're insecure men who wanted to be athletes but never made it. So to make themselves feel better, they take their frustrations out on kids who can't defend themselves. Not the same type of guy as our Officer Kincaid, but not all that different either. If you feel good about yourself, you don't need to bully others."

I sat there like a jerk, as usual, until he said, "Well, we have to stop for today."

The thing is, just like the time with Mr. Reilly, the time with Mr. Leblanc still gets me all worked up every time I think about it. I don't go around smashing things; I just remember it clearly and hate myself for not standing up to him and shouting back. I know most twelve-year-olds don't have it in them to yell at a grown man, especially one like Mr. Leblanc, but I still can't let myself off the hook. That's another one of my problems, by the way. I can never let myself off the hook for anything.

33.

Excerpted from the book *The Maine Murders: What Really Happened in Pierrevert*

By Hayley Blossom
Originally published in the United Kingdom.

Officer Kevin Kincaid usually made his weekly visits to Sunny Singhaboon's house on Friday mornings, his only full day off. He hated to miss the opportunity to sleep in once a week, but his reward more than made up for a few lost hours in the sack.

Kincaid would show up at Sunny's back door promptly at six a.m.—about an hour before her two daughters, Lamai and Lawon, awoke—and the Thai beauty had better be waiting in her black-and-pink kimono, a garment she'd bought in her early twenties when a high-ranking Japanese military officer who'd succumbed to her charms in Bangkok flew her to Tokyo for two weeks of bliss. Kincaid discovered the robe one morning after demanding to see the contents of Sunny's closet, and liked it both for its silky, soft fabric and because he fancied himself an amateur historian on things Japanese. The bookshelves in his apartment were lined with volumes on World War II, including a couple of tomes about geishas in the 1940s. When he knocked on Sunny's door, she was to be standing just inside holding a cup of tea. She was to bow as he entered. She was to be wearing nothing underneath the kimono.

Although breakfast was part of the deal, Kincaid rarely wanted it. He usually just swilled the tea in two or three gulps, then led Sunny into the small den just off the kitchen where the sex act was consummated on a large sofa positioned in front of a television set. This was the place where Sunny spent quiet moments with her daughters, and it revolted her that Lamai and Lawon would be touching a surface upon which Kincaid's sweaty body had writhed. But the sofa was preferable to Sunny's upstairs bedroom, which adjoined the one where the girls slept. The den also had a lockable door.

Kincaid was normally out of the house a maximum of fifteen minutes after he arrived. Sunny would immediately scrub the sofa, whose fake leather surface was easy to clean with a sponge and soapy water, then return to her own bed and stare at the ceiling until she heard the girls stir. After they'd left for school, or during their summer holiday headed off on their bikes to the Pierrevert Swim Club, she'd try to fall asleep for another hour or two before doing the shopping, giving the house a once-over, and leaving for work at the King Richard Inn. Her shift started at two p.m., the hour she began prep work for that night's entrees, readying the ingredients that would later be rapidly assembled. The head chef, Leroy Little, would have already been in the kitchen for at least several hours when Sunny arrived. He often broke into song when she came in, his deep baritone bringing smiles to everyone's faces, especially hers:

> Sun-ny...
> Yes-ter-day my life
> Was filled with rain
> Sun-ny...
> You smiled at me
> And really eased the pain

Leroy had taken over the role of Sunny's unofficial protector, not that she needed one at the hotel—a place where she was liked by all. But there simply weren't many people of colour in Pierrevert, and Leroy knew how difficult that could be. Sunny was also the only female cook in the kitchen, the other women all being waitresses or hostesses. Soon after she was hired, Leroy decided to keep an eye out for anyone trying to take advantage. He flirted with her, of course, and the serenade was part of it, but Leroy flirted with all females under seventy, never crossing the line and endearing himself to one and all. In any case, everyone knew he had a longtime girlfriend up in Hargrove, although no one knew much about her. Whenever anyone asked Leroy to divulge her name, he'd reply "Battle-Ax" and change the subject. Leroy also knew that Sunny had two young girls, so he tried to let her leave work as early as he could, usually by ten thirty p.m. The girls, now fourteen and twelve, knew how to make dinner for themselves, although Sunny planned the menus and made sure everything they needed was on hand.

Kincaid was typically in a chipper, early-morning mood upon arriving. He tried to smile and be friendly, as if hoping he could transform the sexual blackmail into something truly consensual, even warm. Dare he imagine that Sunny would one day fall for him, a Stockholm syndrome scenario in which she would ultimately adore her abuser who, once she saw the light, was in fact a good and kind man who would bring her great happiness? Kincaid certainly entertained such thoughts, although Sunny did nothing to encourage them. It was her strong constitution that enabled her to carry on with day-to-day life as she searched for a way to extricate herself without putting the girls at risk. She thought Kincaid truly capable of harming them and, as a law enforcement officer, equally capable of getting away with it.

On the Friday morning after Chief Cody had teased his deputy about the possibility that he, Kincaid, had been the real target of the alleged poisoning that claimed the life of Angelo Bellino, the young officer seemed to have his usual good cheer when he arrived at Sunny's door. She opened up, bowed, and handed over his tea. He swallowed the beverage down and set the cup on the kitchen table. But instead of leading her toward the den, he suddenly stopped and stared at her threateningly. His eyes darkened. And in a lightning-fast motion that Sunny never saw, his right hand snatched her thin, graceful neck. He squeezed to the point where she could no longer breathe.

34.

O h, Coleman, how exciting!"
       That was Cheryl's reaction when I called to tell
       her about my experience with Officer Kincaid. Then
a couple of nights after we spoke, she picked me up at the
Manor and drove me over to her house for dinner. She cooked
it herself, some pretty decent spaghetti with a salad and Italian
bread on the side, which we took into the small dining room
just off the kitchen. She'd even bought a bottle of Chianti.

"What did he *say*, Coleman?" she asked as we dug into the
steaming pasta. "I want *details!*"

"He wanted to know what Dr. Bellino drank."

"Which was what?"

"Sidecars."

"Mmmm. Love those." She swilled her wine and poured
herself another glass. "What *else* did he say?"

She was really zappy that night, leaning across the table
and lasering in on me. For a change, she was dressed down:
jeans, baggy white sweater, puffy pink slippers, hair tied back
in a ponytail.

"He accused me of poisoning Dr. Bellino's drink. Which is pretty much accusing me of murder. That's when he told me to stand up. Then he handcuffed me."

"Oh my *gawd*! Kevin is *such* an asshole! He and Jason have been best friends since, like, kindergarten. Neither one's playing with a full deck."

"If my shrink hadn't come along, I would've been in jail. At least for a few hours."

The look in her eyes was something close to admiration, or at least a degree of respect for someone who'd been through something tough with the cops. I remember thinking that maybe it made up, at least a little, for my wimp's performance with the mountain man in the parking lot at Erin Go Bragh's.

So we chucked the subject of Officer Kincaid around for a few more minutes and polished off the spaghetti. Then she brought out an apple pie she'd bought in Hargrove. After we finished dessert, a big piece for me and a sliver for her, she said she had to go upstairs and find something. I tried to make myself useful by doing the dishes.

It was a good fifteen minutes before I heard heavy footsteps coming back down. I remember thinking she must have changed her shoes because the slippers she'd had on didn't make that kind of noise. The clomping came to a halt at the bottom of the stairs.

"Go into the living room!" she shouted. "I have a surprise for you!"

I dried my hands on some paper towels and walked back through the dining room into the small salon they had. There was a couch, a couple of easy chairs, and a fireplace that had a smoldering log in it. A dim lamp was lit, but otherwise the room was dark.

"Sit on the sofa! Close your eyes!"

I followed orders and got settled, then caught a strong whiff of perfume as she passed by. It sounded like she was positioning herself in front of the fireplace.

"Open!"

The top piece of lingerie she was wearing was lacy and dark brown with white trim, stopping just shy of her belly button. There's probably a name for it, but I still don't know what it is. Even I knew real stockings when I saw them, though, and hers were attached to a little belt by clasps and thin strips of cloth. The bikini panties matched the top, of course, and that's all she had on except for a pair of red heels that were so high I wondered how she kept from tipping over.

But the outfit wasn't the only reward for the fearless barkeep who'd kept his cool against gestapo-like tactics from one of Pierrevert's men in blue, far from it. Because just in case I was tired of the same old Swedish goddess that was Cheryl Beringer, she'd transformed herself into a different animal, no less ravishing but of a new style entirely.

She was a brunette.

The wig looked completely natural and gave her flowing chestnut locks that touched the tops of her bare shoulders. Her fingernail polish and freshly applied lipstick matched the color of the shoes. One thing I can say for Cheryl: she was a perfectionist.

"Here's your real dessert, Coleman," she said softly. "Black Forest cake."

I know I've told you some stupid stuff before, but this one might be the kicker. Because looking at Cheryl dressed as she was, a fantasy in the flesh, beautiful eyes beckoning, mine for the taking, I didn't feel in the least aroused. Instead, I suddenly felt a deep sadness, one I thought might make my own eyes mist up right then and there if I wasn't careful. It was going to hurt badly enough the day she decided she'd had enough of me. All this just made it worse.

She sauntered slowly over to the couch, sat on my lap, and put her arms around my neck. With her touch, the perfume, and the feel of the lacy garment, my body couldn't help but respond. But go figure: only someone like me could be with someone like her in a situation like that and wish he were anywhere else in the world.

35.

Excerpted from the book *The Maine Murders: What Really Happened in Pierrevert*

By Hayley Blossom
Originally published in the United Kingdom.

"Where is it!" Kincaid shouted, not releasing his grip on Sunny's throat. "Where the fuck is it!"

When he relaxed his hold a few seconds later, Sunny began to cough violently. Her intake of air was a frantic choking sound, not unlike the noise Angelo Bellino made when he stood up from the dinner table at the King Richard Inn just before he died. Sunny bent over forward, placing her hands on her knees as she struggled for oxygen. She thought she might faint.

"What is *wrong* with you!" she cried when she had enough air. "What are you *talking* about! I did not do *anything*!"

"Where do you keep it?" Kincaid seethed, grabbing her by the arms and pulling her upright. "In the medicine cabinet? Under your bed?"

Sunny had been through physical confrontations with customers as a younger woman. She knew how to defend herself to a point. But she was used to dealing with men who'd had too much to drink, whose coordination was off, who could be handled with a swift kick in the groin or a loud shriek that would bring a bouncer—always present in the hotels that catered to her trade—to the door in no time. But Kevin Kincaid, in his present state, possessed by a fury that had turned his face a mild shade of crimson, was not this type of man. Sunny was not close to being a match for him, and there was no bouncer to come to her rescue.

Kincaid dragged her across the kitchen floor into a small hallway, then up the staircase toward the bedroom where Lamai and Lawon might or might not still be sleeping.

"I did not do *anything*, I did not do *anything!*" Sunny screamed, kicking and struggling to free herself.

At the top of the stairs, Kincaid yanked her to the left into a bathroom he had used once or twice when the girls were sleeping at a friend's house or on a school trip.

"Where is it!" he yelled, flinging open a cabinet above the sink where toiletries and plastic prescription containers were lined up on thin glass shelves. Still clutching Sunny with one arm, he swept the entire contents of the cabinet onto the floor. Several glass bottles of perfume shattered on the bathroom tiles.

"Where is *what*? Where is *what*?" Sunny shouted back.

"The fucking *poison*, you little cunt! You think I was born yesterday?"

"I did not do *anything!*"

At that moment Lamai and Lawon peered around the corner into the bathroom, one head above the other, the frilly collars of their flannel pajamas unbuttoned. Sunny screamed something in Thai, and they tore down the stairs at top speed.

Not a stupid man, even if in his frenzy he thought a medicine cabinet would be a logical place for a woman with two adolescent children to store a lethal poison, Kincaid knew he couldn't let the girls out of the house. He let Sunny go and dashed down the stairs, taking them two at a time. He found the girls cowering in a corner of the kitchen next to the fridge, Lamai's hands trembling as she tried to dial a number on the rotary telephone that hung from the wall. Sunny arrived a second or two later, her right foot trailing blood from a piece of glass she'd stepped on in the bathroom. Her face was that of a wild animal trying to protect her cubs.

"Give me the fucking phone!" Kincaid screamed at Lamai, ripping the receiver from her grip and slamming it back onto the hook. Standing between Sunny and the girls, he looked back and forth at them. His heavy breathing seemed to slow down. Perhaps twenty silent seconds went by.

"I did not do *anything!*" Sunny pleaded again.

Something inside Kincaid suddenly clicked. Not the type of individual given to epiphany, it nonetheless struck him that his paranoia about Sunny trying to poison him from the King Richard Inn kitchen—an idea that had gathered steam since the day Chief Cody put it into his head through some innocent joking around—was nonsense. The deputy also realized that the situation he was in was untenable. Two minors had seen him assaulting their mother, and they were feeling physically threatened themselves. Should any of these events ever come to light, well . . .

"Girls," he said calmly to Lamai and Lawon. "I'm sorry for what just happened. Things got out of hand. You have nothing to worry about. Your mother will explain later. I have to go now. So why don't you both skedaddle back upstairs?"

The girls looked at Sunny, who had grabbed a dish towel and begun to clean the blood off her foot. She nodded, and off they went. As soon as they were out of earshot, Kincaid grabbed Sunny's throat again. As with the last time, she never saw it coming.

"Say anything to anyone, you don't want to *think* about what will happen!" he said, his wild eyes bearing down upon her. "I'll be back next Friday. We're gonna *forget* this!"

Sunny tried to nod, and he released her neck. She started rubbing it immediately, to ease the pain. He slammed the back door as he left.

36.

I was so nervous that my hands were shaking. It was Skip's fault because he'd set it up this way. He'd dimmed the lights in his living room, and there was one bright spotlight on the piano.

"You're on a concert stage," he said. "Hundreds of people in the audience awaiting the first move of your hands. The program is in everyone's lap. 'Coleman Cooper, in Concert.' First piece, Prelude number two by George Gershwin, in C-sharp minor. Take a deep breath."

As always, I did as I was told.

"Lower your hands to the keyboard and listen to the total silence. Now begin."

I took another breath and started in on Gershwin's second prelude. It starts with a minor tenth in the left hand, C-sharp up to E in the next octave, and with my big basketball-palming mitts, I could reach that pretty easily. A few minutes later, I pulled my hands up. The penultimate note, the stray B-natural, is my favorite, and I gave it kind of a flourish—at least as much as you can with a single note.

Skip stood and started clapping.

"You *nailed* it, man! Now things are gonna get interesting, 'cause if you can play the second prelude, you can play the first, which is harder but a lot more fun. It's a dazzler. Let me in there for a second."

That's what Skip always said when he wanted me to get up from the piano bench so he could sit down and play. He always looked like he couldn't wait to get in there.

"Here we go," he said, as I stood looking over his shoulder. "Gershwin's first prelude."

The piece starts out with five idle notes. Then another five, like a response. Then *POW*, it takes off like a house afire with heavy bass notes and chords that answer them. The melody and harmonies are so quirky that you know right away it's Gershwin even if no one tells you. At one point the left hand has to cross over the right, as if I could ever do that, and the whole thing ends with a big bang.

When Skip was done he looked up and said, "Whaddya think?"

I burst out laughing, something I do about once a year. He knew what I meant.

"Well, I think you can," he said. "Next lesson we'll take it four measures at a time." He got up and turned on a couple of lamps, then parked himself back on the couch. "Up go the house lights," he said. "And the crowd files out." He looked around the room as if he were mulling something over. "Once you get the first prelude under your belt, we're gonna shift gears and do some jazz improvisation," he said. "I think it's time for you to set a goal."

"Like what?"

"Learning five standards. Hey, you want a beer?"

"Sure."

"They're in the fridge."

I got the beers and joined him on the couch.

"Right," he said. "Five standards. Got any ideas?"

As usual, when put on the spot, my mind went blank. Lucky for me, Skip knew my clueless look well enough to recognize it. "Want some suggestions?"

"Sure."

"You need some bebop. There's a Charlie Parker thing called 'Billie's Bounce.' Twelve-bar blues in F. Tons of tunes fit right into it: 'Au Privave,' also by Parker, 'Straight, No Chaser' by Thelonious Monk. And you need a Latin tune, something by Jobim. Ever hear of Antônio Carlos Jobim?"

"Of course," I said, having never heard the name in my life.

"You don't want 'Girl from Ipanema' or 'Corcovado.' Everybody does those."

He jumped up, got back behind the piano, and started in on something that sounded slightly out of tune.

"It's called 'Desafinado,'" he said. "Not for toddlers, but you're not a toddler anymore."

Oh yes I am, I thought. He stopped playing after about a minute.

"You could use a swing tune, something from the thirties or forties. How 'bout 'Take the A Train'? Billy Strayhorn, same guy who wrote 'Lush Life.' Ellington made it famous. Listen."

He played a few bars with a walking bass in his left hand and the melody in his right. Then he stopped again. "And you need a ballad. Problem is, there's too many to choose from. How 'bout this?" He started to play again, a warm, slow piece. "It's called 'Skylark.' Hoagy Carmichael. Like it?"

"Sure."

"So, how many is that?"

"Four."

"And you're already working on 'But Not for Me,' so that makes five. See if you can repeat 'em."

I surprised myself by remembering them all.

"'Billie's Bounce,' 'Desafinado,' 'Take the A Train,' 'Skylark,' 'But Not for Me.'"

"Son," he said, putting on a grandfatherly tone, "that's as fine a boot camp for a young jazzman as I've ever heard."

I laughed again, God bless him, and took a swig of beer. That's when I noticed a worn-looking copy of *The Northeast Telegram* sitting on his coffee table. There was a big headline that said "Where the Murdered Met" and a photo that looked like it'd been taken in a courtroom. The thing was, Dr. Haynes was in the photo. It wasn't the first time I'd seen that edition of the paper because there were a few copies floating around the front hall at the Manor. I'd already read the article. It'd been on everyone's mind, and they'd even had a special coffee club after dinner one night right after it came out to give the patients a chance to talk about it. Dr. Haynes was there and said it was all speculation and that everyone should just chill, which was pretty much the same thing he'd told me in one of our sessions. The article had mentioned Pearleen Porter, Skip's friend who died.

When Skip saw me eyeing the paper on the table, he spoke right up.

"It's OK, man," he said. "We can talk about it. I read it. Don't know if all the craziness in town has to do with Pearleen, though. She was just a girl with a sweet disposition and a lot of talent. She needed training, but if she'd lived long enough to get it, she'd have gone places. What can you do?"

He went into a little blues riff on the piano, just messing around.

"Cody came to talk to me about the doc who died at the King Richard," he said.

"Me too," I said, because Chief Cody had come around a few days after Kincaid to ask me some questions. I told him pretty much the same stuff I'd told his deputy, but he didn't try to arrest me. Instead, he said, "Thanks a lot," and apologized for Kincaid's behavior.

"I figured but didn't wanna ask," Skip said. "They're just fishin' but they have to. I've known Chief Cody a long time, always thought he was a good guy."

He got up from the piano, picked up the newspaper, and scanned the front page.

"Who knows why things happen, man? All I know is she's gone and shouldn't be."

37.

I could never bring myself to call Mrs. Sorensen "Queen Trish" behind her back like everyone else did. She'd been so nice to me that it felt a little disrespectful. Plus she had such a classy air about her: that straight brown hair, combed and arranged with not a strand out of place, the fine clothes that fit her tall, slim frame so well. Even her voice always seemed sure of itself.

Anyway, not all that long after Dr. Bellino died, maybe around mid-September, she started calling down to the tavern a few times a week at about five o'clock, before we got busy, to ask me to bring a snifter of Grand Marnier up to her apartment. I'd always hop to and bring it right up on a small, round bar tray, maybe playing out a little film noir once I got into the elevator. Some shady character in a raincoat and fedora *had* to be waiting to knife me on the fourth-floor landing. I'd give him a swift jab to the jaw and watch him crumple to the floor, all without spilling one drop of the drink.

The thing was, even though Mrs. Sorensen knew I had to get back to the tavern after I delivered her Grand Marnier, she'd always ask me to sit and chat for a few minutes. Half the time it seemed like she'd already had a drink or two by the time I got there. She'd slur her words a little and bounce from one subject to the next. She'd even ask about where I grew up and what my childhood was like and if I was still in touch with my parents, stuff like that. She wanted to know how I ended up at Buchanan, and I pretty much told her the story, leaving out the part about my wrists. Lucky for me, the scars had healed really well, and you had to look closely to see them. I guess I have that doctor who said he'd played football at Princeton to thank for that.

To be honest, Mrs. Sorensen seemed pretty lonely and depressed half the time. Maybe I'd feel the same way if I'd thrown a fancy dinner and somebody died at it, especially with everyone watching and all. Then one evening, when she was sipping her Grand Marnier and we were chatting away about this and that, she said out of the blue that Mrs. O'Brien of Erin Go Bragh's had called asking about me.

"She'd like you to fill in over there behind the bar from time to time—if you're interested, that is. We're old friends, and she didn't want to contact you without asking me first. I told her we had first claim but what you did on your nights off was your business."

Nobody'd ever wanted first claim on me for anything. I was always last claim if I got claimed at all.

"I think it would be good for you, maybe a night here and there," she said. "Give you a type of experience you don't have. There are lessons to be learned from dealing with that sort of clientele."

"Thank you, Mrs. Sorensen," I said as she scrawled Mrs. O'Brien's phone number on a piece of King Richard stationery.

And a few nights later on a Monday, a day off from the hotel, I found myself behind the bar at Bra's. I had to hitch-hike to get out there, and Erin's son, Seamus, showed me the ropes—like where the booze closet was in the basement, where the key to it was hidden on a hook underneath the bar sink, and how to work the register. He was a big, husky guy but friendly enough. Monday was always a slow night, he said, and he left at around ten o'clock, promising to be back before one to help me close up. I was pretty jumpy, even for me, when I watched him walk out the door. What if the mountain man showed up? Bra's was a pretty rough place anyway. I'd told Cheryl I'd be there, but she said she was going to the movies in Hargrove with her housemates. Only one person I knew came in the whole night, and I didn't see him at first because my head was down in the beer cooler. I just heard him.

"Oh my *God!*" said Fontaine, leaning on the bar and giving me his thousand-watt smile as I straightened up. "What *do* we have *here?*" Then, under his breath, "You know how many girls bartenders get, man? More than *I* get, that for *damn* sure! How'd you *get* this gig? Inquiring minds wanna *know!*"

So I told him the story, and he seemed pretty impressed that Mrs. O'Brien, who by the way was nowhere in sight, had asked Mrs. Sorensen about me.

"Your status in life be risin', man," he said. "I don't know nobody ever tend bar at King Richard *and* Bra's! Do me a favor, get me a beer 'fore your head get too big."

Bottle in hand, which I didn't let him pay for, Fontaine took up his perch on the jukebox, occasionally shooting me a nod that I should check out this or that girl on the dance floor.

By midnight he'd left, and there were maybe twenty people in the whole place. That's when I noticed that most of the bottles in the speed rack were nearly empty. So I thought I'd show what a diligent worker I was by bringing up fresh stocks from the liquor closet in the basement. That way, whoever worked the afternoon shift the next day wouldn't have to do it.

I snatched the key from underneath the sink, told my bar customers I'd be right back, and dashed down the rickety staircase. There had to be rats lurking around down there, and my nose sensed an off-odor that I couldn't place. Plus it was one thing being there with Seamus for a few minutes earlier that night, and another being there all alone with the jukebox blaring upstairs. I've always been scared of basements, like I'm scared of lots of things, and the place seemed ten times darker and danker than it had before.

Anyway, quickly as I could, I unlocked the liquor closet and piled two quart bottles each of the house vodka, gin, scotch, and bourbon into a cardboard box that was lying on the floor. I was back at the foot of the stairs in less than two minutes, and that's when something caught my eye: a door on the other side of the basement that was open just a crack. There was a dim light inside and a few wisps of smoke wafting out. I froze for a moment, holding the heavy box and trying to decide whether to look in. Was the place on fire? Typical me, I figured if I *didn't* check and anything bad happened, it would be my fault. So I put the box down and crept a little closer to the door, the off-odor getting more pungent with every step. It suddenly hit me that the aroma was cannabis, and I should have taken that as a sign to turn the hell around and get back upstairs. Instead, idiot that I am, I inched right up to the door and peered in.

I couldn't see the whole room, but it was a makeshift office. There was a beat-up desk with a small lamp that gave off a little bit of light, an old swivel chair, and shelves on the wall stacked with papers and manila folders. There were some framed black-and-white photographs on the shelves that looked like old family shots, and one of them stood out. I had to squint, but it looked like Erin standing next to Mrs. Sorensen in front of a castle. They both looked a lot younger, at least by twenty years, maybe more. Erin was smiling, and Mrs. Sorensen looked kind of sad. I could see she'd been heavier back then. And that's when I stupidly nudged the door open a few more inches so I could see the other side of the room.

What I saw was a big, grungy-looking sofa pushed up against one wall. Splayed across it at a very odd angle was Erin O'Brien, wearing a pair of wrinkled plaid slacks and a heavy white sweater. A half-eaten sandwich that looked like peanut butter and jelly lay on her chest. There was an ashtray full of cigarette butts on the floor, and perched in one of its crevasses was a smoldering joint. Next to that, lying on its side, was an empty bottle of Old Chaffinch. Erin's eyes were closed, but her mouth was open, and she was breathing heavily. As if on cue because she now had an audience, she started to snore. I hadn't had time to stare for very long when I heard a voice shouting from upstairs.

"Where the *fuck's* the barkeep!"

A typical Bra's comment. But I'm grateful to the guy who yelled because he broke my trance and got me back upstairs with the box of bottles in a hurry.

"Sorry, sorry!" I said, panting for breath, to several pissed-off-looking customers. "Had to get some stock."

At that moment Seamus barreled in through the front door. He glanced at me, nodded, and headed straight for the staircase that led to the basement. I figured what he'd find down there was nothing he hadn't seen before.

.

38.

Excerpted from the book *The Maine Murders: What Really Happened in Pierrevert*

By Hayley Blossom
Originally published in the United Kingdom.

Kevin Kincaid eased his car into the brush just outside Sunny Singhaboon's house, looking in all directions to make sure he had not been observed. As usual, there was not a soul in sight.

Sunny's isolated little street was deserted all day, save for the occasional comings and goings of two other families that lived nearby. None of the neighbours could see each other's dwellings from their own, so the only visual contact was typically a polite wave whenever two cars happened to cross paths on the narrow dirt road. A childless pair in their fifties lived in one of the houses, a young couple with two toddlers in the other. In any event, Kincaid's traditional six a.m. hour of arrival was usually too early for anyone except Sunny to be stirring. And stirring she was on this particular morning, specifically the cup of tea she had just prepared for Kincaid. As required, she wore her black-and-pink kimono. Nothing could appear out of the ordinary when the officer softly tapped on the door.

It had been exactly one week since Sunny last saw Kincaid—the day he'd choked her and threatened untold mayhem if any hint of his sexual blackmail were ever to see the light of day. Since the moment he'd slammed the door to her kitchen and departed in a fury, Sunny had scarcely slept a wink. Whenever she might drift off, she would invariably jerk awake, haunted by nightmares.

In one dream that recurred, Kincaid was grabbing the girls and tossing them down the staircase in her house. In another, she was back at Wonderwomen, not on display but as a seated spectator. On the stage amongst the bevy of Asian beauties gyrating to the thump-thump-thumping disco music were Lamai and Lawon themselves, scantily clad. A few tables in front of her, wearing his Pierrevert police uniform, was Kincaid, smoking a cigar and swilling a cocktail from a tall glass that had hunks of exotic fruit hanging over the rim. He was staring at the girls and giggling. He laughed and laughed until, at one point, he stood up and began to rotate his pelvis to the music. Then he reached for his belt and started to unbuckle it. He unzipped his trousers with one hand and reached in with the other. That's when Sunny would jolt awake.

After nearly a week of such ghastly fare, Sunny's sense of self-preservation finally kicked in. She had taken many risks in her life, and it was time to take one more. The difference was that, in the past, she had put only herself in jeopardy. This time it was the girls too. But she knew she had to do something or lose her mind. If that happened, Lamai and Lawon would go down with her.

That Friday morning, Kincaid knocked lightly on the door and Sunny opened up. He gave her an ingratiating smile. She primly returned it, handing over his cup of steaming tea.

"Could we sit down for a second?" he said.

They both took a chair at the kitchen table and stared at each other. Kincaid's eyes couldn't help wandering toward Sunny's bare ankles, lovely little feet, and turquoise-painted toenails. His mind flashed with vivid images of the soft paradise that awaited him once again. He had no way of knowing that, on this particular day, Sunny was wearing flannel pajamas underneath the kimono, an egregious violation of their rules of engagement.

"I just want to say I'm sorry about last week," Kincaid said. "Let's forget about it, OK?"

After a thoughtful pause, Sunny resolutely said, "No, I will not do that."

"Look, I'm *apologizing*," Kincaid said, his blood pressure instantly rising. "What do you want from me? I'm *sorry*. We're just gonna put this thing behind us and go on like before. Understand?"

"No, I do not understand," said Sunny evenly.

With the second rebuke, Kincaid extended his right arm across the table and pointed a finger into her face from an inch away. "Listen, you little bitch," he said, seething. "*I'm* the one calling the shots here."

Swilling the tea and slamming the cup down, Kincaid rose and took a step over to Sunny's side of the table. He grabbed her from behind, under the armpits, and yanked her out of the chair toward the TV room. What he did not see, because he was facing the wrong direction, was the person who stepped into the kitchen from that small den, blocking his path. He felt sudden contact and whirled around, releasing his grip on Sunny. What he saw was a large Black man wearing work boots, checkered trousers, and a black leather jacket. The man was holding a meat cleaver in one hand and staring directly into Kincaid's eyes.

"You ever touch this girl again," said the deep voice of Leroy Little, "I gonna cut your balls off one by one. Don't matter what happen to me. That what gonna happen to you."

"What are *you* doing here, you fat asshole!" Kincaid shouted. "You're under arrest! Threatening a police officer!"

"I jus' called your boss," Little said calmly. "Soon's he hear the message, he gonna come lookin' for *you*, not me."

"You *what!*" Kincaid screamed.

"I was you," Little said with controlled, quiet menace, "I'd get outta here 'fore I get mad."

Kincaid, who was not carrying his service revolver, stared at Little. Then he turned toward Sunny. A few silent seconds passed by.

"*FUUUUCCCCKKKK!*" Kincaid yelled at the top of his lungs, stretching the syllable into a wailing lament that reminded Sunny of a wild animal—the kind she'd seen as a child in the Thai countryside—cornered by predators. Kincaid dashed out the back door as fast as he had ever moved in his life, jumped into his car, revved the engine, threw it into gear, and rumbled out of the little nest of trees. Clumps of mud flew through the air in his wake.

It was barely six fifteen, and very few cars were on the road that led directly into Pierrevert. Chief Cody's usual arrival time at their office, located in a small building across the street from Town Hall, was six thirty. Kincaid calculated seven minutes to get there if he averaged sixty miles per hour on the curvy route that had a posted speed limit of thirty-five.

All he had to do, according to his frantic reasoning, was arrive before Cody and erase the phone message. Then he'd think of a way out. It would be her word against his on consent, nearly impossible to prove when you got right down to it. And who'd believe a little foreign slut in the first place? He, Kevin Kincaid, was Pierrevert born and raised, a pillar of the community in a powder-blue shirt and navy trousers with a yellow stripe down the side.

The closer he got to the station house, the better he felt. There was no need to worry. Cody would surely back him up after all they'd been through together on the mean streets of Maine. Maybe he shouldn't have flown off the handle with the cook, but that fucking moron had threatened him. A meat cleaver! He didn't have to lie one bit there.

Kincaid careened onto Main Street and sped by the King Richard Inn, braking hard when Town Hall came into view on the right-hand side. His watch said 6:24, and the sun had barely started to come up. The streetlights wouldn't cut off for another six minutes. The station house should be dark and deserted.

But the panic that had fled Kincaid's nervous system came whizzing back when he saw the lights on in the small police office. The chief's yellow-and-white 1962 Thunderbird convertible, Cody's one indulgence, the one expression of style he allowed himself in his otherwise just-the-facts life, sat quietly in its parking space. How many times had Kincaid coveted that car? If he'd been cruising around in such a sleek machine instead of his little Volvo, he'd have had more birds than he could handle. He'd have been fighting them off with his nightstick.

After skidding for a few yards, Kincaid pulled over to the side of the road and sat thinking. It occurred to him that the morning would slowly get brighter, traffic would pick up, and everyone passing by on their way to work would wonder the same thing: *Why the hell's Kincaid sitting in his own piece-a-junk car outside the station house?* Didn't need that on top of everything else.

Five minutes went by. Ten. Then fifteen. Finally, Kincaid pulled back onto Main Street and headed out of town. It took him half an hour to reach the interstate highway, and he drove northward. Within a few hours he would be in Canada. Could they come get him there? He wasn't sure.

By the time Kincaid was only a few minutes out of Pierrevert, Chief Cody had listened to Leroy Little's telephone message four times. Little had not slept a wink the previous night after Sunny had knocked on the door of his small office behind the hotel kitchen at about ten thirty. She'd dissolved into tears and poured out her story in a torrent. Little had listened quietly and told her not to worry. He'd follow her home and watch her go in the back door. He'd be back the next morning at five thirty to await Kincaid, making sure to park his car down the road and out of sight. Little had been so agitated leaving the message, which he'd done from his home around two a.m., that some of the words were difficult to make out. But Cody got it all eventually. And although the chief still felt a degree of loyalty toward the young hothead he had brought on to the police force—despite Kincaid's over-the-top behaviour with the young bartender from the Buchanan Institute— he knew Kincaid was capable of the acts Little described. In his gut, he believed every word of the message.

After sitting quietly with a second cup of coffee, Cody finally rose from his chair, donned his shiny police jacket and cap, and drove up the road to the King Richard Inn. Little was in his office behind the kitchen by then, having spent a few more minutes at Sunny's house following Kincaid's hasty departure to reassure her that everything would be fine.

"I been expectin' you, Chief," Little said when Cody appeared at his door. "Cream, no sugar, right?"

Ninety minutes later, Cody appeared outside another door: Sunny Singhaboon's. He tipped his cap as she let him into the kitchen, where they spoke for over an hour— seated at the same table that had hosted Kincaid earlier that morning. The chief took notes on a yellow legal pad he had brought along.

What Sunny had to say generated a range of emotions in Cody: anger, disgust, and deep empathy for her. Sunny surprised him by saying she did not want to press charges. She had no intention of becoming a public sexual-extortion victim, the center of a spectacle that would be covered in lurid detail by the local paper. She just wanted Cody to know what kind of person Kincaid really was. The chief figured he could live with that if she could, and admitted to himself that her wishes would save the town a great deal of embarrassment.

What he could not live with was the idea of Kincaid getting off scot-free with no punishment for his deeds. So he promised Sunny on the spot that he would fire Kincaid from the force. He said he would give Kincaid an ultimatum: if the deputy ever initiated any investigation of Sunny's immigration status, he would find a way to nail him without bringing her into it. Kincaid had other skeletons to hide, and Cody knew the whereabouts of them all. That would be the deal.

Cody also knew Kincaid well enough to assume he'd done a runner and was already at least a hundred miles from Pierrevert as he and Sunny spoke. But the deputy would eventually touch base with someone, and that someone would be his wingman and drinking buddy, Jason Mason, whom Cody called as soon as he got back to the station house later that morning. "Tell Kincaid to stop hiding and come back home," he told Mason. "Tell him he's not going to jail, at least not yet, and he's lucky as hell for that. But he'd better come back. Now."

Kincaid showed up at the station house two days later, looking and smelling like he'd been on a weeklong bender. His expulsion from the force was short and sweet. He tried the her-word-against-mine argument, but the chief wasn't buying. Kincaid would receive unemployment benefits for three months, and that would be that. Cody's advice to Kincaid was to move far away from Pierrevert and get a new start. There would be no job references coming from the town, but Kincaid had an associate's degree and could always go back to school. "Use the experience to turn over a new leaf and become a different type of person," the chief said. "And don't ever, ever contact Sunny Singhaboon again or speak of her to immigration people."

"You brought this all on yourself, Kevin" were Cody's parting words. "Now get out of here and do something positive with your life."

Kincaid slunk outside and got into his car. He drove straight to the Pierrevert Wine Cellar on Acorn Street, where he bought two half gallons of scotch whiskey, a six-pack of club soda, and four family-size bags of pretzels. The clerk on duty would later say he remembered the purchase clearly. Kincaid had paid in cash and carried everything outside in a cardboard box the clerk provided.

Once back in his apartment on Cheshire Street, Kincaid mixed himself a stiff scotch and soda and emptied one of the pretzel bags into a large bowl. He'd just turned on his television and tuned in a soap opera when Ada Marsh, his eighty-year-old landlady who lived next door, showed up to collect the monthly rent. She found him sitting on the floor surrounded by three jagged knives and a rifle. Just sharpening the blades and cleaning the gun for a hunting trip, he explained. He offered her a drink, which she declined, and wrote out a check for the rent.

"Deer herd needs thinning," he said as he showed her out the door. "At least that's what the state wildlife guys are saying. Weather's supposed to be great!"

He gave her a boyish smile, she later recalled, that would have warmed any grandmother's heart.

39.

My friend Hayley, the newspaper reporter, had been coming into the tavern for a Beefeater and tonic or two almost every night. She always said the way I mixed them was either "smashing" or "cracking" or "spot on." Any ten-year-old can make a good gin and tonic, but I'll take a compliment whenever I can get one because people are always getting mad at bartenders. Believe me, things can get pretty nerve racking in a place like the King Richard, especially if you're the anxious type like me.

The thing is, first, you have to fill orders for about ten waitresses who run around trying to keep their tables happy. Then you have to deal with a bunch of guys on barstools who snap their fingers and shout things like "Hey, barkeep!" And when things pick up, you can get sloppy. You try to mix too many drinks at once, grabbing bottles and pouring with both hands, which means you start making mistakes. Then maybe a diner will send a drink back, which means the waitress will glare at you, and not just because the customer isn't happy and might give her a lousy tip but because it takes her time to deal with the problem. With four or five tables going, she has to walk all the way back to the bar, tell you what's wrong with the drink, then come back a couple of minutes later to get the new drink and take it back to the table. Meanwhile, the dinners for one of her other tables are sitting on the chef's line getting cold, and by the time she picks them up and delivers the plates, *those* customers send them back because the dinners aren't hot enough. Which means she has to carry the big tray all the way back to the kitchen. Then the chefs glare at *her* because she should've picked the dinners up sooner, and *they* have to take time to reheat everything, which makes them late on forty other things they're cooking. And the whole thing started because *you* messed up a drink. Sometimes I wonder why more bartenders don't end up in places like the Buchanan Institute.

Anyway, I thought Hayley's praise about my drinks was just her way of being nice to a loser. But then I started wondering if she had another reason, because she kept pressing me on what my barstool customers were saying about the stuff going on in town. Topic number one was why Officer Kincaid had gotten canned from the police force. Everyone knew it'd happened, but nobody knew why. I'd heard that Chief Cody was saying Kincaid had just decided to move on, but he might as well have said Kincaid was running for governor. That's how much anyone believed him. The only new career Kincaid had was getting hammered every night at Bra's. At least that's what I was hearing at the tavern, especially late at night when it was just the hard-core drinkers. People were saying he'd gone from being a cop everyone was afraid of to being a drunk everyone laughed at, pretty much overnight. They also said he was putting on a lot of weight, really ballooning up. The gist of it was the whole town could see what was happening to Kincaid, but he'd been such an arrogant guy that nobody cared.

Except for Hayley, that is. *She* cared. And not because she was any fan of Kincaid's but because she figured there was a juicy story behind the scenes. She finally got around to admitting it one night at the tavern as she sipped one of my cracking Beefeater and tonics and scarfed down a big basket of Leroy's potato chips, the ones he made for the hotel bars a few times a week.

"Coleman," she said, giving one of the chips a good crunch, "this business about the copper is a load of rubbish. I mean, bloody hell, he's done something the town wants hushed up. You don't have to be blinkin' Sherlock Holmes. God, these crisps are *to die for.*"

"People are talking about it, sure."

If there'd ever been a moment to tell Hayley about my own run-in with Kincaid, that would've been it. I kept quiet, though. The last thing I wanted was to be some sort of background for one of her articles.

"And?"

I think she was on her second or maybe even third highball that night, and I always made them pretty stiff. They didn't make us measure out the booze at the King Richard or Bra's, like they had at the steakhouse I'd worked at before, and I always believed in being pretty generous with the alcohol. You didn't have to be a genius to know that stronger drinks meant better tips. Still, you couldn't go too far, especially at the hotel. The last thing I needed was Mr. Simons giving me the evil eye for overpouring. He'd left me pretty much alone since the night Dr. Bellino died, and I wasn't sure why. Maybe he'd found out Mrs. Sorensen had taken a liking to me.

"I've heard a few people say he deserves whatever's going on with him," I said. "I don't think he's the most popular guy in town." I didn't feel too sorry for Kincaid either, to be honest.

"Coleman, I'd be *ever so grateful* if you'd fill me in on things you hear."

Hayley could be kind of flirty when she wanted something, especially with that British accent of hers. I half expected her to wink at me and say, "I'll make it worth your while." She didn't, though.

"It's just that your work puts you in a rather"—it came out like *rah-thuh*—"privileged position for gossip. Somebody's got to know what happened, and I'm going to suss it out. I'm not as daft"—*dahft*—"as I look."

40.

I hadn't played basketball since the night I'd gotten pushed against the wall and Dr. Haynes helped me back to the BI. He'd asked a couple of times in our sessions why I hadn't been back, and I'd told him the truth: I was afraid of running into Scotty again. I'd be too scared to say anything about the last time and would look like a wimp in front of the other guys. Like any shrink, Dr. Haynes gave me the standard rap about having to face your fears, you can't run away, blah, blah, blah. How many thousand times had I heard *that* one over the years?

"If you *want* to play and you *don't* because of him, then he wins, hands down," Dr. Haynes said.

"Maybe I just don't want to play."

"I think maybe you do."

He was right. I *did* want to play. But I wasn't going to tell him that. Maybe there was hope for me yet.

"Just go and hold your ground," he said. "Watch out for him. I don't think he'll try anything again. If he does, stand up for yourself."

That's when I started to get annoyed.

"He can beat me up and I know it! *You* know it!"

"I'm not suggesting you challenge him to a fight. How else could you defend yourself?"

"What am I supposed to say? 'Scotty, will you please stop slamming me against walls?'"

"Let me give you a sentence," Dr. Haynes said. His voice changed into an aggressive tone. "Why don't you play fair, Scotty?"

I knew this routine. I was supposed to repeat what he said. I always felt stupid doing it but knew I couldn't refuse.

"Why don't you play fair, Scotty," I said, sounding like a little kid on a playground who knows he's about to get his ass kicked.

"Come on, Coleman, put some mustard on it. You can do better than that."

So I gave it another try, adding some mustard.

"WHY DON'T YOU PLAY FAIR, SCOTTY? THEN YOU WOULDN'T HAVE TO DO COWARDLY THINGS!"

I felt like the class nerd with three-inch-thick glasses and a pocket protector trying to stand up to a bully. Dr. Haynes didn't see it that way.

"Yes!" he said. "That's *exactly* the type of thing you say! Because pushing someone from behind when they're not looking is as cowardly as it gets. You want to make Scotty feel stupid."

"Maybe he feels stupid and beats me up anyway."

"Anyone can lose a fight. You'll feel better if you say what you feel."

So two nights later, on a rare Friday when I wasn't working, there I was at the town gym again. And who should come banging through the gym doors after everyone had been shooting around for about ten minutes but Scotty. I decided to ignore him, or at least try to. Next through the double doors was Dr. Haynes.

"Hi, Coleman," he said, ambling right over to me. He was with another Black man who looked about his age. The guy looked familiar. "I'd like you to meet a friend of mine. This is Homer."

"Hey, Willie, I know this fellow," the guy said. "Tends bar at the King Richard, right?"

That's when I recognized him. He'd been one of my bar customers in the tavern the night Dr. Bellino died. We'd talked about music.

"Good to see you again, Coleman."

"Same here."

Homer looked just as good in gym shorts and a T-shirt as Dr. Haynes, even a bit more muscular. I remember thinking they'd better be on different teams or everyone else might as well forget it. And you won't believe who came through the doors next: ex-Officer Kincaid. He was dressed in sweatpants, sneakers, and a sweatshirt, so it was pretty obvious he'd come to play. He didn't look very athletic, though, and you could tell he was working on a major beer gut. He stared hard at me, and I froze. Then I remembered Dr. Haynes was there and exhaled. He gave Dr. Haynes a worse stare than he gave me, which my therapist duly ignored, continuing to chat with Homer like Kincaid didn't exist.

A lot of guys were filtering in, and everyone kept shooting around. I have to admit I've always loved that sound: the bouncing of the balls on the hardwoods, the clang of the rim, the swish of the net, all backed up by the squeaking of sneakers. It's kind of like a symphony, better than anything the East Coast Philharmonic can play, at least for me. So I tried to concentrate on the noise as I stood at the top of the key stretching, not five feet from Scotty. That's when I noticed someone else coming through the double doors, a guy who made Scotty look about as tough as Ruby Calhoun. Just the sight of him sent a beer-and-cigarettes odor into my brain, where the memory of being knocked cold in the parking lot at Bra's was fresh as ever. Kincaid went over and gave him a guy-hug. Jason Mason was here. Two minutes later, the next person to come in put the icing on the cake: the police chief. I looked over at Kincaid, who was staring pure hate at him. Wouldn't Hayley love to see that.

Dr. Haynes took charge of choosing the teams, and you could tell he was trying to make things as even as he could. He'd been playing with most of these guys for years and knew everyone's level, more or less. So we ended up with me, Dr. Haynes, the police chief, and two guys I didn't know—a short one called Hank and another, about my height but bulkier, called Andy—on one side. On the other side were Homer, Kincaid, Jason Mason, Scotty, and a chubby little guy they called Squeegee. There were three people left over, but it was understood they'd play the winners of the first game and get to choose two guys from the losers.

I'm not sure I'd ever felt more nervous before a basketball game, even in the days when Harold Cherry was screaming at me for blowing layups. First, there was Scotty. Then there was Jason, the mountain man, who was cutting death stares at me whenever he could. Then there was Kincaid, who was doing the same when he wasn't glaring at Dr. Haynes or eyeballing the police chief.

Dr. Haynes said our team would play man-to-man defense, and he told me to cover Scotty. He gave me the smirk when he said it. Nothing I could do, and better than covering Jason or Kincaid. Dr. Haynes would take Homer, and Chief Cody would take Jason—a smart move by Dr. Haynes, who wasn't going to ask Cody to cover his former deputy. So Andy would take Kincaid, and Hank would take Squeegee.

Game time.

Once we got started, it was obvious the whole thing would be a shooting contest between Dr. Haynes and Homer. And even though we were playing man-to-man, the other team decided to play a zone defense, meaning each guy guarded an area of the court instead of a specific person. Not sure why they did that when they could've put Homer on Dr. Haynes. The thing was, like a lot of players, Dr. Haynes had a favorite spot on the court to shoot from. His was just to the right of the key about twenty feet from the basket, which happened to be the zone that Kincaid, who was a pretty short guy, was covering on defense. As the game went on, Dr. Haynes was putting one after the other right in Kincaid's face, just *torching* him, as we used to say back then. Kincaid was getting more frustrated by the minute, and he started throwing elbows at everyone under the backboards. One of them missed my head by about an inch.

We were playing to twenty-one, and the score was about seventeen all when Hank threw me a pass in the corner. Scotty was covering that zone and was all over me, waving his arms like a madman and bumping me as I dribbled in place with my back to the basket. I couldn't find a way to pass off, so I took the only option I had: turn around, jump, shoot.

For pretty much the first time in my life, I knew from the second the ball rolled off my fingertips that it was in. And it was, nothing but net. Believe me, when it comes to the aesthetics of life, there's nothing quite like that feeling: turn around, jump, shoot, *swish*. Not even playing Gershwin's second prelude with no mistakes or a jazz solo that really swings. Maybe I just appreciate it more than good players do because it happens to them all the time and never happens to me.

As I made my way back down the court, Chief Cody, running alongside me, looked over and said, "Tough shot, Coleman."

You know, sometimes I think maybe that's all I ever really needed back then: kind of a father or uncle type of guy to look at me and say something like "Tough shot, Coleman." There's nothing quite like that feeling either. My own father died when I was too young for him to be saying stuff like that, and my stepfather would've said, "You got lucky, you idiot."

Anyway, it turned out that Kincaid and Jason, the town tough guys, weren't very good players. No surprise there. Neither was Chief Cody, despite his height, and that *was* a surprise. But he made up for it in hustle, grabbing some rebounds, and encouraging his teammates. Meanwhile, Dr. Haynes and Homer put on a clinic. Neither one could miss. I kind of marveled at them, two men pushing fifty in top shape and making everyone else on the court look like fools. They were just in a different league. They knew it too, but didn't lord it over the rest of us.

Go figure, though, because it was Dr. Haynes' shooting that caused all hell to break loose a few minutes later. He kept firing his jumper over Kincaid's outstretched arms, and after about the tenth time, Kincaid got so frustrated that he boiled over. It happened when Dr. Haynes gave him a pump fake, which Kincaid went for hook, line, and sinker, jumping into the air and screaming, "No way, no way!" But Dr. Haynes sidestepped him and calmly sank the shot, banking it off the backboard. The play made Kincaid look pretty ridiculous, and a couple of other guys sniggered.

"FUCKIN' ASSHOLE!" Kincaid shouted at the top of his lungs.

Next thing we knew, Kincaid had grabbed the ball and hurled it at Dr. Haynes' head. It barely missed. Then he charged him, fists flying, and threw a roundhouse hook. Dr. Haynes leaned to one side to dodge it, like a boxer, and Kincaid had so much forward momentum that he fell flat on his face. He hit the court hard, shook his head from side to side, and started to get up for more. That's when everyone rushed between him and Dr. Haynes, who didn't even look bothered. It was like the whole thing was happening to someone else. Chief Cody took charge.

"Kevin, get ahold of yourself!" he commanded, standing right in front of Kincaid, who'd made it to his feet. "That's enough!"

For a second I thought Kincaid might haul off and try to punch the chief, but he backed away and yelled, "FUCK ALL YOU GUYS!" The ball had rolled around, and he picked it up again, raising it over his head and slamming it down on the court. It bounced nearly to the ceiling. With that, he stomped across the court, banged through the double doors, and left the gym. Jason the mountain man ran after him.

It took a few minutes to get past the whole thing, and everyone kept asking Dr. Haynes if he was OK, but eventually we started playing again. Two guys who'd been waiting for winners took the places of Kincaid and Jason. Our team ended up winning the first game, twenty-one to nineteen, a Haynes layup sealing it. The other team won the second game by maybe five points. I made a few more shots and got some rebounds, but I missed a lot too: three bricks off the rim and one air ball. I didn't have any problems with Scotty after all. Not that he put his arm around my shoulder and said, "Way to play, pal," but he didn't shove me into any more walls.

At the end, it was Homer who suggested we all head over to the Tower, the basement bar at the King Richard, for a beer. The gym didn't have showers, but there were a few towels lying around to wipe the sweat off, and almost everyone had street clothes in their gym bags or in their cars, so most of the guys said sure. Chief Cody begged off, saying he had an early morning, and Scotty left by himself. The idea of having a beer with Dr. Haynes didn't exactly thrill me, but I figured if I said no, he'd trot out his trusty face-your-fears speech again in therapy the next week. I'd heard that one way too many times.

41.

The hotel was a twenty-minute walk from the town gym, and as soon as I entered the Tower through the street door, I knew it would take a while to get a beer. The Friday night gay crowd was in full force on the door side of the fish tank that split the room in two, and I'd have to inch my way through to the bar. It took about ten minutes, same for me as for the other guys who'd been at the gym, and once we all had our drinks, everyone paired off in conversation. As usual, I was the odd man out. Dr. Haynes noticed and waved me over to where he and Homer were chatting. It took another few minutes to reach them.

"Coleman," said Homer, giving me a pat on the back as I arrived. "Nice shooting."

"I second that emotion," said Dr. Haynes, breaking into laughter. I'd never seen him in what you might call a social setting, never mind drinking a beer. And it wasn't like I didn't know they were just being nice. I'd missed a lot more shots than I'd made.

"Thanks," I said.

"Seriously, you played well," Dr. Haynes said. "Any problems with Scotty?"

"No."

"I didn't think you would."

I wasn't too relaxed standing there with those two, so I said I wanted to get closer to the stage to hear the music better. It wasn't Charlie Biggs that night but a young, good-looking Black fellow called Cazzie Peters playing jazz guitar and singing.

"See you Monday," Dr. Haynes said.

"Sure."

Homer gave me a thumbs-up goodbye.

So I found a chair in the main part of the room and gave Cazzie Peters a listen. Boy, was he good. The first song he sang after I sat down still sticks in my mind: "The Days of Wine and Roses." The other thing that caught my attention, get this, was Dr. Nelson standing with a group of women near the fish tank and drinking what looked to be a whiskey sour. She was staring straight at Dr. Haynes, really giving him the evil eye, but he didn't see her because he was too busy talking to Homer. At one point Mrs. Sorensen popped down the stairs from reception, gave the room a quick survey, and headed back up. I didn't think she saw me, so I didn't wave or anything.

Quite a while later, just after Cazzie Peters had sung a bunch of Cole Porter tunes that I'd heard Skip play upstairs— "Just One of Those Things," "Easy to Love," "You'd Be So Nice to Come Home To"—I realized I hadn't paid for my beer. The bartender, a new girl named Nancy, had been so frazzled with the crush of customers that she'd forgotten to ask me for the money. So I made my way back over to the bar, pulled out my wallet, paid up, and introduced myself as one of the bartenders from upstairs. I even gave her a dollar tip on a beer that cost a dollar and a half. We bartenders are good tippers because we know how much people who do our kind of work depend on them.

Anyway, after a last look at the stage, where Cazzie was joking around with a few of the gay guys who kept saying how happy *they'd* be if he'd only come home with *them*, I headed toward the door that led out to Main Street. There must've been fifty people in my way, but I finally squeezed through. The fresh air outside was a rush of relief after all the cigarette smoke. Until I felt a hard tap on my shoulder from behind.

I turned around.

"You think you can get me fired, boy?" said ex-Officer Kincaid.

His face was an inch from mine, just like that crazy doctor years before, except Kincaid had to look upward. The doctor hadn't reeked of whiskey, either.

"I didn't get you—"

"You're gonna PAY, crazy boy," he seethed. "Comin' into MY town with the other fuckin' loonies like ya OWN the goddamn place!"

He grabbed the collar of my T-shirt with both hands and twisted. I flashed to the parking lot at Bra's when the mountain man had made me look like a fool in front of Cheryl, and pushed back, hard as I could. Within two seconds we were on the ground, on the lawn in front of the hotel—pulling, yanking, wrestling, flailing, punching. I heard a loud bang, which turned out to be the door to the Tower, and somebody yelling, "HEY, STOP IT!"

Before anything else could register, two guys were pulling us apart. I jumped to my feet and screamed, "HE STARTED IT!"

I didn't know them but recognized the faces as part of the crowd that had been kibitzing with Cazzie Peters by the stage. Both were big and muscular. *Very* muscular.

"GET AWAY FROM ME, ASSHOLES!" screamed Kincaid, pointing a finger. The two guys just stood there and stared at him.

"Maybe you oughta calm down, buddy boy," said one.

Breathing hard, Kincaid looked at me and said, "You got lucky, Cooper." He brushed himself off, descended the winding ramp down to the Tower, and went inside. The other guy looked at me and said, "You OK?" I nodded, breathing just as hard. "Thanks a lot." And off they went.

It'd gotten pretty late by then, so I headed out on my half-mile walk back to the BI, dazed but otherwise intact.

***

The first thing I saw when I ambled through the front door of the Manor, pretty much as always, was Lenny parked on one of the sofas swilling a bottle of diet soda. He was talking to Marie, who was sipping a cup of tea. A few other patients were hanging around, but I didn't know them. There'd been so many new ones coming and going over the past month that I couldn't keep track. I almost never went to the coffee clubs, where they all got introduced to everybody, because I spent most of my time practicing in the piano room or pouring drinks. I'd bought a secondhand bike off one of the dishwashers at the hotel, and that's how I was getting back and forth to Bra's when I had shifts there. The truth was that after nearly a year at Buchanan, I was starting to feel less and less a part of the place and more a part of the town and the people I worked with.

Freddy Cruz, who was sitting in one of the armchairs reading a copy of *The Northeast Telegram*, looked up as I passed by.

"Where ya been?"

"Playing hoops over at the town gym."

"Dr. Haynes there?"

"Yep."

"I hear he's a helluva player."

"He is."

"Anyone else any good?"

"A friend of his, who was great."

"Sink any shots?"

"A few."

"You look a little banged up. Something happen?"

"Just a rough game."

I trudged upstairs, showered, donned my boxer shorts, hopped into bed, and was just drifting off—my mind full of the struggle with Kincaid—when I heard a loud knock at the door.

"Sorry to wake you, man," I heard Lenny say urgently from out in the hallway. "Got any change?"

I opened up. "Change?"

"I want another soda before I go to bed."

The soda machine was in the snack bar off the front hall, downstairs.

"I was almost asleep."

"I know, I know. Sorry. Forgot to go to the bank today."

I pulled my jeans off the chair I'd draped them over, and reached into the front pocket where I kept my wallet and coins. There were five quarters and two dimes, but no wallet. Then I remembered I'd put the wallet in my windbreaker before going to play basketball. I'd had it at the Tower too, because I'd reached in to pay for my beer just before leaving.

"Here," I said, handing Lenny the coins.

"Thanks man, pay you back tomorrow."

"Don't worry about it."

The thing was, after Lenny left, I checked the side pocket of the windbreaker and the wallet wasn't there. I looked all around the room, even under the bed. Nothing. I didn't have a credit card, but there was over forty bucks in there along with a photo of my dog Frosty I'd kept since I was a kid. Plus a list of phone numbers: the hotel, Bra's, Skip Jones, and Cheryl. It dawned on me that the wallet must have fallen out when I was squeezing through the crowd at the Tower, or maybe when I fell to the ground with Kincaid.

I cut a glance at the clock on my bedside table. One fifteen. All the bars at the King Richard would be closed. But if I threw my clothes on and ran, I'd be there in maybe fifteen minutes. Maybe the new girl would still be cleaning up down in the Tower.

I took the back stairs and the back door out of the Manor to avoid the grilling I'd get from the front-hall peanut gallery, and sprinted to the King Richard. I was sweating like crazy by the time I got there. My wallet wasn't anywhere in sight on the lawn outside the hotel, so I took the walkway up to the big front door. Locked, just as I figured. But I could see one of the night-shift guys, Jeremy, through the picture window. He was sitting in the office behind the front desk going through some folios. He was maybe thirty-five, skinny with sandy hair, and did mainly accounting stuff. I rapped on the window, and he looked right up.

"Kinda late, Coleman," he said as he opened the front door. At least he smiled.

"I think I left my wallet downstairs."

"They're all locked up."

"*Damn* it. You gotta key?"

"Benny might. He's still in the tavern."

"Really?"

Sure enough, Benny was wiping down the bar. He had a Marvin Gaye tape on the sound system, which you could get away with after hours. It usually had to be the *Brandenburg Concertos* or something.

"What're *you* doin' here, man?" he said. "Thought you were off."

"I was. Busy tonight?"

"Slow. Spent most of it in the kitchen shootin' the breeze with the dishwashers."

"Lost my wallet. Can I take a look downstairs?"

"Be my guest." He reached into a drawer and pulled out a key that opened the door to the old, wooden staircase that led to the Tower from reception.

I'll be honest with you. Even though Benny was right there in the tavern and Jeremy was behind the front desk, it was pretty creepy going down into the Tower alone that late at night. Kind of a higher-class version of visiting the booze closet in the basement at Bra's. It was pitch black as I turned left at the bottom of the stairs, and all the light switches were behind the bar along the back wall. That meant I'd have to feel my way past the little stage on the left and through the main part of the room until I got closer to the fish tank, which gave off a glow. I just wanted to find my wallet and get the hell out of there.

With the fish tank's help, I looked under the table where I'd sat listening to Cazzie Peters. No wallet. So I went over to the other side of the fish tank, where I'd squeezed through the crowd to get to the outside door. The tank gave off more light in that part of the room, and I could see a little better, but thought I'd turn on the house lights, anyway. That could only help.

I went behind the bar to flick the switches, which were on the wall to the left of the register, but go figure: I didn't have to flick them after all. Son of a gun, sitting on a little shelf to the right of the register where they kept a big pile of King Richard Inn cocktail napkins was my wallet. Somebody must have seen it on the floor, or outside, and given it to the bartender. I grabbed it like a little kid who'd found a lost toy. The money and everything else was still there, and I was so happy I even *smelled* the brown leather. Maybe things really *were* looking up. Time to get back to my nice, warm bed and think about everything I had to tell Dr. Haynes on Monday.

I was heading toward the staircase that led up to reception when I realized I had to hit the men's room. I could've waited until I got back to the BI, but I knew the walk would be more pleasant if I just took a minute then and there. So instead of turning right to go upstairs, I kept going straight ahead. There was a diagonal corridor there that went off to the left, and the restrooms were at the end of it. The hallway had all sorts of photos on the wall, mainly musicians who played for the East Coast Philharmonic. I hadn't gone to a single concert all summer. How pathetic is that?

Anyway, the diagonal corridor was pretty cool because the photos were all in black and white and you could tell they were professionally done. There were framed dinner menus on the wall too, showing what the hotel was serving back in 1940 and even 1920 when a steak dinner cost thirty-five cents. The place had a history, you had to admit it, and I guess it was good business to put it all on display like that. There were even a few easy chairs in the hallway so people could sit down, relax, and look at all the stuff.

The thing was, the farther I got from the fish tank, the darker it got. I was back in pitch black. But that's when I remembered there was a light switch for the corridor on the left-hand-side wall, just past the staircase. I had to feel around, but finally found it and gave it a flip.

The next instant lives in my brain in a place that's been boarded up for a very long time. It's vivid as ever, though, and comes back to haunt me now and then in a recurring dream. The funny thing is that, for years, whenever I had the dream, it felt like it was all happening for the first time. My blood pressure would explode, my heart would beat like a jackhammer, and I'd wake up shouting without even realizing it. But these days, and I'm not exactly sure when this started, whenever I have the dream I *know* I'm dreaming and I *know* what's going to happen. The other thing is that even though I know what's coming, I'm stupid enough to flick the light switch anyway. You'd think I'd learn that turning right, going upstairs to reception, and heading back to the BI would be a better course of action, but I never do. And instead of bolting awake at what I see, I stay asleep, just standing there inside the dream, staring for a while. I don't know what I'm thinking. Then I turn and walk toward the men's room. When I get there and open the door, I wake up. I'm not shouting or anything. I just feel kind of calm. Strange, but calm.

There was someone sitting in one of the chairs. Not just anyone, someone I knew. To be honest, he knew me a lot better than I knew him, but that was normal for the type of connection we had. On his face was an expression I'd seen at least a hundred times, but there was something different about it. For one thing, the color of his skin had changed. It was tinted a faint shade of red. And there was none of the usual sparkle behind the eyes, which were still open. No taunt that meant, *I know you better than you know yourself.* Not that I think he ever really did.

The smirk.

The natural well-meaningness, even the tenderness he'd let me see just once after I got slammed into a gymnasium wall, was gone too. The look was like a vacant lot. Thinking about it too much, which I try not to do, can get me kind of emotional even today. Because that's how I knew Dr. Haynes was dead.

42.

Excerpted from the book *The Maine Murders: What Really Happened in Pierrevert*

By Hayley Blossom
Originally published in the United Kingdom.

Fourth Murder in Pierrevert
Latest Victim Also Had Link to Buchanan Institute

By Hayley Blossom
Telegram Staff Writer

PIERREVERT—A physician at the Buchanan Institute was found dead early Saturday morning at the King Richard Inn, police said. An early toxicology report indicated cyanide poisoning as the cause of death.

Dr. Wilson Haynes, 49, a psychiatrist at Buchanan for over twenty years and its acting

medical director, was discovered by a hotel
employee in the Tower, the downstairs bar, at
roughly two a.m. The employee's name was not
released. According to several sources, Dr. Haynes
had played basketball with a group of local men
at the town's municipal gymnasium on Friday
night before going to the King Richard.

Dr. Haynes' presumed murder was the fourth
to take place in Pierrevert within the past year,
each of the victims having direct ties to the psychiatric facility located on the outskirts of town.
Of the other victims, Ronald Sanders had been
the institute's chief legal counsel, Dr. Gregory
Frazier its assistant medical director, and Dr.
Angelo Bellino its previous medical director. Both
Sanders and Frazier suffered fatal stab wounds.
Bellino and Haynes were allegedly killed by lethal
doses of potassium cyanide. Bellino, who died
during a Pierrevert Historical Society dinner at
the King Richard Inn over Labor Day weekend,
was succeeded by Haynes as Buchanan's chief
administrator on an interim basis.

At a somber press briefing Sunday evening at
Pierrevert's Town Hall, police chief Chester Cody
called for townspeople to continue their daily
activities without fear.

"What we're looking at are targeted killings,"
he said. "Whoever is doing this is not seeking to
harm the population at large. We're working with
representatives of the Buchanan Institute as well
as with state police to get to the bottom of these
terrible crimes."

Asked whether authorities had any viable
leads in the series of alleged killings that has

rocked Pierrevert, Cody said several "people of interest" had been briefly detained for questioning. He declined to name them.

Zeke Murkowski of the state police barracks in Hargrove said Pierrevert police could count on his full cooperation.

"It's a bad situation and getting worse," Murkowski said. "Several of my men will be made available to Chief Cody if he needs them."

Marvin Glickman, chairman of Pierrevert's Board of Selectmen, told reporters he had confidence in the ability of local and state law enforcement to solve the crimes. Asked whether he felt the fear of more violent crime in the area would hinder the tourist trade, in particular the heavy hotel and restaurant bookings anticipated for the Thanksgiving and Christmas holidays, as well as for the upcoming winter ski season, Glickman said he was guardedly optimistic.

"We'll just have to wait and see," he said. "This region has so much to offer. Hopefully we'll have some arrests soon and we can put this awful period behind us."

Patricia Sorensen, owner of the King Richard Inn, declined comment when reached by the *Telegram* on Sunday night.

A previous *Telegram* article first revealed that Sanders, in addition to Frazier and Bellino, had strong ties to the Buchanan Institute. That article was accompanied by a courtroom photograph taken during an unsuccessful lawsuit brought against Buchanan roughly two years ago concerning the death of Pearleen Porter, who died of an overdose of sleeping pills at the age of 22 while a patient at the institute. Present in the photograph were the three Buchanan physicians—Frazier, Bellino, and Haynes—as well as Sanders, who represented the hospital in the case. Also present was Ruby Calhoun, the institute's chief nurse. With the exception of Calhoun, all have died over the past year. Calls to Calhoun both at her home in Pierrevert and at the institute were not returned.

Dr. Arnold Zinn, a senior psychiatrist at the institute, said the search was already underway for a new chief administrator and that he would be occupying the post on an interim basis. Funeral arrangements for Haynes were not known at press time.

Chester Cody, ignoring the offer of assistance from Zeke Murkowski and the state police in Hargrove, interviewed over twenty people in the days following the alleged murder of Dr Wilson Haynes. All were individuals who had been either at the town gym playing basketball or at the Tower bar on the night the physician died. The "people of interest" he referred to in the press included his former deputy, Kevin Kincaid, and Buchanan's director of admissions, Dr Samantha Nelson, who had a documented history of mental instability.

Sitting in his office later that week, exhausted and discouraged, Cody had to admit to himself that unless he was missing something obvious, something so close he couldn't see it clearly, he had zero leads. Or as Selectman Glickman might otherwise put it: *bupkis.*

43.

It rained for Dr. Haynes' funeral, which happened the following Saturday. The downpour came as everyone was filing into the big white church on Main Street, the one across from the King Richard. I hadn't gone to Dr. Bellino's service even though I'd known him a little, and I hadn't gone to Dr. Frazier's, who I'd met only once, the day I got sucker punched at the Manor. So I didn't know what the turnout was like for those two. But there were so many people for Dr. Haynes that they couldn't fit everyone into the pews. A lot of people had to stand in the aisles or way in back, and others had to stand outside getting drenched or just give up and go home. I'd gotten there about an hour ahead of time, so I had a seat in the third row.

I think every single patient and staff member from the Buchanan Institute was there, because Dr. Haynes was a pretty popular guy. He was always easygoing and friendly outside of therapy, and he made a point of having a presence around the Manor, not like a lot of shrinks who holed up in their offices or just hung around the doctors' building all day. When he'd walk through the front hall, which he did at least a few times a week, he'd always joke around with people. Like he'd say to Lenny, "How many of those sodas have you had today?" Lenny would give him a sheepish look and mumble some number, and Dr. Haynes would say, "Too many, Lenny, too many."

Most of the guys from the basketball game were at the church, along with plenty of folks I'd never seen. I knew Dr. Haynes had grown up in Hargrove and gone to Harvard, so I figured they were from his past. A fair number of staff from the King Richard were there too, which surprised me because Dr. Haynes never hung out at the hotel. Mrs. Sorensen looked bleak in a black dress and long raincoat, a string of pearls around her neck. She also looked pretty shell-shocked, but I guess I would be too if I owned a hotel and people kept dying in it. A lot of folks were coming up to her, putting a hand on her arm, saying nice things. She seemed to be doing her best to keep a stiff upper lip.

Homer Taylor was in the front row next to a tall, light-skinned Black lady whom I assumed was Dr. Haynes' wife. Maybe twenty minutes before the service started, when I first noticed them, he gave me a little wave. The lady looked at me too, and Homer said something into her ear, so I figured he was telling her who I was and that I'd been the one who found Dr. Haynes. Word had gotten around through the hotel grapevine, and Hayley got wind of it too. She even came over to the BI a couple of days later, breezing right in the front door of the Manor and asking around for me. There's a good reporter for you, I guess. It was Freddy Cruz who knocked on my door and asked if I wanted to see her.

To be honest, I was kind of uneasy that Hayley saw the inside of the Manor with all the other patients hanging around. I'd told her I was living there, and that was kind of OK at a distance if you know what I mean. But seeing her standing in the front hall with two or three out-of-it looking guys slouched on the sofa was a little too close to home. I got her out of there as fast as I could, and we took a walk into town.

That's when Hayley said that even though we were friends, she had a job to do and had to ask me a bunch of questions. She wanted to know everything, like how Dr. Haynes was positioned in the chair, what he was wearing, and all the stuff that happened earlier at the gym on the night he died. I'm not the type of guy who ever thinks about making deals or *negotiating* anything, not that I ever had any reason to, but Hayley was pumping me so much for information and getting so exasperated at my one-word answers that I finally said I'd tell her everything I remembered if she promised to keep my name out of the paper. I didn't care if people at the hotel or the BI knew I was the one who'd found Dr. Haynes, but that didn't mean the whole county had to know. That's all I needed, to be branded for the rest of my life as the guy who discovered his shrink dead in a bar.

Hayley had to think for a minute, but she finally said OK. We even shook on it. And she kept her part of the bargain, even though naming me would've given her a leg up on the other reporters who'd shown up in Pierrevert from around the state to cover the story. Chief Cody, who came to Dr. Haynes' funeral in his police uniform, didn't see any reason to share my name with the press either, and I'll always be grateful to him for that. Ex-Officer Kincaid was a no-show.

I was still pretty rattled about the whole thing on the morning of the funeral. I just couldn't get the image of Dr. Haynes in the chair out of my mind. The first thing I'd done when I found him was run back upstairs to tell Benny. Then we'd gone to the front desk to tell Jeremy, the night guy, and he'd called Mrs. Sorensen, who came down in her bathrobe. She said she couldn't bear to look at another dead person, but she called Chief Cody, who showed up in jeans and a flannel shirt ten minutes later. Then the ambulance came, and everything was taken care of in no time. From the look on Mrs. Sorensen's face I thought she was going to crack up, maybe even end up a patient at Buchanan herself, but she just walked into the elevator mumbling and went back upstairs.

That's when Chief Cody sat me down in the reception area and asked me to go over everything that'd happened since we left the gym earlier that night. We talked for almost an hour, and Benny very kindly brought us each a mug of hot coffee from the kitchen before he went home. It was after four in the morning when I finally got back to the BI, and nobody'd even noticed I hadn't been in my room. I didn't get to sleep before six or so. All in all, just another routine night in Pierrevert: a basketball game, a beer at a bar, a lost wallet, another dead shrink.

***

Dr. Haynes' coffin was closed, thank God at least for that. And I'll say one thing: staring at it, all covered with flowers, I knew it was time to leave the Buchanan Institute. I'd saved almost two thousand dollars since I'd started working at the hotel and Bra's, and figured I could afford a small apartment close to town. I even thought maybe it was time to take a break from shrinks, period. I wasn't sure I could deal with getting to know another one, even as an outpatient. Dr. Haynes had been a sane, mature guy, not staring into my face from an inch away or throwing his own sick problems onto me like so many shrinks had done before. But even Dr. Haynes wouldn't have made a difference if I hadn't met Dr. Christie first. He's the one who got me off all the medication and told me to stop trying so hard. He's the one who said the answer was just to be myself, to "let it be." I've never forgotten those things, even if I'm not always very good at them.

The service was short, and Dr. Haynes would've liked that. It was crisp and efficient, no wasted time or movement, just like his jump shot. There was a nice eulogy by one of his Harvard Medical School professors, who said what a special guy he'd been in so many ways. There were hymns, and of course a lot of crying all around. After the last hymn, as people were filing out of the church, Mrs. Sorensen came over to me and said how sorry she was. So did Freddy Cruz, April, and Ruby Calhoun. I saw Lenny shuffling out, but didn't talk to him. He'd hidden a bottle of diet soda under his coat and was taking a pull as he left.

The sun was trying to peek through the clouds by the time everyone was outside, and I was just about to trudge on back to the BI when I felt a light touch on my shoulder. I turned, and it was the tall Black lady who'd been sitting next to Homer Taylor in the front row.

"Coleman?" she said. "I'm Yolanda Haynes."

She reached out to shake my hand, held onto my arm in a very gentle way, and looked right into my eyes. Hers were all red and damp.

"Wilson thought a lot of you," she said. "He said the only thing holding you back was self-confidence. And I just know you'll get there, Coleman. I can tell by looking at you. He thought so too."

"I'm so sorry about everything" was all I could manage, and I'm sure it came out sounding awkward, like I always sound.

"He said you're a better basketball player than you think you are." She even smiled when she said that.

"I guess I'm OK on some nights."

"Good luck, Coleman."

And with that, she turned away and walked toward a group of people waiting by a big black car. I remember thinking how elegant and beautiful she was, and how not very many guys deserve a wife like her. Dr. Haynes did, though.

44.

I just stood there for a while outside the church, watching people walk away or get into their cars parked along Main Street. It was starting to get hot out, kind of like an Indian summer, and I finally decided I couldn't take going straight back to the BI after all, where everyone would be moping around. Plus I was dying of thirst. So I got my courage up and walked across the street to the hotel. Benny was behind the bar in the tavern, and I took a seat on one of the stools.

"A draft, Benny, please. Give me a pint."

"Simons sees you, you're toast. You know you're off-limits here."

"The hell with him."

"You're the boss."

So he poured my beer, the head running over the rim of the mug, and I took a swill. God, it was wonderful. There were a few baskets of Leroy's homemade potato chips on the bar, and I dug into one of those too. They were still warm from the fryer and had just enough salt, but not too much. I made an executive decision right then and there that ice-cold beer and freshly made potato chips were one of life's great pleasures.

"Saw your lady friend the other night," Benny said.

I hadn't seen Cheryl for a while, but I figured that's who he meant since I didn't have any other lady friends. I'd talked to her on the phone and told her about finding Dr. Haynes' body, and she hadn't even seemed that interested. I'd told her I was going to the funeral.

"You mean Cheryl?"

"Yeah, she was all dolled up having dinner with some older guy in the main dining room. Whole place was staring at her. Must have been her dad or uncle or something."

I didn't know if Cheryl had any uncles, but I knew her father was dead. At least that's what she'd told me.

"I should give her a call," I said. "Haven't seen her in a while."

"I wouldn't let that one out of my sight," Benny said. "The stuff dreams are made of."

I'd always been a beer sipper, someone who could make one glass, even a small one, last for an hour. But this time I chugged the rest of the mug right down.

"Benny, how about another?"

"Whoa, the man likes to live dangerously! Simons is here, you know. I saw him fifteen minutes ago."

"Fuck him."

Benny refilled my mug.

"When'd you get such a set of stones, dude?" he said. "Now drink up and get outta here. I don't wanna see the carnage when Fauntleroy waddles in."

I knew I should let Benny's comment about Cheryl drop. But me being me, I couldn't. I've wondered more times than I'd care to admit how things might've turned out if I'd just let it go.

"Tell me about the guy Cheryl was with," I said, taking another swill of suds.

"I thought it was her dad. I mean, she's so freakin' beautiful, and this guy looked like a movie star, all tan, silver hair, dressed to the nines. The two of 'em were laughing their asses off. Somebody said the guy had a big Mercedes parked outside."

I downed my second mug in maybe five gulps and ate a few more potato chips. The only problem with them was they made your fingers all greasy.

"One for the road, Benny."

He gave me a look like I was completely nuts. Guilty as charged.

"Coleman, seriously, get the fuck outta here 'fore you get fired. Maybe me too for serving you in the first place."

I hadn't had breakfast that morning and I almost never drank during the day, so my head was already spinning. I knew Benny was right, but I didn't care.

"Just a half."

"Have it your way," he said, sighing and pouring me another full mug. "Been nice workin' with ya."

I chugged the third pint in about ten seconds, slamming the mug down for effect.

"*Split*, man!" Benny said. "Pay me later."

"See ya."

I nearly fell down trying to get off the barstool, but I managed to make it out of the hotel without Mr. Simons seeing me. The day had turned gloriously sunny, so much that the light hurt my eyes. It must've been about one in the afternoon by then.

When I got back to the Manor, I thought I'd take a nap and try to sleep it all off. But halfway up the stairs, on the way to my room, I happened to look down and see a new patient coming out of the phone booth that was in the snack bar. That gave me an idea, and a few seconds later I snuggled into the booth myself. The little bell chimed as I dropped a dime into the slot. I dialed a number I now knew by heart. She answered after five rings.

"Hello?" Cheryl said.

"Hi, it's me."

"Oh hi, Coleman, how are you? How was the service?"

"Pretty sad, I guess."

"I can imagine."

Silence, a long one. I hate those.

"Listen, can I come over?"

"Oh, I don't know. I'm awfully busy this afternoon and tonight. Maybe another time."

"Are you sure?"

"Yeah, I am. Sorry."

Another long silence.

"Well, I guess I'll see you sometime soon, then," I ventured.

"Sure. Why not?"

"OK, bye."

"Bye."

It took me about ten minutes to get out of the phone booth. And not because I was so drunk that I couldn't open the door. It was the tone of Cheryl's voice that kept me sitting there, ruminating. Especially the "why not," which came out like we were just casual acquaintances, people who might or might not say hello to each other on the street. I wanted to call her back right away and ask if we could talk some more.

Instead, I decided to hop on my bike and ride over to her house. It was all country roads, and there wouldn't be much traffic on a Saturday afternoon. So I changed out of the shirt and pants I'd worn to the funeral, threw on some jeans and a sweatshirt, and took off down Main Street. I was right about the traffic, but hadn't thought much about riding a bike after three pints of beer on an empty stomach. Every ten minutes or so I had to stop and rest because I thought I might black out. By the time I got to Cheryl's front door, almost an hour after leaving the BI, I was sweating like I'd just played a couple of hours of basketball. Not the best way to show up, but I didn't think she'd mind.

I gave the knocker a few whacks, probably too hard, and Cheryl opened the door with a huge smile on her face. She was wearing tight jeans, high-heeled boots, and a white blouse. She was all made up too, with dangly earrings and pink lipstick that matched her nail polish. When she saw who her visitor was, the dazzling smile turned to stone.

"Coleman, what are you doing here?"

"I'm sorry. I just needed to talk. After the funeral and all."

She glanced at her watch and let out an exasperated sigh. "I've got friends coming in fifteen minutes," she said. "That's all the time I've got."

"OK, sure."

"All right, come in then. You're soaking."

"It's just sweat from the ride."

"We can talk in my room."

I followed her upstairs, and we sat on the same little sofa as the night I'd first met her at Bra's. She leaned back, crossed her legs, and looked at her watch again.

"What is it you want to talk about?"

"I just—"

"Yes?"

"I don't know. I guess I just need to know something."

"What's that?"

"Well, are we still . . . I don't know. Going out?"

"Why do you ask?"

"Well, someone told me you were at the King Richard the other night with some man. So I guess I felt a little confused and—"

"Coleman, since we started spending time together, did I *ever* say we were exclusive? Did I *ever* say I wasn't seeing other men?"

At least she referred to me as a man, not a little boy, which is what I felt like.

"No, I guess I just kind of assumed—"

"Assumed what?"

"Well, I wasn't seeing anyone else, so I guess I thought maybe you weren't either."

There was a large bouquet of fresh red roses in a vase on her dresser. A card was nestled inside.

"I'm free to see whoever I please, Coleman," she said firmly. "If I do, even if I sleep with them, that's entirely my business and not yours. It doesn't mean I never want to see you again. But now that you've done what you've done, coming over here when I *told* you I wasn't free . . . I just—"

"I'm sorry."

Another long silence followed, like the one we'd had on the phone earlier that day.

"Who is he?" I finally asked.

"Who's who?"

"The man you were having dinner with at the King Richard."

"None of your business!"

"You can tell me. It's OK."

"I certainly will *not*!"

And here's where I sealed my fate, if I hadn't already. It might've been different if I'd just stood up and said, "Hey Cheryl, you're right. This whole thing with my shrink getting killed, it's made me a little weird. Of course you're free to see other people. So am I. That's the way I like it. Now I'm gonna get out of here and leave you in peace. Maybe see you one of these days. Take care."

If I'd said something like that, I could've imagined her calling me again when she was in the mood for something other than a tanned, good-looking, silver-haired man who drove a Mercedes. Instead, I said something else.

"Did you sleep with him?"

Now defiant: "Since you ask, yes, I did."

"Here in your room?"

"Right over there on that bed." She couldn't resist: "He was wonderful."

"Which underwear were you wearing?"

"Coleman, *STOP!*"

That's when I heard two loud raps of the knocker on the front door. Cheryl looked toward the ceiling, rolled her eyes, stood without saying a word, and scurried downstairs to open up. I remember looking out her bedroom window just then and noticing the sky had darkened. There was a loud thunderclap.

"Hel-*lo* there!" I heard Cheryl say merrily. "*Terrific* to see you both! Come in, come in!"

There was some small talk, and I heard a male and a female voice. They both said how great Cheryl looked. I was trying to stay silent so I could hear everything they said, which is probably why I started to cough. A tickle in my throat came out of nowhere, and I couldn't muffle it. The chatter downstairs went silent.

"Who's that?" asked the woman's voice.

"Oh, nobody," Cheryl said. "Just something I keep upstairs for rainy days."

They all laughed, and I heard them go into the small living room.

That was my cue.

I tiptoed to the top of the stairs, where I could hear the three of them gabbing away about this and that. I moved down very gently, stopped at the bottom, and peered around the corner into the living room. None of them had a clear view of the front door, which I eased open as gingerly as I could. Thank God it didn't creak. I looked in one last time, and Cheryl's head swiveled. She caught a glimpse of me but turned back to her friends without missing a beat. They were older, maybe in their midthirties, but none the wiser. I knew she'd find a way to explain her way out of it easily.

As I mounted my bicycle and headed off in the pouring rain, I held on to one faint hope: that my silent exit might salvage a small grain of respect for me in Cheryl's beautiful blue eyes.

45.

It was just a couple of days later, maybe one fifteen in the morning. I was wiping down the bar at the tavern after my shift, just about ready to turn out the lights and head back to the BI. The phone next to the register rang, and I picked up.

"Is that you, Coleman?"

By then I knew Mrs. Sorensen's voice right away. Plus no one else would call the tavern at that hour unless it was Mr. Simons calling to chew me out about something.

"What can I do for you, Mrs. Sorensen?"

"Would you mind bringing up some Grand Marnier, dear? Take a full bottle and a bucket of ice. And bring a snifter for yourself."

It was the first time she'd ever called me "dear," and it was pretty obvious she'd already been drinking. She was slurring her words a bit. *A shiftner for yourshelf.*

To be honest, the last thing I wanted to do was go up to her apartment. It was late, I was tired, and I'd been up there enough times and listened to her drone on about enough stuff that I really didn't feel like doing it again. I know that doesn't sound very charitable, and it's not that I didn't like Mrs. Sorensen; I did. She'd been a lot nicer to me than she had to, and not every hotel owner hires mental patients. As far as I knew, she never asked any other bartenders to bring a drink up to her apartment and have a chat. I was her pet even if I didn't want to be.

"Sure, I'll be right up," I said.

It was a heavy tray with the full ice bucket and a new bottle of Grand Marnier, never mind that the elevator was broken again, so I had to walk up four flights of stairs to get to her apartment. I almost dropped everything when I knocked on the door because I had to balance the tray against my chest with one arm. Then she opened up.

I'll say this: even though you never really knew what you were going to get with Mrs. Sorensen, I sure didn't expect what I got this time. In the middle of the night, she was dressed up like she was going to the Academy Awards. She had on a long silver gown with beads all over it, matching shoes, even a matching little purse that she was clutching. She had diamonds on her ears and on a couple of fingers, and they weren't small ones. Her face was more made up than I'd ever seen it. Lots of red on the cheeks and some blue stuff on the eyelids.

"Put the tray on our table, Coleman."

Our table. It was the first time she'd ever said that too. She'd put a white tablecloth on it just like they did in the main dining room. There was a big blaze in the fireplace, and that was the only light in the whole apartment.

"Have a seat and pour yourself a drink." *A sheet. Yourshelf.* "Make one for me too, a double."

As always, I did as I was told. And all of a sudden there we were, sitting across from each other next to the big picture window that looked out onto Main Street—the postcard view of downtown Pierrevert. Only it was so dark outside that you couldn't see much. The streetlights went off at midnight.

She took a huge swill of her Grand Marnier, set the glass down, and looked me straight in the eye.

"Coleman, I'm about to do a terrible thing," she said. "Well, two. One to me, one to you."

I think I already told you I'm not a big fan of cordials. Cough syrup with a kick. But the way this was going, I took a pretty big swig of Grand Marnier.

"I'm not sure what you mean, Mrs. Sorensen."

She drank down her glass like it was water and poured another, swirling the stuff around in the snifter for a few seconds before knocking it back.

"I've decided I don't want to live anymore. All these terrible things happening in my hotel. No one will ever want to stay here again, I know it. What'll I do?"

I remember thinking that "What'll I Do?" was the title of a song Skip had played for me at our last lesson. A waltz by Irving Berlin. I wondered if Mrs. Sorensen had ever heard it because I was pretty sure it was from her generation, but it didn't seem like the right time to ask. Then again, it might've changed her train of thought. Given all the loony bins I'd been in, this wasn't the first time someone had said to my face that they wanted to off themselves. It's not like I was out of my element.

"None of it is your fault, Mrs. Sorensen," I said. "When the police find out who's doing this, everything will be back to normal."

"I've got sleeping pills, strong ones," she said. "I'll bet a whole box would do the trick. That would be a peaceful way to go, don't you think? Not like those other people."

"Well, you—"

"I can't do it alone, Coleman. Would you stay with me?"

At that moment, a log in the fireplace fell through the andirons and scattered sparks into the room. I got up, took a new log off the stack just to the side, and laid it in. Then I sat back down and sipped some more Grand Marnier. It was starting to taste pretty good.

"Would you, dear?" she said. "I'd be *so* grateful. You could call Chester Cody in the morning. I won't ask you to do anything against the law. Can you understand?"

Actually, I couldn't. When I'd tried to off myself, the last thing I'd wanted was company. But I wasn't going to tell Mrs. Sorensen my life story.

"I've grown quite fond of you, Coleman," she said, "and I know this is terribly unfair. I just don't have anyone else. The only confidante I have is Erin O'Brien, and we're very old friends, but we have too much of a past for me to ask her for help. She'd never do it. But you, I mean, *you*. Well, you know how I feel."

I had no idea how she felt, so I gave her a quizzical look. "Mrs. Sorensen?"

"Coleman, with all the time you've spent up here, did you think I'd never noticed the scars on your wrists?"

If she'd been a boxer, I would've called that one a knockout punch. It staggered me. I had no wind and no words. She saw it too. But I figured the only way off the ropes was to ignore her comment, or at least try to.

"I'm sorry, Coleman, I should never have said that. Please forgive me."

She turned her head and gazed out the window for a long while. And even though she'd just said what she said, I'm not sure I'd ever felt sorrier for anyone. It didn't matter that she was rich and owned a big hotel because she looked about a hundred years old and like the unhappiest person I'd ever seen. When you think of all the screwed-up people I'd come across in loony bins, starting with the one I saw in the mirror every morning, that's going some. But I just kept sipping my Grand Marnier, trying to think of something else to say.

The silence lasted for about five minutes, a hell of a long time, but it felt like we were communicating in *some* way. I was just *there* and hoped that counted for something. The room was getting pretty hot with the fire crackling away, and I remember noticing that her makeup was starting to run.

"Mrs. Sorensen, why don't you just turn in for the night?" I said. "I'll stay for a while, until you're asleep. The sun will come up in the morning, and you'll feel much better."

She reached into the ice bucket for a handful of cubes, dropped them into her snifter, and filled her glass again with Grand Marnier. She took a huge swill.

"My goodness, Coleman, I *am* drunk," she said. "I don't think I've been this bad since the day I got the telegram saying my husband was dead. It was the winter of 1944. There was a song on the radio when I opened the envelope: 'Rum and Coca-Cola.' The Andrews Sisters, Patty, Maxene, and LaVerne. My, they were good. Such lovely voices. Did you ever hear of them?"

"I'm not sure, ma'am. But I think I've heard the song." I was suddenly calling her "ma'am" again.

She started humming the tune, and her face brightened up a little.

"Of course, you're right, dear," she said with a deep sigh. "What on *earth* was I thinking? My goodness, whatever would I do without you?"

She gave me a bleak smile that almost broke my heart. And maybe she was right after all. I *did* understand how she felt. At least in some way.

"You'll be fine, Mrs. Sorensen. I'm sure of it."

"Do me a favor, dear, help me up and lead me to the bathroom. I can change clothes in there. It won't take a minute. Promise me you'll wait."

"I promise."

I figured I'd get out of there, fast as I could, after she was all tucked in. But I was going to tell Jeremy down at the front desk what'd happened. I'd leave it to him to check on her during the night. There was a master key to every room in the hotel in a drawer down there, even to Mrs. Sorensen's suite. I knew because she'd told me about it one time. I even knew where it was, not that I'd ever used it.

"Come on then," she said. "Help the old girl up."

I tried to lift her out of the chair gently, but she was like dead weight. Never mind that I hadn't ever touched her before except to shake hands. The whole thing was getting *way* too intimate for me. I even remember the odd smell of her perfume, nothing like the kind Cheryl used to wear, more the type you'd expect your grandmother to use. I guess that made sense, given her age.

We eventually got her standing and made our way slowly over to the bathroom. It was huge, about the size of the living room in the house I grew up in. The bathtub looked like three people could fit inside, and there were two sinks with a big mirror and a medicine cabinet above. The wall of drawers looked straight out of a magazine about fancy houses. I remember starting to sweat because I'd kind of had to *drag* her part of the way, what with the fireplace throwing off so much heat. Given the state she was in, I wasn't sure if she'd really be able to get undressed and put on something to sleep in without falling and maybe hurting herself. But if you think I was going to unzip the back of that gown and help her climb out of it, you've got another thing coming.

"Thank you, dear," she said as she shut the bathroom door, locking it with a loud *clack* of the latch. "I won't be long."

"Just yell if you get into trouble," I said through the door. "I'll be right here."

I figured if anything *did* happen, there *had* to be a female on duty somewhere in the hotel. Don't ask me who, though. Everything was closed down for the night, and even housekeeping left at ten o'clock. Maybe I'd have to call one of the staff at home.

Anyway, I didn't want to just stand there listening at the bathroom door, so I went back to the table, sat down, and poured myself some more Grand Marnier. I could hear Mrs. Sorensen moving around, and it seemed like things were going OK. Drawers were opening and closing, water was being turned on and off, and I thought I heard her brushing her teeth. I definitely heard the toilet flush. My mind was wandering all over the place, I can tell you that. How the hell did I end up in a hotel room in a town called Pierrevert, Maine, with an old lady who wanted to kill herself? Par for the course if you're me, I guess. I also knew I was getting pretty tanked myself and that I better stop. But I'd decided that Grand Marnier was, after all, a highly misunderstood, wrongly accused substance that was absolutely delicious once you got used to it.

About ten minutes later, I heard the latch. The door opened, and Mrs. Sorensen appeared in a pair of flannel pajamas, face scrubbed and clean, not a hair out of place, bedroom slippers on her feet. She'd taken all her jewelry off too. I started to rise to help her across the room, but she held up her hand.

"I'm fine now, Coleman, thanks to you. But I'm still going to have a nightcap before bed. Is there any Grand Marnier left?"

"Yes ma'am."

We'd drunk most of the new bottle, and I don't know how much she'd had before she called me. She took a few careful steps and sat down at the table with a loud exhale.

"Pour me one more, dear, with lots of ice. It'll be the last, I promise. And heavens, don't worry about me. I'll be fine in the morning, just as you said."

Once again, I did as I was told. And I noticed she'd stopped slurring her words. This was a woman who could put it away like a sailor.

"Jiminy crickets!" she suddenly said. "I *declare* I am *famished*. Are you hungry, Coleman?"

Actually, I was starving. I nodded.

"There's some cheddar cheese in the fridge, crackers in the cupboard on the side, plates above the stove," she said. "I'm afraid you'll have to serve us."

I looked over at the kitchen, which was small. You could see into it from the living room.

When I opened the fridge, I saw the cheese on the top shelf. It was in one of those packets where the wrapping really clings to what's inside, and it hadn't been opened yet. There wasn't much else in there, but I'd never thought Mrs. Sorensen did a lot of cooking. I'd seen Leroy prepare a tray for her plenty of times and send it up with one of the waitresses. But I was pretty surprised at how dirty the inside of her fridge was. It looked like the shelves hadn't been wiped down in months, which kind of offended my bartender sensibilities. It also seemed off-key for a woman who always looked so well tended.

The crackers were in the cabinet just where she said, and I grabbed three plates—one for each of us and one for the cheese and crackers. The thing was, typical me, I couldn't get the cheese packet open. You know how sometimes you pull and pull and try to rip the corner and it just won't open? Then you use your teeth, which is what I did next, and it *still* won't open? Mrs. Sorensen saw me struggling and yelled, "There's knives in the second drawer next to the stove!"

There sure were, as it turned out—lots of them—but it was so dark in there that I couldn't find a small one. So I grabbed a big one with a jagged edge, like the kind they used down in the kitchen, and tried to slit the corner of the cheese packet. As usual, I screwed everything up. I was pressing so hard to pierce the wrapping that once I finally did it, the knife kept going and sliced into my left index finger.

"Damn it!" I shouted, dropping the knife and packet onto the counter.

"What happened, dear?"

"I *cut* myself!"

"Rinse it in the bathroom! There's disinfectant in the medicine cabinet!"

I squeezed the finger hard as I hustled over to the bathroom, and the water from the faucet was ice cold, which dulled the pain. The cut wasn't all that deep, but I still wondered if I might need a stitch, maybe even two. The main thing was whether it would hurt when I played the piano. Skip had been working me out on diminished scales, and I'd thought I was getting the hang of them. Just my luck. Anyway, I grabbed some toilet paper to dry the finger because I didn't want to stain one of Mrs. Sorensen's nice white towels that were hanging on a rack next to the sink. Then I opened the medicine cabinet to look for the disinfectant. There it was on the bottom shelf.

And that's when I saw something else.

I think I already told you I was the best chemistry student in my whole grade in high school. Don't ask me why, the subject just came naturally to me and I always got As without having to study.

On the top shelf of Mrs. Sorensen's medicine cabinet was a small green glass bottle. There was one of those old-fashioned labels on it, the kind you used to see stuck on big jars behind the counter at drugstores. The Ye Olde New England look. The script on the label spelled out a chemical compound in three big letters that looked like they'd been written about fifty years ago with the type of pen you had to dip into an inkwell. Just like the chord symbols that Skip had taught me for the piano, this one wasn't too hard to figure out if you knew what the letters stood for.

There's no way I would've done this if I hadn't been so hammered, but I reached up and grabbed the green bottle, brought it back to the table where Mrs. Sorensen was sitting, and put it down in front of her. Then I took a seat and swigged my drink. I'd forgotten all about the disinfectant, never mind the cheese and crackers. Blood was starting to seep through the toilet paper wrapped around my finger.

When she saw the green bottle, Mrs. Sorensen downed the rest of her drink and poured herself another. Don't ask me why I did this, but I reached into the ice bucket with the hand that wasn't bleeding and put a few extra cubes into her glass. That was the last of the ice and the Grand Marnier. She leaned back in her chair, looked out the window again, and we sat silently for another few minutes. For the second time, she was the one who broke the trance.

"Coleman, did I ever tell you about my husband?" she said.

"No ma'am, you haven't."

"Rupert was his name, after the grandfather on his mother's side, but everyone called him Robby. Had a shining career ahead of him as a chemist, could have worked for any company or taught at the university. He made up what's in that bottle before he left for the war. Took another one just like it with him in case he ever needed it. By the time he realized I'd kept some for myself, he was halfway across the ocean. I wanted it in case something happened to *him*, and it did. Shot down, dead. I never had the courage to use it, mind you."

Man, I was drunk. But I still knew what those letters on the bottle meant. KCN. That would be potassium cyanide. And I still said what I said, which was very unlike me.

"You mean you never had the courage to use it on *yourself*?"

She took another swill of Grand Marnier and shook her head like someone who can't believe the denseness of whoever they're talking to. And at that moment, dawning on my foggy brain, I felt a dire need to relieve myself. I'd drunk nearly half the quart bottle of Grand Marnier, but the discomfort hadn't registered, especially after cutting my finger. When it finally did, it packed a wallop.

"Excuse me, Mrs. Sorensen, I'll be right back," I said, rising clumsily from my chair and stumbling toward the bathroom.

After using the facilities, I turned on the cold-water faucet full blast and splashed my face a few times. The guy I saw in the mirror was someone I barely recognized. He was out of focus, like the reflection of the bathroom. The walls seemed to be moving on their own. A terrible dizziness set in, and I thought I might be sick then and there. At least I was in the right place for that. But the wave of nausea passed, and I reached for one of the towels. The hell with the blood on my finger, which anyway was starting to congeal. The soft fabric felt wonderful on my face and had a nice, fresh smell, like a good hotel towel should. I inhaled deeply. The thing was, as I reached for the door handle, I don't think I was absolutely sure of one word Mrs. Sorensen and I had said to each other for the past half hour. It was like a dream. I still knew where I was, though, and knew she'd be sitting at the table when I returned.

Except she wasn't. When I stepped out of the bathroom, her chair was empty. She was nowhere in sight. I stood there looking all around the room.

"Mrs. Sorensen?"

The blow came from behind, on the top of my head. It was a lot worse than the time I got sucker punched at the BI, because instead of a fist, it was a metal ice bucket that came crashing down. I could tell by the feel of the impact and the sound it made in the instant before I lost consciousness. We bartenders know our ice buckets.

When I came to, I don't know how many minutes later, I was lying on the floor in front of the fireplace. Both of my arms were stretched out behind me, and my wrists were bound together with a sort of twine that seemed like it was attached to something else, something heavy. I tugged hard but couldn't separate my wrists or move my arms. And this time it wasn't a guy standing over me grinning, but an old lady—Mrs. Sorensen, to be exact—straddling my chest and holding the razor-sharp point of the jagged-edged knife to my throat.

"Well, look who's awake," she said.

"Wha—"

"There's something you don't understand, Coleman."

"Why'd—"

"They deserved it. Every one of them. Don't ever say they didn't."

The self-assured glint had returned to her eyes, but it wasn't like the one I'd seen before.

"That fat lawyer prancing about like a *peacock* in the court-room," she said, seething. "How *long* I waited! 'Could I please stop by, Mr. Sanders? I need some legal advice.' We were in his den. He looked into a cabinet, never saw it coming. Ha!"

She pushed the blade downward.

"DON'T!" I shouted.

I winced and felt a tiny trickling of blood. She pulled the knife back.

"That *Frazier* fellow. Parking out back so no one would see him *crawl* to his car, *blind drunk* every night! Not another soul in sight. Lovely."

She was getting more and more animated, her eyes burn-ing with recollection. I was frozen, tied down, paralyzed by fear and alcohol, staring up into her face.

"*Bellino* was the worst," she said, bristling. "Could not have cared *less* what happened to that poor girl. But *you* gave me my chance!"

"*What?*"

"You left the *cocktails* on the *tray*! I know what Angie Bellino drinks. He and his Sidecars. Nobody saw me slip the cyanide in. All too drunk on *my liquor*! The knives were messy anyway. Here's to biding one's time."

The knives. Like the ones in the drawer. Like the one she was holding to my neck. Like the stabbings in Hayley's articles.

Mrs. Sorensen tossed her hair back like a femme fatale in a film-noir picture. "I didn't know if the crystals would work," she hissed. "They're *old*, like *me*. What a fine chemist my Robby was!"

My wrists felt cemented together. Then I realized I could move my fingers. I started feeling around, grasping.

"That *Haynes* was her *doctor*," she said. "Should have *known* about her past. You saved the day again!"

"*Me?*"

Her face was lost in a thousand-yard stare. "You were in the Tower, all alone, Cazzie Peters singing. Haynes at the bar. I came down later, asked him to stay after closing—to talk about *you! That's what got him!* Was just the two of us, all dark. Offered him a drink. He said club soda. Didn't see when I made it up, drank it right down. You should have *seen* him *gyrating* all over the place!"

The idea of Dr. Haynes gasping for breath from a cyanide mickey was a bit much for me. Whenever the image pops into my head, as it still does sometimes, I try to push it right out.

"I wasn't going to hurt the Calhoun lady. I'm no *monster*. Not that she didn't deserve it."

The fingers on my right hand found a stray piece of the string that was tied around my wrists. I pulled at it. It started to give.

"Take the knife away, Mrs. Sorensen," I said. "I'll listen to you."

"You won't say anything to anyone, will you, Coleman? I've rebuilt your life. We have a special bond. Don't we, dear?"

My fingers were finding more slack in the knot, and that's when it hit me. What she'd been saying. *That poor girl.* Dr. Nelson's supreme annoyance at a patient suicide. The frame hanging in the hotel above the piano. Skip's face at the mention of the name. The court case in Hayley's articles.

"Wait a minute!" I demanded, as much as anyone in my position could demand anything. "This is all about the *waitress?* The Black girl who sang like Billie Holiday? The one who committed suicide? Pearleen Porter?"

"SHE DIDN'T COMMIT SUICIDE!"

The fire was fading and the room getting darker, but I kept my eyes on Mrs. Sorensen's. Then I felt my right wrist brush against the woodpile next to the fireplace. I'd forgotten all about it.

"SHE WAS SPECIAL!" Mrs. Sorensen screamed, pressing the knife harder, piercing my skin again.

"STOP!"

A surge of adrenaline kicked in, and I tugged with everything I had. My wrists broke free. And I'll say this: to this day, I'm grateful for my big hands. The ones Skip Jones coveted, the ones he said would let him play like Oscar Peterson, the ones that allowed me to palm a basketball even if I didn't know what to do with it once I had it.

Mrs. Sorensen was still talking, but I have no memory of what she was saying just then. My right hand was groping for a grip on a medium-sized log. What I *did* hear, or *thought* I heard in the back of my mind, was Dr. Haynes' voice. *Come on, Coleman. Put some mustard on it.*

My arm swung forward, and the impact of the log on Mrs. Sorensen's shoulder sent her tumbling onto the wooden floor. She howled as the knife flew out of her hand, and I jumped to my feet. She was splayed every which way for a second but gathered herself quickly. I watched as she slid herself across the room and found a sitting position, back against the wall, underneath the big picture window. That's when I saw it was the long, thick laces of her gumshoes, the ones she kept where the sun could dry them out, that she'd used to tie up my wrists. She'd attached the laces to the two heavy andirons in the fireplace. Not a bad piece of scouting for a woman of a certain age, never mind one with more than half a bottle of Grand Marnier under her belt.

"I'm sorry, Mrs. Sorensen," I said, trying to catch my breath. Typical me, even though she'd cut my neck twice with a large knife, I was feeling guilty for hitting her with the log. "Are you all right?"

"I think I am, dear," she said, rubbing her shoulder. She was winded and shell-shocked but somehow calmer. "Are you?"

Wiping the blood off my neck with my shirtsleeves, I walked slowly toward the door that led out to the hallway. I opened it, then turned back to gaze at Mrs. Sorensen one last time before leaving.

"Coleman," she said. "Maybe someday you'll understand. You have no idea."

"No idea of what?"

She sighed heavily and looked straight into my eyes. "Coleman?"

"Yes?"

"Pearleen Porter was my daughter."

46.

Excerpted from the book *The Maine Murders: What Really Happened in Pierrevert*

By Hayley Blossom
Originally published in the United Kingdom.

Author's Note

The sources for this book were personal memory, direct interviews with many of the principals, and research.

As a reporter for *The Northeast Telegram*, I covered the Pierrevert murders as they happened, and was acquainted with many of the people chronicled in the book. I was also physically present at some of the events described. In that era, the *Telegram*'s small bureau in Pierrevert was located around the corner from the King Richard Inn, placing me at ground zero for information gathering. The articles reprinted in the book, with the kind permission of the *Telegram*, have been duplicated word-for-word from the paper's editions of that day and time.

In the year that followed Patricia Sorensen's confession to the murders of Ronald Sanders, Gregory Frazier, Angelo Bellino, and Wilson Haynes, I conducted multiple rounds of interviews with people involved in events that surrounded the crimes. Many of the conversations amongst the principals reported in this book are as they were personally described to me by interviewees. In cases where exact words could not be recalled, I paraphrased what was either said or likely to have been said based on interviewee recollections. In some cases, dialogue in the book is reproduced as it was overheard by me, owing to physical proximity, at the time the conversations actually took place. I also exercised a degree of poetic license regarding the inner thoughts of certain people, based on personality and circumstance.

In addition to the principals, interviewees included patients and staff (both former and current) at the Buchanan Institute, as well as employees (both former and current) at the King Richard Inn and Fegelmann's Department Store. The Buchanan Institute generously permitted me to view Pearleen Porter's medical records, including her personal diary, as part of my research.

Patricia Sorensen, despite numerous requests and the permission of the penal institute in which she was serving a life sentence at the time of this book's writing, declined to be interviewed. In her written confession to the murders, she merely said she carried out the crimes "in memory of Pearleen Porter." If she had deeper motives, other than her obvious psychosis, they will apparently go with her to the grave.

Part of my research involved a tourist trip to Bangkok, Thailand, during which I visited the Wonderwomen nightclub and spoke with people who had known Sunisa Singhaboon during the years she worked there. The names of these individuals were provided in advance by Ms Singhaboon, who, after a good deal of hesitation, ultimately agreed to be interviewed in the hope that speaking out would encourage other victims of sexual blackmail to do the same. I express my deepest thanks to Ms Singhaboon for permitting me to tell her story.

I would also like to thank the National Football League Players Association, which was very kind in helping me locate people who had known Henry "the Helmet" Porter during his playing days. The former teammates and opponents with whom I spoke were extremely giving of their time and remembrances, as well as saintly patient with a British female trying to grasp the mysterious arcana of American football. Before meeting them, my only comment when watching an NFL match had been something along the lines of "My, what pretty costumes they wear!" For my broader acquaintance with the National Football League, in particular its history during the era in which Henry Porter played, I thank *The New York Times*, whose microfilm I spent many hours poring over in the Hargrove Public Library.

Finally, I would like to thank Martin Taft and Jerome Kolner, the editor and publisher, respectively, of *The Northeast Telegram*. They not only granted me the leave of absence I needed to write this book but let me have my job back, as promised, after the writing was completed. I may not have stayed long on my second go-round, but I'll always have Pierrevert.

Hayley Blossom
Great Missenden
Buckinghamshire
England

47.

It all happened so long ago, I guess about ten years now, that I might have screwed up some of the story, like I still screw up a lot of things. But I think I got most of it right. I'll never forget the headline in *The Northeast Telegram* a couple of days after I saw Mrs. Sorensen up in her apartment that last time. It was in big black letters across the top of the front page: **"Confession in Pierrevert Murders,"** by Hayley Blossom. I still have a copy in my closet, but it's gone all yellow now.

And just so you know, it was Mrs. Sorensen who decided to call Chief Cody and tell him she was the one he was looking for. I never said anything. I just left her sitting there on the floor that night and went back to the BI. Well, first I went downstairs to the bathroom next to the reception desk and got washed up. The cuts on my neck looked like I'd done a very bad job of shaving, even though they *felt* a lot worse when the knife was piercing my skin. My finger wouldn't need stitches after all. That said, there was a lump on my head that hurt like hell, courtesy of the ice bucket Mrs. Sorensen had crowned me with. Otherwise, I was presentable. I rolled up my shirtsleeves to hide the bloodstains, and the all-night stragglers in the front hall at the Manor didn't say a word when I passed by and went up to my room.

You want to hear something crazy? If Mrs. Sorensen hadn't confessed, I'm not sure I ever *would* have said anything. Nothing was going to bring Dr. Haynes back, and I didn't see myself as the kind of guy who goes to the police with a tip that solves a bunch of murders. It's a decision I never had to make. The thing is, about a week after the night with Mrs. Sorensen, I had a thought I couldn't get out of my head. I finally realized that the only way to get rid of it was to make a phone call, so I did. To Erin O'Brien.

The next day, my night off from tending bar in the tavern, Erin took me to dinner at the King Richard, white tablecloths and all. It was technically off-limits for me to be in the main dining room, but no one was going to say anything after everything that'd happened. Erin told me a story I've never told anyone. Until now.

What I couldn't stop thinking about was the photograph of Erin and Mrs. Sorensen in front of the castle, the one I'd seen at Bra's the night Erin was drunk and snoring on the couch in the basement. I just had a feeling the photo had something to do with the last thing Mrs. Sorensen had said to me, about Pearleen Porter being her daughter. I had to tell Erin I'd peeked into her office that night and seen her, but she wasn't mad. She liked me, and don't ask why older ladies take a shine to me—at least they did back then. Maybe it's because they felt sorry for me.

We had our drinks in front of us, Old Chaffinch for her and a beer for me, and had just ordered dinner when I asked Erin about the photo. She told me the castle was in Ireland, outside Dublin, and that she and Mrs. Sorensen had gone there together for a specific reason.

"Patsy's husband was killed in the war," she said. "T'was then she started to drink. We had that in common."

She called Mrs. Sorensen "Patsy." I'd never heard that one before. "She never cared for another after Robby, but she was human as any other lass and pretty as a picture, even in her forties. T'was what she was in that photograph. There was a bloke around the hotel, a handyman, fine thing, handsome, built like the Rock o' Gibraltar. I'd have given 'im a few bob meself. Ah, but it wasn't right. In those days, luv, you just couldn't . . ."

Erin let her voice trail off, looked lost in thought for a few moments, and took a gulp of whiskey. Then she picked up again.

"She called 'im up to her room one night to fix a light. 'Tis what he did, fix things 'round the place. She was langers, she told me, couldn't help herself. Happened just the once, but once is all it takes, luv. T'was Lamont, his name. Lamont Little. Had a shed o' tools out back, where they now call the courtyard. Had a son, Leroy, worked in the kitchen. Still does, doesn't he?"

Erin wasn't really asking if Leroy still worked in the kitchen at the King Richard. She knew he did. She just liked to put questions at the end of sentences, like Hayley used to do.

"Well, soon's Patsy knows she's got herself up the pole, Lamont scarpered. Left town, never came back. I took 'er to Ireland when she started to show. We must've stayed six months. Me mum gave us the run of our old family house, and that's where Patsy had the child. What a fine little thing! Patsy wouldn't leave 'er there, she wouldn't, so we brought her back 'ere. T'was me took the baby to the orphanage, near Hargrove. Patsy felt better knowin' the girl was close by where she might catch a gander one day.

"Then she learnt the girl'd been adopted, and it made 'er happy. Found out she was at Buchanan too, all those years later, and sent money all secret. Made sure she got a job at the hotel, where she could see 'er every day. When the girl died, I thought Patsy would too. What she did about it after, the revenge killin', all them blokes she thought responsible, she never told me that. Wasn't anyone's fault what 'appened to that child, it just 'appened. Patsy went gone in the head. I'm gobsmacked as anyone, luv."

Erin polished off her Old Chaffinch and signaled the waitress for another. It was Gladys who got our table, just my luck. You could tell she didn't like having to treat me like a human being.

"'Tis only three people in the world knows that tale, Coleman," Erin said. "Patsy, me, and you. Gi' it the respect it deserves."

And that was that. The only person who ever asked me if I could think of a reason for what Mrs. Sorensen did was Hayley, even though I bet Chief Cody tried to figure it out too. Hayley said the hole in the story, "wide as the blinkin' English Channel," was that no one ever found a motive that made any sense. When Mrs. Sorensen confessed to the murders, all she said was she did it for Pearleen Porter. But Hayley said a rich hotel owner doesn't turn into a killer over a young waitress she hardly knew.

I never told Hayley what Mrs. Sorensen and Erin O'Brien had told me, though. I didn't think it was my story to share. It's kind of funny because Hayley ended up writing a book about the murders, and part of the title was *What Really Happened in Pierrevert*, or something like that. The thing was, Hayley never knew the real truth—that Pearleen Porter was Mrs. Sorensen's daughter, by Leroy's father. And that she started killing people because she blamed them for Pearleen's death. Only *I* knew.

I'm a little embarrassed to admit this, but a while after everything happened, when I was still tending bar at the King Richard and Hayley was still a reporter for the *Telegram*, I kind of fell for her. It was hard not to because she was so smart and so British, always saying things like "crikey!" and "it's all sorted" and "sod that." We got to be good friends, at least I thought we were, so one night at the tavern as she sipped at one of my cracking Beefeater and tonics, I found the nerve to ask her out for dinner. She gave me this sisterly smile and said, "Coleman, I think you're very sweet." Believe me, anytime a girl says, "You're very sweet," it really means "I wouldn't go out with you if my life depended on it." I got the hint.

***

And you know, every time I think back to those days, I kind of wonder where I'd be now if I'd been a better wrist slicer and kicked the bucket right there in the bushes at the Plains Clinic. I'm not religious, but I'm still pretty sure we all go somewhere else after we die, and something tells me they're not too cool up there on young guys who bump themselves off. I'm sure they forgive you after a while, but I bet when you first get to the door there's someone waiting who looks like a six-foot-ten, 260-pound power forward in the National Basketball Association. I bet he's dressed in high-top sneakers, sweatpants, and a T-shirt that shows off all his muscles. There's a whistle around his neck and a clipboard in his hands. I can just hear the conversation.

"You Cooper?"

"Um . . . yes."

"You fucked up big-time, boy. Get your ass on in there. I'll see you first thing in the morning. Be ready to run."

I know it sounds a little crazy, like I always sound, but I've read a few books on this stuff, and I think the next life is like a school where you sit around, talk about things you did when you were here, and try to figure out how you could've done better. I bet classes for the suicides—at least for guys like me—start at about five in the morning, and they probably keep you going until nine or ten at night, seven days a week.

I wouldn't even be surprised if they make you run killer drills, like we did on my high school basketball team. That's when you start at the base line, run to the foul line and back, then to mid-court and back, then to the *next* foul line and back, and finally all the way to the *other* base line and back—all in thirty seconds. At least that's the goal. We did hundreds of them when Mr. Glover was the coach, and they don't call them killers for nothing.

The thing was, sometimes at the end of practice, Mr. Glover would yell, "OK, Cooper at the foul line!" Then he'd gather everyone around and say, "Cooper gets four foul shots. Each one he misses, you run one killer." I was a terrible foul shooter and the whole team knew it, so every time he screamed, "Cooper at the foul line!" they'd all let out this huge groan. I don't know why Mr. Glover put the whole thing on me like that, because he could've just said, "OK guys, we're gonna run four killers, let's go." He never sent anyone else to the foul line, only me, which didn't do any wonders for my popularity because I usually made maybe one out of four. Then one time in my senior year I sank them all, and the guys fell onto the court like they were delirious or something because the impossible had happened. So I was a great guy for one day, until I missed them all at the next practice and we had to run four killers.

***

Anyway, in case you're wondering what happened to all the people I've talked about, I'll tell you what I know. My stepfather, Terry, died about five years ago. Got drunk and crashed his pickup truck. He never found out where Mom was living, but then she died a couple of years later of an aneurysm in her brain. I like to think I gave her some happiness during the last few years of her life, because I'd drive down to see her maybe once every couple of months and play the piano for her. She'd kept the old upright I learned on as a kid, and she'd just sit there on the sofa with a blanket around her shoulders and listen with a smile on her face. When I think about her, I think about my real father too, even though he died when I was only seven. I just wish he'd lived long enough for me to get to know him better. I *do* remember he was a real disciplinarian, but I know he had a good heart.

Over at the Buchanan Institute, Ruby Calhoun and Freddy Cruz retired and left the area, at least that's what I heard. April got married a while back, moved to Boston, and opened a sporting goods store with her husband on Newbury Street. She invited me to the wedding and I went. It was quite the affair, and we drop each other a letter every now and then.

Lenny lives in New York City and is off the diet soda, or so he said a few years ago in a Christmas card. I think he's working at an accounting firm. He said he'd gotten obsessed with fitness and had even started running marathons. As an old baseball radio announcer I used to listen to when I was a kid was fond of saying, "How about that?" I don't know what happened to Marie, the only person I ever met who ate almost as many potato chips as I do. And somewhere along the way I got a letter from Mark Williams saying hi and apologizing for decking me in the snack bar. How about that too?

Hayley moved back to England a few years after everything happened and started working for a newspaper called *The Daily Telegraph*, doing investigative reporting. At least that's what she wrote me in a letter. She said she'd had a hard time finding a publisher for her book here in the States, but that she'd found one in London. The book eventually came out over here, though, and when I saw it in the window of a bookstore in Hargrove, I couldn't resist picking it up. She told the whole story pretty well, even if she never knew the real truth about Mrs. Sorensen and Pearleen Porter. And bless her, she kept a promise she'd made a long time before about her newspaper articles: she never mentioned my name.

I still see Chief Cody every now and then. It's usually when he's walking around town, or maybe over at the Cauldron Café where I treat myself to lunch sometimes. He even shows up occasionally at the town gym to play basketball, which I still do on Monday nights. He ended up marrying Sunny, the Asian lady who worked in the kitchen at the hotel, and they have twin daughters. Their girls are really cute, always skipping around town in matching little outfits. Sunny's two older daughters, the ones who served the spring rolls the night Dr. Bellino died, both moved away. Somebody told me one was in medical school and the other was a schoolteacher.

The younger policeman who tried to arrest me, Kevin Kincaid, a pretty complicated guy who maybe should've been a patient at Buchanan himself, was killed in a motorcycle accident in Mexico about a year after everything happened. There was a notice in the *Telegram* when he died, and a lot of my bar customers talked about it for a long time afterward. He hadn't been the most popular guy in town. I never told anyone about the day he slapped the handcuffs on me and tried to shove me into his police car.

Mrs. Sorensen died in prison about a year ago. The article in the paper didn't say what she died of or how old she was, but I think she was pushing eighty. Believe it or not, I went to the prison maybe three or four times a year to see her, from the time she was sent to jail until she passed away. Even though she did what she did, I saw her as a sick person, so I tried to have some compassion. And I don't think she ever really would've dug the knife deeper into my throat when she had the chance. Push wasn't going to come to shove, not with me, even though I was scared as hell at the moment.

I never let on to her that I knew the whole story about Lamont Little, Pearleen, and Dublin, the one Erin O'Brien told me. I figured if Mrs. Sorensen had wanted me to know, she'd have brought it up herself. She got thin as a rake in her last years, almost like Amy used to look back in the old days, and maybe that had something to do with her dying. But her face would light up when I came into the visiting room. They'd let us have lunch together, and she wasn't in handcuffs or shackles or anything. It was a minimum-security type of place, and just for women. She always called me "dear."

Leroy Little moved to New Orleans a few years ago and opened a small restaurant of his own, a Cajun joint, just outside the city. He said the Maine winters were just too much at his age. He even sent me some photos of the place, called the Boondocks, and said anytime I wanted a bartending job I could have one. I could never bring myself to tell him that Pearleen Porter had been his half sister. It just wasn't my place, and I don't know if he ever knew.

But Leroy being Leroy, he gave me a wonderful gift just before he left town: his recipe for apple crisp. He had to reduce all the quantities so I could make it in my apartment, and it took me a while to get the hang of how to make it come out right, but I finally did. I make it all the time, especially in the autumn apple season. If you put a scoop of good vanilla ice cream on it when it first comes out of the oven, you've got something that really makes you glad you're a bad wrist slicer.

My jukebox-leaning buddy, Fontaine Perkins, is still around, and I run into him once in a while. I found out he's a lot older than I thought he was. He must be pushing sixty by now. He still has the great smile, the cool clothes, and the soulful strut when he walks down the street. He still says, "Yo, Coley, what's hapnin' my *man*!" when he sees me. The thing is, we can't lean on the jukebox anymore because Bra's shut down when Erin O'Brien passed away a couple of years ago. The bar died with her. The whole county went into mourning when that happened because Bra's was kind of a special place, and nothing else ever opened up where people could get together and dance. Not that we'd all be trying to get down these days even if we had somewhere to do it, because everyone's older now and might feel too stupid. Well, maybe except for Fontaine. I bet he can still dance like the guys on that old Saturday morning TV show.

And Cheryl, go figure, ended up marrying Jason the mountain man about three years after I knew her. I'd see the two of them every now and then, maybe on Main Street or at Bra's, and she'd try to give me a smile. Then I didn't see her for a long time, and I think it was Fontaine who told me she'd divorced the mountain man, moved to Virginia, married a surgeon, and had a couple of kids. To be honest, once I got a little distance, I didn't blame Cheryl for dumping me when she did. I'd have dumped me too. I think the reason she decided to go out with me in the first place was that she'd already been with confident guys and wanted to try a card-carrying dork, kind of like you'd order something unusual at a restaurant to be adventurous. Once she'd tried the strange dish and decided she didn't like it, she sent it back for something more familiar. Fair enough. And she gave me an awful lot.

Which brings me to Skip Jones, whose old apartment across from the Pierrevert Wine Cellar is now mine. Skip died of emphysema a couple of years ago, up into his seventies, and I'm still not over it. Not sure I ever will be. I studied piano with him right up to the very end. He was still playing at the King Richard and had an oxygen tank next to the piano so he could take a dose whenever he needed it.

Skip did the nicest thing anyone has ever done for me: he gave me his Steinway Model B grand piano. And he asked if I wanted to take over the lease on his apartment. So I left the little studio just outside of town where I'd lived alone since I checked myself out of Buchanan right after Dr. Haynes died, and sold the dinky upright piano I'd bought at the Hargrove

Music Center. Actually, I hadn't lived totally alone. I had a dog, a mutt that I named Smoky, who I bought on impulse one day when I went to Pritchard's Orchard to get some apple cider. The Pritchards' dog had just had a big litter, and there was this one puppy with a look on his face I couldn't resist. He was a great friend for a long time until he got sick and I had to put him down. I like to practice the piano in the morning, and Smoky was a late sleeper, so whenever he'd wake up and amble over to say hello, I'd play "Smoke Gets in Your Eyes." I know it's silly and that he was just an animal and all, but I still think somewhere down in his little dog brain he knew it was *his* song.

Anyway, Skip had no living relatives and no one to leave anything to, so he left his place exactly like it was, including all the black-and-white photos of jazz piano players on the wall. I've kept them exactly where they were, from left to right on the long side of the living room: Thelonious Monk, Oscar Peterson, Erroll Garner, Bill Evans, Bud Powell, Horace Silver, Duke Ellington, Dave Brubeck, Vince Guaraldi. There was one classical player up there, Chopin, a print of an old painting, and I've kept him too. Skip always used to say Chopin would've been a monster jazz player. Bach too.

As for my own playing, I still have a hard time relaxing at the keyboard, and in my whole life too. But I like to think I'm getting better at it. I've kind of *had* to because in addition to giving me his Steinway and his apartment, Skip gave me his job.

A bunch of stuff happened at the King Richard before that, though, the main thing being that Mrs. Sorensen had to sell the hotel when she went to prison. The people who bought it are really nice, an English couple called Nigel and Tiggy Lister-Cheese. They did a lot of redecorating and made Bosworth's Tavern look like it was around the corner from Piccadilly Circus or something. Boy, did Hayley ever love that. They even started serving English-pub food in the tavern, all the stuff Hayley had told me about like bangers and mash, bubble and squeak, and toad in the hole.

Mr. Simons left the hotel a few years after the Lister-Cheeses took over, and they hired a new food and beverage manager, a redheaded lady named Laura. That happened to be the name of an old song Skip used to play, and once she and I got to be friends, I'd sing a few bars when passing by her in one of the hallways. And go figure, a few months after she started at the hotel, Laura made me the head bartender. That meant I had to order all the liquor, make up everyone's weekly schedule, and train any new guys she hired. She even gave me a raise. I liked the training part of the job, but I was a bad boss because I was too soft. I could never yell at anyone no matter how badly they screwed up. Maybe it's because I didn't want to be like Mr. Simons.

Then right before Skip died, he told Nigel and Tiggy that I should replace him at the piano. They gave me an audition, and I played the first five standards Skip had taught me all those years before—"Billie's Bounce," "Desafinado," "Take the A Train," "Skylark," "But Not for Me"—plus Gershwin's first prelude, which gave me a lot more trouble than the second. I guess I passed the test, because kind of overnight I went from being a fixture behind the bar to a fixture behind the piano. The money was about the same, and let's face it, playing the piano is more fun than mixing drinks.

***

The thing is, I'm still here today, five nights a week and on Sundays for brunch. I have my days free to practice, which I do all the time because if you play the same stuff every night you drive the staff and the customers crazy, not to mention yourself. So I try to learn a few new songs every week. I know I'll never sound like Skip, and even though I play for a living now, I still don't consider myself a real professional. Skip could sight-read anything, play classics almost like a concert pianist, and sound like Oscar Peterson playing jazz. As for me, I like to say I'm good enough to know how bad I am—a halfway decent amateur, emphasis on the halfway.

Still, after so many years of living alone except for Smoky, the piano helped me meet someone I've gotten pretty close to. She's ten years older than I am, and her name is Molly. She came to the hotel on one of those leaf-peeper tours a couple of years ago, just after getting divorced, and liked Pierrevert a lot. So having plenty of money and no kids, she decided to move here and buy a house.

In the beginning, she'd come in to hear me play almost every night, and she really knows her music. These days she comes in maybe three times a week, orders a Southern Comfort on the rocks, and says something like "I'd really love to hear some Hoagy Carmichael." Or some Gershwin or some Richard Rodgers. I think she knows just about every song ever written for the Broadway stage, probably because her grandfather was a theatrical producer in New York in the 1930s and 1940s, and she says they were really close.

She's a small woman, maybe five foot three, so we look kind of funny walking down the street, arm in arm. And we don't live together. She has her house, I've got Skip's apartment. It's better that way. Her place is only a fifteen-minute walk from the King Richard, so everything's nearby. Her favorite song is "I'm Old Fashioned" by Jerome Kern and Johnny Mercer, and sometimes she sings softly in the side parlor when I play it. The words are some of the prettiest I've ever heard:

> I'm old fashioned,
> I love the moonlight,
> I love the old-fashioned things . . .

The sound of rain,
Upon a window pane,
The starry song that April sings . . .
This year's fancies,
Are passing fancies,
But sighing sighs, holding hands,
These my heart understands . . .
I'm old fashioned,
But I don't mind it,
That's how I want to be,
As long as you'll agree,
To stay old fashioned with me.

Those lyrics knock me out, they really do. And Molly is into film noir too, so that's another thing we have in common. Which kind of reminds me of something.

The other night we were watching a movie that wasn't what you'd call *real* noir because it wasn't made back in the 1940s or 1950s. But it was still all about crime and murder, and there was a femme fatale, so pretty much the same idea. It was about this lawyer who meets a beautiful woman who's married to a rich guy she hates. The lawyer and the woman have this steamy affair and decide to kill the husband so they can take off with his money. But after the lawyer does the deed, the lady double-crosses him, makes sure he gets nailed for the murder, and runs off with the dough to some exotic place where she lies on a beach in a bikini sipping drinks with little umbrellas in them. She'd planned it that way from the very beginning.

Anyway, before the lawyer offs the husband, he realizes he'll need a way to get rid of the body. He decides to leave it in a big deserted building near the beach. But he also decides to set the place on fire after he gets out of there, figuring that'll take care of his fingerprints and any other evidence-like stuff he might forget about and leave lying around. So he goes to this street guy who knows all about arson and asks him how to make a firebomb he can set to a timer. The best part is the street guy doesn't want anything bad to happen to the lawyer, who's kept him out of jail a few times. He tries to talk the lawyer out of the whole thing. He even offers to plant the firebomb himself as a favor. The lawyer's kind of flattered but says no, thanks, he'll do it himself.

"I sure hope you know what you're doin'," the street guy says. "You better be damn sure, 'cause if you ain't sure then don't do it. 'Course that's my recommendation, anyway. Don't do it."

I like that line a lot because it's exactly what I'd say to anyone who's thinking of lying in some bushes and slicing up his wrists, or maybe putting a gun to his head, or jumping off a bridge or something. The thing is, you never know how fast things can turn around, and in ways you never thought of.

When I think of all the stuff I would've missed if I'd been a better wrist slicer—like meeting Dr. Christie and kicking all the medication I'd been on for years. Like knowing Dr. Haynes, one very cool guy and a helluva point guard. The two of them taught me that all shrinks aren't bad and that some, go figure, can actually help you out quite a lot. Even living for a while at the Buchanan Institute, which maybe wasn't a picnic every day but was the right place for me at the time and gave me a perch for a do-over in life that I'll always be grateful for.

Lenny and his diet sodas. Leaning on the jukebox at Bra's with Fontaine. Leroy's deep voice and his smile, not to mention his apple crisp and homemade potato chips. Skip's soft touch on the piano, and everything he taught me. Château Lynch-Bages. Swishing the jumper in Scotty's face. Chief Cody saying, "Tough shot, Coleman." Hell, even listening to Charlie Biggs work his way through "Bar Room Buddies." And it's never been lost on me that not very long after I thought I had nothing to live for, I found myself in bed with the most beautiful girl I've ever seen to this day. If something like that can happen to me, it can happen to anyone. Believe me.

The thing is, if I'd been a better wrist slicer that night outside the Plains Clinic, I'd probably still be up there in the great beyond running killer drills. The power forward would be standing off to one side, whistle around his neck, stopwatch in hand, shaking his head in disgust at my performance.

"Let's MOVE IT, Cooper! You owe me MORE!"

So if it ever occurs to you to crawl into a row of bushes on a cool fall evening—well, all right, it *occurs* to just about everyone a few times in their lives. But if you ever feel really close, just remember what the street guy said to the lawyer: don't do it. Because that's my recommendation too. Take my word, you don't want to find yourself running killer drills next to someone like me.

ACKNOWLEDGMENTS

Many people helped give this story the light of day, and I would like to sincerely thank each one. First, numerous friends and former colleagues were kind enough to read early drafts and offer valuable feedback: David Applefield, Clare Gaffney, Jonathan Gage, Elisabeth Kehoe, Mary Kole, Bob Plant, Claude and Nicole Rivière, Sally Seymour, Charles Starks, Shari Tanguay, Nicholas Thaw, Walter Wells, Janice Willett, and Julian Young. My wife, Nicole Crawford, as candid a critic as ever was, also weighed in.

I'd also like to thank the following: Amherst College for accepting me as a sophomore when I was thirty-one years old; the late professor Nora Crow of Smith College, who gave me confidence in my writing at a time when I needed it; the late professor Klemens von Klemperer of Smith College, for his friendship and mentorship; the late Richard Todd, former editor of *New England Monthly*, for running my first magazine piece and for his thoughtful advice on the writing game; Larry Parnass and the late Steve Szkotak, mentors at my first journalism job at the venerable *Daily Hampshire Gazette* in Northampton, Massachusetts, for teaching me how not to bury the lede; Claude and Nicole Rivière, without whose friendship and support I could never have made a go of it in Paris; Walter Wells and Martin Baker for opening the door to my job at the *International Herald Tribune* (*IHT*), Jonathan Gage and Sam Abt for pushing to change my status from stringer to staff editor, and John Vinocur for making that change official; David Ignatius of *The Washington Post*, formerly of the *IHT*, and author of many successful novels, for his friendship and advice; Anne Bagamery, former *IHT* colleague, for introducing me to my wife—best blind date I ever had; Rene Sonneveld, Chicago Booth classmate, for thoughtfully sending me a magazine ad for a new writing and editing job that he thought might interest me; Barry Adler for opening the door to that new job, and for a great London walkabout; Alan K. Rode, for lifelong friendship and film-noir inspiration; piano teachers Andy Jaffe and Ahmet Gulbay for keeping me inspired and practicing; Jane Friedman for her excellent advice on the modern world of book publishing; the late Robert L. (Bob) Hansen for his big heart; my late uncle, Col. J. Philip King, US Army, for introducing me to Bangkok more than thirty years ago; the Texas dream team of Maria Loukas, Anne Figueiras, and Sondra Jo Battle, for looking after my nonagenarian mom so wonderfully; and finally, my friends at Le Suffren in Paris—a neighborhood brasserie where much of this book was written sitting on a barstool—for their handshakes and the way they say *"Bonjour Philippe!"* each time I walk through the door.

I would also like to thank my collaborators at Girl Friday Productions (GFP) for their expertise and professionalism: Sara Addicott, Paul Barrett, Jasmine Barta, Ingrid Emerick, Christina Henry de Tessan, and Georgie Hockett. Likewise for GFP associates Patty Economos, Jennifer Kepler, Valerie Paquin, and Faith Black Ross. Likewise for my friends at Copy Write Consultants, Kathryn Steed and Christopher Hoffmann, for helping me obtain the permissions I needed. And likewise for Joshua Schwartz and Ashley Durrer at Pubvendo for helping me find an audience.

I'm also extremely grateful to Laurent Chneiweiss, who one day said to me, *"Pourquoi pas essayer d'écrire un roman?"* (Why don't you try writing a novel?) Thanks to my late dad for giving me discipline. Thanks to my terrific mom for giving me more things than I can remember (including the gift of countless philosophical discussions over a bottle of Champagne and large bowls of salty snacks).

And finally, *merci mille fois* to my wonderful wife, Nicole, and to our two children, Fanny and Ollie, who give me reasons to smile every day.

PERMISSIONS FOR SONG LYRICS

SEPTEMBER

Words and Music by Maurice White, Al McKay and Allee
   Willis
Copyright © 1978 EMI April Music Inc., Steelchest Music,
   EMI Blackwood Music Inc. and Irving Music Inc.
All Rights Administered by Sony/ATV Music Publishing
   LLC, 424 Church Street, Suite 1200, Nashville, TN 37219
International Copyright Secured All Rights Reserved
Reprinted by Permission of Hal Leonard LLC

EVERYTHING HAPPENS TO ME

Words and Music by Matt Dennis and Tom Adair
Copyright © 1941 (Renewed) Onyx Music Corporation
   (ASCAP)
All Rights Administered by Music Sales Corporation
International Copyright Secured All Rights Reserved
   Reprinted by Permission
Reprinted by Permission of Hal Leonard LLC

SUNNY

I'M OLD FASHIONED

I'M OLD FASHIONED

PERMISSION FOR MOVIE DIALOGUE

ABOUT THE AUTHOR

Philip Crawford is a former writer and editor for the Paris-based *International Herald Tribune* (now *The New York Times International Edition*). A graduate of Amherst College and the University of Chicago Booth School of Business, he divides his time between Paris and Aix-en-Provence.

Made in the USA
Middletown, DE
04 November 2020